Animal 5:

Executioner's Song

T0014954

Animal 5:

Executioner's Song

K'wan

www.urbanbooks.net

Urban Books, LLC
300 Farmingdale Road, NY-Route 109
Farmingdale, NY 11735

Animal 5: Executioner's Song

ISBN 13: 978-1-64556-507-9

First Mass Market Printing December 2023
Printed in the United States of America

10 9 8 7 6 5 4 3 2 1

This is a work of fiction. Any references or similarities to actual events, real people, living or dead, or to real locales are intended to give the novel a sense of reality. Any similarity in other names, characters, places, and incidents is entirely coincidental.

Distributed by Kensington Publishing Corp.
Submit Orders to:
Customer Service
400 Hahn Road
Westminster, MD 21157-4627
Phone: 1-800-733-3000
Fax: 1-800-659-2436

Animal 5:

Executioner's Song

K'wan

Part I

RIDERS ON THE STORM

Chapter 1

A few days earlier . . .

Ashanti let out a deep sigh of relief when he could finally pause and take a breath. It had been a trying last few days, especially the previous forty-eight hours. It felt good to have on a fresh set of clothes after spending the entire night soaked to the bone. The gray sweatpants he wore were a bit too big, and the white T-shirt, tighter than he was used to about the chest, but they were all that he had access to in the apartment. It was a three-bedroom in a high-rise building on Manhattan's Upper West Side. The place was on loan from a friend who owed him a favor. Friends were in short order those days, but Ashanti had always been a man of few comrades. It was him and the Dog Pound against the world; at least, that's what it felt like. Everybody was out for their pound of flesh, and he welcomed them to try to claim it.

He plucked a half-smoked blunt from the ashtray and pulled a metal folding chair over to the window. Then he flopped in the chair and fired up the weed, frowning when he cupped his hands near his nose and caught a whiff of the stench coming from his skin. Though he had showered when arriving at the apartment, he still stank of the blue chemicals they'd all been soaked in when they raided the boat dubbed the *Red Widow*. What the substance was, where it came from, and where it would lead were the questions that plagued him as he smoked and stared out the window.

The Manhattan skyline poked from behind the thick gray clouds that had settled over the city that morning. It had been laden with the threat of rain lingering. The city was blanketed in gray, save for a low flickering patch of orange, imitating from somewhere in the distance. The dancing orange flames were like a lone match struck in a smoke-filled room. The smoldering chemical fire was what remained of an explosion that had occurred a few hours earlier that had rocked the whole west side of Manhattan.

Various news outlets had been reporting on it all morning. It was a tragedy that had claimed the lives of several crew members aboard a ship called *la Viuda Roja*—the *Red Widow*. According to reports, the cargo vessel had originated in Puerto Rico, carrying a shipment of sugar. Its final destination was Canada, but not before stopping in New York to refuel. However, that was just a cover story. The ship's true destination, as well as its cargo, was a truth only known to a select few. By that point, none of it mattered because both truth and lies had gone up in flames.

There were several running theories about what had caused the massive explosion. Some said a fuel leak caused it, while others claimed it was another terrorist attack. There was plenty of chatter about it on the news and the streets, but none of the theories or rumors came anywhere near the truth. The sinking of the *Red Widow* and the murder of its crewmen had been a message from a grieving father to those responsible for his pain. Ashanti knew Animal better than anyone involved, so he understood that this was just the warning shot. They called him the "Bastard Son of Harlem," but his rage would stretch further than a few dozen Manhattan blocks before it was all said and done. The entire city would come to know his full fury. He was a genie released from its bottle, and there was nothing anyone could do to put him back.

The plan had been to cripple his enemy's operation and rescue his kidnapped children, but things went south, and the situation went from bad to worse. Not only was he now further away from rescuing his kids than when he started, but he had lost the only real leverage he had against the cartel, which was a messenger bag containing a chemical formula that would shift the balance of power in the drug trade on two continents. Ashanti was just as pissed as any of them when the bag had gotten snatched, but he understood. It happened under unforeseen circumstances, so there was no blame to place, but you couldn't tell that to Animal.

Ashanti had tried to console his mentor, but how does one tell the devil they won't receive their due? This was an even harder sell when it was the devil's fault. They had managed to come into possession of the very thing that had not only started the war and got the kids snatched but also had the power to end it all. The ball had been in their court . . . until it wasn't. Now, they were all fucked, all because Animal tried to handle a snake and thought he wouldn't get bitten. The whole situation was fucked up, but Ashanti was committed to riding it out until the end, even if he disagreed with how it had been handled. Blind loyalty was a muthafucka, and had it been anyone else asking him to enter a fight he knew they had little chance of winning, Ashanti would've told them to eat a dick and go on about his life, but this wasn't just anyone. This was Animal.

Though only separated by a few years in age, Animal had been the closest thing to a father figure Ashanti had ever had. They were products of the same circumstances, born into a world that didn't love them. Ashanti's mother had been an addict who had sold him and his sister, Angela, into bondage to pay off a drug debt. When Ashanti finally liberated himself from his captors, he returned to the only place he knew—the hood. Barely a teen with no friends, family, or anyone else who cared enough to look after him, Ashanti found himself at the mercy of the streets. He would sleep in stairwells and steal what little food he could to sustain himself. It was hardly a life for a child. This was about when Animal found him and took him under his wing. Animal had protected Ashanti and taught him how to defend himself. Under his mentor, Ashanti had grown from prey to predator. His résumé was extensive, and before he reached the legal drinking age, he was one of the most feared young dudes on the streets. He owed everything that he was and everything that he had to Animal. This meant if he had to pull a Thanos and murder half the universe in his name, Ashanti would happily do it.

A soft knock on the bedroom door drew Ashanti's gaze from the fire in the distance. He didn't invite whoever it was in, but it didn't stop them from pushing the door open. It was Cain, one-half of a set of fraternal twins that Ashanti had been raising, as Animal had done for him. Cain stepped in, his thin frame nearly swallowed by the oversized black hoodie he was wearing. The hood was pulled tightly over his head to obscure his badly scarred face. One side of his face was burned from an accident he'd had as a kid, which left him blind in one eye. His mother had always called the scar *the mark of the beast,* and Cain tried his best to live up to that. On the streets, Cain was the equivalent of the monster hiding under your bed.

"He's here," Cain said in his gravelly voice.

Ashanti nodded. He saw the faintest hints of what could only be assumed was a smile touching the corners of Cain's mutilated mouth. "What?"

"Nah, I was just thinking how lucky you were that me and Abel came along to make the ranks of the Dog Pound resemble something close to respectable because the last litter of pups looked kind of weak." Cain snickered. It sounded like a car motor that was having trouble turning over.

"Shut up and send him in," Ashanti laughed.

Cain moved aside for the guest to enter the room. He was a tall man with a thin build. His skin was brown and pockmarked from the acne he had suffered ever since Ashanti had known him. When he walked, he favored his right leg a bit. The faintest wisps of a beard were starting to sprout on his chin, and his braids had thinned at the top. Still, he held on.

He stopped short of Ashanti, and there was an awkward pause as if he weren't sure what to do or say. It had been quite some time since they had last seen each other, and they both had grown into different people than the ones they'd known back in the day. He was an original member of the Dog Pound, a holdover from the days when Tech was still running the show. At one point, he and Ashanti had been as thick as thieves, but now, they felt like strangers. The silence between them swelled, and Ashanti finally broke it.

"You gonna keep standing there like the ugly girl nobody wants to dance with or give your boy some love?" Ashanti spread his arms. There was a brief pause before his guest stepped forward and accepted his embrace. "Man, it's good to see you, Nef."

"Likewise, bro." Nef smiled. "Damn, looks like your skinny ass is finally trying to gain some weight." He patted Ashanti's developing potbelly. "All that good eating, I guess."

"Nah, man. This is all beer." Ashanti rubbed his belly. "You don't know how good it is to see a familiar face. Even one who doesn't keep in touch with his people."

Nefertiti, known to his friends as Nef, was one of the original five-man team who raised so much hell in Harlem. Back in the days, Nef, Ashanti, Animal, Brasco, and Tech had been young outlaws who lived off the fat of the land and played by their own rules. Those had been some good times before life and death had pushed them in different directions. When Animal had retired to the West Coast, and Ashanti was off with Kahllah learning a new skill set, Nefertiti found himself alone in the game. He'd taken a fall and ended up doing a skid bid. When he was released, he realized he no longer had a taste for the life and squared up. It was probably for the best. Nef was the homie, but he had never really been like the rest of them. Murder didn't live in his heart as it did theirs, and it would've likely only been a matter of time before their lifestyle would've made him a casualty.

"It ain't like that. I just been caught up. I wanted to reach out, but . . ." Nef began awkwardly.

"You don't owe me any explanation, homie. You did your tour of duty and always served honorably. So, what you been up to?" Ashanti retook his seat at the window and invited Nef to sit on a milk crate pushed against the wall.

"Trying to stay out of the way and enjoy life," Nef replied.

"I'll bet. I heard the city cashed you out behind that bum wheel." Ashanti nodded at his gimpy leg. At the time of Nef's arrest, he had taken a bullet to the leg from an overzealous cop. Nef sued the city, and he had a settlement waiting for him when he was released from prison.

"Yeah, man. It was the least they could've done for popping me. After the lawyers took their third, and then I paid back the high interest loans I was letting my baby moms take out while I was away, wasn't but a hundred grand or so left."

"That's still a good piece of money, Nef. I hope you did the right thing and didn't blow through it," Ashanti said.

"Between the cost of living in New York and trying to care for these kids, a hundred thousand don't last as long as you might think."

"Shit, how many kids do you have now?"

"Five," Nef said with a sigh.

"I still can't figure out how a nigga like you went from getting no pussy to fathering a tribe," Ashanti laughed.

"I was getting pussy. I just wasn't trying to stick my dick in everything like you and Brasco," Nef said good-naturedly, and then he remembered why he had come, and his mood darkened. "I still can't believe my nigga is gone."

"Me either." Ashanti shook his head sadly, thinking how Brasco had gone out. He died the same way he lived, gun blazing and screaming fuck his enemies. "He went out like a soldier, though."

"With Brasco, I wouldn't expect anything less than a soldier's death," Nef said with a smile. Brasco had always been one of the hardest cats in the hood. He had never met a challenge he wouldn't face head-on. He was one of a kind, and Nef would miss him dearly. "So, we got access to his body for a proper send-off?"

"Nah, it went up with the fire," Ashanti said sadly. "Even if it hadn't, trying to recover his body from the police would've likely ended with one, if not all, of us going to prison."

"Right. I heard y'all been tearing shit up. When I heard through the grapevine that Animal was back in the city, I thought it was bullshit, but as soon as I saw those bodies start dropping, I knew there would've only been one man behind the trigger. Where is Animal? I'd like to see him and offer some words over what happened to his wife."

"I'm sure your words will be appreciated, but I'm afraid they'll have to wait. We're going ahead to the send-off, and Animal will meet us there. He's gone to see a man about a dog."

Chapter 2

Thomas Clark, Junior, known to those closest to him as Tommy Guns, sat on the front lawn of his family's estate, slow-sipping three fingers of Hennessy from a red plastic cup. In any of the multiple cabinets inside his manor, Tommy could've found any number of cups or glasses that better suited a man of his standing, but he liked the red plastic cups. They reminded him of winter days when he and his crew used to play the block, and the only thing they had to fight off the biting cold was a bottle of brown. It had only been a few years, but it felt like a lifetime ago since Tommy had found himself playing anything except the odds. Life had changed for Tommy Guns when his father passed and left him, one of three heirs, to a multimillion-dollar realty empire. While the children of Poppa Clark were afforded a good life because of their father's post-criminal investments, Tommy said his pledge of allegiance to the game that had provided them with the start-up capital.

The oak tree he was sitting beneath provided shade from the slowly setting sun. It was a monstrously ugly thing with a thick trunk that almost doubled over on itself. Gnarled branches sprinkled with leaves seemed to return less green with each passing season. The tree was an eyesore, and had it been up to the rest of the family, they would have had it cut down when they had taken ownership of the property, but Tommy had lobbied against it. The tree was hideous against the rest of the well-maintained landscape, but it had a quality about it that Tommy especially could appreciate. The oak was twisted and broken . . . just like him.

Usually, Tommy would've been enjoying his afternoon drink anywhere but the front lawn. His favorite place to drink and think was at the rear of the property, where the lagoon had been erected. It was a small patch of land, lined with palm trees and blanketed by white sand dunes. In the center of it was a small pond with lights in the bottom that, when switched on, illuminated the water in emerald light. It was like someone had taken a slice out of a tropical island and dropped it in suburban New Jersey, which they technically had.

The lagoon was the only holdover from their old house. Everything else had been sold off or demolished, but Tommy had insisted that the lagoon move with them. Every tree, every grain of sand, and every rock were all coming with them. His brother and sister argued that it would be cheaper to build another lagoon rather than move that one, but Tommy wouldn't hear it. He relented on everything else but stood firm on the lagoon. It was more than just a luxury to him, but a thing of sentimental value. It had been the passion project of their late father, Poppa Clark.

Poppa had been a native of Trinidad before moving to the States and eventually settling in New York City, where he would start building his fortune. The city was now his home, but a part of Poppa's heart always longed for his native soil. So he had it brought to him.

When Poppa finally managed to climb to the top of the food chain, he immediately took precautionary steps. He isolated his then wife and children from what was happening in the city. To do this, he made his first significant purchase: an entire block in an affluent section of North New Jersey. Poppa had all the houses in the neighborhood demolished and erected what would be the first Clark Estate on top of their bones. The lagoon had been Poppa's favorite place and would eventually become Tommy's too. There had been some life-changing decisions made sitting around the emerald pond, including the one to sell their original family home and uproot the lives of the Clark children.

Sitting in the front never felt right to Tommy at either house, especially the new one. Even on those rare occasions that the family held gatherings on the lawn, Tommy always played in the back. It wasn't that the front of the house wasn't nice. The family had spared no expense on the landscaping. It boasted acres of manicured grass that stopped just short of the iron gates surrounding the property. The trees had been imported from different places and cared for by specialists to survive the harsh Jersey winters. In the spring, they bloomed nearly every color of the rainbow. There had even been a feature done in *Homes & Gardens* about the estate, a fact which the lady of the house was sure to mention whenever they had guests over. It was indeed a serene place, just not Tommy's style.

For Tommy, it was too out in the open, and his PTSD made him suspicious of open spaces where he could be an easy target. Not that an assault of any sort was something they would likely have to ever worry about, considering the amount of money the Clarks had spent on securing the property. If you were tough enough to make it past the half-dozen armed guards, you'd still have to make it over the iron fence that enclosed the property. And let's say, for the sake of argument, you were fortunate enough to make it through the first two lines of defense, you'd still have to contend with the dogs.

The hounds had been Tommy's idea. The pack consisted of seven pit bulls, an entire litter that Tommy had purchased from a respected Dog Man named Fat Tone he knew through K-Dawg. They were the product of the last stud from a four-time champion and a bitch that was up and coming. The pups were born of exclusive blood, bred to either die in the pit or make their owners rich off the lives of their victims in the pit. However, Tommy had another purpose for them. His brother once questioned why Tommy spent so much money on the backyard brawlers rather than invest in properly trained security dogs. Tommy's answer was simple: *"Some dogs will kill for you because that's what they've been trained to do, and some dogs will die for you because they love you."* His father's killers had taught him that.

The wind picked up, ruffling the pages of the newspaper across his lap. It was a copy of the *Star-Ledger*. The periodical was folded open on a page detailing an explosion that had rocked the Port of Newark the night before. The official cause was a gas leak, but Tommy suspected differently. This was part of what brought him to the front yard that afternoon. Sitting under the oak not only provided him with a measure of cover but also gave him the perfect vantage point to see who was coming and going on the property. That day had been busier than usual.

His little brother, Shai, had just emerged from the main house. As usual, he was dressed in a suit but had forgone the tie. At his side was a tall man with skin that was deeply tanned. He wore plain, black slacks and a white shirt rolled up at the sleeves. Tommy had never seen the man before. As he thought about it, he probably wouldn't have recalled if he had. The man had what you would call an "unremarkable" face. So much so that he forgot it every time he took his eyes off it. It was as if something about the tanned man played tricks on Tommy's senses, and he didn't like it. There was only one other person he had known to have that effect on people, and he had been dead for years.

"And the plot thickens," Tommy mumbled under his breath.

"What was that? You need something, boss?" Moose asked from his vantage point, standing behind Tommy. He was a burly man but had the uncanny ability to move softly. He had been so quiet that Tommy had forgotten that he was there.

"No, I'm good," Tommy said in an irritated tone without bothering to look over his shoulder at his bodyguard. He knew Moose meant well and was only doing his job, but Tommy could never get comfortable about somebody up his ass 24/7 like some wet nurse. It had been at the insistence of his brother that each family member has an extra set of eyes in the back of them at all times. As if the millions of dollars in security and surveillance equipment placed all over the property weren't enough. Shai had become increasingly paranoid after "the incident," as they referred to it.

It was awhile back, a few years after they had taken up residence at the new estate. Shai had just been crowned king and was still trying to find his way. It was a rough transition for everyone, and the troops were spread thin, dealing with the vultures trying to pick over Poppa Clark's bones. They had only taken their eyes off the ball for a second, but that was all it took for an assassin to breach the estate. Thankfully, no one had died that night, but the message sent to the Clark children had been received. Anybody could be touched . . . including them.

Shai had damn near broken the bank on security, and since then, none of them had been allowed to move around alone. Tommy understood that his baby brother was only trying to ensure his family was safe, but it didn't do much for Tommy's already bruised ego. Tommy was used to dealing with threats to the family, so being forced to take a backseat made him feel weak. Had it been up to him, he'd have forgone hiring extra security and cowering behind an iron gate. Instead, he'd have taken it to the streets. That's how Tommy Guns would've done, but he was no longer sitting at the head of his father's table. Shai was the new king, and Tommy was an afterthought.

Tommy continued watching his brother and his guest skulk across the yard and speaking in whispers. For an instant, Tommy thought he saw a smile touch the tanned man's lips. Shai had always been the charmer of the family. The boy could sell water to a whale. When the two finished whispering, the tanned man got into a plain-looking Honda and departed. Shai stood at the top of the driveway until the Honda was through the gate before turning back to the house. It was then his eyes landed on Tommy, and he switched directions.

"What's good, Nappy Black?" Shai greeted his older brother with the nickname he had been calling him since they were kids.

"Ain't shit, Slim. Just out here enjoying my daily paper and sip." Tommy tipped the cup at Shai.

"Oh yeah," Shai took the cup from Tommy and downed the liquor. "You usually do your brooding in the back. What brings you out into the sun in the daylight?"

"Told you, enjoying my paper and drink," Tommy repeated. "You see this?" He held up the article about the cargo ship that had exploded.

Shai barely scanned it. "Yeah, I think I did hear something about that. Some type of gas explosion, right?"

"So they say," Tommy replied in a disbelieving tone.

"What? You think it was something else?" Shai asked his brother.

"All depends on who that was who you've been snuggled up in your office with for the last hour."

Shai hesitated. It was only for a beat but enough to tip his hand. "That was a friend of ours from Virginia. I've been looking at some beachfront property down there, and he will help me secure the permits I need to build on it. I'm thinking about taking a trip down there in a few days. You should come with me. We can stay in a shitty motel and get drunk every day like when I was a shorty, and you used to take me to Virginia Beach for Memorial Day weekend. Lie in the sand, fuck with some broads . . . It'll be just like old times."

Tommy laughed. "Appreciate the offer, little brother, but I don't think these wheels are made for off-roading on sand." He patted the rubber tires of his wheelchair.

Shai's face darkened at the remark.

"Lighten up, Slim. I didn't mean nothing by it," Tommy said good-naturedly. The subject of his paralysis was a touchy subject in the Clark house, especially with Shai. Shai held a measure of guilt behind the assault that had put Tommy in a wheelchair and their father in the ground. He blamed himself for not being there when it went down, but in truth, there was nothing he could've done even if he had been there. It took Tommy awhile, but eventually, he came to grips with the fact that he and those bullets had been destined to meet.

"I know. Sometimes, it's hard to be light when your spirit is heavy," Shai said with a deep sigh.

"Then let your big bro help you carry that load." Tommy reached into the small knapsack that hung from his wheelchair and fished out the small bottle of Hennessy. It was already half empty. He poured a healthy amount into Shai's cup and sipped from the bottle. "Something going on that I need to know about?"

"Nah, nothing for you to stress over, T." Shai sounded more confident than he really was.

"That's not what I asked you. Just because I spent the majority of my time locked away in the library of this grand, old house doesn't mean my ear ain't still to the streets."

"And what are the streets saying?" Shai asked.

"They're saying what you ain't," Tommy said flatly. "I hear there's a storm brewing."

"No worries. We got plenty of umbrellas," Shai assured him.

"They won't do us much good in a flood," Tommy countered. "What happened to the Clarks getting out of the game?"

"We are . . . I mean, we have. So what's with the twenty questions all of a sudden?" Shai was getting irritated.

"Because I don't believe in coincidences. No way in hell that one of Poppito Cruz's ships goes down, and less than twenty-four hours later, you're meeting with an assassin at the house, and they're not related," Tommy pointed out.

"Moussa isn't an assassin. I told you, he's helping me with some building permits and—"

"Bullshit," Tommy cut him off. "From that nondescript outfit to how he moved all light-footed, that's a man skilled at moving unnoticed. He's got 'killer' written all over him, and I'm sure not even you're naïve enough not to pick up on it. I taught you better than that."

Shai started to lie but decided against it. "Okay, Moussa is connected, but my business with him is legit. One of his associates sits on the zoning committee in Virginia, and they will make sure we get approved for the permits I need so we can do our business with no questions asked."

"And what did you promise him in return?" Tommy asked.

"Cash, what else? This deal is about money, not blood," Shai assured him.

"It's always about blood when it comes to this family."

"Either that brown liquor or spending so much time in the house is starting to make you paranoid," Shai downplayed. He made to walk away, but Tommy's next words gave him pause.

"*La Viuda Roja*," Tommy said in almost perfect Spanish. "*The Red Widow*. It was the name of the ship that went down."

"Is that supposed to mean something to me?" Shai asked, not liking where the conversation was going.

Tommy shrugged. "Probably not since you were still out chasing bitches with Swann the first time Poppa and I had seen it. That's back before you wore the crown, and I was still being groomed for the big chair. Being Poppa's right hand often put me in the presence of many heavy hitters in the game, including Poppito. Me and Poppa had flown to Puerto Rico to meet with the old-timer about potentially doing business. One of the things he tried using to woo us was the small fleet of ships he employed in moving his drugs from the island to the mainland. His pride and joy was the *Red Widow*. He had named it after his daughter, Red Sonja. Now, *that's* a name you might be slightly more familiar with since she was the side bitch of a certain homicidal friend of ours for some years. Not to mention, it was her who helped smuggle this same friend back to the East Coast, and shortly after, he tried to kill you. Feel free to stop me when this starts to sound familiar."

"Tommy, it's not what you think."

"Shai, you don't even wanna know what I think," Tommy chuckled. "Like I told you, my ear is always to the streets. I know all about the broad trying to snake her way into taking over Poppito's business."

"We don't deal with Poppito. So what does it matter to you who's running his operation?"

"It doesn't. What matters to me is that chick's little coup has started a domino effect that could put us on the to-do list of a serial killer. According to my sources, someone or something has reopened Pandora's box, and quite a few people have started turning up missing. So, Shai, I can only hope you haven't been stupid enough to have your hands in whatever has set that li'l nigga off again."

"Tommy, I'd be lying if I told you that I didn't know why Animal was back, but I can tell you that it isn't because of anything I've done. His beef is with Tiger Lily, not me."

"So, you've never heard the phrase 'guilty by association'? Shai, it ain't no secret that I was salty when you ended up in Poppa's chair, and I ended up in this one . . ." He touched his wheelchair. ". . . but never once have I tried to undermine your rule or questioned your decisions. For the most part, I've allowed you to do your own thing and learn from your mistakes, but when those mistakes threaten the well-being of this family, I have to speak up."

"I know, Tommy. I value your council, but you're calling this one wrong. This is between them. The Clarks don't have a dog in this fight." Shai patted Tommy's shoulder reassuringly. "Now, I'm about to have the chef whip up a late lunch. You wanna join me?"

"Nah, I ate already," Tommy said, sipping from his bottle.

"Okay, well, I'll see you later then," Shai said, but his brother didn't respond. Instead, he waited for a few ticks before returning to the main house.

Tommy sat on the lawn for a while longer, replaying his conversation with his brother. He wanted to believe that Shai wouldn't have been stupid enough to place the family in a war again inadvertently, but something didn't feel right. He'd have to keep a close eye on the situation, not only for the sake of the family but also for the sake of Tommy's own plans. Though a deal hadn't been struck between Poppa and Poppito on their trip to Puerto Rico, Tommy had kept in contact with the cartel boss's son, Chris.

Some years after Poppa had been killed and the opportunity had presented itself for Tommy and Poppito's son to scratch each other's backs, so to speak, a bargain was struck. The woman they called Tiger Lily taking over Poppito's business and Chris turning up dead had compromised their arrangement, but it didn't necessarily kill the deal. One thing that Tommy still had on his side was the element of surprise. For obvious reasons, Chris and Tommy had kept their arrangement from their families. It was *their* thing. There were only three people who knew about it, and one of them was dead. Tommy had one last trump card to play if he had any hopes of salvaging the deal, but his chances at success would depend on Animal. His latest temper tantrum was threatening to destroy years of Tommy's hard work, planning, and scheming. This, Tommy couldn't have.

"I need to think. Take me back to my room," Tommy said to Moose over his shoulder.

Moose pushed Tommy across the grass, up the porch ramp, and through the front doors of the massive house. Usually, he'd try to engage Tommy in small talk about sports or some other irrelevant topic just to fill the dead air, but that day, Moose remained silent. He knew that Tommy was in one of his moods. His boss was hardly ever the picture of happiness, always seeming to be sour about one thing or another, but even then, Moose could still strike up a conversation with him. It was when Tommy was in those especially dark moods, like that day, which made Moose edgy. When he was like that, the slightest thing could set Tommy off. Moose had seen that anger and had no desire to be the target of it. People were under the misconception that because Tommy was in a wheelchair, it made him less dangerous when, in fact, it was the opposite. Since being crippled, Tommy had learned to do way more damage with his voice than he ever could with his pistols.

The staff must've also picked up on Tommy's mood because none of them spared them more than a glance as they passed through the foyer on their way to the elevator, which would take them to the third floor. That level of the house was Tommy's private domain and off-limits to everyone except the cleaning staff, and even they had to get approval from Tommy before venturing to that floor.

They exited the elevator and went down the hall to Tommy's room. Tommy wheeled himself the rest of the way with Moose leading. Moose pushed the slightly open door wide enough for Tommy's wheelchair to fit through. Tommy got to the doorway and paused, studying the entrance. He never left his bedroom door open. Pulling it closed behind him when he came and went had become second nature to him. Even if he'd authorized one of the staff to go in and clean up, they'd have known to make sure that the door was closed when they finished or risked Tommy's wrath. This was wrong.

Moose led the way into the room, with Tommy cautiously bringing up the rear. The caretaker went to the nightstand and retrieved one of Tommy's stashed pre-rolled blunts that he kept in the drawer. He knew Tommy liked to have a smoke after his drink. It had become a part of his routine. Moose had once asked why he didn't smoke on the lawn with his drink. Tommy gave him a tongue-lashing that was legendary, and ever since, Moose knew not to question Tommy's habits and just comply with his orders.

As he was about to turn and pass the pre-rolled to Tommy, Moose's eyes landed on something on Tommy's bed that hadn't been there before they went out previously. It was two shards of broken wood.

"What the heck is this?" Moose picked up the pieces and examined them. Both were only slightly longer than a ruler and nearly as wide.

It took Tommy's brain a few seconds to register what Moose was holding in his hands. They weren't two random pieces of wood but a wooden crucifix that had been broken in half. He had only seen a broken cross once before in his life. It was on the same night that the Clark fortress had been breached when he found it, a broken cross lying in the foyer. It had been a message left for Tommy by an assassin, a message that only Tommy would receive. The cross symbolized a broken God, the nickname given to Tommy by one of the Clark family's greatest adversaries—and the man who almost proved to be their undoing. "Moose!" Tommy shouted a warning, but it was already too late.

The bedroom door slammed closed behind them. Tommy was pretty sure who he would see long before he spun in his wheelchair but prayed that he was wrong. He wasn't. His face was almost exactly the same as the last time Tommy had laid eyes on him. It had to have been several years, but he seemed to have not aged a bit in that time, save for his eyes. His eyes had always held the dull sign of a kid who had seen too much, too fast, but there was still a faint flicker of life behind them. Now, that flicker had died in the eyes of the kid who had seen too much and was replaced with those of a man who had seen it all.

Chapter 3

Moose was the first to react. He dropped the broken cross and went for the gun holstered under his arm. For a man of his size, Moose was fast, but unfortunately for him, Animal was faster. Faster than anyone he had ever or would ever encounter.

Animal kicked Tommy's wheelchair, sending it flying across in Moose's direction. Instinctively, Moose moved to keep Tommy from falling from the chair when the wheel skipped, and it tilted. That was just what Animal had intended for him to do. However, while he was trying to save his boss from wiping out, Animal was leapfrogging the chair with his fist fired like an anime character. Moose's head snapped, but the blow from Animal's bony fist didn't do much more than irritate the bigger man. Moose assumed that it was the best Animal had to offer him and had already planned his victory celebration in the back of his mind . . . when things took a turn.

Apparently, Animal's initial strike had been the warm-up . . . He was tenderizing the meat before cooking it. Never taking his eyes from Moose's face and the triumphant look plastered across it,

Animal drew his arm back, muscles coiled like a jackhammer about to crack the first layer of ground of the day. Then like the wake of a grenade pin being pulled, Animal's arm fired out and buried his fist into Moose's chest. There was a transference of kinetic energy, almost like a small explosion from Animal's fist that passed through Moose's chest and sent him stumbling over his feet . . . and falling out the window. A shrill scream was followed by what sounded like a garbage bag full of hamburger meat slapping against the ground.

Tommy pushed off the bed, sending himself speeding backward as fast as his wheelchair would carry him. Even if he had been whole, it would've been a dogfight in such close quarters, but in his condition, broken, he had no chance of survival. He would need to get out of that room if he hoped to live. Tommy's hand had just landed on the doorknob when he felt himself being snatched back. Animal grabbed him by the shoulder and almost lost a finger when Tommy came up swinging the hunting knife he kept stashed in his chair. He got in two good swipes before Animal clocked him in the side of the head with a pistol. Tommy's world went loopy, and he dropped the knife.

Apparently, Animal had gotten meaner as he got older and stronger too. Tommy learned this when the killer snatched him from his wheelchair and body-slammed him onto the floor with the ease of a sack of laundry. Pain shot through the parts of Tommy's body that could still feel it. He wanted to hop up and defend himself, but without the use of his legs, all he could do was lie there helplessly and glare up at Animal.

"I see the Clark security is still top-notch, huh?" Animal said in a mocking tone.

"Little nigga, are you out of your mind?" Tommy snapped.

"Nah. For the first time in a long time, I know exactly who and what I am," Animal said sinisterly.

"You know, in less than sixty seconds, this room is gonna be filled with armed men looking to blow your fucking head off, right?" Tommy said confidently. If they hadn't yet seen what was going on through the cameras, Moose's body in front of the house would surely bring security running.

"Then I guess I better handle my business in fifty-nine," Animal replied, pushing Tommy's wheelchair against the door and jamming it under the knob. "Been a long time, Tommy Guns." He moved toward him.

"Not long enough," Tommy spat. "What do you want here?"

"The same thing I wanted the last time I penetrated this place's shitty security." He reached for Tommy, and to his surprise, the eldest Clark child flinched. He'd never known Tommy Clark to fear anything, including him.

"Relax." He gripped Tommy under his arms and helped him onto the bed. "You might come from a family of bitch-ass niggas, but you've always been solid. I'd never address you at a disadvantage or any other way not befitting a man who I still hold some measure of respect for."

"Do you always murder employees of men you claim to respect?" Tommy looked toward the window Moose had exited through.

Animal glanced out the window. "A man of his size from this height . . . a few broken bones maybe, but he'll live. Or so I hope. If I were you, I'd be more concerned about my own well-being than that of the help."

There was a brief silence between them, and the two men sized up each other. It was still hard for Tommy to process how the shadow of death standing before him and the little kid he used to send on missions were the same person. He'd heard the stories about what Animal had become, but seeing him up close and personal, he understood why the streets feared him. The boy radiated violence. Over the years, Tommy had often wondered what would have happened if he had taken Animal under his wing instead of leaving him to Swann. Animal had grown up to be the ultimate guard dog, and he had no doubt that had the youngster been with him that day at the restaurant, Tommy would still have his legs, and Poppa Clark would still have his life.

"I'd be lying if I said I didn't know why you were here," Tommy finally spoke up. He was thinking about the conversation with his brother and the *Red Widow*.

The admission stung Animal. Before breaking into
the house, he had wanted to believe what Shai had
told Abel about not having a hand in the events that
had transpired. He hoped there was still some honor
left in the Clark family and their years-long feud was
truly over, but apparently, he had been wrong.

"If you know why I'm here, then that means your
family has once again contributed to my grief." He
pointed his gun at Tommy. "I thought better of you,
Tommy. Beef aside, you've always been the honorable one of your stinking lot, but honorable men
don't murder innocent women and kidnap children."

"Fuck are you talking about?" Tommy was confused.

"I'm talking about the people your family and that
cock-sucking brother of yours have chosen to do
business with. The same people who murdered my
wife and kidnapped my children," Animal snarled.

This caught Tommy totally by surprise. He had
assumed Animal was there because of whatever
happened to the *Red Widow*'s cargo. Whatever in-
volvement Shai had been lying about, he had no idea
that Animal's wife had been murdered, let alone his
children being abducted. Now, everything was starting to make sense. The revelation made him dizzy.
Had it not been for him holding onto the bedpost,
he'd have fallen on the floor, and it was doubtful that
Animal would help him up again.

"You don't look so good, Tommy. I guess getting
caught with your hand in the cookie jar can do that to
a man. No worries because I'm about to take away all

your pain." Animal jammed his gun under Tommy's chin. He cocked the hammer back with his thumb and paused. He heard footsteps outside the bedroom door, followed by something heavy slamming against it. Someone was trying to break into the room.

"Tommy, what's going on? You good?" Shai could be heard yelling through the door, followed by more banging.

"Baby brother to the rescue, huh? Better late than never, I guess." Animal nudged one of Tommy's useless legs with the barrel of his gun. "Looks like I'll be getting a Clark two-for-one special today and the opportunity to end you both. That door seems pretty sturdy, so it should give me at least a few minutes with you before I give your little brother and whoever is out there with him my undivided attention. Today is the day that I end the Clark bloodline once and for all."

"You're about to make a huge mistake, kid," Tommy warned him.

"I've been making mistakes all my life, but this feels right." Animal tightened his grip on the pistol. "How would you react if somebody touched one of yours?" he asked. He didn't expect an answer from Tommy, but he gave him one anyway.

"I'd kill them and everybody they loved," Tommy said honestly. "But before I got to the business of killing, I'd make sure my guns were pointed in the right direction."

"So, you trying to say that your brother ain't in bed with the bitch who snatched my babies?" Animal pressed.

Tommy thought about the question before answering. "Honestly, I couldn't tell you for certain. Even if I could, I wouldn't. That's still my brother, and I got no illusions about how this is all gonna play out for all parties involved, big or small. But, no, I could never give my brother up to die."

"You either talk, or you bleed," Animal threatened.

"Blood it is, then," Tommy said calmly. "I'm a gangster, so if you expect me to give my brother up or beg for my life, you're wrong on both counts. I think you already knew that before you came here, though. I'm still in the dark about a lot of this, but the pieces are starting to come together. The only thing I can tell you right now, with absolute certainty, is that the Clarks had nothing to do with what happened to your family."

"And I'm supposed to believe you because you respect me enough to keep it real?" Animal asked sarcastically.

"No. I expect you to know me well enough to know how I get down," Tommy told him. "In all the years our two sides have been at it, we've always kept it within the unspoken rules of war. We've dropped bodies on your side, and you've knocked off a few of ours and—"

"I'd say I've sent more than a few of yours back to hell," Animal cut him off.

"You gonna keep stroking your own dick or let me finish?" Tommy was becoming irritated with him.

There was a loud thud at the door. It still held, but the wheelchair had shifted. Animal knew it wouldn't be long. "Make it quick, and I'll do you the same courtesy. Get to the point."

"My point is, we've always kept the bloodshed amongst the soldiers. Civilian blood has never been spilled, at least not intentionally. That's because we were raised to respect the code. Now, Shai might not be cut from the same slab of concrete as you or me, but my brother was still raised as a man of principle because my father wouldn't have it any other way. What happened to your family was some sucker shit, and regardless of how you might feel about us, you know in your heart that sucker shit ain't in our DNA."

Animal studied Tommy for what felt like forever. He searched the lines of a man's face who he had once idolized, searching for signs of deception. He knew he likely wouldn't find any but went through the motions anyway. Animal wanted to catch Tommy in a lie, wanted a reason to gun it out with whoever was on the other side of that door, and let them feel his pain. Not because they were involved but because it would be easier than the alternative. The Clarks were real and tangible enemies, ones he could fight head-up. Lilith was a different story. Trying to strike at her had proven to be about as easy as trying to hold water in his palms. After a while, Animal lowered his gun. "Let's say I buy the shit you selling and spare your life. What do I get in return?"

"My favor," Tommy said flatly.

"I don't need nothing from the Clarks," Animal spat.

"I'm not speaking for my family. I'm speaking for Tommy Guns. A man like you can never truly know what he needs until he needs it."

Animal thought about it. "And if it turns out one of yours was involved in this?"

"Then they burn," Tommy assured him. "If it's within my power, you have my guarantee that I'll make this right."

"How? You're a powerful man, Tommy, but I don't think even you're capable of resurrecting the dead." Animal thought of Gucci.

"You'd be surprised at what I'm capable of these days." Tommy flexed his hand.

"For all I know, you could be trying to line me up. I don't trust none of Poppa's kids."

"As you shouldn't. This is why I'm prepared to offer you a show of good faith. Have you visited your old man since you've been back?" Tommy asked quite unexpectedly.

Animal's face became hard. "See, I was just thinking about letting you live, and now you wanna change my mind." He leveled his gun. "What do you know about what happened to my father after we banged out at the church?"

"Unfortunately, not much. Had I been able to retrieve his body, I'd have made sure Priest was given a proper send-off. I made a place for him next to the plot where you laid your mom to rest. It's an empty box, more symbolic than anything, but it was the least I could do. You and I may have had our differences, but Priest was family to me. I owed him as much. When you get a second between catching bodies, go visit your people. I don't know if you'll find any peace there, but there's a chance you'll find something else there that will aid you in your mission."

"Don't play mind games with me, Tommy Guns," Animal warned.

"You know I've never been one for games. Do it—or not. That's your call to make."

"What the fuck ever, nigga. Anything else?" Animal asked sarcastically.

"Actually, yes. How the hell have you managed to breach our security not once but twice?" It was a question that had been nagging at Tommy since the first time Animal had done it.

Animal gave him his golden smile. "If I told you, it would ruin the surprise if I find that I need to pay you a third visit. I don't think either of us wants that, though."

"Agreed."

The bedroom door finally opened, bursting from the hinges under the weight of the heavy guard throwing himself against it for the last few minutes. Tommy's bedroom was flooded with men wearing black and carrying guns. Shai brought up the rear.

"Big bro, you good?" Shai asked, checking his brother for injuries.

"Man, quit pawing at me. I'm straight," Tommy assured him.

"I thought I heard voices coming from in here," Shai said, looking around the room. It was empty save for Tommy, who was still seated on the edge of the bed. Before Tommy could offer an explanation, one of the security guards interrupted them.

"What the hell happened to Moose?" He was looking through the broken window. Below, a medical team, which they kept on staff, was hoisting the bodyguard onto a gurney. All eyes in the room turned to Tommy, including Shai's.

Tommy shrugged. "Clumsy nigga tripped and fell."

Chapter 4

Kahllah awoke with a start. She had been so deep in her sleep that the point of waking felt like drowning. She sucked in air, letting it fill her lungs, and frowned when she picked up on staleness. It was like she was in a room where the windows hadn't been opened in weeks. She peered around, attempting to make heads or tails of where she was. It was a small room, barely big enough to hold the massive bookshelf that dominated one of the walls. There was no light except the candles that burned on the small night table beside the bed she was lying in. Something else was mixed in with the musty smell. It took her a minute to put her finger on what it was. It was death.

Instinctively, she rolled out of bed and was on her feet. She lasted about ten seconds before the room started to spin, and her legs felt like they couldn't support her. Her vision started to double, making it hard to focus. When she tried to take a step, one of her knees buckled, and she found herself falling. Had it not been for a firm hand grabbing her about the arm, she would've smacked her face on the end table.

"Easy," a calming voice urged her. "The sedative hasn't completely worked its way out of your system. You should be fine in a few hours."

"Nicodemus." Kahllah recognized the voice of her elder. She allowed him to help her back into the bed. After a few moments, the room stopped spinning long enough for her to regain her focus.

Nicodemus lowered himself into the wooden chair that was at the bedside. It was a simple thing, but it looked like it had taken him some effort to do so. He was huddled in the folds of the dark robe he wore most of the time, but only now, the garment seemed ill-fitting. It hung loosely over his frame, threatening to fall off if he moved the wrong way.

In the flicker of candlelight, she caught a glimpse of his face and could see that some of the color had returned to it, but his cheeks were still drawn, and heavy bags were under his dark eyes. He hadn't fully recovered yet. To look at him, you would have never known that until the day before he had spent weeks wasting away in the same bed that Kahllah now occupied, a victim of a failed assassination attempt. It was made to look like he had been bitten by one of the snakes he kept in his lab, which he used to make his poisons. The council ruled it an "accident," but some whispered otherwise.

Nicodemus was known as the Master of Poisons. He had been handling venomous creatures for decades and had been bitten so often over the years that his body developed a natural immunity to most of the bites and stings of the animals he handled. Even still, he kept a variety of antidotes and antivenoms at the ready, which is what made it so suspicious that no one could seem to find one to treat whatever was afflicting him then.

For weeks, they all sat by and watched as Nicodemus deteriorated from whatever toxin was attacking his system. He lasted longer than anyone would've thought, but it would only be a matter of time before he succumbed to his injuries. Nicodemus would've surely died had Kahllah not shown up when she did, bringing with her a dark gift. Where science had failed, it had succeeded.

"How long have I been out?" Kahllah winched as she pushed herself into a sitting position. She was in a great deal of pain but tried her best not to show it in front of the elder. Within the Brotherhood, pain was for the weak.

Nicodemus thought about the question. "About twenty-four hours, give or take. I must say that I'm impressed with your durability. I can't think of too many who have gone head-to-head with Bastille and lived to suffer the pains of it, let alone with all their limbs still intact."

Bastille . . . At one time, he and Kahllah had been allies, both faithful servants of the Brotherhood of Blood. Bastille had always been a man to toe the line of right and wrong, but never to the point of committing acts that could be considered dishonorable. That changed when he threw in his lot with Khan and

Tiger Lily in their plot to overthrow the Brotherhood.
Bastille had been responsible for trying to assassinate
Nicodemus, but it had been on Khan's orders, no
doubt. In the end, the attempt had failed, and Bastille
had lost his life for it, but not before beating Kahllah
to within an inch of hers.

"A beautiful death," Kahllah smirked, recalling
the sight of Nicodemus's diamond-dusted bullwhip
taking Bastille's head off. Nicodemus gave her a
disapproving look. It was frowned upon to celebrate
the death of one of their own unless they had fallen in
service to the Order. "My apologies."

Nicodemus nodded, accepting her apology. There
was a brief silence between them. The elder sat as
still as a statue in the shadows. She could barely see
him in the candlelight. Kahllah noticed a reading
lamp on the nightstand and reached to turn it on.

"Leave it," his voice was low, but she could feel the
weight of the command in his words. "My eyes are a
little sensitive to light as of late."

"Are you okay?" Kahllah asked, genuinely concerned.

"Truthfully, I don't know," Nicodemus said dream-
ily. He held up his hand in the candlelight and
curiously studied the veins beneath his skin. There
was something off about him, and they both knew it.
"What is happening to me?"

"A side effect of what has brought you back to us,"
Kahllah told him.

Nicodemus stopped his examination of his hand and turned his attention to Kahllah. "What have you done?"

"None of the healers or even our doctors seemed to be able to stop the poison from spreading. The rest of the Order may have been willing to sit by and watch you fade, but I wasn't. Science had failed us, so I turned to my only other alternative."

"Blood magic?" Nicodemus gasped in horror.

"Yes," Kahllah confessed shamefully. "It was the dark gift that snatched you from the jaws of death."

"You had no right," Nicodemus shouted.

"I had no choice," she countered. "What was I supposed to do? Sit back and watch you die?"

"If it was God's will, yes."

"This was not the will of God but that of greedy profiteers who would corrupt our most sacred Order."

"And this is what pushed you to traffic with demons?"

"Demons?" Kahllah raised an eyebrow. "I would remind you that these *demons*, as you call them, are the ones who helped us build this mountain stronghold. When the church we had served faithfully for centuries decided that we had outlived our usefulness and forced us from our original home, it was the Blood Tribes who gave us refuge. When our members were being hunted and exterminated by Vatican soldiers so that the secrets of the dirty deeds we had done in the name of His Holiness would die with us, it was the House of Gehenna who answered our call to arms.

We have always been the Brotherhood but became the Brotherhood of Blood to honor those who had given their lives to ensure our survival. Not just the natural, but the supernatural as well."

"I know our history better than you, little girl. That was a time long before you or I and when our interests and those of the Blood Tribes were the same."

"And what are our interests now, Poison Master? To become drug dealers? Maybe join the Arms Race? These last few years, you've spent so much time huddled amongst your books and potions that you don't see what's happening to us. Or maybe you see and just don't care anymore," Kahllah accused.

Nicodemus was on his feet in a flash, hand drawn back to strike her. Kahllah never batted an eye. "Have a care, Lotus. My patience with you can only be stretched so far."

"Yet, my love for you knows no bounds," she said with a dramatic sigh. "Why else would I have done what I did to save you, even knowing it could have cost me my life?"

"Your stay of execution is temporary. I owe you a debt for saving my life, but there is still much that the Black Lotus must answer for." He retook his seat.

"We are under siege, Master Nicodemus, and this time, our enemies are not descending on us from Rome but from under our own roof."

Nicodemus sat quietly and listened as Kahllah told him what she knew of Khan's plans to usurp the Brotherhood's leadership by killing him so that he could move the Order into the business of drugs and guns. He wished he could say he was surprised but couldn't. Nicodemus wasn't so far removed from the goings-on within the Brotherhood that he was unaware of the unrest amongst some of the younger Brothers. The elders may have been content with living by the time-honored traditions, but the youth were getting restless. They were tired of living in the shadows, only knowing service, and were eager to sample the forbidden fruits that grew in the new world.

Nicodemus knew it would only be a matter of time before something like that happened, but he hadn't expected it to come from Khan. He had handpicked Khan to bring into the Brotherhood. Nicodemus had pulled him out of the gutters of Cuba and made him a man of influence and wealth. Raffa Khan was possibly one of the greatest of his students, but he was flawed. He always had too much ambition and too little patience.

"So?" Kahllah realized a few moments had passed since she filled Nicodemus in, but he hadn't said anything.

"So, I will speak with the Brothers about these accusations. In time, this will be handled accordingly," Nicodemus said as if it were that simple.

"Time? Have you not been listening to what I've said?" She was on her feet. "Khan has made his play, and now, it's time we make ours. We must put him down and those loyal to him before we find ourselves overrun by these traitors," Kahllah warned.

"Khan is strong, maybe the strongest of us, but we are still the Brotherhood. It will take more than one rogue Brother and a few of his disciples to overthrow something that has stood for nearly a thousand years. He can attempt, but he would need an army to succeed," Nicodemus said confidently.

"He already has one. Khan isn't the only one of your old students who are conspiring against you," Kahllah informed him.

Nicodemus had only had two students in his time of service, so he knew who she was referring to. "Impossible. She's been dead for years, killed by the same rabble she was selling our secrets to."

"I assure you, Tiger Lily is very much alive and doing more than trading in weapons and information now," Kahllah insisted.

That was a name that Nicodemus hadn't heard in many years and thought he would never hear again. He and Tiger Lily had a history that stretched back many years, long before she became one of the Brotherhood's most celebrated assassins and eventually its greatest traitor. In those days, she had been called Lilith and was making her coin as a thief and prostitute. Her hunting grounds were the high society circles of South Beach, Miami. She would lure men in with the promise of sex, only to drug and liberate them of their goods. Nicodemus had been one of her intended victims. He had been visiting Miami on Brotherhood business when the then young Latina beauty had caught his attention.

He had watched her applying her trade for two nights before approaching her under the guise of a trick looking for a good time. She greedily took the bait and went to his hotel room with him, which would be her undoing. When she awoke two days later, she was miles away from Miami.

Nicodemus spent days breaking Lilith's body before he started on her mind. She needed to be *reconditioned,* as he called it. It took longer than he had expected because she was incredibly strong-willed, but she eventually broke, as they all did, and submitted to his will. Nicodemus remade her, body and soul. They started as master and student before eventually becoming lovers. Nicodemus taught her the ways of the Brotherhood, including his mastery of chemistry. This was how she developed such an intricate knowledge of manufacturing drugs. It was the drugs that would eventually drive a wedge between the two of them. He became the catalyst of her exile from the Order.

As a child of the streets, Lilith understood that money was to be made from drugs, but the Brotherhood would never back such a venture, so she went rogue. She began selling her services and Brotherhood technology to the highest bidders. When word of her exploits made it back to the elders, they branded her a traitor and passed a death sentence on her. However, before the execution order could be carried out, Lilith was murdered by one of the same cartels she had been in bed with, or so

Nicodemus had been led to believe. However, according to Kahllah, his lover was still very much alive and up to no good.

"And you're sure of this?" Nicodemus asked.

"Absolutely," Kahllah confirmed. "She is backing Khan and behind the kidnapping of my adopted brother's children."

This caught Nicodemus by surprise. "Priest's bastard still lives? This day is just full of surprises."

"Yes, he lives. Had it not been for Lilith trying to kidnap his daughter, I would've never known any of this."

"What use could Lilith have with the child of the Bastard Son?"

"Her blood," Kahllah told him. "Though Animal was never initiated into our Order, he is descendant from a member of the Black Hand, and by extension, so is his daughter. On the other side of her genetic makeup, her mother is the heir to a very powerful cartel chief. Celeste is next in line to inherit the drug empire if the mother dies. To put it simply, by right of birth, this little girl has a place at both our tables."

"And when the child comes of age, she could possibly shift the balance of power on both fronts." Nicodemus picked up on where Kahllah was going with it. "Brilliant strategy. By using the girl, Lilith gets to have her cake and eat it too, without starting an all-out war."

"We need to move against the traitors while we still can. I can take a small battalion of some of our most skilled Brothers out into the world to hunt down Lilith and Khan, and we can end all this with a swing of my blade." Kahllah made a slicing motion with her hand.

"I agree." Nicodemus nodded. "A team will be dispatched immediately to bring these accused traitors before the council to answer for their crimes."

"Thank you, Master Nicodemus. I can be changed, armed, and ready to leave to lead them within the hour," Kahllah told him.

"And who says that you'll be leading them? This is something that will be handled by the Black Hand."

"And I am a member of the Black Hand," Kahllah reminded him.

"You *were* a member of the Black Hand," he corrected her. "As I said earlier, there is still much that the Black Lotus must answer for. Quite a bit has been said about you in your absence from us. I think you should remain here until we figure out what is fact and what is fiction."

"And my brother?" she questioned. She knew that Animal would need her for what was to come.

"Is of no concern of ours until he becomes a concern of ours. Right now, I need you where I can see you until I say otherwise."

No sooner than Nicodemus had made his decree, someone knocked on the door. A few seconds passed before a young man stepped in. He was tall with skin the color of bronze and rich black hair that he wore tapered on the sides. His youthful face was covered in a thin five-o'clock shadow. A long-sleeved linen shirt clung to his well-defined chest and muscular arms. Honey-colored eyes studied Kahllah quizzically as if she were some exotic animal he saw for the first time. Kahllah knew his face from when she had met him years before when she was visiting the Mountain on business. She had never bothered to learn his name, but she had seen the damage he could inflict with the two rods dangling from his belt inside a custom holster. Inside them were retractable bullwhips, similar to the old-fashioned leather one used by Nicodemus, only these were powered by Brotherhood technology and quite lethal.

"So, I'm a prisoner now?" Kahllah was speaking to Nicodemus, but her eyes were on the man with the spears.

"Not a prisoner, but a guest . . . at least until we can get this sorted out." Nicodemus stood. "I have some other business to attend to that may keep me away for a day or two. When I return, we will settle this. In my absence, you may look to my apprentice, Artemis, to attend to any needs you may have." With that, Nicodemus left the two of them in his chambers.

Kahllah looked at Artemis, who was standing as still as a statue, still watching her with those eyes. She knew that behind those soft, inviting eyes was a stone-cold killer. If Nicodemus had left him to watch over her, that meant he was confident that Artemis could handle her if she got out of line. She planned to put Nicodemus's confidence to the test the first chance she got. Had Kahllah thought that Nicodemus would try to confine her instead of helping her, she would have let him die rather than giving him the precious gift meant for her. There wasn't too much she could do about it now except bide her time.

When she was done with the staring contest between her and Artemis, she decided to break the ice by offering her hand. He glared at it for a minute as if he suspected it might have been some trick. When he had decided that she was sincere, Artemis shook her hand.

As soon as Kahllah's skin contacted his, it produced a spark strong enough to make her wince. The stone face had faded when she looked at him, and he was smiling at her like the cat who had swallowed the canary. Something about the way he was looking at Kahllah made her uneasy. She wondered if one of Artemis's gifts had been the ability to read minds, or was she so transparent that he could tell that a man hadn't touched her in years? Either way, she hoped Nicodemus finished his business early. She wasn't sure how she felt about spending an extended period in close quarters with Artemis.

Chapter 5

The damp grass made a sloshing noise under the soles of his Converse as he hiked over the hill. He had been walking around for the last twenty minutes or so. It wasn't that he didn't know where he was going. He just wasn't sure that he was ready to go there. In truth, he wasn't even sure why he had come. There was something about Tommy's suggestion that had been nagging at him since he'd left the Clark house.

He was too weary to think, but he felt like he had to keep moving to keep his hold on his sanity, so he allowed his body to carry him where it would and found himself at a cemetery. It had been years since Animal had been there, and the one time he did come, he only stayed long enough to ensure the work he had ordered on his mother's burial site had been done to his specifications. Outside of that instance, he had been avoiding the place for years. Gucci had always tried to urge him to visit her, but he always made an excuse about why he couldn't. He hated cemeteries almost as much as hospitals because they both represented death.

It was funny how something he had dealt with day in and day out for most of his life could still make him uncomfortable. Killing men in battle was something that Animal had come to accept and gotten used to. Still, it was a horse of a different color watching someone you cared for wither away in a hospital or getting together to say your final goodbyes to a loved one right before you tossed dirt on them. Unfortunately, he had been throwing dirt over loved ones far too often lately. Animal was no stranger to loss, but losing his wife and best friend back-to-back hit differently.

So much was happening that it felt like a weight had been placed on his shoulders. A weight so heavy that he often found himself wondering how long he would be able to carry it. He was at his breaking point. Animal could not say for sure where the things he was going through would lead, but in an attempt to establish some clarity, he had to start where it had all begun.

He crossed the cemetery leisurely, running his fingers absently over the headstones as he passed them. As Animal neared his destination, he could feel his legs tremble. It wasn't that he was afraid; more like uneasiness washed over him. The plot he was looking for was on a hill in the shade of a willow tree. In life, his mother had never been one for sunny days, so Animal wanted to ensure she was laid to rest in the shade. There had only been one headstone the last time he visited, but now, there were two. The larger of the two was rose-hued marble steeped at the top like a church roof. Sitting atop it was an angel carved of the same stone. Clutched in one hand was a sword and a shield in the other. He stood vigil over the soul of the woman who rested there. The second grave was unremarkable. It was a simple black plaque with no name but three words: *Sword of God.* It had been a moniker given to a man who Animal had hated growing up, but by the time of his death, Animal had discovered a newfound respect for him.

It had been several years since he was slain, and Animal still had no idea what became of his body following the shootout at the church. Tommy claimed that they hadn't taken it, which left the off chance that the police carted it off and buried it in an un-marked grave in Potter's Field when no one had come to claim it. A more likely outcome was the Brotherhood had claimed it. The secret order of as-sassins, which his father had served for so many years, had their own way of laying their own to rest when they had fallen in the line of duty. The thing was, Priest hadn't fallen while in service of the Brotherhood. He had sacrificed himself so that Animal and Gucci might live. It was still hard for Animal to digest that a man he had always thought to be selfish could've proven him so wrong with one act of selflessness. Maybe he had been wrong about the man who gave him life but hadn't stuck around long enough to watch him live it. It wouldn't have been the first time he had been wrong in assessing someone's character.

Animal dropped to his knees at the foot of the angel. The moisture from the wet grass soaked through the knees of his jeans. He had felt the cold touch of the Reaper on more than a few occasions, but that was the first time it was different. Death had almost taken hold of him, and to that day, he still couldn't figure out how he had made it off the sinking ship. Then as his hand went absently to the scar behind his ear, he had an idea.

He had been avoiding coming here, but he knew he would have to make the pilgrimage one day. There was so much that he wanted to say . . . *needed* to say to his parents, but he now found himself at a loss. His fingers traced the letters of the rose headstone marked *Marie Torres*.

"Hello, Mother," he began. The word felt alien coming from his lips in reference to the woman who had given him life. He couldn't remember the last time he had called her anything other than by her name or an explicative behind her back. Animal and Marie hadn't had the best relationship growing up. In life, she had been an addict and a whore who, more often than not, put her own needs before those of her children. As a result, she kept a revolving door of men coming in and out of their lives. Some were okay, but for the most part, they had all been assholes who weren't interested in anything beyond getting their dicks wet. Animal hadn't particularly cared for any of the men Marie kept time with, but there was one who he came to hate above all the others.

Eddie's tenure in the Torres household had lasted the longest. To that day, Animal couldn't remember where she had found him or when they had started seeing each other. It was like he had just woken up one day, and Eddie was there with no plans of leaving. Eddie was the one who brought the drugs to the table. Marie wasn't a saint. She chipped here and there, experimenting with cocaine in social settings, but it was Eddie who turned her into a full-blown addict. Those years spent with Eddie were some of the worst of Animal's life. He was a special kind of cruel who seemed to get his kicks off finding creative ways to torture young Animal.

One of Eddie's favorite forms of punishment had been to lock Animal inside the small dog cage they kept in the living room. Animal would be caged for hours, sometimes for a full day with no food or water. Eddie wouldn't even let him out to use the bathroom. Instead, he instructed him to handle his business on the newspaper that lined the cage. As Animal reflected on those times, he reasoned that Eddie's treatment of him had as much of a hand in transforming him into The Animal as anything else he had gone through in the streets.

Years after Animal escaped, he still carried the hatred for Eddie for what he'd done and was no great lover of his mother for letting him. He couldn't understand how a parent could allow such things to be done to their child and not intervene. Back then, his young mind was ignorant of the evils of addiction and how those caught in its thrall became someone else. All he saw when he looked at Marie was a mother who didn't love her son, so, in turn, he tried his best not to love her. In a perfect world, his stance would've softened, and time would've healed the rift between mother and son, but thanks to Eddie, this wasn't to be. He had murdered Marie, not with beatings or drugs, but with the infection he had transmitted to her. Marie died in the hospital at the tender age of 36 from AIDS-related complications. Animal never even had the chance to say goodbye.

Some time would pass before Animal could balance the scales on that account. His and Eddie's paths had crossed entirely by chance. This time, Eddie wasn't confronted by a frightened child who he could beat at his pleasure but the monster he had helped to create. In those early days, Animal was a novice killer and hadn't learned to savor the small moments that came just before the end of a man's life, which was fortunate for Eddie. He was dispatched swiftly and violently. Killing Eddie for his actions brought Animal a measure of satisfaction but no real peace. His life couldn't get his mother back nor reset the clock on the time they had missed while feuding. The only thing it really did was complete the transformation Animal had been slowly undergoing. He had set out on the devil's road, and there would be no turning back. Then he met Gucci, and everything changed.

From the moment Gucci had walked into his life, she became the light of it. She was the one thing that gave him hope in a world of hopelessness. The woman taught him how to love when it seemed that he would never know love again. Gucci had gifted him with a slice of heaven, and in return, he dragged her with him to hell. Animal destroyed everything they had built together with the simple act of opening his front door . . .

When his ex-lover, Red Sonja, showed up at his beach house unannounced, he should have kicked her ass to the curb before even allowing her a chance to open her mouth. But instead, he let her in. With Sonja, trouble always followed. This time was no different, except that trouble had come in the form of the little redheaded girl who was clinging to Sonja's leg. She had her mother's steel-gray eyes and a face that Animal saw every time he looked in the mirror.

As it turned out, when Animal had fled Puerto Rico to return home to Gucci, he had left Sonja behind with more than a broken heart. His leaving her had rocked Sonja's world, and here she was years later . . . looking to return the favor. Letting Animal in on the fact that he had a daughter he knew nothing about was one part of it. The second was that someone was trying to kidnap her.

That night, Animal listened as Red Sonja spun the tale that would move him to do something he had long ago forsaken—shed blood. Her father, Poppito Suarez, led one of the most powerful drug cartels in the Eastern United States. Animal first met Sonja when her father employed him as a part of K-Dawg's mercenary crew, *La Peste Negra*—The Black Death. Animal and the hired guns had been instrumental in Poppito removing one of his top rivals and seizing control of Old San Juan. Animal hadn't seen Poppito in years but always remembered him as a man who, when he spoke, people listened, so it surprised Animal to learn that it was no longer his voice being heard.

Poppito had taken a new wife, a woman named Lilith. She was a dark-haired beauty who was a few years Poppito's junior. At the time, little was known about Lilith outside the fact that she was a player in the game. It was said that she had the power to change the fortunes of the men she shared beds with. Lilith's words carried influence in rooms where women had no place, let alone a voice. It didn't take long before her whispers in Poppito's ears began to manifest themselves as orders handed out throughout his organization. Within a few months, she carried more favor with the cartel boss than those loyal to him for decades.

The old-timers whispered about Poppito's new love interest being some kind of *bruja* who trafficked in the dark arts and suggested that her hold over him was supernatural. Unfortunately, Poppito's health suddenly started to decline around the time he got involved with Lilith, which did little to dispel the rumors. Lilith was, without question, more than what she seemed, but by the time anyone realized how serious of a threat she represented, the balance of power had already shifted.

Lilith had taken Poppito's position, but it was his blood that she would need to secure his power. By becoming his wife, she gained power of attorney over his legitimate holdings, but so long as his heirs lived, her control over the cartel could be contested at any time. Poppito's only son and next in line, Christopher, was the first to go. He had been cut down on the streets of Old San Juan, and his body was left to be discovered by tourists. This left Sonja, who Lilith had planned a similar untimely demise, but Poppito's daughter had proven far more challenging to get rid of. With the help of a few still loyal to her father, Red Sonja managed to escape from the island with her daughter, Celeste. The mother and daughter had dodged a bullet, but it was only a temporary reprieve. So long as they remained a threat to Lilith's plans, they would never be safe, which brought them to Animal.

For Animal, the decision to get involved wasn't an easy one for him to make. When he'd gotten out of prison, he promised his wife that he had put down his guns for good, but after Sonja had laid everything on the table, he found it hard to ignore their cause. Though he had only just met Celeste, she was still the fruit of his tree. He felt obligated to protect his newfound daughter the same as he would have done his son. Against his wife's advice, Animal had agreed to come to Sonja and Celeste's defense and stand against the wicked stepmother. As a result, he now found himself a widower with two missing children, betrayed by one of the two women who claimed to love him.

Something wet splashed on the back of Animal's hand. He touched his fingers to his cheek, and they came away wet. When he realized that he was crying, he found himself filled with shame. However, the time for crying had passed. Actions were what was needed. He looked at his father's grave, and for a minute, he could almost hear his voice, as he had that night on the beach. *"Every minute that those involved are allowed to breathe God's good air is a mockery to not only your pedigree as a harbinger of death, but it's an offense to the memory of every soldier who has laid down their life in the name of your survival. Go forth, my son. Pick up your guns and cleanse this world in their vengeful fire."*

"Yes, the fire." Animal nodded. Priest hadn't been right about much in life, but he was right about that. Gucci was dead, and Animal did not know if he would ever see his children again. All he had left was the fire; he would let it wash over his enemies and dance gleefully in the flames while they burned.

As Animal was preparing to finish his visit, he spotted something near his father's headstone. It was so small that he wouldn't have noticed it had the sun not struck it at just the right angle. He cleared away the dirt and grass and plucked the thing from the grave. It was a golden rosary. He knew it well, as it had been one of his father's favorite killing tools. Animal ran the rosary over his fingers and found the touch of it comforting. Tommy had been right about him finding the trip helpful. The rosary was a reminder of where he came from and what he was.

He was pushing himself up from the ground when he felt something. It was the bite of cold steel behind his ear. Animal knew the touch all too well. He could hear the distinct sound of a gun's hammer being cocked in his ear.

"Had this been a few years ago, there was no way I'd have been able to sneak up on The Animal," a familiar voice said. "Guess the rumors of you going soft have some truth to them. Now, get up. On your knees is no way for a man of your reputation to die."

Chapter 6

After spending the last couple of days cramped in the house, plotting, it felt good to be outside. The fresh air was just what she needed to help her think, and she had a lot on her mind. Lilith Angelino-Suarez sat in the back of her expansive Westchester, N.Y., home, enjoying a cigar and a glass of rum while watching the sunset. It was a beautiful property that sat on just over an acre of green grass, bordered by cherry blossoms. She'd had them planted when she first purchased and renovated the property several years before. She had fallen in love with cherry blossoms since she first saw them at the Brooklyn Botanic Garden. One of her male suitors had taken her there on a date when she was younger. It was entirely too hot for them in her native Cuba or her primary home in Puerto Rico, but the climate in New York was just right for them, at least in the spring. Sometimes, she forgot how beautiful and peaceful it was because she was hardly ever there.

Outside of when she wanted to go shopping, Lilith had no real taste for the Rotten Apple. New York was one of her cartel's biggest drug markets but one of her least favorite cities. It was too big, too busy, and frankly, too dirty for her liking. For a girl from a small village such as herself, being mashed amongst the tall glass towers and bustling people was like culture shock. You would think that with her spending a good part of her adult life in Miami, she would have been able to adjust to New York, but it and Miami were two different animals. The only reason she had even purchased the property in Westchester was out of spite. Lilith was someone who valued her privacy, and for this reason, she didn't stay in hotels. In each city she visited, she kept a rental property, and New York was no different . . . up until a few years ago when she met a man who she needed to show the error of his ways.

It all happened purely by chance. At the time, Lilith was renting a five-bedroom unit inside a high-rise building on the Upper Westside of Manhattan, which she absolutely loved. She had been renting the apartment for a year or so back then and was content to make that her New York base of operations until she met him. A man of wealth and influence sought to take out a contract with the Brotherhood of Blood. This was back when she was still in good standing with the Order. He had requested that they dispatch the best of the best, so the contract was given to Tiger Lily.

Generally, contracts were negotiated and paid for using a broker, but for reasons that Lily couldn't remember, she had met with the man in person.

From the moment she laid eyes on the squat, white man, she knew she didn't like him. He carried an arrogance that came with most men who had money but had never had to work for it. She had visited with him in the very yard where she sat that evening and gone over the details about her intended target, which happened to be the person who afforded him such a lavish lifestyle—his wife. The woman was the heiress of a hotel baron and had inherited a great deal of wealth upon his passing. When she married her husband, she afforded him a lavish lifestyle and showered him with everything he wanted, and still, he wanted more. They had no children, so everything she owned would be passed to him upon her death. The woman was already on in years and sickly, so she likely didn't have many years left on earth anyhow, but he was eager to expedite her passing.

The more he talked, the less Lilith cared for him. He was a worm and a parasite, and the very sight of him disgusted her. It wasn't bad enough that he was plotting to have his wife murdered, but how he treated the employees who worked at the home pushed her over the top. One of the maids, a cute, young Black girl of about 20, had accidentally spilled one of the drinks she had been bringing out to the yard for them. The man flew into a rage, hurling insults and racial slurs at her. Then for good measure, he kicked her in the ass as she was cleaning up the mess. The girl cried, but Lilith knew that they were not tears of hurt—but rage. At that moment, Lilith decided that there was no way she could perform a service of any kind for this man. Still, she had taken a sacred oath to the Brotherhood, and a life paid for was a life taken.

Against her better judgment—and her oath—Lilith went to the heiress and exposed her husband's plot to have her killed. The woman didn't take it well at all. Lilith had expected her to be broken up at finding out about the man she loved, but instead, she was furious. She offered to pay Lilith three times the sum of the contract's value to kill her husband instead. Lilith compromised with her. She wouldn't take the woman's money but would ask for something else in return. She wanted their land. The woman happily agreed. It was one of many such properties she owned, and she wouldn't miss the Westchester home.

Once Lilith carried out the execution of the husband, the heiress stayed true to her word and signed the property over to one of Lilith's shell companies. Lilith would have the home demolished and the property renovated. In place of the impressive residence shared by the couple, she would have one built to her specifications. Once the deal between Lilith and the woman was closed, she would murder her anyway, fulfilling the original contract. After all, a life paid for was a life taken.

The elders were livid when they found out what Lilith had done. Not only had she violated the terms of the contract by exposing the identity of the man who had contracted her to the intended target, but she had done it for personal gain. Regardless of whether she eventually killed the woman, she had still broken her vows, so she had to be punished. For what she had done, she was tossed into a dark hole, devoid of light or human contact save for the times Nicodemus would visit her once every other morning to flog her with his whip. She had strayed from the path and needed to be "reconditioned." It was a steep price but well worth it.

Those six months in the hole were long and hard ones for Lilith. The only thing that helped her keep her sanity was her dreams for the property that now belonged to her. Before coming to the Brotherhood, Lilith had been a broke hustler, and even after joining, she still didn't have much. She had money, rental properties, and even a few pieces of jewelry she held onto for nostalgia's sake, but the Westchester property was the first thing she ever really owned that had real value. It was in her isolation that Lilith first began to question whether the path the Brotherhood had laid for Tiger Lily was one Lilith wanted to follow. It was then that the seeds of doubt were planted that would eventually lead her to the point where she found herself that afternoon.

A flicker of motion on the iPad resting on the table pulled Lilith from her reflection. She picked up the sleek device and looked at it. The sound was muted, but she didn't need to hear what was happening, only see. On the screen, a live feed from one of the rooms in the house played. It was a room painted in soft greens and yellows. Toys were scattered about, and the large television on the wall played some random cartoon. It was a spare room to accommodate Lilith's occasional overnight guests at the house. For the last few days, it had been occupied by two very special guests.

The boy, a bright-eyed, brown-skinned toddler, sat content on a bean bag chair watching television. There were two gaming systems on the floor in front of the chair, which he sometimes entertained himself with. He hadn't been much trouble during his stay, save for the occasional crying for his mother, as children separated from their parents over periods were prone to do. He could usually be pacified by sweets or a shiny new toy. But the second occupant of the room proved far more difficult to please.

She was older than the boy, having not long ago crossed her third year but carried herself with the soul of someone who had been here before. She looked to have recently risen from her chemically induced slumber. She spent most of her time there sedated, as she was a bit rambunctious. She ran her thin fingers through the mop of matted red hair on her head. It could stand a good combing, but the girl wouldn't allow anyone to touch it, so they let her be. Then after making a visual check of her brother, she curled her knees to her chest on the bed and locked her steel-gray eyes on the door. That's all she did when she wasn't sleeping . . . brood and watch.

The door to the room opened, and Lilith watched as one of the girls who worked for her, Maggie, entered the room. She pushed a wire cart holding two plates of whatever was on the dinner menu that night. Standing in the doorway was one of Lilith's soldiers. Both of them looked uneasy. The toddler rushed to the cart happily to receive his dinner plate and juice box, but the girl remained on the bed. Maggie nervously picked up the second plate and tried to coax the three-year-old to eat, but she continued sitting silently, glaring at her. Maggie glanced nervously over her shoulder at the soldier before timidly approaching the little girl's bed.

The redheaded girl didn't seem opposed to Maggie's presence and even allowed her to sit on the bed. Maggie smiled warmly, said something Lilith couldn't hear, and held up a spoon full of food as if offering to feed her. The little redhead mustered a small smile and scooted forward a bit, mouth wide and prepared to accept the food. When Maggie let her guard down is when Lilith spied the child's hand slipping beneath the pillow. What transpired next happened so fast that Lilith would have to go back and watch the feed later to analyze the turn of events.

The redhead produced the cord from one of the gaming controllers she had pulled loose and hidden under her pillow, slipping it around Maggie's neck. Maggie was caught totally off guard as the redhead twisted her body to tighten the cord around her neck and dropped all her weight to secure it. She was tiny but quite strong, as Maggie realized once the cord constricted, and her air was cut off.

The soldier guarding the door rushed into the room to help. Maggie's arms were flailing, and her eyes were rolling in her head as the 3-year-old was strangling her. The soldier tried to get to the little girl to pull her off Maggie, but she had wedged herself tightly into the corner, using Maggie's body as a shield, so it wasn't easy. He finally managed to free Maggie but now found himself the target of the rabid child's anger. She sprang from the bed and clawed onto his back like an angry monkey. The soldier howled in pain as the girl's teeth bit deep enough into his neck to draw blood. With some effort, he managed to get the girl off him and threw her violently across the room. Unfortunately, she bounced off the wall and came right back at him. It took the combined efforts of Maggie and the soldier to hold the girl down and inject her with another dose of sedative. After a few more minutes of thrashing, the drug finally kicked in, and she went still.

Lilith couldn't help but beam proudly as she watched the whole fiasco. Even at such a young age, Celeste was already proving to be the perfect blend of both her parents: resourceful and ruthless. If what she was showing at 3 indicated who she would grow to be, Lilith had made the right choice by risking it all to snatch her from her parents. Celeste resented Lilith abducting her, but it was only because she didn't understand the part she was born to play in the Grand Design. In time, she would come to embrace her destiny, as well as her power. Through Celeste, Lilith would change not only the course of the Brotherhood but also the world. Everything Lilith had been trying to build rested on Celeste, but her brother, T.J., was a different story. The only reason Lilith even had him was that he had the misfortune of being in the house when Celeste was kidnapped and his mother murdered. Other than that, he had no real value to Lilith or her plans. Nevertheless, she knew that she would have to make a hard decision sooner or later.

"Mother?" A soft voice called from behind Lilith. Standing in the doorway was a statuesque, brown-skinned girl with dark eyes and full lips made for kissing. Her long dreads hung loosely down her back, stopping just short of her plump rear end. As usual, she wore fatigue pants, a long-sleeved T-shirt, and boots. She was a natural beauty with a model's shape, but she always chose to hide what God had given her under grungy, baggy clothes. Lilith had always encouraged her to embrace these things, but Ophelia was reluctant. Instead, she went out of her way to hide how beautiful she was, hardly ever showing any of her skin, and got defensive if a man complimented her. Most considered her behavior strange, but that was because they didn't know what Ophelia had suffered in her old life before Lilith gifted her a new one.

"What is it, child?" Lilith asked.

"My apologies for disturbing you, but I wanted to let you know that all has been made ready for your guests to be received."

"Excellent," Lilith said, going over her mental preparations. This visit was an expected one, but not this soon. There was still so much to do, so many wheels that had yet to be set in motion. The visit would push up her timeline, but she couldn't do much about it. To try to avoid it or ignore the request would've been to tip her hand. At that point, the element of surprise and uncertainty were the only things she had working on her side.

"Are you sure about this?" Ophelia asked as if reading her mother's mind.

Lilith thought about it before answering. "No, but the greater the risk, the greater the reward."

"Or the loss," Ophelia added.

"No need to worry, daughter. The rite of hospitality will ensure our guests mind their manners while under our roof. There is nothing to fear," Lilith assured her.

"I fear no one but the Almighty," Ophelia said confidently.

"Then why the long face?"

Ophelia was hesitant.

"Speak," Lilith ordered.

"It's the *Red Widow,*" Ophelia began nervously. "It's been—"

"Sunk," Lilith finished her sentence for her. "I've seen the news. Were we able to salvage any of the shipment it was carrying?"

"Some, but not much. We also lost almost every man we had on the ship. I'm sorry, Mother." Ophelia lowered her head in shame.

Lilith stood and approached her adopted daughter. She was shorter than Ophelia, but her presence felt much larger. She used her index finger to force up the girl's head and looked into her dark eyes. "What have I always told you about eye contact?"

"To look people in the eyes is a sign of confidence. Even in our final moments, we look death in the eyes so that he knows we aren't afraid," Ophelia recited. It was one of the first things Lilith had taught her. When Ophelia came to Lilith, she suffered from very low self-esteem and had always had a problem making eye contact with people. Again, this was a result of the abuse she had suffered. She had been free from bondage for years, but the girl still struggled with some of the lingering mental scars.

Lilith nodded in approval of her answer. "And you don't have anything to be sorry for. The lives lost on the boat are of no consequence. The cargo was my concern. Had my Nightshade overseen our shipment, our enemies wouldn't have stood a chance. That was my fault for entrusting the task to those not worthy. It's a mistake I won't make again." She touched the girl's cheek affectionately. Then she noticed something else behind her eyes. There was more that she needed to say. "Something else?"

"We also lost the bag. Sonja double-crossed Animal's people and fled with it before our agents could spring the trap you set for the dock," Ophelia told her.

This disappointed Lilith. She had anticipated Animal and his crew making a play for the *Red Widow*. She'd have been disappointed if he hadn't, considering how formidable of an adversary he had proven to be thus far. It had all been a part of her plan. The information about the *Red Widow,* which she was sure would be discovered in the satchel, would act as the bait to lure Animal and his bunch close enough for her to wipe them out and retrieve her property. Just when they thought they had achieved a measure of victory, her soldiers would swoop in and snatch it from them. But it hadn't gone as planned. She knew Animal and his group would cause some collateral damage, but she hadn't expected a group of gangbangers to be creative enough to sink an entire cargo ship. It was further proof of the assassin's resourcefulness.

Losing their shipment hurt, but it would've been a loss she could recover from if she retrieved the bag and the chemical formula inside that held the key to mass-producing the drug that sparked their little war. Without the shipment or the formula, she stood to lose everything. "It would seem that I have underestimated this Animal," Lilith said.

"Then why continue to toy with him?" Ophelia questioned. "Release your Nightshade. I will go into the city and bring back the heads of Animal and all who stand with him."

"I know you would try, my Nightshade, but I'm not confident you would be able to deliver on that promise . . . at least not as a whole," Lilith told her.

"Is this about the boy?" Ophelia asked angrily. Seeing Ashanti had stirred repressed memories in her, and Lilith was aware of this. "He means nothing to me, Mother. On my honor." She knelt before Lilith. "Whatever I was in my old life is dead. I am reborn in the image of the Order and live only to serve. I have shown this repeatedly, yet you still doubt my ability to do what needs to be done?" She was so angry that her body trembled, and her eyes became moist with tears. She wanted nothing more than to prove herself to her adopted mother.

Lilith pulled the girl to her feet. She cradled her brown face in her hands, wiping her tears away with her thumbs. "My Ophelia, you are by far the best of us. It isn't your ability that I doubt, but your heart. Worry not about Animal's soldiers. The wheels have already been set in motion, and very shortly, the blood of Animal's crew will stain the streets of New York. As far as their leader, he will be allowed to live for a time longer. Animal still has a role to play in this."

Ophelia pulled away. "What role can Priest's bastard have in this other than to bleed at your feet? Whatever plans you had for him died with his father. It is done."

"It is done when I say so," Lilith countered.

"I warn you, Mother; to continue to toy with this man is to put all we have worked for at risk," Ophelia said in frustration. She didn't like the game her mother was playing.

"Who are you to give *me* warnings? I have been in countless battles and faced far greater adversaries than this brokenhearted boy, and I am still here to talk about it, little girl. You would do well to remember who you are speaking to, lest I have to remind you," Lilith warned.

"I meant no disrespect, Mother. It's just that . . . I have looked into the soul of this Animal and found it empty. Even if we were to return his children to him, his code of honor would not allow the death of his wife to go answered. Besides the kids, he has nothing left to live for," Ophelia explained.

"In that case, let's give him something to die for," Lilith said wickedly, toking her cigar. "I agree with you that the only way to end this will be with the death of Animal, but it will be on *my* terms and when *I* am ready. I will allow him to go peacefully into the fields, but first, I will make him reap the harvest."

Ophelia turned to leave without bothering to respond. It was pointless by that point. Her mother's mind was made up.

"Will you not be staying to receive our guests?" Lilith asked.

"If it's all the same to you, I'd rather not. Unfortunately, I'm not skilled in smiling at people I plan to kill," Ophelia told her.

"Don't be proud of your weaknesses," Lilith shot back.

"As you say, Mother." She bowed and left the woman to her cigar and her sunset. Her mother was playing a dangerous game that could cost them more than just a few soldiers and a business opportunity. There was far too much at stake to leave anything to chance. If her mother couldn't see it on her own, Ophelia would have to show her the light.

Lilith was finishing her cigar when the iPad tied into her security system alerted her to motion in the front of the house. She adjusted the view and found Ophelia storming out of the front door carrying a dark-colored bag. She tossed the bag into the backseat of her rental car before climbing behind the wheel and peeling down the driveway to the main road.

"Should I be concerned about this?" a voice spoke softly behind Lilith. She never heard him approach, but his presence didn't alarm her. She had been expecting him but had grown accustomed to his unannounced visits by then. He was one of the few people who could sneak up on her.

Lilith didn't turn to acknowledge him when she replied. She simply shrugged. "Children are rebellious by nature. Every parent must eventually go through it."

"Spoken like someone who still has room for error, which you don't. I need to know that you still have this under control."

"You will still have what was promised to you; no worries on that account," Lilith assured him.

"And if the girl thinks differently?"

This time, Lilith did face him when she answered. Her eyes were hard and unflinching. "She is not your concern, and I hope this is the last time I'll have to remind you of that. Sometimes, you must let children make a mistake so they learn from it before you step in and correct it."

Chapter 7

The place where they had chosen to honor the memory of their fallen comrade was not a funeral home, cemetery, or anywhere else one would typically gather to say farewell to a loved one. Instead, they chose an empty lot behind one of the new markets that had popped up in Harlem. It was one of those stores that mainly sold organic products at prices that most locals couldn't afford, but it hadn't always been. They hadn't chosen the spot because Ashanti had an understanding with the owner and would be able to conduct their business uninterrupted, but because of what that one-square city block represented to the members of the Dog Pound, especially Ashanti.

Long before the market had come along, an abandoned building had stood on that patch of land known to those who dwelled inside as "The Below." It was an eyesore that the city had been neglecting for years, but it was home to children squatting inside the property. The Below was a place that Animal had created for the wayward children of the ghetto who had no place else to go. At any given time, as many as a dozen or more homeless kids could be occupying The Below. Animal served as their surrogate big brother and caretaker. He ensured they had a safe place where the evils of the outside world couldn't touch them. Then the war came, and everything changed.

Ashanti had been the only survivor of the fire that had consumed The Below, and one of the only two children left from the flock Animal had given shelter there. Men sent to kill Animal had set the fire as revenge for taking out one of theirs. To that day, Ashanti was still haunted by the screams of the dying children trapped inside and burned alive when the building went up. So many young lives were needlessly snuffed out. Their deaths earned them a mention in the newspaper, but it was Animal's vengeance that covered the front page. Animal's wrath wasn't just limited to the men who had set the fire, but those closest to them as well. Their wives, brothers, sisters, and sometimes even their dogs were all put to death. It was the only time Animal had broken his rule against killing women, but besides their children, everyone else was meat.

Witnessing the things that Animal did in the name of the kids who died in The Below was the one time Ashanti had ever been frightened of his friend until now. The moment Tiger Lily and her minions touched his wife and kids, they had let the devil out of his cage, and Ashanti feared that there would be no putting him back in this time.

"Where you think he is?" Nefertiti snapped Ashanti out of his thoughts.

"I don't know," Ashanti answered. It was already dark, and they had been scheduled to meet at sunset. "He should've been here by now."

"You think somebody may have gotten to him?" Nefertiti asked in a concerned tone.

Ashanti chuckled. "Or more like he got to somebody. Fuck it. Let's get started."

Five of them gathered in the alley; former and current members of the gang known as the Dog Pound and one other. Cain was his usual stoic self, huddled in his hoodie, wearing a blank expression. He had always been the hardest of them to read. The only hint that he felt anything at all was that every so often, he would wipe his nose with the back of his shirt sleeve. That was as close as you would get to an emotional response from him. Cain hadn't known Brasco as long as Ashanti or Nefertiti, but in their short time together, he had come to have a great deal of respect for the slain man. They fought side by side against impossible odds back at Cain's apartment, where Brasco had been killed. It was largely in part to him that they had escaped. Brasco was a soldier, the same as Cain.

Standing next to Cain was his brother, Abel. He was the easier of the twins to look at. He was a handsome youth with a brilliant smile who sported his hair in neat box braids. His Yankee cap was pulled down so low that you couldn't see his eyes, but Ashanti knew he was watching. That's all Abel did as of late, watch and brood. He used to be a jovial young man who loved to crack jokes, but that was before the incident in a nightclub that left the blood of a police officer on his hands. He hadn't meant to do it, but the cop had the drop on Animal, so Abel did what he had to do to save the big homie. Killing that cop had stolen whatever innocence that Abel had been holding onto. It seemed like every day since then, he slipped a little bit deeper into the darkness threatening to consume him.

Nefertiti stayed close to Ashanti. He was trying to appear the picture of calm, but from the way his eyes kept darting around nervously, you could tell that he was uncomfortable, and rightfully so. Nefertiti found himself the alley cat in a den of lions. The longer he hung around, the more obvious it became that he no longer had a place amongst them, but he was still Dog Pound and had as much right to be there as anyone. Nef tried to put up a strong front in front of the others, but Ashanti knew that inside, he was probably in bad shape. The original members of the Dog Pound were all close, but Nef and Brasco shared a different kind of bond. Brasco gave Nef more shit than anyone, but he was the only one who could. If anyone else bothered Nefertiti, they would have the bruiser to deal with. Brasco had been like a big brother to him, so it was only natural that he was taking his death harder. It had probably hit him harder than anyone there, except for Bizzle.

The whole time they had been gathered, Bizzle hadn't said much outside of uttering the occasional explicative between sips of the bottle of Hennessy that he was putting the hurt on. He wasn't quite drunk yet but was getting there. Bizzle wasn't an *official* member of the Dog Pound, but he was family. He was Brasco's uncle, the third oldest of four brothers. Each of them was a career criminal and stone-cold gangster, making it easy to see why Brasco turned out the way he did. When Animal first ran away from home, Bizzle and his brothers took him in. Each of the brothers had contributed something different to Animal's criminal education, but it was Bizzle who he most connected with. Animal respected all the brothers, but he looked up to Bizzle. They all did, even his older brothers. He was a man of few words, but his actions spoke volumes.

The five men stood around a memorial they had built for Brasco: a milk crate draped in a red bandanna and surrounded by burning candles, mostly red but a few white ones sprinkled amongst them. A small metal trash can was off to the side. Inside it, a small fire burned. It would be to the fire that they would give their offerings, things from each of them that they wanted Brasco to carry with him on his journey to the other side. On top of the crate was a picture of Brasco and the original members of the Dog Pound: Tech, Silk, Chyna, Animal, Ashanti, and Nef. Ashanti remembered the night it was taken. They had put a Harlem cab on hold for the day and had the driver take them to Six Flags for Fright Fest. The day stuck out to Ashanti because Brasco had gotten them kicked out. He got drunk and fought with one of the actors posing as the guy from *The Texas Chainsaw Massacre*. Brasco was still holding the fake chainsaw in the picture. Outside of them getting kicked out, it had been one of the best nights of Ashanti's young life.

Looking at the framed Polaroid made Ashanti sad. Of everyone in it, the only ones left were Animal, Nef, and him. Brasco died in the line of duty, defending his friends, Chyna was killed during a robbery, and Silk lost her life in a shootout with the police. All their deaths hurt, but Tech's probably stung the most. He was killed by a man they had once called a friend, Swann. To that day, the fact that Swann was never made to answer for his crime bothered Ashanti, but sparing him had been a necessary evil. Swann had been instrumental in brokering the truce between the Dog Pound and the Clark crime family, ending a war that had decimated both sides. Still, Ashanti wanted to blow Swann's head off, but Animal forbade it. He had given his word that there would be no retaliation as long as he was the leader of the Pound, but when, and if, the day came when that changed, Ashanti planned to do Swann filthy, just as he had done Tech.

They all hovered around the makeshift memorial in awkward silence. When someone passed, it was usually Animal, or maybe even Zo, to set it off with an offering of words, but they were both absent. Animal was God knew where, and Zo had to go make sure his home was secure, and his lady was good. They were up against a different type of enemy, who had already proved that they didn't have a problem touching a man's family. Nothing was off-limits. He would link with them later.

Ashanti didn't blame him. He had done the same with Fatima once shit started getting thick. He sent her off to stay with one of her cousins on Long Island until it was all done. Of course, she tried to argue against it, but for Ashanti, it was nonnegotiable. He couldn't risk something happening to Fatima, especially with her carrying his seed. He had seen how what happened devastated Animal, and Ashanti didn't think he could handle that loss without losing his mind. On the other hand, the fact that Animal was still standing and handling business gave Ashanti a whole new level of respect for him.

With Animal and Zo being gone, this left Ashanti as the elder statesman, and everyone was looking for him to lead the prayer. He had never been comfortable with public speaking, even if it were only amongst a few. Ashanti had been far better with his gun than with words, but he would give it a try. Nervously, he stepped up, trying to think of something to open with about his departed friend. Surprisingly, Nef beat him to it.

"My nigga, 'Sco . . ." Nef wrung his hands anxiously. "If you'd asked me about a hundred niggas I thought might've gotten laid out, your name would have never entered my mind. We been in a hundred firefights, and you ain't never took more than a scratch . . . well . . . except for that one time."

"Shit, don't remind me," Bizzle picked up. "Fool-ass nigga almost lost his whole leg fucking with that 9 mm."

"Brasco been shot before?" Ashanti asked in shock. He had never known this.

"Even better, he shot himself," Bizzle managed a chuckle. "This was years ago, probably back when you were still shitting in rubber pants. Brasco was still a little shitbird himself, barely into grade school but always into some shit he had no business in. I used to get my money off hammers, so I always had a bunch of them in the house. I usually kept them secured pretty well, but I guess this day I slipped, and Brasco got hold of this baby 9 mm I was holding onto. Me and Vernon came in one night and found him in front of the TV, trying to spin the gun like the dude on whatever cowboy-ass show he was watching.

"When he saw Vernon, he got spooked because he knew big bro would fuck him up for playing with the tool, so he tried to hide it behind his back. His finger must've hit the trigger or something because the next thing you knew, the shit went off, and we were rushing Brasco to Bronx Lebanon Hospital. We took him all the way up there instead of Harlem because everybody in there knew me and my brothers. We were always either in that hospital or putting some-one else there," he laughed. "You should've heard that little muthafucka hollering and crying the whole cab ride up there. We made up a bullshit story about him taking a stray on the way to the store. When the police questioned Brasco, he told them the same thing. He was young, but he wasn't stupid. We put the code in ours from birth."

"I'll drink to that," Cain chimed in. He approached Bizzle and extended his hand for the bottle. Bizzle studied him for a few ticks before relinquishing his drink. Cain took a deep drink before approaching the memorial. "You know I used to study y'all niggas when I was a kid," he spoke to the picture. "I used to be the fly on the wall when y'all were destroying shit left and right in the city. The name Dog Pound rang like Sunday mass in every hood. I wanted that . . . I wanted to be a part of that. Animal was my favorite because he was a monster like me, but it was you who I respected most. Your loyalty to your team gave me something to aspire to.

"My time with you was far too short, but I'm thankful to have had it." Cain removed a knife from his pocket and sliced off the end of one of his braids. "When you get to hell, show this to the devil so that he knows you were one of mine while you were on earth. That'll make sure you get treated right, and let him know he and I will settle up shortly." He tossed the lock of hair into the fire. Then Cain wiped the sleeve of his hoodie across his nose and moved on.

"Well said." Ashanti embraced Cain. He gave him an approving nod and then took the bottle. Ashanti stood amongst the candles, trying to keep himself composed. This was the first time since the shooting that he had a chance to process that one of his closest friends was gone. "Damn," was the first thing that came out when he finally opened it to speak. "They say that every time a real one passes on, it opens up a vacancy for a sucker to take up occupancy in his place. That ain't true because I can't name a hundred niggas living or dead who could fill this void you don' left in the world or this crew. There isn't too much that I can say to you in death that I haven't already said to you in life.

"In the Pound, we always gave each other our flowers while we could smell them because we knew none of us were long for this world. Me, you, Animal . . . We came into this world prepared to die young, so it ain't no big surprise when it happens, but that don't make this hurt any less. For each one of us that dies, it leaves the rest of us one step closer to being alone. I only pray that I never end up the last man standing because I can't go through this again," he said emotionally.

He pulled loose the red bandanna that had been tucked into his sweatpants and tossed it into the fire. He then took a healthy swig of the bottle, spilling liquor over his chin, before hoisting it in the air. "For my brother, who left this world the same way he lived in it—busting his fucking gun. He died the way we should all hope to, looking his enemies in the eyes. It was a soldier's death."

"A soldier's death!" they all chimed in.

One by one, the rest of them came forward to offer to the fire the things they wanted Brasco to take with him. When the offerings had been made, they cracked a few more bottles and talked shit around the memorial as they waited for the fire to go out.

Putting it out before its time would have been disrespectful. Everybody seemed to have a story about Brasco, even the twins, but it was the dialogue between Bizzle and Nef they really paid attention to. They really knew Brasco and had stories about him that showed Ashanti a side of his comrade he wasn't familiar with. Ashanti knew Brasco better than many folks, but he was still the baby of the crew. Before Ashanti got down with the Dog Pound, Brasco's life was largely a mystery outside of what he had been told. To Ashanti, Brasco was the asshole big homie who sometimes played too much, but he seemed to be so much more to everyone else.

"This is some bullshit," Nef spoke up. He was two stops on the train from intoxicated. "How some niggas gonna smoke my bro and ain't on borrowed time?"

"Who says they ain't?" Abel took it upon himself to answer the question. "If me or my brother thought this was a gang that didn't take care of their own, we'd have stayed neutral or flipped the other side when Danny-Boy approached us."

"Straight like that," Cain agreed. "If you can't remember that the Dog Pound never leaves a debt unsettled, then maybe you been away too long."

"Don't matter how long I been gone, I'm Dog Pound for life . . . *original* Dog Pound," Nef shot back. His bloodshot eyes were looking Cain up and down. "Y'all the little homies under my little homie. When did you pee-wee gangsters start thinking y'all had a voice in this?"

"When we started killing niggas, bitches, and police for this," Abel replied. "Out of respect for Ashanti, I ain't gonna make this a thing, but next time you open your mouth on some Dog Pound shit, remember that it was me and my brother who picked up the torch when you dropped it."

"Enough," Ashanti interjected when he saw where things were about to go. "This is about Brasco, not you two dumbasses."

"My fault. I'm just in my bag a little bit over this," Nefertiti said apologetically. "I meant no disrespect to the youngster or anybody else. I just think that we need to deal with whoever did this sooner than later. If y'all wanna wait, that's cool. Just put that thang in my hand, and I'ma get busy. That's on the hood," he boasted.

"Whole lot of gang shit. I hear it, but I can't see it," a voice called from the mouth of the alley. A female appeared, seemingly out of nowhere. She was dark-skinned with a curvy frame mostly hidden under a pair of baggy black jeans and an oversized Champion sweatshirt. Her jet-black hair was streaked with red highlights and parted into eight thick braids. A red bandanna hung loosely about her neck, and a menacing gorilla head with its fangs bared was tattooed on her right temple, just shy of her hairline. "Only two amongst y'all I know to be reputable members." Her eyes touched Bizzle, then Ashanti. "As far as the rest of y'all, where you from? Who brought you home?

PART II

THE UNKNOWN SOLDIER

Chapter 8

Home . . . For many years, that's what Kahllah had called the Mountain. From when she first arrived in the United States as a girl to many years later when she would take the "Long Walk," a rite of passage for all graduate initiates of the Brotherhood, this was the only place that she ever felt truly safe. She loved every inch of the cold stone walls and the bloodstained earth. They had forged Kahllah into the woman she was, and when she walked beneath the Mountain, it filled her with pride, but that was a lifetime ago . . . before her home had become her prison.

Before leaving, Nicodemus had advised that Kahllah keep herself confined to his quarters, but it hadn't been a command. However, even if it had been, it was doubtful that she would've followed the order. She felt like the walls were closing in on her, and she yearned to stretch her legs. It had been years since she roamed the halls of the Mountain, and she was curious to see what had become of it in her absence.

Of course, Artemis was against the idea of venturing outside Nicodemus's chambers. Rumor had it that word of her presence had spread throughout the Mountain and was met with mixed emotions. Things were tense amongst the Brothers, so Nicodemus had suggested confinement in the first place. But Kahllah refused to hide. Regardless of what Nicodemus had tried to suggest, she was Black Hand, and to do anything less than facing whatever dangers would await wasn't in her character. Like the rest of the Brothers of the Order, Kahllah had been named in the shadow of the Mountain, and her blood stained its sands. She feared nothing or anyone which dwelled there.

It took a bit of negotiating before Artemis finally agreed that they would leave the chambers for a short walk, and it wasn't without a few stipulations. The first being that she had to change her outfit. The street clothes she had come into the Mountain wearing would draw unwanted attention, so Artemis insisted that she dress in something that reflected what most everyone else wore, white linen pants and a white top with sandals. She drew the line when he offered her the white mask to hide her face. The white masks were issued to initiates, those still in the first circles of their Brotherhood reconditioning. Kahllah was a master, maybe not of the same status as Nicodemus or even Tiger Lily, but she still held rank and would not allow herself to be disrespected by wearing the mark of an initiate.

When they emerged from the chamber, they were greeted by two guards outside, holding long spears and swords strapped to their waists and wearing

identical silver masks. These were members of
Nicodemus's honor guard, who he had brought in
to replace the previous two who had held the post
before clashing with Kahllah. These two weren't random soldiers like the last but well-trained assassins.
Moving like a set of bookends, they crossed their
spears to block Kahllah's path.

"It's fine," Artemis told them.

"By order of Master—" one of them began, but
Artemis waved him silent.

"Nicodemus has left the Black Lotus in my care.
She is my responsibility. This door is yours," Artemis
spoke with authority.

"As you say, m'lord," The guard gave a half bow and
allowed them to pass.

"You're kind of young for a lordship, aren't you?"
Kahllah asked once they were out of earshot of the
guards. The title of lord was just shy of being dubbed
a master. Both titles were reserved for the Brothers
who possessed unique skill sets, like Nicodemus
being the master of poisons, or even Kahllah, who
was hailed as a master botanist. She wondered what
Artemis's gift was.

"Things have changed since you sliced your way
through the ranks, Lotus. As the need for leaders of
men has increased over the years, those of us who
are capable are ascending quicker. Make no mistake,
though; I have earned my rank. Nothing was given to
me," Artemis clarified.

"And what might I ask, are you a lord of?" she asked curiously.

"That is a conversation that will keep for another time," Artemis said and walked ahead.

It felt good to finally be out of the cramped chambers of the Master of Poisons, with its stale smell and moldy books. Kahllah inhaled deeply once they were on the other side of the door, taking in a chestful of the fresh air. One would've thought that because of how deep inside the Mountain they were, it might've significantly affected the air quality, but it didn't. Instead, the Brotherhood engineers had designed a sophisticated ventilation system that pumped natural air from outside through the entire mountain.

They had just cleared the corridor that led to Nicodemus's chambers when Kahllah stopped short. Her eyes were cast toward something dark, staining the rough stone floor. They had managed to scrub away most of it, but remnants of the blood lingered. This was the spot where Anwar had fallen.

"Did he die well?" Artemis asked as if he could read her mind.

"He died honorably," Kahllah said without taking her eyes off the stain.

"Then he received the best death of them all, a beautiful one," Artemis said. They lingered for a moment or two longer, then continued walking. They walked in silence for a while before Artemis started speaking again. "It is said that Anwar was your first."

"And my last," Kahllah confirmed.

"No heart for playing the role of the instructor?" Artemis wondered.

"Too much heart, actually," she corrected. "Anwar became more than just my student. He was my friend, and it became a problem. As instructors, we must be able to separate our feelings from the development of our students. The elders were never comfortable with the personable nature of our relationship. They feared our being friends compromised his development and prevented him from becoming a perfect weapon, as all Brothers are. So, I released him."

"Did you agree with their assessment?"

"Not at first, but the fact that he died trying to help me proves that the elders weren't wrong in wanting to separate us. Anwar's blood is on my hands," Kahllah confessed.

"If that's the case, then your hands aren't the only ones soiled in this. I was the one chosen as the elder for a second circle initiate group that Anwar found himself in," Artemis told her.

"Yet another high honor for someone so young," Kahllah said.

"Not an honor, a punishment," Artemis revealed. "I have always been . . . opinionated, for lack of a better choice of words. I am a Brother of the Blood, dedicated from when I was named until the day I leave this body, but I am no sheep. I have trouble following blind directions, but some would confuse my need to understand with insolence. None were more critical of this quality of mine than your father, the Priest."

This took Kahllah by surprise. "You knew my father?"

"For a time," Artemis confirmed. "The Priest was supposed to be the handler during my Long Walk."

The Long Walk was one of the final steps in re-conditioning a member of the Brotherhood of Blood. During your first few years as a member of the Order, your time is spent almost entirely under the Mountain or at whichever of several Father Houses around the globe you were brought in by. Except for training exercises or executing a contract, no one left the halls of the Order until it was deemed that they were ready. This is when the fortunate of them would embark on The Long Walk. The Long Walk was a year in which you were allowed to leave the Order and go into the world of men to figure out where, if anywhere, they belonged in it. At the end of your year, you would return to the Brotherhood draped in the fantasy life you'd created for yourself. Only when you could prove that you could convincingly wear more than one skin were you deemed fit to serve the Order. Unfortunately, it had taken Kahllah two years to prove herself instead of one.

"If my father was your handler, then how come we've never met outside the Mountain?" Kahllah asked curiously. Her father had introduced her to many of her peers, but she could never remember seeing Artemis outside of that one time when she visited the Mountain.

"Because it was a very short-lived arrangement. Priest gave me an order, and when I questioned him, everything went to the left," Artemis recalled.

"Sounds about right." Kahllah knew all too well how her father felt about being questioned. He hated to have his authority challenged. "If you don't mind me asking, what did he order you to do?"

"Take a life."

Kahllah was confused. "Isn't that what we do? Take lives?"

"Yes, but this was different. See, this wasn't a contract killing. This was a woman whose only crime was falling in love with a man she couldn't have. An associate of your father's. A drug lord, if I recall correctly."

Poppa Clark. The name exploded in Kahllah's head. She knew well her father's relationship with the former patriarch of the Clark family. It never sat well with her because Poppa Clark was the only man she had ever seen her father subservient to. She could never understand what kind of hold the drug dealer had over him that made Priest weak for that family.

"The woman had been seeing the drug lord behind his wife's back and became pregnant. They tried to pay her to get rid of the child, and when the woman refused, the drug lord deemed that she had to die. Priest charged me with committing the killing. Unlike some, I have no problem killing men and women alike if it's in service to the Order, but this was not. Priest took my defiance personally and used his influence with the elders to have me punished."

"Was the punishment harsh?" Kahllah asked.

"More of a blow to my ego than anything else. For one year, I was stripped of my position as a part of Nicodemus's honor guard and his protégé while I was made to train initiates. Not just any initiates but a group of hopeless misfits on the verge of being euthanized if they couldn't graduate to the next circle of reconditioning. I was tasked with either getting them ready or disposing of them. Anwar was amongst this group."

"I'm assuming it was a success since Anwar finally made it to being a full member of the Order."

"Of the six students, two crossed over, including Anwar. The rest . . ." Artemis patted the whips at his sides.

"A beautiful death." Kahllah understood his meaning.

"During my time with the little prince, I grew quite fond of him," Artemis continued. "We weren't necessarily friends, but I respected him. Anwar came to us late in life, so there was still much of the outside world in him, but by the time I got done with him, he was ready to take the next step. I was proud of my accomplishment, successfully reconditioning someone the elders had deemed hopeless. I was certain that I had stripped him of all outsider weaknesses and that he was ready to take the next step, but I was wrong. The fact that he lost his life over an emotional attachment proved that."

Kahllah lowered her head in shame, thinking of the part she had played in his death.

"I'm not blaming you, Lotus." He noticed her mood darken. "Anwar loved you like family, so I understand why he took up arms in your name. If I were in his position, I can't say that I wouldn't have done the same. We are a brotherhood and therefore honor-bound to protect one another, or at least we're supposed to. Sadly, some amongst us have no honor, such as the bastard who murdered our ward. Bastille should count himself fortunate that it was Nicodemus who he encountered in that hallway instead of me. The Master granted him a quick death, but I would not have been so kind."

They walked silently for a time, each lost in their thoughts of Anwar and what might've been. A group of people was coming down the same corridor from the opposite direction. They were a group of young initiates that looked to be somewhere in their pre-teens, give or take. Leading them was their instructor, a man whose mask Kahllah didn't recognize. The instructor greeted Artemis but bypassed Kahllah as if she were invisible. The smallest of the group of initiates lagged behind the group a bit, staring at Kahllah curiously. Kahllah touched her forehead before giving a curt nod, to which the initiate responded by scampering off as if a ghost had just saluted him.

"What was that about?" Kahllah asked Artemis.

"Forgive the little one, Lotus. It's not every day they encounter a real live bruja," Artemis told her.

The remark reminded her of the nickname Tiger Lily had given her years ago. "I'm no witch."

"There are some under the Mountain who think differently. They say that you were seduced by demons who taught you the black arts during your time in the outside world. Some believe you are indeed a witch and used blood magic to bring Nicodemus back from the dead."

"And what do you believe?"

Artemis measured the question before answering. "I believe there is more to the Black Lotus than meets the eye."

They continued their walk, down one corridor and up the other. Kahllah would run her hands over the stone walls every so often, letting their rough grooves bring back memories of happier times for her under the Mountain. Kahllah's nose picked up a familiar scent as they strode deeper. One that was totally out of place this deep belowground. It smelled of grass and rain. Her eyes lit up in recognition, and before she knew it, she rushed off toward the smell.

"Lotus!" Artemis called after her, but she ignored him. "This girl is going to get me fucking killed," he cursed before running after her.

Kahllah followed the corridor until it opened into space easily twice the size of a football field. The chamber was overgrown with grass and trees that stretched as far as the eye could see. It was as if a rain forest had sprouted in the heart of the Mountain. It was the most beautiful thing anyone fortunate

enough to see would ever behold. Kahllah knelt and
picked up a handful of dirt, which she rubbed between her palms, taking in the familiar feel of the soil.
Then cupping her hands around the soil, she brought
it to her nose and inhaled deeply. It smelled so . . .
familiar, as it should have. Because of her mastery
of botany, Kahllah had at one time been one of the
Brothers charged with maintaining the home-grown
forest. It was called the Hanging Garden; once, this
chamber had been one of her favorite places under
the Mountain. It was the one thing she missed most
about being away.

"What are you doing?" Artemis asked when he
finally caught up with her. "We had an agreement.
No wandering into places that could present a threat."

"Stop being so dramatic, Artemis. I know this
place as well as any chamber under the Mountain.
The Hanging Garden has always been one of the few
places under the Mountain that represented peace
and not war," Kahllah told him.

"Lotus, this has not been the Hanging Garden for
some years now," Artemis said in an edgy tone. His
eyes constantly swept the treetops as if expecting
something to jump out at them.

"If this is no longer the Hanging Garden, what is it?"
Kahllah asked, not understanding. She wouldn't have
to wait long for the answer.

The trees above them began to rustle, causing
leaves to fall on them. This was followed by belching.
Not the belching you'd expect to hear from someone

who had consumed too much soda too fast, but the deep, prolonged rumbling produced something wild and powerful. Something large enough to block out the artificial light that shone in the garden moved over Kahllah's head. It was so fast that she hadn't even been able to make out what it was. What she did know was that it wasn't alone. Suddenly, the branches in the trees all around them began to shake and rain down more leaves.

"Behind me!" Artemis grabbed her by the arm and put himself between her and whatever was coming.

A man appeared on a tree limb a few feet above them. At least, Kahllah *thought* that it was a man. He wore a mask, but not the steel or fiberglass designs sported by most of the Brotherhood. This one was carved from the bones of something that had once walked the earth but was too large to have been a human. He wore a vest of coarse fur over his upper body and fatigue pants. He noticed Kahllah and Artemis watching, so he put on a show, leaping from one branch to another, drawing closer to them. There was no way a man of his size should've been so agile, which told Kahllah that he was dangerous.

The bone-faced man let out another belch, this one louder and more aggressive. One by one, faces covered in white masks began to appear all around them. They were the same white, barren masks worn by Brotherhood initiates. Only theirs were all decorated with red palms across the faces. Though they weren't yet inductees of the Order, they had all been touched by blood.

Kahllah stood back-to-back with Artemis in a defensive stance. She looked at the hostile souls surrounding her, her brain racing, trying to calculate her odds of survival. She could feel the hostility rolling from them in waves threatening to drown her. All of them seemed to hate her, but the greatest hatred came from the man in the bone mask. He despised her, and she had no idea why.

"What the hell is this?" she finally asked Artemis. He was standing with his back touching hers and doing his best to ensure they weren't blindsided.

"It's what I tried to warn you about before you ran off like a girl just offered free candy." Artemis snatched both his whip handles from their sheaths. "This hasn't been the Hanging Garden in some time. Now . . . It's known as the Planet of the Apes."

They were trapped. The path they had chosen to enter the garden was blocked, and there was no way to determine where the foliage ahead of them would lead. The initiates were a volatile lot, but it was the one in the bone mask who had his finger on the button. It was he who would determine where this confrontation would go. "You should have known better than to bring that witch into the jungle," Bone Face said after a time. His voice carried the weight of a man used to giving orders.

"She's under the protection of Master Nicodemus. She walks where she pleases so long as that order stands," Artemis told him, casually flipping his whip handle back and forth in his hand. "Don't make this something it doesn't have to be, Prime."

Prime, short for Primate, was a man-made being notorious under the Mountain for his skill at violence. In his Brotherhood file, he was listed under the code name Primate, but those who knew him well called him the Mad Ape. During his time as an exile of the Brotherhood, Prime had been a prisoner of the Warrens. The things he'd seen and done in the Warrens had fractured his mind and made him unstable. "Don't come into my house trying to flex the word of a man who I hear is hardly feeling like himself these days."

"What's that supposed to mean?" Artemis asked.

"It means that the dead shouldn't have a vote in the decisions of the living," Prime clarified. "All they've been talking about under the Mountain is Nicodemus's miraculous recovery and the circumstances surrounding it. In truth, it would've been more honorable had you let him die. From what I hear, you've allowed a once great man to be experimented on like some lab rat instead of allowing him the honor of death."

"I've never known the great and powerful Apes to trade gossip like schoolgirls. I've already told you that the Lotus is under the protection of my master, and let that be that," Artemis said, tiring of going back and forth.

"Nicodemus is also gone and likely never to stand in the shadow of the Mountain again," Prime shot back. "The old ways are dying, Lord Artemis, and we are approaching the dawn of a new age for the Brotherhood. The weak will be rooted out, and the strong will be elevated to our rightful places of honor. You are a man of great respect within the Order. You're no ape, but still a true warrior. Men like you are in short supply, so I would rather have your support than your head. Your place is with we who will embrace the future, not those who will die in the past. Let your new life begin with the death of this traitor. Stand aside and let me do what must be done."

"You know I can't do that, Prime," Artemis told him.

"I had hoped not to have to kill you to get to her, but either way, the witch will never leave this mountain alive." Prime brandished his club.

"I have two reasons why your theory is flawed." Artemis drew both his whip handles and activated them. The metal rods made a low humming as they came to life.

Prime gave Artemis an amused look. No one challenged the second in command of the mighty Apes, even one of Nicodemus's puppets. "Apes!" The sound of his voice brought the initiates to attention. "You want to earn your totems and be done with the white masks of your novice stations? Now is your chance to prove how badly you want it. A commendation to him who brings me the skull of the traitor." He pointed his club at Kahllah.

None of the ape initiates had ever had the pleasure of laying eyes on the legendary Black Lotus, but her reputation preceded her. All under the Mountain knew what she could do, but the promise to earn their mask totems and no longer be faceless trainees was too much to pass up. So, they obeyed . . . and attacked.

"Lotus," Artemis said over his shoulder, never taking his eyes off the surging group of Apes, "earlier, you asked me what I was the lord of. I was named Artemis in the shadow of the Mountain, but those who have fallen at my feet know me as the Lord of the Lash."

The twin whips sprang from the handles Artemis held like two vipers. They were similar to the one Nicodemus had made so infamous, but these were made of some flexible metal. From the advanced technology used in creating them, they had to be Brotherhood designs, like the technology that powered the weapons that had almost killed her several years earlier when she'd faced off against the outlaws called Wizard and Sable. She had encountered them while trying to solve the Francis Cobb murder and clear her name of the cop killing. The weapons Wizard and Sable had used against her had been stolen from the Order and sold on the black market, but Artemis's had been gifted. As the Apes moved closer, Artemis struck the ground between them, sending up sparks and the smell of scorched grass. The whips would throw off electrical pulses from whatever empowered them every few seconds. The whips were quite lethal, but it was clear that Artemis didn't really want to use them. They were Apes, but still Brothers. Unfortunately, they didn't leave him a choice.

The first of the initiates to attack was met by one of the lashes across his face. He screamed like a man set on fire and staggered back. His mask smoldered where the whip had made contact. The second initiate was swifter and more battle savvy than his predecessor. He waited for Artemis to swing the whip high, then ducked under the strike, tackling Artemis to the ground. He rained blows on the young lord, beating him about the face and chest with his fists. Kahllah was about to help, but it wouldn't be necessary. Artemis raised one of the whip handles, flashing the blade that had sprung from the end of it before driving it into the ape's back. Within seconds, Artemis was back on his feet, weapons bared, and moving on to his next victim. The restraint he showed at the beginning of the attack was long gone. He was now fully committed to the game of life and death Prime had started.

Only once had Kahllah seen Artemis's signature whips put to use, which had been a part of a training exercise, and he had held back. Seeing Artemis use the lashes against inanimate targets was impressive, but seeing him slice through flesh and muscle was pure poetry. Artemis pirouetted through the cluster of initiates, laying into them with his whips. The steel bands moved like extensions of his arms, bleeding and burning everything they touched. The Lord of the Lash wasn't just a title given to him. It was who he was.

Kahllah was so focused on watching Artemis that she almost didn't see the ape spring from the bushes behind her. He was a wiry initiate, swinging a battle-ax. Kahllah had barely dodged the strike meant for her head. She stumbled backward and tripped over the bark of the tree she had been standing closest to. Seeing that he had her at a disadvantage, the ape pressed his attack . . . which would be his undoing. Kahllah waited until he was right on top of her before shooting the heel of her foot out and striking him in the balls. She smiled inwardly as she felt his testicles explode in their sack.

The ape stumbled, one hand holding his ruined nuts and the other his ax. With a roar, he came at her again, swinging wildly. Kahllah sidestepped his attacks as if she knew where each one would be launched before he threw it. She saw his arms begin to drop, indicating that he was tiring from his wild swinging and moved in on him. When the ax went up, she fired her index and middle finger into the space where his shoulder and collarbone connected. She turned her fingers, and as if she had a key to his nervous system, the ape lost the use of that arm, and the ax fell to the floor. Now crippled, the ape tried to retreat, but there was no escape when the Black Lotus came for you. Kahllah shot her foot out and tripped him, sending him crashing face-first to the dirt.

The wounded ape forced himself onto his back with his good arm. He watched in horror as the Black Lotus scooped his discarded ax from the dirt. He wasn't sure if it was due to the adrenaline working overtime or the near-blinding pain in his balls, but when he looked at her, he thought that he might've been hallucinating. Inky waves of black energy poured over her hands like dripping tar. "What are you?"

"I am death," she replied before splitting his skull with the weapon.

After dispatching the initiate, Kahllah turned her attention back to Artemis. He was outnumbered but holding his own against the initiate Apes with his whips. She had to admit that she was quite impressed. While admiring his combat skills, she spotted an ape coming at him from the trees at his blind side, sword raised for the killing blow. She threw the ax two-handed, sending it flipping end over end until it eventually found its mark in the back of the ape who had tried to blindside Artemis.

The Apes were strong, but even in force, they were no match for the combined efforts of Artemis and Black Lotus. They were too inexperienced, and it wasn't long before the duo began to drive back the Apes.

"Cowards!" Prime snarled at the fleeing Apes. Seeing his initiates retreating not only infuriated him, but he was embarrassed. It had been his duty to train that particular group of initiates, and they were making him look like a fool. "I'll claim the witch's skull myself." He slammed his club against the ground, sending up a spray of dirt.

"If it's all the same to you, I've grown quite attached to my skull . . ." Kahllah picked up a discarded blade and tossed it from one hand to the other and back. ". . . but by all means, give it your best shot."

The Black Lotus and Artemis took up fighting stances, keeping Prime between them. Kahllah and Artemis were highly skilled fighters and could best most men, but Prime was no man. He was an ape. Long before Prime had ever donned the fur cloak of the gorilla tribe, he had been only a little animal. His induction into the Apes only seemed to pull his base nature to the forefront. Even with the combined efforts of the two masters, there would be no way for them to stop Prime short of killing him, which Artemis figured had been his end game all along.

The Lord of the Lash was no fool. Only one of them would leave the Garden that day, and no matter which it was, the death of the loser would likely shatter the already fragile peace between the Apes and the other factions of the Brotherhood. It would be all the excuse either side needed to ignite a civil war under the Mountain. That would be reason enough for the Apes to break away from the Brotherhood and pursue their own agenda . . . an agenda Prime had been pushing for since taking his oath. Artemis had two choices: kill or be killed, and both would lead to war. And then, he was presented with a third option.

He dropped from the treetops and landed in a squat directly between Prime and Kahllah. His back was to her so that she couldn't identify him right off, but she got the feeling that he was a part of the tribe. While the others of the tribe dressed in garbs to make them look like Apes, the man between them had the physical appearance of one: broad, stooped shoulders and muscular, gangly arms that were so long that he probably never had to stoop much to tie his shoes. He wore a camouflage vest with matching pants and black combat boots. What stood out most about this newcomer was a bronze gauntlet covering his left hand and part of his forearm. When he raised the gauntlet over his head, the Apes who hadn't already been run off began to retreat as if they were vampires standing before a brandished cross. They all fell back, except Prime. He stood in the presence of the newcomer as defiant as ever.

"What are you doing?" Prime snarled angrily at the man who had come between him and those he meant to kill.

"Preventing you from doing some dumb shit and dragging the rest of us into it with you," the man with the bronzed glove replied. His voice sounded like that of a very young man with a hint of an accent that marked his place of origin as somewhere in the tri-state. "Nobody else bleeds today—not on my watch."

"Need I remind you of the crimes she stands accused of against this Order?" Prime pointed his club at her accusingly.

"You need no more remind me who the Black Lotus is than I need to remind you that I am the elder of this tribe," the man responded.

"The Apes are free people. There is no king in this jungle," Prime snapped.

"No, but every zoo needs a keeper." He held up his right hand and brandished a ring that bore the insignia of the Brotherhood. Every sect leader was presented with one when they first took up their stations.

"Metal and jewels don't make leaders; steel and blood do," Prime said in a challenging tone.

"This we can agree on. As I've told you before, any time you or any of the tribe feel like challenging my authority, I ain't turning down no fades. You got a problem with something I've said today or any other day, then let it be known, and let's settle it." He flexed his hand in his bronze gauntlet.

Prime just glared as if he was weighing his odds of success. Reasoning that he couldn't, he humbled himself. "I spoke out in anger and meant no disrespect, but you must understand my concern. This woman is a threat, dubbed so by our own elders. By the laws that have governed this Order for nearly four centuries, she must die."

"Laws which are bent and broken all the time at the convenience of the old men," the man reminded him. Soothingly, he laid his hand on Prime's shoulder. "We have bigger battles that we need to prepare for, brother, but not this one. You know as well as I do that this is a war between men, not Apes."

Prime shrugged his hand away. "This is where you are wrong, *brother*. This war will touch us all, even if you like to convince yourself otherwise. Ignore the warnings all you like, but I plan to make sure that the Apes are ready for what's coming." Prime turned on his heels and headed back for the trees. He stopped short and shot a murderous glare at Kahllah, who was still holding the blade she'd picked up. "Consider this stay of execution a temporary one. I meant what I said about you never leaving this mountain alive," he threatened before disappearing into the trees.

Kahllah watched the newcomer watching his comrades. He kept his eyes on the tree line until he was sure Prime wouldn't rile the initiates to a second attack. Apparently, even he didn't trust the Mad Ape. Even when the threat had passed, the tension remained in his shoulders, a trait born from someone who had been at war all their lives and didn't know how to stand down—someone who had been battle-tested. He finally turned enough for Kahllah to get a good look at him, and her heart leaped. His mask was made of the same rusted bronze as his boxing gloves. At the forehead was a totem Kahllah had only heard whispered about but never thought she would see in person. It was of a carving of a gorilla baring its fangs . . . the mark of the Iron Monkey.

"The Legend of the Iron Monkey"
Until recently, the legend of the Iron Monkey, sometimes called the Iron Monk, had been a fable

whispered about amongst the elders. It was a ghost story told to initiates as a warning not to stray from their studies. According to the lore, the Iron Monkey had been promised to the Brotherhood at birth as payment for a blood debt owed by the boy's father. In return for letting him live, he had offered up his begotten son to the Order. The deal the father struck wasn't because he didn't love his son; in fact, he was the most important thing to him, but giving him to the Brotherhood provided him with a better life than the father ever could, as well as clearing his debt.

The bargain was struck, and the boy who would grow to be known as the Iron Monkey was now the property of the Brotherhood. Generally, when the Brotherhood adopted children into their Order, they were brought to the Mountain for conditioning as soon as they were old enough to swing a blade, but this isn't how it was done with the Iron Monkey. He was to be the first group of experimental agents who would give the Brotherhood a firmer hold over urban communities. Soldiers that were products of the hood but loyal to the Order.

The boy was cast into the harshest conditions the American ghettoes had to offer: a poor education, a poverty-stricken home, no life skills, a murdered mother, and a drug-addicted father. The deck was stacked so high that the boy was never meant to see over the top. All these things and more were thrust at him during his developmental stages to directly influence who he would become. All hope of anything

good happening in his life was snatched away, and
he was dared to survive under those conditions.
However, not only did he survive, but he also thrived.

The Iron Monkey started at the bottom, stealing
and committing petty crimes to keep his belly full.
He eventually got his hands on a pistol and entered
the robbery game. Not long after, he was introduced
to a local hustler who used him as muscle. Because
of his natural gift for violence, he excelled in his
position as an enforcer until the time came when he
started to dream bigger. Then the Iron Monkey went
from taking orders to giving them. During his rise
to power, he even unknowingly helped eliminate a
target on a Brotherhood kill list. The boy was in the
prime of his greatness, and it was the perfect time
to bring him in finally . . . and then the unthinkable
happened. The kid whose life the Brotherhood had
been monitoring and manipulating for two decades
simply . . . vanished.

It was nearly a year before the Brotherhood could
track down their experiment. By the time they found
him, he had been reduced to a shell of what they'd
watched him become over the years. The loss of his
one true love had driven him to the bottle for comfort.
Alcoholism had taken him to the top of a mountain
and thrown him down as hard as possible. He'd
gotten himself tied into some cats who played heavy
in the mixed martial arts scene and spent the next
few months of his life drowning his sorrows in booze
and blood. In the shadows of these back-alley brawls

and the stained canvases where underworld coins were wagered on the lives of men who wouldn't be missed, he first earned the moniker of "Iron Monkey." Those who had been fortunate enough to be hit by the young man and recount the experience always described him the same way: an ugly kid who looked like a gorilla but hit with the force of a wrecking ball.

Such extensive time and punishment in the streets had fractured the young man, but he was not broken and, therefore, still of use to the Brotherhood. They rescued him from the captors and returned him to the Mountain, where he was debriefed. A complete reconditioning proved to be out of the question by then. He was too far gone from so much time spent in the urban jungles. He was street poisoned.

When he arrived at the Mountain, the elders weren't very hopeful. He still proved to have the capacity for violence and was quite capable of snuffing out lives, but being able to kill didn't make you an assassin, at least by Brotherhood standards.

After some debate, it was decided that the experiment was a failed one, and the young man was exiled to the Warrens, catacombs deep beneath the Mountain reserved for the Brothers who were considered unredeemable. Those banished there were castoffs of the Order, the violent, morally corrupt, and criminally insane. Men who had proven far too volatile to ever have a purpose in the Brotherhood other than to be used as weapons of mass destruction and chaos. Many expected the Warrens and the things that dwelled there to break him, but once again, he proved that he was indeed made of iron . . . and iron does *not* break.

Not only had the Iron Monkey managed to survive, but he also had established himself as the leader of the lunatics and deviants who haunted the Warrens. His ascension couldn't have come at a more opportune time. When a battalion of rogue brothers launched an attack within the Mountain, it wasn't the Black Hand who had won the day for the Brotherhood but the Iron Monk. With a small group of his new followers, they escaped the Warrens and came to the aid of the Brothers, who had left them to die.

The selfless act by the Iron Monkey was his final test and proof to the Order that he deserved of a place amongst them. The elders offered him a full pardon and a place within the Brotherhood, but he would only accept it if the same offer were extended to his fellow exiles. He also had one more stipulation. He had been a prisoner while in the fighting pits and again in exile. He would never again be another man's captive; the only way to ensure this would be if he were the one calling the shots. He wanted a seat at the table. After some deliberation amongst the elders, they reached an agreement. The Iron Monkey would not be given an official place at the table of elders but would have command over his own sect of the Brotherhood to be made up of prisoners of the Warrens. The small group of warriors would be beholden to the sacred oaths taken by all members of the Brotherhood but recognized as an independent entity. From then on, they would be known as exiles no more, but the tribe of the Iron Monkey, known as "the Apes."

"It wasn't smart to bring her here, Artemis," Iron Monkey addressed Nicodemus's protégé.

"It wasn't intentional. An unexpected detour," Artemis told him. "Do your Apes make it a habit of attacking their seniors unprovoked?"

"Cut the bullshit. We both know that Prime was attacking *her,* not *you.* Had I not been here, both of you would likely be ape food right now," the Iron Monkey told them.

"Or ape killers," Artemis countered. "I wasn't aware that you had arrived back at the Mountain. The last I heard, you'd gone off to hunt down your rogue initiate." There was a rumor circulating that one of the ape initiates under Iron Monkey's care had left the Mountain without authorization, which was forbidden for an initiate until they had completed their first three circles of training, and it was time for their Long Walk.

"Ape business is not Brotherhood business. Just count yourselves lucky that I was. This situation could've been avoided had you not brought someone here who was branded a traitor," Iron Monkey said.

"I'm no traitor," Kahllah said defensively.

"No disrespect to you, shorty. I'm only telling you what the word around here is," the ape leader clarified. "My tribe keeps to the jungle, but the wind whispers to the trees, and the trees whisper to us. What the trees have been saying for the last few months has been causing concern."

"And what are the trees saying?" Artemis asked.

"They're saying that not everybody is okay with the current seat of elders and the direction they're taking this Order. Change is coming, and votes won't make these changes but blood and steel." The Iron Monkey looked at Kahllah.

"Civil war," Kahllah voiced what he was insinuating.

Iron Monkey nodded in agreement. "And if this civil war comes to pass, on which side will the Black Lotus stand?"

"Side of the righteous," Kahllah said with confidence.

"As will the Apes," he agreed.

"Can you speak for your tribe?" Kahllah asked. She looked up at the trees as if expecting another attack.

"I could, but I won't. I am the chief of our tribe, but we Apes have our own free will. There are no masters in the jungle," Iron Monkey said honestly. "I can't be certain which way the wind will blow us, but what I can tell you is if it threatens this Order, it dies. Man, woman, or flower."

"This we can agree on," Kahllah assured him.

"Well, if this war the two of you speak of does come to pass, it'll likely spill beyond your precious jungle and out into the real world, where there are few trees for you to hide in. What then?" Artemis challenged. He had never liked the fact that the Apes were separatists and more concerned about affairs in the jungle than Order as a whole. He felt the elders had given them too much freedom compared to the rest of the sects.

"We will rise to the occasion; what else? Unlike some of you who have been sheltered in the shadow of the Mountain, I'm a child of the streets—born and raised in the gutters of Harlem. If you listen closely enough, you'll hear my name rings louder on the streets than in the jungle. So you ever find yourself doubting how far my reach goes, you have only to look for my mark." He tapped the gorilla totem on his forehead.

Artemis seemed clueless about what the Iron Monkey meant, but Kahllah had an idea. She knew his history and who he was before he became the Iron Monkey. "Still got a touch of your old life in you, huh?"

"As do you, or else you wouldn't be risking your life for a nigga who ain't long for this world anyhow," Iron Monkey said in half jest. The trees above them moved, letting them know they weren't alone. They couldn't see the Apes, but they were there. Watching. Waiting. "The natives are getting restless, and I'm not sure how long I can keep them pacified, even wearing this ring."

"I'll be certain to tell Nicodemus how you helped us here today. Your deeds should be recognized," Artemis said sincerely. He didn't know the Iron Monkey very well outside the few brief times they had met in passing, but he had proven to be as honorable and brave as the legends said.

"Thanks, but I'm not gonna hold my breath for that pat on the head," Iron Monkey said.

"Meaning?" Kahllah questioned, remembering Prime's remark about the elder not returning from his trip.

Iron Monkey just shrugged. "That's above my pay grade and, honestly, my scope of care. The world is full of uncertainties, but one of the few things certain is that your presence here threatens to upset certain plans that have been too long laid to allow anyone to derail, even if that someone is a member of the Hand."

"Should I take that to mean that my life is in danger?" Kahllah asked sarcastically.

"Stop acting like you don't know we all signed up to die young when we took the oath," Iron Monkey chuckled, "but bullshit aside, you ain't got a lot of friends here. Even less now that you've put yourself on Prime's shit list. My advice is that you don't trust anyone here that you haven't shed blood for or with." He looked toward Artemis.

"And why would the ape chief care whether someone who has been branded a traitor of the Order lives?" Kahllah wanted to know.

He shrugged his broad shoulders. "Call it a hunch I hope I'm not wrong about."

Kahllah nodded. There was an unspoken understanding that passed between them. Like her, the Iron Monkey was an outsider who had been pulled into the Brotherhood through unconventional means but had come to love the Order to the point where they would kill or die for it. With the warning issued, the Black Lotus prepared to leave. The Iron Monkey had already given her plenty to think about, but he wasn't done.

"They say that outside of myself, you've spent the most time dealing with the good folks in the slums," Iron Monkey said. It wasn't a question but a statement. "I'd guess your ties to the Bastard Son of Harlem have placed you in some very interesting company."

"I've met a few people. Why?" Kahllah wondered where he was going.

"Depending on how this all plays out, my next move will be to pay an unfriendly call on someone who may be an acquaintance of you and yours. Goes by the name of Savage . . . Fire Bug, if memory serves me."

Kahllah knew the Savage family name quite well, besides the particular member he'd mentioned. She'd become familiar with the family of outlaws during her time helping Animal. Outside of the middle brother, Keith, she didn't care for the Savages. Fire Bug, especially. He was a wild and disrespectful kid that loved to blow up shit.

"I know the name but wouldn't call him an acquaintance. Even still, I'm not in the way of gossiping about other people."

"I would expect no less from the Black Lotus. So if you ever happen to make it into his company, tell him that he's got to answer for that business with Tiffany," Iron Monkey told her.

"I'm no messenger," Black Lotus said.

"Of course, you aren't, but a part of me feels like you'll find a way to get my words to his people. Until we meet again, Black Lotus." He started toward the tree line whistling a tune.

When Kahllah heard the song he was whistling as he disappeared into the brush, it made her blood boil. The first time she had heard it had been while watching old Looney Toons reruns with her nephew, T.J., and the last had been while at the wrong end of a shotgun. The song's title was the "Camptown Races," but she knew it as the "Executioner's Song."

Making it safely out of the Hanging Garden did little to ease Kahllah's tension. They had barely made it out of a very volatile situation that had the makings of going left. Prime was clearly a formidable opponent and would've no doubt given both Kahllah and Artemis runs for their money, but Kahllah had an edge that would make her a favorite to win most battles. Prime was fighting for status, while Kahllah was fighting for family. He was willing to take one life, but Kahllah was prepared to snuff out every soul under the Mountain to get her niece and nephew back. Civil war be damned. She had been ready to push all her chips to the center of the table before the Iron Monkey intervened.

The ape chief had proven to be just as much of a co-nundrum as she had heard, loyal to the Brotherhood but still holding onto his old life. It was evident that they had that in common, but what else? More accurately . . . who else?

De Camp-town race-track five miles long . . . The lyrics played in her head.

She turned her attention to Artemis, who was walking slightly ahead of her. He hadn't said much since they had left the Garden. He didn't have to because what was on his mind was written across his face. Unlike Kahllah, who had come to live amongst the Brothers when she was older and had already tasted life, Artemis was a Mountain child. This, or some other Brotherhood Motherhouse, had likely been the only home he had ever known. As a resident, he was more vested in the political games played within the Order and more informed than Kahllah, who was only slightly above a guest. The confronta-tion with the Apes had him rattled. Not so much the battle but the Pandora's box the confrontation had opened up.

"What was that all about? Back there with the Apes?" Kahllah broke the uncomfortable silence.

"Nothing for you to concern yourself over, Lotus," Artemis said.

"Wait. Was that not me fighting alongside you against the Apes not even an hour ago? You're gonna have to do better, Artemis. I respect your loyalties to the Brotherhood, but how about a little loyalty to the chick who saved your ass? I think it's obvious that this rabbit hole goes far deeper than either of us thought. What did Prime mean by that remark about Nicodemus not coming back? Have the elders been compromised?"

"I don't know," Artemis said in frustration. He was trying to hold his composure but struggling.

"Then find out," Kahllah insisted. "You're Nicodemus's right hand. I'm sure you can reach out to him."

"Don't you think that if I could, I would have by now?" he snapped. Then he continued in a more even tone. "We believed you from the moment you showed up spewing conspiracy theories. Nicodemus and some of the elders had been aware of the unrest for a while, but they failed to give the threat the credibility it deserved. The attempt on Nicodemus's life showed them the error of their ways. It was confirmation that the Order had indeed been compromised, but none of us could be sure who was involved. This is why Nicodemus kept his trip a secret. The only people who knew he was leaving the Mountain were his escorts and me. Not even the other elders were aware of the trip."

"Then how did Prime know?" she questioned.

"Isn't it obvious? We have been betrayed." Finally, Artemis gave voice to what she was thinking.

"Any idea by whom?"

He thought before answering. "I have a few suspicions but can't come at these people with allegations. To lay such a claim, I would need solid proof. I have much to do, and I can't do any of it until I get you out of harm's way. I'm still sworn to protect you." He turned down the corridor they'd come down earlier when leaving Nicodemus's chambers.

"Artemis, with everything that we've just learned, there's no way you can expect that I will allow you to lock me back in that room and hope that I live long enough for you to figure it out," Kahllah said defiantly. She had played nice up until then, but the stakes had been raised. If she were to die, it would be with a blade in her hand and not hiding like some coward.

"We're going back to the Master's chambers, but we won't be staying longer than it takes for me to gather a few things I'll need for our journey," Artemis told her.

"Journey? Where are we going?"

"I've got a lot to figure out, but I can't do it here. Much like you, I have no plans of staying here and waiting to die. We're getting the hell out of this Mountain."

PART III

WILD CHILD

Chapter 9

It was after dark when Alonzo, aka Zo-Pound, made it home. The place where he lay his head those days was a quiet, tree-lined street in Westchester County. It was a quaint two-bedroom house with a driveway large enough to fit two cars if you put them nose to end. It wasn't the largest or most luxurious house, but it was his. The two-story house was a far cry from the roach-infested project apartments where he spent his childhood and a good chunk of his adult life.

To say that Alonzo came from humble beginnings would've been putting it nicely. He was a child of Harlem, hailing from the General Grant Housing Projects. Alonzo started out as a stick-up kid, banging anything and everything moving to help put food on his table. His skill with pistols was how he had earned the moniker of Zo-Pound. It came from his preferences when it came to firearms. He was partial to .357s and .45s. Five was his lucky number, or so it had been. A stint in a state correctional facility had derailed his young criminal career. Zo hadn't done a lengthy bid in comparison to some of his friends, but his time in prison taught him that he wasn't cut out for a life of twenty-three and ones.

Upon his release from prison, Zo squared up and joined the workforce. He landed a job working in the storeroom of a supermarket and eventually graduated to the assistant manager position. It wasn't the most glamorous job, but it was legit and kept his parole officer from tossing him back behind the wall. Zo was okay with living the life of a workingman, but he was never content. He always felt like there was something more out there for him, but a part of him was hesitant to risk a regular paycheck to chase something else. Then he met her . . . and everything changed.

From the first time he laid eyes on Porsha, he knew he loved her. Kids in the ghetto were taught that love at first sight only existed in fairy tales, that it wasn't real, but it was the only thing he could describe that he felt that day Porsha walked into the supermarket where he worked and asked him where to find the cereal. She stirred something low in Alonzo that made him feel queasy, and his palms would sweat every time he saw her. Back then, he always felt like Porsha was out of his league. She was a hood celebrity and ran with all the cool kids. What could she possibly want with a box boy making a hair above minimum wage? Still, he put his best foot forward and pursued her.

Time and circumstances would eventually push the two of them together. They would teach each other the lessons of love. In Zo, Porsha would learn that good men still existed, and in Porsha, Zo would learn that a man's character said more about him than his W-2. Their union, no matter how unlikely, was a genuine one, and their love for each other was pure. This isn't to say that their relationship was always the stuff of fairy dust and unicorn tears. The young couple would experience more than their share of ups and downs, especially when Zo found himself back in the streets for a time. That was a period that really put what they had to the test.

Zo's older brother, Lakim, ran with a dude named King James and a crew that was heavy in the game. When King James returned from prison and hooked up with Lakim, these two dudes hit the streets. They had Harlem clicking like the '80s. They had come from nothing and were well on their way to having it all. One person who was primarily responsible was a kid who ran with them named Ashanti. Zo could never put his finger on why he had taken such a liking to the baby-faced shooter; he just did. Ashanti was young, brash, and didn't give a fuck about too much of anything other than a dollar, but he was genuine. What you saw with him was what you got, and he never changed up. Zo respected that. He came to love Ashanti like a little brother, so whenever he came to Zo with a problem he needed help solving, Zo didn't think twice about agreeing to ride with him. One such problem was a blood debt owed to a kid named Animal. Those months he had spent fighting the wars that had nothing to do with him directly were rough. Zo had been in battles before, but this was his first taste of a full-scale war.

There were nights when Zo didn't think he would make it home, but through the grace of God, he always did. And every time he came in off the streets, Porsha was there waiting on him. It was she who held him when he had night terrors and she who habitually lied to the police on his behalf whenever they came sniffing around. Porsha had never touched the front line, but she bore as many war scars as he did and never once complained. He had always promised her that one day, her loyalty would be rewarded with a normal life, and in time, he would give it to her.

Zo had taken his street money and made some sound investments that had started paying off for him to the point where he didn't have to be in the streets anymore. The day Zo had closed on the house and had Porsha sign off on the deed, he promised her that he was officially retired. He built the dream life for them that Porsha had always wanted, and now, he had to tell her that he was about to possibly tear it all down and ask her to be okay with it.

Zo drove around his block twice before parking his car on a side street two blocks away. He walked the distance back to his house, head constantly on a swivel and his hand gripping the .357 shoved into his jacket pocket. He spotted Porsha's Toyota Sequoia in the driveway when he got to his house. She'd been dropping hints to Zo about a Benz truck, and when he pulled up with this, she had mixed feelings. Zo could remember her disappointment until he broke down why keeping it simple would make them lesser targets. She understood and respected it, but she also persuaded him to give her the difference in price in cash. To this day, Zo couldn't tell you what she did with the extra money, and he never asked. However, he trusted her enough to know that it hadn't been squandered. It wasn't that Porsha couldn't blow through cash, but she'd been through enough rainy days to learn to be prepared for them when they came.

Seeing her whip in the driveway was no surprise. Zo hadn't expected her to be there, and a part of him was glad about it. She was booked for a modeling gig in Texas and scheduled to fly out at six a.m. that morning. He had promised her that he would drive her to the airport, but, of course, that was before he got roped into helping Animal and Ashanti sink a cargo ship carrying a shipment of designer drugs. He couldn't tell her that over the phone, so he made up some bullshit excuse about why the sun was about to catch him still in the streets.

As expected, Porsha went up top on him and called Zo everything but a child of God. She thought he was out cheating, and he couldn't convince her otherwise without coming clean. Suspecting he was with another broad versus her knowing he was out dropping bodies with Ashanti and had broken his promise was the lesser of the two evils. So instead of taking his lady to the airport as he'd agreed, he let her jump in an Uber and hoped he could sort it out when she returned.

"Motion detected at the front door," Zo's phone alerted him as he put in the key. His home security camera and alarm systems were synced to his mobile phone so that he could always have his eyes on the things precious to him.

When he crossed the threshold, he cursed as he tripped over a pair of Porsha's shoes in the foyer. That girl had a serious problem keeping her clutter in one area. Normally, Zo would've been tight about it, but it was a welcomed sight that night. The fact that she still had clothes in the house or hadn't gathered his belongings meant that he still had a boxer's chance. He knew that he would have to make up for this big time when she came back.

He reset the alarm system and jogged upstairs to the master bedroom. A quick peek in the closet revealed that Porsha's travel bags were gone. He went into the master bathroom and stripped off his clothes in preparation for a shower. Zo placed his phone on the sink and jumped in. The water was turned to its highest degree, but Zo held fast under the scalding spray. He welcomed the burn and hoped it would help wash away the sins he had committed in the name of loyalty.

As Zo got out of the shower, he heard his phone go off: "Motion detected at the front door." Zo knew that Porsha was gone and wasn't expecting anyone to visit him, but it wasn't uncommon for the occasional passerby to set off the system if they crossed within range of the sensor. Zo wouldn't have thought too much about it had the following alert that came through not been: "Front door ajar."

The first thing that popped into his mind was the bounty. Tiger Lily had placed a price on the heads of all those who had joined in Animal's cause. He learned this from Ocho. Ocho was a kid Zo had seen great potential, so he took him under his wing. The kid reminded him of Ashanti without the homicidal streak. Ocho was a true hustler and a wizard at committing fraud. When Zo had first found him, Ocho had been risking his life and freedom passing off counterfeit bills. Once Zo got behind him, he could graduate to bigger things, such as credit card and check fraud. With Ocho's knowledge of scamming and Zo's financial backing, they built a nice operation. Thanks to Zo, Ocho found himself able to make a lot of money, but it wasn't enough to stop his young protégé from trying to collect the reward for Alonzo's head. Ocho had rocked Alonzo to sleep, and that's how he had caught him slipping. If it hadn't been for Cain showing up when he did, Alonzo's brains would've decorated the trunk of that car instead of Ocho's. That act of betrayal taught Zo two very important lessons: trust no one and always be prepared.

Alonzo hustled across the bathroom, still naked and wet. He slipped and almost busted his ass, getting to the cabinet under the sink. He flung the doors open and began frantically sifting through Porsha's seemingly endless supply of hair products and rolls of extra toilet tissue until he found what he was looking for—a small .38. His years of running with Animal and his crew had shown him the importance of always having access to a weapon. He'd have rather had his .45, but the pocket-rocker would have to do.

Zo quietly opened the bathroom door and slipped into the hallway. He tiptoed down the stairs, leaving a trail of damp footprints in his wake. When he reached the bottom, he could hear someone rummaging around in the closet where Porsha kept her jackets. That was also where they kept one of two safes in the house. The one upstairs held all their good jewelry and important papers, but the one downstairs was stuffed with pistols, ink, blank check booklets, plates, and other tools used in Zo and Ocho's fraud business. The fact that the closet was the first place the intruder went meant it was likely one of Ocho's bunch. Besides Zo, Ocho was the only one who knew what was in that safe and what to do with it. He'd more than likely run his mouth to his boys while plotting to snake Zo right before he'd gotten himself killed. No matter, though. A few counterfeit plates and some guns weren't all they would get from breaking into Zo's house.

Silently, he slipped into the living room. The intruder was hunched over in the closet and looked like he was struggling with something. It was likely the safe. Zo crept up behind the intruder and aimed the .38 at the back of his head. "Young, dumb nigga," he hissed. His finger was about to press the trigger when the intruder spun around, holding their own pistol. Zo barely could move his head before the intruder's gun went off. In the muzzle flash, he caught a glimpse of a familiar face. "Porsha?"

"Zo?" Porsha asked in surprise, still on one knee with the gun raised and ready to fire again. Her hand was trembling but steady enough to hold the pistol level with his head. "What the fuck, Alonzo?" She lowered the gun after confirming his identity.

"Girl, what the hell are you doing creeping around in the closet?" Zo asked, relieved that he hadn't shot his lady by accident.

"Putting my bag away," Porsha pointed to the suitcase sticking out of the closet. That's what she had been struggling with. "Why do you have a gun, and why are you naked?" She looked him up and down suspiciously. "You got a bitch in my house?"

"Hell no. I was in the shower and thought you were a burglar," he explained. "What happened? I thought you were supposed to be in Texas for that shoot for the next few days."

"My flight got canceled. There's a bad storm out there, so everything flying into Houston is grounded until morning. I didn't want to sleep at the airport, so I came back home. Why? Is that a problem?" Porsha asked, noticing the leery expression on his face.

"Of course not. I just expected you to be gone for a couple of days," Alonzo said honestly. With Porsha gone, he would be free to handle his business with

Animal and the others, but her presence complicated things. He didn't know who else would be coming after him or how much they knew about him, so there was no way to ensure her safety.

"You probably planned to go fuck off in the strip club or maybe go lie up with whatever bitch kept you from taking me to the airport," Porsha said with a roll of her eyes. She walked into the kitchen and turned on the light. Porsha was a beautiful girl, five foot something with chocolate skin and long legs. Her hair was pulled back into a tight ponytail, and the only makeup she wore was a hint of lipstick.

"You know I only got eyes for you, baby. So stop acting like that." Alonzo followed her.

"Then why didn't you keep your word and come take me to the airport?" Porsha fished around in the refrigerator and pulled out a plastic container of orange juice. She didn't bother with a glass, just sipped straight from the container while watching Alonzo over the rim.

He leaned on the counter and sighed. "It's complicated."

"Really? All these years we've been together, and you still on that?" She slammed the container onto the counter, splashing it with juice. "I see what kind of games you're playing, and I'm not with it." She turned to walk away, but he stopped her.

"On everything, I ain't trying to play you. I just got some shit going on that I can't really talk about. So the less you know about it, the better," he told her.

"Yeah, right. I been helping you bury your bones for years, and now, you wanna act like you're trying to protect me? Get the fuck out of here. You think you're so slick, Alonzo, but that's word to my mother. If I find out you're out here creeping on me, your ass is grass." She pressed two fingers against his forehead and pushed hard enough to snap his head back. Porsha stormed up the stairs with Alonzo hot on her heels. She grabbed a pair of pajamas from the drawer and laid them on the bed.

"What are you doing?" he asked, watching her start to strip off her clothes.

"About to take a shower and relax. What does it look like?"

"It's still kind of early, I was thinking maybe me and you can go out and grab a bite," Alonzo said while sliding into his boxers and then a pair of jeans. He needed to get her out of the house.

"I'm tired and have a flight to catch in the morning. I don't feel like it," she said.

"C'mon, baby. I can take you out to City Island. Or we can go to that other seafood spot you like in Manhattan. You know your greedy ass can't say no to lobster tails," he joked.

Porsha cracked a half smile, even though she wanted to be mad. "Don't be trying to bribe me with food because you know your ass is in the doghouse. I still think there's some funny shit going on that you're trying to keep from me."

"Listen, let me take you out, and I can explain everything. I promise it isn't what it . . ." Alonzo's words trailed off. A red dot appeared in the center of Porsha's chest. It only took his brain a second to register what was about to take place and less than that to prevent it. Alonzo tackled Porsha at the exact moment the first round of bullets came ripping through their bedroom window. He covered her with his own body as a spray of glass rained down on them.

"What the fuck is happening?" Porsha shouted.

"Stay low," he responded, pulling her across the room. Alonzo shoved her into the closet and closed the door before scrambling toward the bed.

"Alonzo!" Porsha shouted. She tried to yank the door open, but he had locked her in. She couldn't get out but could see through the slits in the closet door. What happened next would stay with her for a long time.

Three of them kicked in the front door of their home, all wearing stocking caps over their faces and carrying firearms of varying sizes. The leader was a beefy man carrying an assault rifle and wearing black boots. He waved his hand, motioning for them to go upstairs, where he knew his prey was. Following the big man's lead, they made their way upstairs. The bedroom was a mess of broken glass and feathers from the pillows they had aired out, but there was no sign of the ones they had come to kill. Then he heard someone moving inside the closet. Gun cradled, he moved toward the door. His hand had just touched the doorknob when someone called out.

"You looking for these?" Alonzo was lying on the floor between the bed and the window. In his hands were two massive guns. The .45 and .357 rang out in unison. The slugs hit the man in the chest, holding the assault rifle, and knocked him off his feet. He crashed through the closet door, nearly landing on Porsha, who was huddled in a ball and screaming her head off.

As Alonzo got up from the floor, a bullet whizzed past his face, nicking his cheek and drawing blood. He fired low, hitting the second man in the crotch with the .357 and then knocking his head off with the .45. Seeing his comrades down, the third man bolted, but there would be no escape.

The third man made it halfway down the stairs before something heavy hit him in the back and sent him flying the rest of the way. He crashed into the front door with so much force that it splintered. His back burned from where the bullet had hit him, but he still found the strength to crawl for the exit. He spared a glance over his shoulder and saw Alonzo taking his time making his way down the stairs. It wasn't supposed to go like this. When they accepted the contract, they had been assured that Zo-Pound would be the easiest of the group to take down. He wasn't a killer like the rest of them. *"A sheep trying to run with wolves"* was the exact quote. Unfortunately, they had been wrong about Zo-Pound . . . so very wrong.

"Nah, don't try to dip off, muthafucka. We're just getting started," Alonzo growled, grabbing the man by his legs and pulling him into the living room. Then with his bare foot, he kicked him over onto his back. "You come into my home and try to violate?" Next, he stomped him in the face with the heel of his foot. He was enraged.

"Hold on. If you let me live, I'll tell you who sent us," the third man tried to barter for his life.

"No need. I already know who sent you, and that bitch will join you shortly." Zo rested the barrels of both guns over the third man's eyes and pulled the triggers. The bullets ripped through his skull before cracking the floor beneath.

"Zo," he heard Porsha timidly call his name. She had managed to climb out of the closet and descend the stairs. When Alonzo turned to her, he looked like something out of a horror movie. His eyes had a wild look, and his face was smeared with blood. She had never seen him like this before.

"This is all fucked up. We gotta go," Alonzo told her, never taking his eyes off the dead man at his feet.

"Men just shot up our house, and that's the *best* answer you can give me? What's going on? What have you let Ashanti and Animal pull us into?" Porsha began rambling nervously.

Zo felt his temples throbbing. He'd just had a shootout in a residential neighborhood and was in a house full of dead bodies and all kinds of fraud paraphernalia. He didn't have time for this. Zo tucked one of his guns into his waistline, grabbed Porsha with his free hand, and gave her a good shake.

"Porsha, if you love me, you'll shut your mouth and do as I ask. We need to leave before . . ." His words trailed off.

"Alonzo," she said his name softly. His expression had suddenly gone blank, and a vacant look filled his eyes, scaring her.

"Fuck," he strained, coughing blood in her face. His arms turned into noodles, and he lost feeling in his hands. His pistol clattered to the floor, and he seemed to be having trouble standing. Finally, on shaky legs, he turned to look at something behind him, and it was then that Porsha noticed two things: the blade protruding from his back and a shadowy figure standing directly behind him.

The figure was tall, not as tall as Alonzo, but taller than Porsha. It wore a one-piece camouflage bodysuit with two gun belts slung across its narrow hips. Long dreads hung from beneath the green cowl draped over its head. A green mask with a flower carved into the forehead covered the shadow's face. There was also a blade in its hand that was identical to the one sticking out of Alonzo's back.

Porsha had no idea who this person was or what they wanted, but Alonzo seemed to. He summoned up what little energy he could and went for the remaining gun tucked in his waist. He managed to clear it but never got a chance to use it. He hadn't even seen the assassin move, but he heard the air whistle. Alonzo never felt a thing. In fact, he hadn't even realized that he had been cut until he saw his hand fly across the room with the gun still in it. His head swam, and he collapsed to his knees, clutching his bloody stump.

"On your knees is no way for a member of the Dog Pound to die." The assassin helped Zo to his feet and pulled him into an embrace. The gesture was almost a tender one. "Your loyalty to the Bastard Son is why death has visited you tonight. But before it's all said and done, death will have visited all who rallied to his cause." The assassin looked at Porsha, who was in the corner, frozen with fear.

"She's a civilian," Zo rasped.

"But you are a soldier." The killer looked Zo in the eyes before pushing the blade deeper into his back and severing his spine. His end was swift and painless. "A soldier's death," the assassin whispered before letting Zo's body fall.

"No!" Porsha howled like a wounded animal. She was generally passive, but seeing the man she loved murdered so coldly caused something inside her to snap. She lunged for the gun that Alonzo had dropped. Her fingers were just closing around the handle when a heavy boot landed on the back of her hand, breaking several bones. Ignoring the pain, Porsha clung to the assassin's leg and sank her teeth into her thigh, drawing a scream from the killer. If she were going to die, it wouldn't be without a fight.

The assassin fired a knee into Porsha's chin with so much force that it knocked her jaw off its hinges. Then she grabbed Porsha by the hair and spun her in a full circle before letting her fly across the room and crash through the glass coffee table. That should have ended it, but Porsha wasn't finished. The girl pushed herself to her feet, dazed but still ready to go. The girl had fire.

Next, the assassin grabbed Porsha by the throat and drove her into the wall with so much force that it knocked several pictures to the ground, breaking the frames, one of which was the photograph she and Alonzo had taken at Animal and Gucci's wedding. Finally, the assassin placed the blade to Porsha's throat and looked into her eyes, searching for signs of fear. Instead, she found only defiance. "You love him so much that you would join him in death?"

"Happily," Porsha mumbled through her broken jaw. Without Alonzo, she had nothing . . . was nothing. She closed her eyes and began to pray as she waited for the killing blow, but it never fell. Then unexpectedly, the assassin released Porsha and allowed her to fall to the floor. When she opened her eyes, she found the killer standing across the room near the door.

"The debt here has been settled," the assassin answered the question on Porsha's face. "There will be no more death here tonight—at least not by my hand. In time, your bones and your heart will heal. If you still long for death, come find me, and I will accommodate you. I am called Nightshade."

Chapter 10

"Am I the only one wondering who this knockoff version of Animal is supposed to be and why she thinks she can come through talking crazy?" Nef moved forward, ready to lay hands on the girl and put her back in her place.

"Don't!" Ashanti stepped into his path. He did it more to protect Nef than her.

The girl in the bandanna walked cockily into the circle of men, recklessly eyeballing them as if trying to figure out which one to swing on first. Finally, she stopped before Ashanti and looked him up and down. "What's popping?"

Ashanti shrugged. "You, sometimes me. Been a long time, Diabolique."

"Too fucking long. I hate the fact that this was the thing that had to bring us all back together." She hugged Ashanti tightly.

At one time, her name had been Rose, but for the last few years, she had been going by Diabolique. It was a nickname Animal had given to her years ago because he said she had a touch of the devil in her. Diabolique had been the second survivor of the flock from The Below. She was a secret that Animal kept close to his chest. Ashanti knew about her because she came into the fold about the time he was first cutting his teeth. The circumstances under which Diabolique came to stay with them at The Below were sketchy, and Animal never really talked about it, only to say that she didn't have anyone else. Years later, Ashanti would learn that Animal shared some connection with the girl's late mother. Ashanti didn't think it was sexual, but whoever the girl's mother had been, she must've meant a lot to Animal for him to be as protective of the child as he was.

One thing that had always been obvious to Ashanti from the first time he had met the girl was that she had issues. Diabolique was full of piss and vinegar, always angry over this or that, and always on "go." She was cursed with a violent temper and would explode over the simplest things. Her short fuse was likely because of all she had been through at such a young age. The hardheaded young girl gave Animal fits, more than Ashanti ever had, but he never stopped trying with her. Diabolique never stuck around long enough to be officially inducted into the Dog Pound when it was formed, which explained why Nef didn't know her.

Diabolique had spent her life as an outlaw in the truest sense, never planting roots in one place and living outside the lines of the law to get what she needed from one day to the next. Every so often, when she found herself in a bad way or needed a few dollars, she would seek out Animal. No matter how many random guest appearances or how much time had gone by, he never questioned or denied her when she came. Over the years, her visits became less frequent and eventually stopped altogether. Animal never went out of his way to look for her because he knew that she generally didn't want to be found when she disappeared. It had been a few years since any of them had seen her. The last anyone had heard, Diabolique had gotten arrested somewhere in the Midwest over a shooting and had to do some time. The story had always seemed sketchy to Ashanti because none of his contacts had ever been able to find a record of her having ever been arrested outside of New York, but Animal didn't press it, so neither did he.

Just beyond Diabolique, her guardian angel lingered. Animal was still wearing the stained, damp clothes from the night before. His shoulders sank slightly more, and his eyes held a weary look. By that point, he had been moving off sheer will. Nevertheless, his spirit pushed him on.

"Where you find her?" Ashanti asked, giving Animal some dap.

"She found me," Animal informed him. "I was visiting with some people when she showed up."

"You mean when I caught you *slipping*," Diabolique corrected him. "Old age got you niggas getting sloppy."

"Dog Pound ain't never been sloppy," Nef said. However, he didn't know the girl and wasn't feeling her attitude.

"Oh yeah?" Diabolique turned to him. "Is that why muthafuckas is on the street calling y'all weak for letting all this shit go down? I can't say that I blame them. I'd think y'all were a bunch of bitches too for letting somebody touch the big homie's family, and they're still breathing."

"Shorty, you're out of line," Abel spoke up.

"The hell I am," she shot back. "Ain't no way in the fuck this was supposed to happen to Animal's people, and the streets ain't bleeding. I know I speak for everyone here when I say that the OG has been watching our asses for years. He's the sole reason a lot of us are even still alive, and in return, we have failed him miserably. So this shit doesn't sit right with me."

"D, I see where you're going, but you need to slow up a bit until you get all your facts straight," Ashanti interjected. "You been gone for a while, but we been doing this war shit for years. We can't just jump off the porch without a plan."

"I got a plan. Kill every muthafucka that had a hand in snatching this man's children and laying his wife. On mine, I bet that nigga, Shai, was behind it. We need to go holla at that dude," Diabolique said venomously. She had been away during their conflict with the Clarks and had always regretted not being there for Animal when he needed her.

"I already spoke to Shai," Abel told her. "That shit is like beating a dead horse. I don't know if doubling back right now is such a good idea. We don't want to poke a hornet's nest unnecessarily."

"Dig this, Blood . . . I don't give a fuck about no Shai, his crippled-ass brother, his crack whore mama,

drunk sister, or his dead daddy. But unlike my pre-
decessors, I bang this Dog Pound shit for real. All
my Apes already on deck and ready to do what y'all
couldn't! If there's to be blood, let it be." Diabolique
pounded her chest.

"Enough!" Animal said, finally tired of Diabolique
getting everyone riled up. The girl meant well, but
sometimes she could be a bit much. "I appreciate you,
baby sis, but I can't have you running around stirring
up random shit. Not while my kids' lives are hanging
in the balance."

"My bad, big homie," Diabolique said apologetically. "I just feel so fucking helpless right now."

"You aren't the only one," Ashanti assured her.
"We're all twisted about the way this shit has played
out. But to be honest, I'm not sure what our next
move should be." He looked at Animal.

"Let's go over what we know so far." Animal ran
down the events as they had happened for Diabolique . . . Sonja showing up at his house, the kidnap
plot, the drugs, and finally, Gucci's murder. His voice
was heavy when he spoke about his wife, and for a
minute, he felt like he would break down while re-
counting the events.

"I'm sorry . . . about your wife and all." Diabolique
rubbed Animal's arm comfortingly. "I'd only met her
that one time in passing, but she seemed like a good
woman. Hell, she had to be to have tamed the beast."

This made Animal smile. "Gucci was the best of
us."

"And her killers will answer for it. You got my word," Diabolique promised. "So, where are we at with it now?"

"Kahllah is still in Virginia trying to petition the Brotherhood to help us figure out how to stop Tiger Lily. But she hasn't checked in recently, and I'm getting a little worried," Animal said. She had been gone a few days, and no one had heard from her. He was beginning to wonder if something had gone wrong. Since his retirement, he had gotten to know the Brotherhood and their methods intimately, thanks to Kahllah. But even with what she had taught him, he still didn't have a firm grasp on the secret order of assassins and their methods. What he did know, though, was that they were a dangerous lot who distrusted outsiders.

Though Kahllah was one of theirs, she was currently campaigning to kill another respected member of her Order in the name of an outsider, which complicated things. Lilith had been branded a traitor by the Order. Her name still carried a great deal of weight under the Mountain, and there was no doubt some were still loyal to her. It was impossible to tell how many other members she had brainwashed already, and for all they knew, Kahllah could've very well been walking into a trap.

"The Lotus can handle herself," Ashanti said, trying to sound more confident than he really felt. "Whether she can get the Brotherhood to help is anyone's guess, but we've got to leave her to it and focus on doing our part, tracking down Sonja and that damn formula."

"Anybody know where to start looking?" Cain asked. He had been silently watching the exchange.

"I've got a few ideas. I know some people in the city who did business with her father's cartel," Animal said. "Sonja is alone in a foreign city, so she will need allies. I say we shake all the trees we can and see what falls out. Not the soundest plan, but it's all we've got for now."

"We got the kid," Abel reminded them. By the "kid," he spoke of Lilith's youngest son, George. He had been the reason Animal and Abel had been at the club when the cop got shot. George was currently a hostage of the Dog Pound and the only bargaining chip they had left now that Sonja had stolen the messenger bag containing the chemical formula that Lilith wanted.

"Wait, is it true that y'all got this dude locked in a storage unit?" Nef chuckled.

"Not exactly the smartest place to stash somebody who might be your last hope of making shit right. You better hope the nigga is even still alive after all this time," Diabolique said.

"She's right, but since our apartment and half the building got blown to shit, we're kind of short on options," Abel replied.

"We can take him to my place," Nef offered, to everyone's surprise.

"Dawg, I thought you were married with kids? We ain't bringing this around your family," Ashanti told him.

"Don't be an idiot, Ashanti. I got a little out-of-the-way spot that not many people know about," Nef said slyly.

"A *jumpoff* crib," Diabolique mumbled in disapproval.

"You need somewhere to stash this nigga or not?" Nef shot back. He was trying to help and didn't appreciate the chick judging him.

"Yes, and thank you," Animal answered. "Once we get him out of the storage unit and somewhere secure, we can really put the screws to him and see just what kind of value we can get out of this hostage."

"That's an idea I can get behind. Sitting around and waiting for the other shoe to drop drives me crazy. I need some action," Bizzle said.

"And you'll have it," Animal replied. "You go with Cain and Nef to secure that package. Cain, you think you can get him to talk?"

Cain flashed his twisted grin, twirling his knife between his fingers. "Is a pig's pussy pork?"

"My man." Animal gave him dap. "I don't give a fuck if you peel that nigga to the bone to get him to spill, so long as you don't kill him. His life might still count for something."

"Animal, you know I only got two gears—go and go harder," Cain reminded him.

Animal stepped up and eyed Cain. "That sadist shit you be on ain't got no place on this train. When my kids are safe, we gonna swim in the blood of all these sissies, I promise you that. But for the time being, I'm going to need you to practice some restraint. Can you do that?"

Cain gave Animal a look that bordered on defiance. Those who knew him watched him closely because the scarred twin did not take orders well. It wasn't that he was looking to challenge Animal, but he had been looking forward to impressing him. Cain had come up following Animal's career closer than an athletic scout looking for the next LeBron James. Since Ashanti had introduced them, Cain had been going out of his way to show the elder murderer how far he was willing to go to prove that his name belonged in the same conversations. He opened his mouth to deliver the response that came naturally, but a look from Ashanti gave him pause. This wasn't the time nor the place for a pissing contest. "You got it, big homie," was his edited reply.

Animal didn't necessarily believe it, but he accepted it.

"Don't worry. I'll make sure your orders are carried out to the letter, like always," Nef said, trying to ease the tension.

"I trust you will," Animal addressed Nef but kept his eyes on Cain. "This is why I'm leaving you in charge of guarding him while we out here getting to it."

Nef was thankful to have watchdog duty instead of Animal calling on him to participate in something more sinister, but he didn't miss the looks coming from the other members of the Dog Pound. He was an original, and being relegated to the role of babysitter in front of the pups wouldn't make them respect him. "Animal, if you're going to be out there in the thick, then I need to be at your side, same as Ashanti, same as we always mob."

Animal picked up on what was happening. Nef hadn't been in active combat in years, and even back when he was running with Animal, he had always been squeamish about mayhem. Drawing first blood wasn't in his nature, and Animal wouldn't toss his friend in over his head or embarrass him by indicating as much. "Nef, the fact that you been Pound since the beginning is why I'm asking this of you." He placed a hand on Nef's shoulder and gave a squeeze. "Considering what's at stake, you're one of the few people I'm comfortable enough with to assign this task. Who can I trust more than my brother?"

Nef looked at him with thankful eyes. "I'm a little disappointed that y'all are gonna have all the fun, but whatever part you need me to play, I got you."

"While they're handling that, I got something I need you to do," Animal addressed Ashanti.

"Just tell me who it is, and he's dead," Ashanti declared.

"Not just yet," Animal said, to Ashanti's disappointment. He loved putting in work. "You still fuck with those stickup kids from up on the Hill? You know the ones I'm talking about."

The question took Ashanti somewhat by surprise. Animal spoke of a small group of dudes who did stickups and other hustles. Animal had been long gone from the city by the time the crew's names started ringing, so Ashanti didn't expect that he even knew who they were, let alone Ashanti's affiliation with them. It just went to show that no matter where Animal was, he always had his finger on the pulse of New York. "They ain't Dog Pound. What you want with them?"

"Information," Animal told him. "Those thirsty muthafuckas are always sniffing around for somebody to rip off, so it stands to reason that they may have heard of new players in the game trying to set themselves up in the city. So go holla at them dudes and see what they know."

"Animal, I don't do recon. I do murder." Ashanti was sour on the idea of being sent on an errand. A task like that should've been delegated to one of the pups, not his most trusted shooter.

"I mean no slight to your character, li'l brother. I'm asking you to do this because you're highly respected in these streets. If you ask a nigga a question, they'll be inclined to answer without trying to bullshit you." Animal soothed his ego. "Rattle that cage, and then I need you to get a line on Zo and link back with me. If he's done securing his lady, I need him and those pistols back on the front lines with us."

"You got it," Ashanti agreed.

"And me?" Abel asked, not used to being separated from his brother.

"You're with me and Diabolique," Animal said to everyone's surprise. To ride at Animal's side was a place of honor, but Animal wanted Abel with him for a different reason. He'd seen something in him at the club when he'd shot that cop. He couldn't quite put his finger on it, but he wanted to keep Abel close, so he had eyes on him. "Us three are gonna hit the streets and see if we can get a line on my baby mama."

"I think I can do you one better than a random search." Diabolique offered. "You said all this is about some new designer drug she's trying to flood the streets with, right?"

"And?" Animal wanted her to get to the point.

"Well, shit like that isn't like crack, coke, or dope where you'd be hitting up different hoods trying to get it out. We gotta go where the pretty people play, the nightclubs."

"That narrows it down," Ashanti said sarcastically. "You know how many clubs there are in New York City? We'll be at this for days."

"We don't have to go to every club, big bro. We just need to hit the one that will be the most popping." Diabolique dug in her back pocket and pulled out a flyer that she handed Animal.

Animal read the party flyer, and a smile crept to his lips when he saw who one of the specially invited guests would be. "I hope everybody's got their rabies shots."

The statement confused most of them, but Ashanti knew what it meant and wasn't unhappy that he would miss the reunion.

PART IV

ROADHOUSE BLUES

Chapter 11

It was a beautiful night in New York City, not too hot but not too cold either. It was the perfect weather for a gathering, and that's precisely what was happening in Midtown—a spot known simply as The Club was selected to host an amateur music showcase. None of the artists who would take the stage that night had more than a local buzz, but it wasn't the talent that would be the draw that night, but the expected guests expected to attend. Of course, there would be A&Rs and a few celebrity judges who would bring out the women and a slew of acts thirsty for a deal, but another person was scheduled to be there to bring out the goons. This was the person that anybody with sense would make sure to stand next to at some point during the night. That's what had brought most of the people out that night—opportunity. That was the very thing that had brought Valentino out that night.

"Yo, you see the ass on that bitch?" Valentino exclaimed as he watched a thick girl in a too-tight dress saunter past him on the line. He was a youthful, light-skinned dude with curly hair and hazel eyes—a real pretty boy.

"Huh?" Zion had only been half-listening. He was dark-skinned with a husky build. He wore his hair in a coarse Afro full of naps that could stand a shape-up.

"Bro, what planet are you on right now? All these bitches coming back and forth, and your eyes been on your damn shoes the whole time," Valentino said.

Zion just shrugged. It was true. His eyes had been glued to his shoes the whole time. He was wondering if he had done a good enough job of scrubbing all the stains out of the old construction Tims. Unfortunately, he couldn't afford to buy new footwear for that night, so he found the least busted pair of boots in his closet and took a soapy rag to them, hoping he could at least make them look presentable.

"Look, Z, I hope you don't plan on being on your strong, silent shit the whole night. We're supposed to be here to have fun and fuck with some bitches," Valentino capped.

"I thought we were here to get some money," Zion reminded him.

"Nigga, we gonna do that too, but that don't mean we can't have fun while we're at it," Valentino told him. Zion was his best friend but could sometimes be a pain in the ass. The kid was always brooding. He had a good reason for his sour disposition, though. Zion hadn't had the easiest home life. His mom had walked out on them when he was a kid, and his dad was in and out of rehab, and even during the stretches when he was home, he paid little attention to his son. Zion spent a good deal of time at Valentino's. His wasn't the most functional household, but at least there, Zion was guaranteed a decent meal every night and somewhere that wasn't infested by vermin to lay his head. Valentino's mom had never been too fond of his scrappy young friend, but she was locked up, and his uncle was now running the household and family business. He didn't care if Zion crashed at the house so long as he contributed, and he did by way of going along with whatever harebrained schemes they came up with in the name of a dollar.

"How did you find out about this place again?" Zion asked, peeping the high rollers who were easily allowed entry while they were forced to wait in line. Zion felt like they were out of their depth.

"I told you, one of my peoples put me onto this spot. They said it was the best place to be for what we need to do," Valentino answered slyly. It was true that The Club was a happening place to be that night, but he hadn't discovered it through anyone he knew. He actually found out about the function from a promotional flyer he'd found in his house while looking for something to break his weed up on. So when he saw the names of some of the people invited to attend, he knew it would be the perfect spot to test-drive his latest money scheme. He didn't like not being honest with Zion, but he knew that if he told him, his friend would've been more likely to talk him out of the plan rather than agree to tag along as his muscle.

After what seemed like forever, the two youths had finally reached the front of the line. The guy at the door was a thin dude with a pencil mustache and greasy, black hair. He looked like one of those cartoon villains who was always trying to tie the damsel in distress to train tracks. He took one look at Valentino and his friend and made a face like he had just smelled something foul. "Fuck y'all want?" he asked.

"Same as everybody else. To get in on the action." Valentino gave him a toothy grin.

The Villain chuckled. "Shorty, you gotta be 21 or older to get in here, and y'all don't look a day over 16. You got some ID?"

"Fosho!" Valentino went into his pocket and produced a driver's license, bearing his face but the name and birthday of someone else. He watched the Villain as he studied the identification before sticking it into the handheld device to check it for authenticity. Valentino glanced over his shoulder at Zion, who looked nervous, and gave him a confident wink. After a few seconds, the machine blinked green, and he returned it to Valentino. "Good looking." He tried to step inside, but the Villain stopped him.

"Fifty cash . . . each."

"What? The flyer said twenty," Valentino replied.

"I don't give a fuck what the flyer says. If you two shitbirds wanna come in, it'll cost fifty." The Villain held out his hand.

Valentino was about to raise a stink, but Zion stepped up. "Here." He slapped five beat-up twenties into the Villain's hand. That money was supposed to feed him for the rest of the week, but he would've rather part with it than cause a scene and possibly be embarrassed in front of the crowd in the line.

"A'ight, now, y'all can go in." The Villain parted the ropes for them.

"Bitch-ass nigga," Valentino mumbled under his breath once they had passed through the entrance. "Yo, why you give that nigga the money when you know he was trying to beat us?"

"I know, but it ain't that serious. Besides, we're gonna make that back, and then some once we sell off the shit you're holding, right?" Zion questioned.

"Sho, you're right, Z . . . Sho, you're right." Valentino slapped him on the back confidently. He had told Zion that he was sure they would make a killing pushing product in the club, but in truth, he wasn't sure. The drugs he had stashed on him were new and untested, which he was counting on to be the big draw.

He'd swiped the strange blue crystals from the stash his uncle, Louie, had in the crib. Louie was a master chemist, at least before getting busted and kicked out of college for using the science lab for manufacturing MDMA. He did two years in jail behind it, and when he came home, he made his money cooking crack and cutting heroin for the local dealers. Not long ago, he was approached by someone looking to put a new type of product on the streets. Louie's job was to help the new connect manufacture the drug and get it street-ready. Valentino, being a student of chemistry himself, served as his uncle's apprentice. He didn't know much about the strange blue crystals his uncle was making, but he did know that the fiend his uncle used to test them damn near stroked out in their living room. That was enough to tell Valentino he could profit from it. So he hit the streets and started whispering into the ears of a few cats he knew who would purchase the new drug from him.

The problem Valentino was facing was that the drug was still untested. There was no telling what the long-term effects would be. Not that he really cared. For him, it was all about turning a quick profit. He reasoned that he would do a quick test run at The Club and see how it affected people. This would give him a better idea of what he was dealing with before he sold it to the guys he had waiting in Harlem. The Club run would be a gamble, but a worthy one. As far as he was concerned, if it went badly in the club, he wouldn't have to worry about ever seeing any of the random people he sold to again. If it went well, it would be the first step in building his clientele. Valentino was forever the opportunist, just like his mom.

"I thought for sure he was gonna shut us down when he swiped your ID," Zion whispered to Valentino once they were out of earshot of the Villain.

"I told you to stop doubting my skills, bro. My mom had me making fake IDs since I was a shorty. I'm so nice with it that I can get past TSA with my cards, so you know I ain't worried about no candy-ass bouncer," Valentino boasted. Scamming ran in the family. Forgery was a gift he had inherited from his mother. She could duplicate identification, credit cards, checks, and just about anything else if you gave her time and the right materials. She was a master forger, a skill she had passed on to her children. It was her gift at forging things, sprinkled with a bit of greed, that had gotten her locked up. She was running a rent scam, subleasing an apartment she no longer had claim on to a group of girls. The money they gave her every month went into her pocket instead of the rent office. The shit eventually hit the fan, and the girls got evicted for lack of payment. When the hoodrats tried to run down on Valentino's mom, intent on whipping her ass for stealing their money, she played the victim and called the police. The girls were arrested, but the dispute was far from over. One of the girls blew the lid off the rent fraud she was running.

When law enforcement arrived at Valentino's apartment, they hit the mother lode. They found ink cartridges, blank checks, card-pressing machines, and all sorts of other illegal paraphernalia. Just like that, the case became a federal one. Because it was his mom's first offense, she only caught five years in the Feds. She'd been gone for almost four already.

After getting past the Villain, they had to be searched by a bouncer posted up near the metal detectors. He was a big-headed, dark-skinned dude with a gold tooth in front of his mouth. The bouncer searched the pockets and waistlines of everybody who came in after they cleared the metal detector. For the guys, he made them take off their shoes to make sure they weren't hiding anything in them. Valentino went through with no problem, but Zion couldn't say the same. When he removed his boots for the bouncer to check them, things took a turn for the awkward.

"Damn, shorty, how long you had these mutha-fuckas on?" The bouncer held the boot at arm's length while turning his head to avoid the strong odor—the inside of the boots stank of sweat and mold.

"It's your job to secure this bitch, not be a come-dian." Zion snatched the boots from the bouncer and quickly stepped back into them.

"Don't get mad at me because ya joints smell like you walked barefoot in shit before you put them on," the bouncer joked. This drew a laugh from a group of pretty girls waiting to go through the metal detector behind them.

Fire burned in Zion's eyes as he stared at the bouncer, who was doubled over laughing. He could feel the demon that slept in the back of his head begin to stir. When he awoke fully, it would be feeding time. Zion's ashy hands came alive, curling into tight fists. At such close range, he was sure he could break the bouncer's jaw without even trying. He looked at Valentino, whose eyes pleaded for him not to do it. He knew what Zion was capable of when provoked, and this situation had the potential to go from bad to worse in an instant. With some effort, he swallowed his rage.

"You got it," Zion unclenched his fists. "I'm gonna let you rock, but best believe our paths *will* cross again," he told the bouncer before bumping past him and going inside.

Once they were inside the club and swallowed by the music and the thick smell of weed smoke, sweat, and alcohol, some of the tension had drained from Zion. He was still mad, but not enough to let it ruin his night. Valentino had promised him the spot would be jumping, and for once, he hadn't been lying. Until then, the closest thing Zion had ever experienced like this were neighborhood house parties, and they were rated PG compared to the scene unfolding inside The Club. Half-naked women abounded, as far as the eye could see, dancing on thirsty dudes and doing things that Zion had only seen in rap videos. One of the girls dancing on the floor rubbed her ass against Zion, and he blushed in embarrassment as he felt himself getting hard inside his jeans.

"Didn't I tell you this was the spot to be?" Valentino shouted over the music. All Zion could do was nod dumbly. "C'mon, let's hit the bar."

The two youngsters bumped through the crowd on their way to the bar on the far side of the room. It took them nearly ten minutes to reach it. The bar was crowded with people trying to order drinks or loitering. One dude, wearing a neck full of fake jewelry, was leaning against the bar, nursing a drink that was mostly water because he'd had it so long that all the ice had melted.

"Excuse me, but you think we could get in there for a second?" Zion asked him.

"Nah, this me," the dude with the fake jewels said dismissively, giving the youngsters his back. He was being an asshole for no reason.

"C'mon, Z. I think I see a spot down there where we can get in." Valentino was ready to relent and move on, but Zion wasn't.

Zion grabbed the dude's arm and bent it behind his back with enough force that he could feel his shoulder pop. Then he discreetly whispered, "Homie, right now, you fronting for nothing, but I'll tell you like this. If you don't move, I'm gonna take this arm and them fake-ass chains home with me tonight."

"You got it . . . You got it," the dude in the fake chains whimpered. Zion gave his arm a painful twist for good measure before releasing him to slink off and lick his wounds.

"Damn, Z. You amaze me at how you can go from zero to sixty in a matter of seconds," Valentino laughed as they occupied the spot the dude had vacated.

Zion gave a fake laugh, but inside, he felt terrible. He could inflict great pain on people when he wanted to, but violence was always a last resort for him. Growing up, he had watched his dad beat his mom, and when she left, his dad beat him until he was old enough to start hitting back. Once, he had lost control and almost beat his father to death. That was the first time the demon had ever spoken to him. "*Break him,*" the voice in his head had commanded, and Zion did as he was told. He broke his father's jaw and cracked two ribs. The incident had traumatized Zion. But even though his father was a piece of shit, he was still his parent, so he loved him.

Once Zion understood what he was capable of, he worked on getting it under control. Over the years, through meditation and weekly anger management sessions, Zion got better at blocking out the voice in his head that pushed him to hurt people. Still, every so often, the demon in his head managed to get loose and demanded to be fed. During those times, God have mercy on whoever was the object of his rage because only God could stop the wrecking ball of the young man when he went there.

"Let me get a bottle of Hennessy and a couple of waters," Valentino told the bartender once she got around to taking their orders.

The bartender looked at the light-skinned boy and his scruffy friend. "You know bottles are three-fifty, right?"

"No problem." Valentino slapped a credit card bearing someone else's name on the counter. The girl looked at the card suspiciously before running it through the machine. The transaction was approved without a problem, and the boys were presented with their bottle and a couple of glasses. "Is it okay if I tip you in cash?" He pulled a knot of bills from his pocket and fanned them.

"Cash is king," the girl said playfully. Her mood had softened now that she saw that he was handling.

Valentino peeled off five twenties and slid them across the bar. "There's more where that came from if you down."

"I get off at two a.m.," the girl told him while stuffing the bills into her bra.

"See you then," Valentino winked and slid the bottle off the bar.

"Man, why did you let me break that dude off my last hundred dollars, and you're holding that big-ass bankroll?" Zion asked when they were away from the bar. If he had to guess, he'd say that Valentino was holding onto at least a few grand.

"Chill out, Z. That's prop money. I printed it up this morning," Valentino informed him.

"You mean counterfeit?" Zion was shocked.

"That bitch is gonna be big mad when she tries to spend that bit of change," Valentino laughed.

Chapter 12

Valentino led the way as they bumped through the crowd again, trying to find somewhere they could occupy and do their thing, but it wasn't easy. The place was stuffed with people wall-to-wall, and it was hard for them to move, let alone chill. Finally, there was an unoccupied table marked RSVP sitting near the stage. Valentino made a beeline for it, with Zion on his heels. He had just beaten a group of girls in skimpy clothing to the spot and parked himself before they could. The girls looked pissed, but Valentino didn't care.

"Yo, you sure we can sit here?" Zion asked, looking at the RSVP sign.

"You see anybody else in these seats?" Valentino asked, filling up two glasses with Hennessy. He took one and slid the other to Zion, who was still standing. "Look, man, if whoever these seats belong to shows up, we'll just move, but for right now, sit your ass down. You're blocking the pussy." He craned his neck to get a better look at a female who was twerking on the dance floor.

Zion reluctantly took a seat, but he didn't relax. The whole time his eyes kept sweeping the faces of anyone who came in the direction of the table, think-

ing they were the ones the seats were being held for.
The last thing he needed was to be embarrassed for
a second time that night. Half an hour passed, and
they were able to enjoy the seats without incident.
Valentino had even managed to scrounge up a couple
of hoodrats to join them. They weren't the most
attractive girls in the club, but they were entertaining.

"So, what kind of name is Valentino? Sounds
Italian or something. You got some white in you?" the
leader of the girls asked. The boys assumed she was
the leader because she had done most of the talking
since they sat down. Her name was Shay. She was
light-skinned with full, pink lips and wearing a long,
black wig. Her heavy breasts sat damn near on the
table.

"On my daddy's side." Valentino sipped his liquor.
"What gave it away? My lack of pigment?" He ran his
hands down his cheeks jokingly.

"I think light-skinned dudes are sexy," another one
of the girls said, throwing back the healthy shot of
Hennessy she had poured from their bottle before
refilling it. She was slim, with slightly bucked teeth
and sporting braids that could stand to be done over.
Her name was Tasha.

"You think anything with a swinging dick is sexy,"
Shay said with an attitude. She had already laid her
claim to Valentino and saw Tasha's thirsty ass trying
to step on her toes.

"So, y'all must be some big-time players to have
your own private table in here tonight." Shay kept

talking to Valentino and ignored the dirty look her friend was giving her.

"Shorty, my name ringing in these streets," Valentino boasted.

"Then how come I never heard of you?" the third girl in their group asked sarcastically. She was short, with a honey complexion. Her natural hair was styled into a cute, curly Afro with purple highlights. Her name was Tess, and from the moment she'd sat down, it was clear that she really didn't want to be in the company of the goons, but her friends had pressured her.

"Because we probably don't run in the same circles," Valentino told her with an attitude. Tess was blowing his. Shay and Tasha had already let it be known in not so many words that they were down for whatever, but Tess would be a tougher nut to crack. There always had to be one in the group.

"Tess, why don't you chill out? We came here to have some fun, remember?" Tasha reminded her.

"Some of us are having a little too much fun if you ask me. It's still early, so why don't you slow down a little?" Tess suggested, watching Tasha throw back another shot. She was a bad drunk and knew where the night would end up going if she got too twisted.

"Nah, she got it. And it's plenty more where that came from. Ain't that right, Z?" Valentino nudged his friend.

"Um-hmm," Zion mumbled. Unlike Valentino, who was outgoing, Zion was shy around girls.

"Your friend doesn't talk much, do he?" Shay observed.

"Who, Z? He's the strong, silent type, but he's loads of fun once you get him going." Valentino refilled Zion's glass before he finished his first drink.

Zion looked at the liquor but didn't pick it up. He already had a nice buzz going on and didn't want to get too drunk. When he was drunk, he had less control over his demon and a sneaky feeling that he would have to keep his wits about him that night. "*Pussy*," he could hear his visitor snickering in his head, but Zion ignored him. He knew better than to play a game he would likely lose.

"Damn, everybody sitting around all stiff and shit. I thought this was supposed to be a party." Tasha threw up her hands and started dancing in her seat. The liquor was starting to kick in.

"Oh, you a good-time girl, huh?" Valentino gave her a sly smile.

"I've been known to turn up a little under the right circumstances," Tasha told him.

"I got just what you need." Valentino dug into his pants, rummaging around in the sandwich bag he had pinned to the inside of his underwear. He looked cautiously around before pulling Tasha's hand to him and placing something in her palm.

"What's this?" Tasha examined the blue crystal curiously.

"It's called Blue Dream." Valentino recalled what he had heard his uncle's connect call it.

"Looks like molly to me, only blue," Shay remarked. She wasn't big into designer drugs but dabbled here and there.

"Nah, that shit is way better than molly. The high is easier to control, and the buzz lasts longer. Blue Dream is gonna be the next big thing, and I got the line on it," Valentino said proudly. "Y'all want some? I got more than enough for everybody." He pulled some more crystals from his underwear and extended his hand to Shay.

"Nah, we good." Tess shoved his hand away before Shay could respond.

"What's the matter, baby? You don't like to party?" Valentino asked.

"I'm down for a good time, but if it ain't weed or liquor, I ain't fucking with it," Tess told him.

"Speak for yourself." Tasha popped the crystal into her mouth and washed it down with liquor. "Y'all ain't fucking with it?" she asked the boys.

"Z don't get down, but I'll take the ride with you." Valentino opened his mouth and acted like he popped the crystal but really palmed it.

Zion was the only person at the table who peeped what Valentino had done, which bothered him. It wasn't because he didn't know the girls from a can of paint or that they gave two shits about him. It was the principle of it. Zion had gotten down with plenty of the slimeball shit that Valentino was known to pull, but that didn't mean that he agreed with it. He lived his life by a particular code of ethics that Valentino may have been able to recite but wasn't bound to as he was. This is where they often butted heads. When Valentino went too far out of bounds, Zion would check him, but for the most part, he let him do whatever. He might not have agreed with some of the stuff, but he often hesitated to speak up. For all Valentino's faults, he was the only one who provided Zion with food and shelter when he had nowhere else to turn, and it was hard to argue with someone who brought you in out of the cold time and again. And for this reason, Zion held his tongue more often than he spoke up.

As the night wore on, things got a bit more relaxed. Tasha seemed to have caught Dance Fever from the Blue Dream. The bouncers had to visit their section twice because she kept climbing on the table and twerking. Valentino was amused by her antics, while Tess looked pissed, and Shay was just bored. Zion had finally let down his guard enough to try to have a good time. He even finished the glass of liquor Valentino tried to force on him and was considering another one. He had just reached for the bottle when something gave him pause.

He felt him before he saw him. It was like the built-in sixth sense in Zion's head had started ringing the alarm, alerting him of a potential threat. So Zion stopped his sipping and swept the crowd for the source of his growing anxiety.

As he approached the table, the crowd seemed to part for the white man. Now, standing over their table, Zion could see he was taller than he'd thought when he first spotted him across the room. He stood up straight at about six foot two, possibly six-three. He was of a stocky build, likely genetic rather than from time spent in the gym. He had a mop of slicked-back hair and the beginnings of a beard covering his jaw. In his tracksuit, white sneakers, and gold chains, he reminded Zion of the old mobsters he'd seen sitting outside the shops in Little Italy once when his dad had taken him to the feast of San Gennaro.

His eyes locked with Zion's, and there was a silent exchange between them as if they were trading their life's stories without uttering a word. Zion could feel the demon that lived inside him. He was fully awake now and thrashing against the walls of his mind. *"Fight or flee . . . fight or flee!"* the demon shrieked over and over, but Zion remained still. He wasn't sure that he could move even if he wanted to. There were certain people who you could tell exactly what they were about without them having to open their mouths. Their sheer presence could convey more about them than their words ever could. This man glaring down at him was one such person.

"You boys lost?" the Italian asked Valentino and Zion.

"What kind of question is that?" Zion asked, trying to sound tough. But in truth, he was nervous. He was sure he could take the man in a physical fight, but there was something else beneath his physical appearance. Something that he couldn't put his finger on, but it had his demon unnerved. *Fight or flee . . .*

"It's a question asked of kids who find their asses parked where they don't belong," the Italian replied. "Or maybe you can't read?" He motioned toward the small sign that read *Reserved*.

"If you wanted us to move, all you had to do was say so," Zion replied.

"Well, I'm saying so," he shot back in a nasty tone.

"You know what? We're gonna leave you boys to your sausage party and find somewhere else to sit," Tess volunteered. She sensed the mounting tension between them and wanted no part of what was about to go down.

"Chill. Y'all ain't gotta skirt off like that," Valentino tried to encourage them to stay. He had planned on getting his dick sucked and maybe getting into an orgy, but the Italian was blocking his action.

"No, it's fine. We're out," Tess insisted. She rose to leave but found her girls hesitant. "I suggest y'all get your asses up and follow suit unless you plan on taking the train home since I'm the one who drove us down here." At the prospect of getting left to their own devices and missing their ride, the girls got up and left, much to Valentino's displeasure.

"Nigga, what the fuck is your problem?" Valentino asked angrily as his plans for the evening scurried off.

"My problem is, I'm trying to be nice, but in a minute, you boys are going to make me get nasty," the Italian replied.

Valentino looked at Zion. He was sure that he and his friend could take the man. He was by himself, and there were two of them, one of whom was a brute. Zion, however, didn't seem so sure. There was something in his eyes akin to fear, and Valentino wasn't used to seeing that in someone he knew didn't fear much. If this Italian had Zion spooked, maybe it would be best for them to bow out. "Fuck it. We ain't wanna sit here anyhow." He rose to leave, but a feminine voice gave him pause.

"Afraid I'm going to have to insist that you stay." She stepped into view. They had been so focused on the Italian that they hadn't noticed her watching the exchange. She was gorgeous, but the way Valentino looked at her, you'd have thought she had just been spewed up from the bowels of hell. Valentino was a fair-skinned dude as it was, but as he stood in the woman's presence, all the color bled from his face.

"Oh fuck," Valentino muttered.

"Is that any way to greet the person who is no doubt sponsoring your little party?" The woman looked over the table with the half-empty bottle. "I don't know why I'm surprised. You're so typical of your species, a dog-ass nigga. You get what you want from a woman without so much as a kiss goodbye. Shame on you, Valentino."

"I can explain—" he began, but she cut him off.

"I'm sure you can, but I'm also sure that anything that comes out of that lying mouth of yours will probably tempt me to cut out your tongue, so I suggest you don't," she said coldly, slapping him on the cheek. "You wanted to be a player in the game? Well, you're all in now, shorty. So, sit your high-yellow-ass back down so I can give you a crash course in the rules."

Chapter 13

As soon as Ashanti crossed into Harlem, his whole demeanor changed. He sat up straighter in the driver's seat of his Jeep Wrangler and adjusted his mirrors. He tapped the complex combination of buttons on the dash before punching the seat belt release, which revealed the hidden compartment beneath the glove box where his gun was stashed. Ashanti was a feared killer, but he was also a recognizable face in the town. Under normal circumstances, he would've been good in Harlem because everybody knew how he gave it up. Still, with the escalating climate of the war and the bounty Tiger Lily was said to have placed on all their heads, you never knew when a man would decide to put a payday above common sense and try to collect on it. Wrapping his fingers around the gun handle brought him a measure of reassurance but not comfort. Comfortable men were dead men. His years of running with Animal had taught him that.

The dudes he was looking for lay their heads in a housing project known as the Polo Grounds. He wasn't sure which building they stayed in, but most nights, you could find them posted up in front of the store across from Rucker Park, up to no good. So this was the first spot he hit.

The weather was good that night, so there were quite a few locals out and about. He pushed north past Rucker Park before making a U-turn and heading south. A red light caught him near the corner store. A cluster of young men and women loitered in front of the bodega. A few dudes threw hard stares at the Jeep, trying to peer through the tint to see who was inside. Ashanti rolled down the passenger-side window enough for them to see who was behind the wheel. The sight of him was enough to kill whatever big ideas the guys may have had, but not the girls. All the young hoodrats in Harlem knew who Ashanti was and how he played, and they were always trying to get next to him. A light-skinned girl with a big ass separated herself from the crowd. She made sure to throw a little something extra into her sway when she approached the Jeep. Her eyes never left Ashanti as she closed the distance. She leaned her elbows on the car door and poked her head in to speak. "What up, Hollywood?"

She was a local who Ashanti knew as Bay. They called her that because her pussy was said to be deep and wet like a bay. Men lucky enough to have sampled it could attest to the truth in the myth. Ashanti was one of those men. It was never too serious for either of them, just something to do at the time. Life had pulled them in different directions, but occasionally, under the right circumstances, they still found themselves on the wrong side of a bad decision. Bumping into Bay that night could be a gift or a curse, depending on the way the conversation swung.

"There you go with that bullshit. You know I'm Harlem to the heart." Ashanti gave her a devious smile.

"I can't tell. Word on the street is that you too busy rubbing elbows with famous people to show the hood love anymore," she teased him.

Ashanti shrugged. "I'm here now, right?"

Bay smirked at his wit. There was a slight pause where they just looked at each other before Bay replied. "So, what's up? You usually pull up on me on the late night and after you've had way more to drink. You ain't out here looking for a good time, so I'm guessing it's a problem."

Ashanti laughed. "C'mon, why can't I just be sliding through, trying to enjoy the weather and the scenery?"

"Because niggas like you don't know how to have fun. All you know is fucking or killing. So, which one is it?"

"I'm really not looking for either one. It's your dude I'm actually trying to holla at," Ashanti told her. The guy Bay was seeing was an associate of Ashanti's, not so much a friend. Their relationship was strictly business, so Ashanti never felt bad for fucking his girl behind his back.

"What you want with him?" Bay asked suspiciously. She knew how Ashanti gave it up, and there was no telling how a conversation would end between him and her man.

"Relax, I ain't on that." Ashanti read the fear in her eyes. "I'm just trying to holla at the nigga right quick."

Bay weighed it for a few ticks. Ashanti was a killer, but he wasn't a liar. "He's around the corner at the dice game. I'll get in and show you where it's going down." She tried to open the door, but Ashanti hit the locks on her.

"Bet, but if it's around the corner, we ain't gotta drive. Let me park, and we can walk," Ashanti told her. Then without waiting for a response, he pulled farther up the block and parked his car. He wasn't trying to shit on Bay, but Harlem was small, and everybody knew everybody. The last thing he wanted was for someone to see Bay getting in his car and saying something to Fatima. Though nothing was happening now, Fatima knew his history with Bay, so you wouldn't have been able to tell her anything different. That was a headache he didn't need.

Ashanti had just parked his Jeep and was about to get out when his cell phone rang. He looked at the caller ID and couldn't help but laugh when he saw who was calling. "You must've known you were on my mind." He tried to sound cool when he answered.

"Yeah, right, nigga. So much on your mind I had to call you three times before you picked up? What's really good?" Fatima cut right into him. She was a woman who didn't believe in holding her tongue when she was feeling something and was one of the few people who could check Ashanti.

"Relax, ma. I'm good. How are you?"

"Pregnant and stressed out," she sighed.

"What you mean? I thought you'd have your feet up, enjoying the quiet of the suburbs."

"That's the problem. This shit is too quiet. You know I'm a Harlem chick. I need the sights and sounds of my city to keep me sane," Fatima said seriously. She was born and raised in the trap, and the hood was all she knew.

"Well, you might want to get used to it. As soon as this shit is over, I'm moving you and my son out of this fucked-up-ass city," Ashanti promised.

"There you go, swearing it's going to be a boy. It's still too early for us even to find out the sex," she laughed.

"It's gotta be a boy. My sperm too strong to make a girl. This kid is going to be my warrior prince," Ashanti declared.

"Whatever it is, boy or girl, this child will *not* be a warrior. It's going to be a scholar and grow up to be great just like its dad," Fatima said.

"Shit, ain't nothing great about me. I'm just a street nigga trying to live from one day to the next," Ashanti said honestly. For as much boasting and bragging as Ashanti did in the streets, he actually suffered from low self-esteem, as did many young men from similar walks of life. Their over-the-top behavior was to compensate for what they felt they were lacking.

"You know I hate when you do that, put yourself down. You may not have had the easiest upbringing, but you're making incredible strides as a man. You've accomplished a lot, and you haven't even begun to scratch the surface of what you can become."

Ashanti beamed. "You always know the right things to say, baby." He was about to add to it when his phone beeped. "Hold up," he said, checking to see who was on the other line. Porsha was calling. She was likely trying to find out where Zo was. Unfortunately, her game of twenty questions would have to wait until he finished with Fatima.

"Who was that? One of your shorties?" she half-joked.

"Nah, that was Porsha. She probably looking for Zo," he told her.

"You mean your shadow isn't with you?" She was surprised. Over the last few years, Ashanti and Zo have become inseparable.

"No, he had to go check on his crib. I'm dolo."

"I don't like it, Ashanti. You know, in times of war, y'all are supposed to stay at least two down at all times," Fatima reminded. It was something she always heard Ashanti tell his underlings.

"Listen to you sounding like a little general." Ashanti was amused.

"I learned from the best. But seriously, I'd feel much better if you had somebody out there with you. Zo . . . even one of the twins."

"Our numbers are stretched pretty thin right now. Everybody is out handling their parts trying to get these kids back," Ashanti said.

"Any luck?" Fatima asked.

"Not really, but we've turned up some interesting leads. I'm following up on one now. Gotta see somebody who might have some information."

"That means you're out there looking for one of your old chicks," Fatima said with an attitude. She knew that females were the best sources of information when you were trying to find out what was going down in the streets.

"Don't be silly. I'm about to pull up on our friend, the gambler." Ashanti knew better than to use certain names on the phone in case something went left and the police needed a trail of breadcrumbs to follow.

"Where are you exactly?"

"I'm up in the Polo Grounds."

"Don't that dusty whore you used to mess with live up there too?" Fatima asked. She was speaking about Bay.

"Man, I ain't seen shorty in forever," Ashanti lied. A knock on his window startled him to the point where he almost dropped his phone. Bay stood outside with her hands thrown up as if to ask what the holdup was. "Baby, let me get out here and handle this business. I'll hit you back."

"Why you sound so nervous all of a sudden?" Fatima pressed.

"You bugging. I told you I'm out here in the mix," Ashanti reiterated while holding his finger up to tell Bay to wait a second.

"Yeah, okay," Fatima said, clearly not believing him. "But before you go, let me tell you something. If you got me squirreled away out in West-Bubble-Fuck, pregnant and paranoid so you can run around chasing pussy, you ain't gonna have to worry about your ops catching you. I'm gonna lay you down myself."

"Man, why you always gotta be so extra?" He was getting aggravated.

"Because I'm an extra bitch. You knew that when you hooked up with me." She matched his tone.

"Look, calm down. I ain't trying to get you all riled up. Not in your condition," Ashanti softened his tone. "I love you, Fatima . . . and only you. You ain't never got to worry about losing me to no other broad. That's on Brasco."

"It ain't another woman I'm worried about losing you to, Ashanti. It's these streets. These people y'all into it with ain't like no corner hustlers. These cartels are a whole different animal than any of us are used to," she warned.

Ashanti took a deep breath before responding. "This will all be over soon. When it is, I'm falling back. No more penitentiary chances. I just gotta take this one last ride with the homie."

"I know you do, Ashanti. You've always been loyal to a fault."

Bay tapped the window again, frustrating Ashanti. "Look, I gotta go see this guy before he disappears. I'll call and check in with you later."

"Okay, I'm gonna let you go, but before I do, I need you to make me a promise."

"Anything," he said sincerely.

"Promise me that you aren't gonna die in the streets. I need you to see this child come into the world. Make it back to us, Ashanti."

"I promise. Ain't nothing gonna stop me from seeing my baby born," he said, trying not to get emotional. "I put that on Brasco."

"I love you, Ashanti."

"I love you too, Fatima," he said, ending the call. Ashanti took a few seconds to compose himself. Bay knocked on the window again, obviously getting impatient. "Muthafucka, wait," he snapped, startling her. He slipped the phone into the pocket of his sweats and grabbed his gun. As he got out of his Jeep, he never felt his cell phone slip from his pocket and fall between the seats.

Chapter 14

Tess found herself experiencing a mix of embarrassment and irritation. Getting, in not so many words, kicked out of the section they had been sitting in had her uptight. She knew from the moment they had sat down with the two dudes that nothing good would come of it. She had seen through them from the moment they had opened their mouths—wannabe gangsters in the club trying to stunt. They had proven her right when the truth came out in the wash, and it was revealed that they had parked their asses somewhere they hadn't paid to sit. That was the embarrassing part, getting kicked out. What irritated her was that she was the only one who seemed to have an issue with it. Tasha and Shay carried on with the rest of their night as if it had never happened. She loved her girls. They had been down since middle school and been there for one another through the best and worst of times. Tasha and Shay were more like sisters than friends, but love aside, the older they got, the more obvious it became that they weren't on the same page. Tess moved through life in search of a better way, but the only thing Tasha and Shay seemed to be searching for was the next good time.

They wouldn't have to wait long to find it. No sooner than they had exited the section Valentino had appropriated than they received an invitation to sit in another. This one came in the form of a short dude with a shaved head who was rocking a ton of jewelry. The piece that caught Tess's eye was the Rottweiler medallion hanging from his chain. She wasn't impressed by him, but she had seen the chain somewhere before. Dude smelled like trouble, so Tess was ready to step around him and keep it pushing, but not Shay. Instead, she stopped and exchanged a few words with him. Tess couldn't hear what he was saying to her friend over the loud music, but whatever it was enticed her to take the bait. The next thing Tess knew, she was hustling to keep up with Shay as the dude led her and Tasha to where his party was sitting . . . And what a party it was!

At least ten of them occupied a corner booth near the stage. Most of them were jeweled out, just as the bald kid had been, but a few stragglers looked like they had just been pulled from a street corner before arriving at the event. That made it easy for Tess to tell who was connected and who was just a straggler. As a whole, they were a less-than-savory-looking lot, all looking at the girls like bones set before a pack of starved dogs. The entourage of young men gave Tess pause, but it was the man resting at the center of the group that shot off a warning bell in her head.

He was a husky dude draped in an expensive-looking black sweat suit made by no designer Tess had ever heard of. This was obviously a custom piece. A black-on-black White Sox hat sat cocked on his head at an angle that a gust of wind could have knocked off. A bottle of champagne dangled lazily in one hand, a thick blunt in the other. He whispered into the ear of an older man sitting to his right. He must've felt Tess's eyes on him because he stopped his conversation and turned his attention toward her.

She couldn't see his eyes behind the dark sunglasses, but she could feel his gaze washing over her. When he moved, the jacket shifted, and she could see the thick diamond chain hanging around his neck. At the end of it was a Rottweiler head similar to the one the bald dude was wearing, only three times as large and flooded with diamonds. When the club's lights hit it, it had the effect of a Snapchat filter. It was then Tess realized why the other chain had looked so familiar.

They had gone from the frying pan into the fire.

"Low, I see you've returned bearing gifts," the dude with the big chain said and flashed a sinister grin. "Who do we have here?"

"This is Tasha and Shay," the man with the bald head made the introductions, "and . . ." He looked at Tess and paused. "I'm sorry, I never caught your name."

"That's because I didn't give it to you," Tess replied.

"This one has got a little spice to her. I like that." Big Chain nodded in approval. "Why don't you come sit by me." He patted an empty seat on the padded bench next to him.

"Mama always said never to play strangers too close," Tess told him.

"I'm no stranger, love. Everybody knows me," he said confidently.

"Ain't you a rapper or something?" Tasha asked. Her eyes were glassed over, and her words slurred a bit.

Big Chain removed his sunglasses and looked at the girl with weed-slanted, red eyes. "C'mon, shorty. You really wanna play this game? If you know my face, then I'm sure you know my name. Just in case you don't . . ." He snapped his fingers.

A short, light-skinned dude with a low Afro stood up on command. He was wearing a black T-shirt with the print of a butler's tuxedo on the front. He was momentarily hesitant as if he didn't know what would come next. Big Chain glared at him, and this helped him to find his voice. "You are in the presence of the exalted, highest in the room, Boss of bosses and King of Harlem . . . Don B.," he recited from memory. He had given the introduction more times than he could count.

"That's better, Hollywood. Next time say it with a little more enthusiasm," Don B. scolded him like a child, which drew laughter from everyone except Tess. Don B. could feel Hollywood shooting daggers at him, but the minion knew better than to lend voice to his displeasure. Being somewhat of the court jester for Big Dawg had been a cross he'd carried for the last few years. Awhile back, he had sold Don B.

some beats that didn't belong to him and ended up getting Big Dawg Entertainment sued by the rightful composer. Even though Don B. settled out of court, it still cost him a grip. Since it was Hollywood's fault, he was on the hook for the money, so Don B. made him work it off as an indentured servant.

"That is so cool. Does he know any more tricks?" Tess giggled.

"Bitch, don't get your head knocked off," Hollywood snapped. It was bad enough that he had to take shit from Don B. and his crew, but he wouldn't allow some random THOT to disrespect him.

"Relax," the large man standing next to Don B. warned in a gravelly voice. He was well-built with a hard face that bore the scars of the many battles he'd been in.

"Why you checking me instead of the bitch, Devil?" Hollywood complained.

"Because she doesn't know any better, and you do," Devil replied.

"Both of y'all keep it cool. We wouldn't want the ladies to think we're a gang of savages, would we?" Don B. asked.

"Shit, we are," Low joked, which got him a dirty look from Don B.

"On my honor, you girls are in good company. Have a seat," Don B. phrased it like a request, but it felt like an order.

Tess still didn't move, but Tasha and Shay happily joined the group. With no other choice than to join them or make good on her earlier threat to leave, Tess sat down. She made sure to occupy an empty chair out of Don B.'s reach. She parked herself next to the member of their entourage, who seemed to be the most harmless. He was a handsome, brown-skinned dude with a clean-shaven face. While the rest of the men were dressed in high-end designs and heavy jewels, he wore a simple pair of jeans and white sneakers with a blazer. Tess tried to give him a friendly smile, but he turned away as if she were bothering him. Apparently, he was an asshole who just didn't look the part. Tess would learn later that this was Tone, Don B.'s best friend and manager.

"What's the matter with your boy? He doesn't like pussy?" The old-timer sitting near Don B. joked. His name was Sammy, and besides the hoodrats, he was the only one in the section who wasn't on the Big Dawg payroll. Though he wasn't a member of their crew, it didn't stop him from enjoying the hospitalities of the record label. He'd been chugging champagne like it was water for half the night.

"Stay in your lane, old-timer, before you find your invitation into this circle revoked," Devil warned. Sammy's joke had been harmless, but Devil didn't take it as such. To him, Sammy was as big a leech as the women, if not more so.

Never one to back down from a challenge, Sammy matched Devil's tone and glare. "I was only busting your balls a bit, but if you got your panties in a bunch over it, I can cut out. I got more pressing business that requires my attention tonight, but I took time out of my schedule at your boss's request." He jabbed his thumb at Don B.

"And your time, as well as your presence, is appreciated," Don B. said to defuse a potential situation. Sammy was a pain in the ass, and had he not currently needed the old man's assistance, he'd have gladly let Devil slap his head off.

Sammy had been running the streets for longer than most of the members of Big Dawg had been alive. He started out as a number runner in the late seventies and then got into gambling heavily. Sammy could count cards, manipulate dice, or figure out how to rig just about any game you could place a wager on. The last few years, his claim to fame had been a franchise of underground gambling spots all over the five boroughs. Outside of the casinos and the mob, Sammy hosted the biggest games in town. But it wasn't his underworld ties that had him enjoying Don B.'s hospitalities that night, but his biological ones.

The tensions finally eased, and everybody was back in party mode. Even Tess had managed to loosen up a bit. Don B. watched from behind his sunglasses as the girls drank his liquor and smoked his weed. Outside of Tess, he could tell that they were straight leeches, which was okay by him. It was all a part of the game for him: give and take. What they didn't know but would soon learn was that the Don usually took more than he gave.

"I can't front; y'all niggas are way more lit than
the other two dudes we were with earlier," Shay said,
helping herself to another glass of Hennessy from
the dozen or so bottles lining the table. After filling
her glass, she went to fill her friend's. Tasha looked
like she'd had enough, but it didn't stop Shay from
pouring her up anyhow. When she went to add liquor
to Tess's, she covered it with her hand, indicating
that she was good.

"Oh yeah, what happened to them?" Tone asked
curiously.

"Their front-o-meter expired," Shay laughed.

"Well, we don't do no fronting on this side. We're
what the rest of these niggas aspire to be," Don B.
boasted, drinking champagne from the bottle. A bit
of it trickled down his beard, but he didn't notice.

"What's up with your homegirl? She good?" Low
asked, pointing to Tasha. He noticed that she hadn't
touched her liquor. Instead, she was just sitting there
with a dreamy look in her eyes, staring out at nothing
like she was in a trance.

"Yeah, she just a little faded. She'll be okay," Shay
said dismissively. "Why you so worried about her
when you got all this right here?" She had never been
one to mince words when she was after something.
Then discreetly, she placed Low's hand on her inner
thigh.

Low took the liberty of running his hand up her
flesh and under her dress. He was pleased when he
discovered that Shay wasn't wearing panties. He let

his fingers graze her unshaven pussy, slipping one inside her. She let out a soft moan as he explored her box. Low knew what time it was, and the hungry look in her eyes said she did too. "Yo, me and baby girl about to take a walk. Be back in a few." He got up and took Shay by the hand.

"Wait, where do you think you're taking my friend?" Tess asked protectively.

"To have a grown folk's conversation. Why, you wanna come?" Low asked hopefully. He would've loved to break his dick off in both of them.

"She good," Shay answered for her. "We'll be right back."

Tess watched as her friend allowed a stranger to lead her outside into the unknown and sadly shook her head. "Thirsty bitch," she mumbled.

"Don't stress," Tone told Tess, noticing the concerned look on her face.

"Huh?" Tess asked.

"I said, don't stress," he repeated. "Low is a thirst bucket, but he's also an honorable man. He ain't going to go any further than your homegirl allows him to."

"And what is that supposed to mean?" Tess asked, not really liking the sound of it.

"What it means," Don B. cut in, "is you can chase after them and try to stop something that none of us have control over, or continue enjoying the Don's hospitalities until they return. Who knows? You may even find yourself inspired to let your hair down and try to have a little fun, Big Dawg style." He offered her a glass of champagne that no one had seen him pour.

"Nah, I'm good," Tess declined. She had never met Don B. personally, but his reputation preceded him. She wasn't foolish enough to drink from any glass he handed her without seeing him pour it.

"Why did they turn the A/C off?" Tasha asked randomly, fanning herself with a napkin.

"Girl, what the hell are you talking about? The air-conditioning is going full blast," Tess said, rubbing the goose bumps on her arms. The Big Dawg table was placed directly under one of the vents, so it was super chilly where they sat.

"Probably all our free liquor getting to her thirsty ass," Hollywood remarked.

"She had some drinks earlier but never touched that Henny," Tess pointed at the still full glass of brown liquor on the table. "It was probably that Dream shit," she said offhandedly.

"Look, if she can't hold her liquor and is gonna start tweaking, then y'all gotta bounce. We don't need that kind of heat on us," Tone said. The Big Dawg crew had a reputation when it came to chicks partying with them and finding themselves getting out of character. Their lawyer had settled two lawsuits over similar situations, and they'd been warned about incurring a third. Their brand was already dirty, and they couldn't afford to soil it further with another questionable incident.

Tess ignored Tone and turned her attention to Tasha. "You good, ma?" She noticed the girl had started sweating.

"I don't know. I think I might be sick." Tasha began to teeter in her chair.

"Maybe she needs some air. I'll walk her outside," Don B. offered. From the moment he saw the bug-eyed look in the girl's eyes, he knew that she was on something more than liquor and weed. If he played the situation right, he could spend the next twenty minutes skull-fucking Tasha, and she probably wouldn't be any the wiser. He had been plotting on Tess, but Tasha would do.

"The hell you will." Tess read his mind. She stood and then pulled Tasha to her feet. The girl's legs could barely support her, and she almost fell, but Tess held fast. "I got you, sis. I got you," she promised, steering Tasha toward the bathrooms.

"Leave it to Low to find a bunch of pillhead bitches to invite into the circle," Tone laughed, summoning over three more girls from the crowd to replace the ones they had just lost. A Big Dawg party didn't stop.

Chapter 15

"Damn, why you gotta be all stink and shit?" Bay asked once Ashanti had gotten out of the ride.

"It ain't about me being stink. It's about you rushing me. You see I was on the phone, right?" Ashanti retorted.

"For you to be all in your feelings over me fucking with you while you were on the phone, you must've been talking to your little girlfriend," Bay teased.

Ashanti turned and looked at her seriously. "Dig this. Anything involving my girl ain't got no business coming out of your mouth. Don't overstep your bounds, Bay," he warned.

Bay threw up her hands in surrender. "Damn, take it easy. I was only joking with you, Ashanti. There used to be a time when you knew how to take a joke."

"Those were different times, and I'm a different man now," Ashanti said harsher than he'd meant to. "My fault," he offered, seeing that he had offended her. "I just got a lot of shit riding me right now, so my temper is a little short."

"Don't trip, Ashanti. We've both said worse to each other. Ain't no thang." Bay started walking, and Ashanti followed.

"So, how's the fam? What's up with your little sister? She still on her genius shit?" Ashanti made small talk.

"Yeah, Tess is still smart as hell, but she's starting to feel herself a little bit," Bay told him.

"How you mean?" Ashanti asked. He'd always known Tess to be a smart and focused little girl.

"Since she's leaving for college in a min, she's decided to spend her summer making up for lost time. That girl has been in the streets more than a little bit lately, especially with those two stoop rats she hangs around with. Them bitches are bad influences."

"So, these girls holding a pistol on Tess to make her run with them?"

"No, of course not. I mean that they aren't the same as Tess. She's got plans, and all them hoes have is the block. Five years from now, they'll still be doing the same shit."

"The same could be said about us when we were their ages, but look how we turned out," Ashanti pointed out.

"Right. A shooter and a salesgirl at Macy's. Thanks for making me feel better," Bay joked.

"Honest work ain't nothing to thumb your nose at, Bay. We could be a lot worse off. I'm thankful for all my blessings, big and small," Ashanti said.

"Listen to you sounding all grown up." Bay gave him a playful shove.

"I told you, I'm not the same kid," Ashanti reminded her.

"I guess you're not." She smiled, wondering what could have been.

Ashanti and Bay walked down to 151st Street, where she told him they would find her boyfriend in the lobby of one of the buildings. The whole time, Ashanti felt queasy in the pit of his stomach, like something was off. He doubted Bay would be dumb enough to try to set him up, but with the state of things on the streets, you couldn't help second-guessing anyone, not even an old friend. He reflexively checked his pistol, secured in the waistline of his sweatpants by a leather belt he wore underneath. The belt ensured the gun didn't move too much or accidentally drop. It was a trick he had learned from Zo-Pound. Thinking of his friend reminded him that he had never returned Porsha's call. When he searched his pockets for his phone, he found no trace of it. It must've fallen out in the car.

"Fuck," Ashanti cursed, startling Bay.

"What's wrong?" she asked.

"Nothing," he said, mad at himself for not checking for the phone before he left the car. He'd walked too far to go back for it. He hadn't planned to be there any longer than he had to, so the phone would keep for a few minutes.

A blue and white police car made its way down the street they were walking on. They slowed at the sight of the couple, one of the cops giving Ashanti an exploratory once-over. He said something to his partner, who was behind the wheel and nodded in

Ashanti's direction. Ashanti felt his heart quicken in his chest. He hadn't done anything, at least not that day, but it didn't stop the natural sense of unease experienced by most young men of color when they spotted police. "*1558*," he mentally noted the number on the side of their squad car. It might come in handy if this shit went bad. There were a few beats where Ashanti and the cop just stared at each other from a distance. Ashanti wasn't trying to antagonize him, but breaking eye contact would've made him appear guilty. Only when the cop felt confident enough that Ashanti wasn't an immediate threat and told his partner to push on did Ashanti let go of the breath he was holding.

"Where this dude at?" Ashanti asked impatiently. His stomach was now doing cartwheels, and he wanted to meet up with who he had to see and get ghost as swiftly as possible.

"Right in there." She pointed to a building with the front light burned out. Shadows could be made out in the lobby, but the lack of light made it hard to see who it was.

"Ladies first." He made a sweeping gesture for her to lead the way.

"Damn, after all these years, you still don't trust me?" Bay half-joked.

"I don't trust no bitch but my own, and sometimes I even question her motives," Ashanti said seriously.

Bay shook her head in amusement and proceeded up the half-dozen steps leading to the building's entrance. He held the door for her to enter and followed, staying directly behind her so that anything that might've been waiting for him would've had to go through her first.

The first thing Ashanti noticed when he entered the lobby was the heavy smell of weed. The smoke was so thick that he was sure they could smell it on every floor of the walk-up building, likely to the tenants' displeasure. He doubted the young men in the lobby smoking cared too much. There were about eight of them, ranging in age from about 16 to early twenties. Everybody was huddled over the dice game that was going on in the middle of the lobby floor. Ashanti glanced at the pot, and if he had to guess, it amounted to maybe $1,500. That was chump change to a man of Ashanti's standing, but the guys watching the game were eyeballing it like *The Last Supper*. It was unlikely that any of them would make a play for it, considering the dude who was holding the bank.

He was an older dude, probably close to 30, give or take a few years. His skin was fair and blemish free. A plain, white T-shirt hugged his muscular frame, and a long gold chain hung from his neck. The medallion at the end brushed the floor when he bent to scoop up the dice. He shook them in his hand, whispering to them as if casting a spell. Ashanti knew what the results of his roll would be before he even tossed them. The three spun gracefully before hitting the wall and coming to a stop near the pile of money:

three, three, three . . . trips—another winner. The losers cursed and complained as their money was snatched up. All Ashanti could do was chuckle. They were obviously novices or naïve. Anybody with good sense knew you didn't gamble with the man they called Dice and expect to win.

The gambler must've felt Ashanti's eyes on him because his head jerked up. A scowl crossed his lips when he spotted Ashanti standing there with Bay. It only lasted for a second before he fixed his expression, but that was long enough for Ashanti to peep it. He knew what Dice must've been thinking seeing his girl with one of her exes, and under different circumstances, he might've been right. Lucky for him, that night, Ashanti didn't have pussy or murder on his mind.

Dice whispered something to the man at his right, who pulled out a cell phone and texted—likely, calling for backup. Once the text had been sent, Dice picked up his money and moved in Ashanti's direction. Bay intercepted him and draped her arms around him. "What's good, boo?" She kissed him on the lips passionately. No doubt she knew what Dice was thinking too and wanted to put his insecurities at ease.

"You tell me?" Dice was speaking to Bay, but his eyes were on Ashanti. It wasn't a challenging look. Dice knew better than that, but he wanted his displeasure at seeing them together to be known.

"I see you're still up to your old tricks," Ashanti said in the way of a greeting.

"They're only old to those who have seen them already," Dice said with a shrug. "You trying to get in the game?"

Ashanti chuckled. "You know I'd never bet on a fixed fight unless I were sure the odds were in my favor."

"Take a chance. Today might be your lucky day," Dice said.

Ashanti looked past Dice to the players, who were all looking at him with expressions ranging from fear to curiosity. If it went down, they would probably throw it all away to try to help Dice and would likely find themselves on the way to either the ER or the morgue. Ashanti could use a little wreck, but that wasn't the time or the place.

"Thank you, but no. I just need to bend your ear for a second. In private. Take a walk with me right quick." He nodded in the direction of the door. He could see that Dice was hesitant. "If I was on that type of time, I'd have come in here blasting, and there wouldn't be nothing these niggas, or whoever you had your man text, that could stop me from doing it to you. You ain't got nothing to fear from me, Dice. I just wanna talk."

Reluctantly, Dice allowed Ashanti to lead him outside. Bay was also with them. Dice was trying to hide it, but Ashanti could tell that he was jumpy by the way he kept looking around, no doubt expecting Zo or one of the twins to jump out from behind a car and smoke him. Once he was sure that there weren't any monsters lurking, he addressed Ashanti. "So, what's up?"

Ashanti opened his mouth to speak, then thought better of it when he realized Bay was lingering around being nosy. "Bay, why don't you take a walk? This shouldn't take but a few minutes. Then you can have your man back."

Without so much as a question, Bay nodded and walked off, which angered Dice. Had he told her to leave while he talked business, they would've argued, but she obeyed Ashanti like a loyal dog. Dice didn't think that the two of them were still messing around, but the fact that he still had that type of hold over his girl bothered him.

"Look, I know if you came up here looking for me, it can't be for nothing good. I ain't scammed or robbed nobody out your click that I know of, so I gotta ask myself what you want from my life, Ashanti." Dice got right to it.

"I need your ears," Ashanti told him. A terrified look sprang to Dice's face. He'd no doubt heard about Cain cutting the face from one of their enemies and running around with it like a mask. "Not like that. I'm trying to get a line on somebody and wondered if you heard any scatter on them in your travels."

"Ashanti, you know me well enough to know that I ain't in the business of talking other people's business or pointing no fingers at them," Dice told him.

"Nor are you in the business of dying."

"You ain't gotta be shooting no threats, homie," Dice said defensively. He wasn't a killer like Ashanti, but he was no choir boy either.

"You need to calm down, Blood. I don't throw threats. That's too much like giving a man a heads-up that he's about to die. Why don't you listen to why I needed to talk to you before you change the circumstances under which we part company?" Ashanti said. He hadn't meant it as a threat, but it had the same effect because Dice wisely closed his mouth. "You and your boys still robbing the rich to feed the poor?"

Dice didn't answer right away. "We do what's necessary to put food on the table. Why? You looking to get somebody took?"

"Nothing like that. The Dog Pound handles its own. I'm wondering if you or your people have heard about any new players looking to move some major weight. Somebody trying to go big enough to get the attention of your band of merry thieves."

Dice took a long pause before responding. "You know, every nigga with an ounce of white is out here trying to be the next Azie." He referenced the old Harlem hustler.

"No, this wouldn't be no niggas trying to push no powder. These would be people looking to push designer shit, and it'd probably be a bitch at the head of their table."

"I'm not a drug dealer, fam," Dice said innocently.

"But you are a robber of drug dealers," Ashanti reminded him. "Dice, I know you make it your business to keep an eye out for new faces trying to set up shop so they can meet the business end of your gun or your hustle. That's how you get your coins, and I ain't mad at you. All I need to know is where to lay hands on these people. It would be looked upon favorably with me and Animal if you had a hand in helping us do that."

When Ashanti dropped Animal's name, it changed things. Dice knew who Ashanti was, but he had actually seen Animal in action firsthand. It was an incident he'd worked hard to forget over the years. Dice weighed it. Having the leader of the Dog Pound in his debt was a tempting prospect, but that would also put him on Animal's radar. He didn't know what would come of helping Animal get next to the people Ashanti was pressing him about, but he did know that if the aftermath turned into a mess that needed to be cleaned up, he would likely find himself thrown out with the trash. Men like that never left witnesses. "If I haven't heard anything?"

Ashanti's eyes bore into Dice. He searched his face for signs of a lie but knew with a seasoned gambler like Dice, he was wasting his time trying to read him. "A'ight." He nodded. Ashanti still wasn't sure whether he believed Dice but didn't want to spend more time than he had on that block trying to figure it out. "If you do hear something, hit me up." He started back down the block.

"How am I supposed to contact you if I hear something I might want to share?" Dice called after him.

"Ask Bay. She knows how to reach me," Ashanti called over his shoulder. He didn't have to turn around to see how deep the remark had cut Dice. Instead, he could feel the heat at his back.

At the same time Ashanti was returning to the ave, a man came in the opposite direction. He was dark-skinned with a pockmarked face that bore a wound under his eye that had never quite healed properly. He had a bop in his step, usually reserved for walking a state prison yard. Ashanti didn't know him, but they had seen each other before. He was Dice's right-hand man and streets-proclaimed knockout artist. He gave Ashanti a hard stare as they passed each other, to which Ashanti just shook his head and chuckled while continuing on his way.

"Yo, wasn't that the little blood nigga who be with them twins? I can't remember his name." Woods walked up to Dice, who was still standing outside the building, shooting daggers at Ashanti.

"Ashanti," Dice said as if it pained him even to speak the name.

"What did he want?" Woods asked.

"Funny enough, he was pressing me about the same thing you tried to bring to the table. New faces with new product." Dice had known who and what Ashanti had been asking about, but it hadn't yet suited him to reveal that. He gave Woods a serious look. "You still wanna hit that spot, knowing that Ashanti's ass is tied up in this now?" Woods had come to Dice with a plan to take off a spot that was supposed to be holding a stash of some sort of new wave drug. It was supposed to be an easy lick, as there would be little to no security, and the cat who lived in the spot wasn't known as a shooter. He was supposedly tipped off to it by an old buddy of his.

"You know this a game of chances. You backing out on me when we've come this far?" Woods wasn't happy. He couldn't hit the spot alone, and it was too late in the game to try to find someone else. He needed Dice.

"It doesn't feel right," Dice told him.

"That's fucked up that you would back out on me. You just make sure you keep that same energy when I hit this spot and get rich from this work I'm about to snatch," Woods said angrily.

Dice was still staring in the direction in which Ashanti had departed before responding. "My life has been a less-than-savory one, and I like to think that the only reason I've survived this long is that I'm a man who knows how to play the odds. A true gambler knows when the percentages of him winning have shifted out of his favor."

Chapter 16

"That nigga, Low, been gone for a while. You think he's good?" Devil asked after a time.

"He's probably knee-deep in shorty guts," Don B. laughed, wishing it had been him outside smashing. "Relax and let the man bust his nut, Devil."

"The li'l sober one who took her friend to the bathroom seemed cool, but I don't trust them other two. They stink of scandal, especially the one Low slid out with. She's the type of bitch that will set up a nigga for failure."

"Everybody knows that if you cross a Dawg, you're liable to get bit," Hollywood boasted while sipping a glass of champagne.

"Fuck you know about being a Dawg?" Devil grilled him. "Shit, you ain't even a pup. As a matter of fact, you're on the clock and ain't even supposed to be drinking." He slapped the glass of champagne from Hollywood's hand. Violating Hollywood wasn't necessary to put him in his place, but Devil was in his bag. Devil was a paranoid man by nature, but he had been especially on edge that night. Don B. and the others carried on like they didn't have a care in the world because their ears weren't to the streets anymore. Devil, however, was out there in the trenches, day in and day out. He knew that something wicked had been brewing and wanted to make sure neither the Big Dawg crew nor he got caught up in it.

"Man, why all y'all young niggas so tense? Back in my day, when we stepped out, it was to have a good time and get some pussy," Sammy said coolly. He always compared how they did things back in his day and the present time, which irritated people. It was like he was stuck in a certain year and refused to leave.

"No disrespect, but Big Dawg concerns ain't your concerns, old head," Don B. told him in a respectful but firm tone. "Let's get back onto why you're sitting here drinking up my shit. I greased your palm because you said you could guarantee me a meeting with your nephew before his set tonight, yet I find myself still waiting. What up with that?"

"Nathan moves on his own time, but don't you worry none. He'll speak with you," Sammy assured him.

"I need him to do more than speak. I need him to recognize my vision for him and fuck with the Dawgz," Don B. stressed. The only reason that Sammy had even been allowed into his space was that he happened to be the uncle of an artist named Inferno that Don B. was trying to sign to Big Dawg. Don B. had been trying to cut into him for months with no luck. When he found out that the old gambler was related to him, Don B. figured to use Sammy as his way in. In exchange for cash, Sammy promised to get Inferno to sit down with the Big Dawg boss, but it had yet to happen. If it turned out that Sammy was bullshitting him, Don B. would let Devil take out his frustrations on the old man.

"I can lead a horse to water, but it's you who are going to have to convince him to take a drink," Sammy capped. He was just motioning for the waitress to fill his glass again when something across the room caught his attention. "You've got to excuse me for a few, Don. I got another meeting I need to take." He got up from the table.

Don B. followed Sammy's eyes. He spotted a statuesque redhead lingering by the DJ booth. She was fair-skinned but tanned like she had just stepped off some tropical island. The corners of her full red lips were curved in irritation. The black leather pants she wore were so tight on her thick thighs that Don B. couldn't help but wonder if she needed help getting into them. Though dark sunglasses covered her eyes, he knew she was watching them. He was the Don. How could she not be? "There you go again, putting pussy over business."

"Sometimes they're one and the same," Sammy said slyly. "Don't worry, Don. You're gonna get your meeting with my nephew just as soon as I'm done with this."

"A'ight. Just don't get so caught up that you forget about me, and I have to send Devil to look for you," Don B. warned.

Sammy gave him a grin. "I didn't get to be this old by not knowing which dogs bark and which bite. You're definitely the biting kind, so I'm gonna make good on my end." He strode off to meet the redhead.

"I don't see how a nigga that old and ugly can still manage to pull the baddest young bitches," Devil said, ogling the redhead.

"Yeah, the old head stays knee-deep in something." Don B. watched as Sammy tried to greet the redhead with a hug, but she kept him at arm's length. "Somehow, I doubt whatever they're talking about got nothing to do with pussy, though."

Before Don B. could ponder it further, the Villain assigned to the door appeared. He whispered something into Tone's ear that seemed to surprise him. "*Who?*" Tone could be heard asking. The Villain repeated what he had just said and pointed to the door. "A'ight, I'll take care of it."

"Everything good?" Don B. asked, noticing the look of uncertainty on Tone's face.

"Too soon to tell," Tone said in an uneasy voice.

"If you ain't back in five minutes, I'm coming with the Dawgs," Devil said.

"I appreciate it, but if I'm gone that long, that'll mean there wasn't much y'all could've done for me anyhow. So my advice, if I ain't back soon, grab the Don and hit the closest exit," Tone told him and followed the Villain through the crowd toward the entrance.

PART V

END OF THE NIGHT

Chapter 17

"You are the worst driver," Abel said in an irritated tone, bouncing around in the backseat of the candy-red Dodge Challenger as it wove recklessly in and out of traffic. They flew down the West Side Highway, going at least thirty miles over the posted speed limit.

"Nigga, quit bitching," Diabolique, who was behind the wheel, barked over her shoulder. "This a muscle car. It ain't meant to be driven like no city bus." She yanked the wheel hard left to catch the exit, screeching the car's tires.

"Ease up, li'l mama. We get pulled over with these straps, all this will have been for nothing," Animal told her.

"Police jump on us, then it's court in the streets. That's on the hood." Diabolique picked up the large 9 mm wedged between the driver's seat and the center console.

"We all gonna die eventually, but I'd rather it not be while I still got business to finish. Slow down." Animal's tone was stern this time.

"You got it, big homie." She eased her foot off the pedal, then cast a dirty look at Abel through the rearview mirror, only to find him returning her glare. They'd only known each other for a few hours but had already taken to arguing like an old married couple.

Thankfully, Diabolique navigated the local streets with more caution than she had done on the highway. They drove past their destination to case the joint. The line was halfway down the block with people looking to get in, but there weren't many cops about. This was a good thing, especially considering what they were planning. They spent the next twenty minutes looking for a parking spot, which they eventually found on a residential street five blocks away.

"Why the fuck you park way up here? You should've just pulled up by one of those hydrants. I'd have paid the bum-ass ticket," Abel scolded her.

"Spoken like a nigga who ain't never participated in an extermination," Diabolique chuckled. "We post by a hydrant, and we run the risk of getting more than a ticket. You know how one of these thirsty-ass traffic cops are. That ticket ping back to my registration, and homicide gonna be kicking my door in after we lay these fools, and that'll be bad for all of us."

"Only bad for all of us if you fold under pressure," Abel shot back.

"Scary nigga, don't ever disrespect my gangsta. Steel don't fold or break. This Dog Pound until they lay me." With the fingers of her right hand, Diabolique threw up a D, and with the fingers of her left hand, threw down a P. "Animal, I wish you'd did a better job of training these wet-behind-the-ears-ass pups!"

"And I wish I'd brought Ashanti and Cain with me instead of you two knuckleheads," Animal snapped, finally tiring of their bickering. "Y'all can work out the obvious sexual tension lingering between you after we take care of the business at hand. Until then, tighten the fuck up." He got out of the car and started walking.

Diabolique turned toward Abel and gave him a playful smile. "Is that what it is, young pup? You trying to smash?" she half-joked. She didn't much care for Abel but couldn't deny the fact that he was handsome.

Abel studied her before answering. She had taken out her large braids, and her thick hair now hung in loose waves around her shoulders. She had traded in her jeans and sweatshirt for black leggings, a short leather jacket, and a tank top that showed off her flat stomach. Her face was lightly dusted with makeup, not much, just enough to bring out her natural glow and a dab of lip gloss over her lips. Of course, she was still rocking her grills, and the bandanna was now braided around her wrist like a fashion accessory instead of her flag. As much as he hated to admit it, when Diabolique cleaned up, she had the potential to be something, but her aura was just so gangsta. Whenever he looked at her, he couldn't help but see Animal. Still, whenever their eyes locked, there was no doubt that he felt something, and it was weird for him. "Don't flatter yourself," he grumbled and exited the car.

Diabolique laughed to herself as she watched young Abel hustle to catch up with Animal. Despite her hard-ass presentation, she was fully aware of her effect on men when she applied her natural gifts. She was two sides of the same coin, which she could flip at will . . . which is what made her so dangerous.

"So, what's the plan?" Abel asked Animal as they walked down the block.

"We go in there and see if we can get a lead on my trifling-ass baby mama. Considering the cast of characters who will be there, it's a good bet that Sonja will be there trying to beta test her product. If we see her, we pack up her ass and move out," Animal told him.

"And if she won't go quietly?" Abel asked a bit too enthusiastically for his tastes. He hadn't forgotten how Sonja had knocked him over the head and made off with the messenger bag, and he was eager for some get-back.

Animal stopped walking and turned to face the twin. "Let me make something clear to you. This is not the time or place to be pulling no cowboy shit. We don't need a repeat of that shit you pulled at the other club. This ain't some rinky-dink joint we'll be able to slide out of unnoticed if you kill another cop."

"See, I *knew* you were still holding that shit over my head," Abel said. He had been catching the funny looks from Animal and the fact that suddenly, he wanted to keep him close.

"Li'l nigga, tuck your muthafucking feelings," Animal barked. "We don't lay blame in war. We learn from our mistakes and try our best not to repeat them. You think I'm trying to punish you, but I'm really trying to keep your eager-to-die ass alive. Sonja is about a foul broad who needs to answer for what she's done, but she is also very dangerous. That little knock she gave you on the head was a love tap. You should consider yourself fortunate that you walked away with a bruise on your skull instead of a hole in it. You come at Sonja like she's weak because she's a female, and I can promise that we'll be pouring out liquor and burning bandannas in a trash can for *you* next."

"Don't worry. I'll keep the pup in line." Diabolique tried to throw her arm around Abel's neck playfully, but he shrugged her off. "What you think the numbers are gonna look like, Animal? Should we expect her to be alone or with company?"

"Sonja is a lone wolf, but when her back is against the wall, she's good at recruiting idiots to do her bidding." Animal recalled all the times her sweet whispers had driven him to jump out the window to do her bidding. "We prepare for the worst but hope for the best."

The trio was making their way across the street, with Animal taking the lead, flanked by Diabolique and Abel. The two continued their banter while Animal tried his best to drown them out. Diabolique was so focused on the insult that she was in the pro-

cess of hurling at Abel that she didn't see the silver
Denali that sped through the intersection, attempting
to beat the yellow light before it turned red. Animal
snatched her back just before the truck could clip her.
As the vehicle passed them, Animal made eye contact
with the driver. A light of recognition went off in both
men at the same time. Animal reached for his strap,
but the Denali was through the intersection before he
could draw.

"Fuck," Animal cursed, angry at missing his opportunity.

"I know, right? You see that muthafucka almost
hit me!" Diabolique said, thinking he shared in her
anger at the driver for almost killing her. "I wish I
had thrown one at his nondriving ass!" She shaped
her fingers like a gun and pointed it at the Denali's
shrinking taillights. The speedy driver had to swerve
to avoid hitting a slow-moving car ahead of it.

"You and me both," Animal mumbled.

At least two dozen people waited in line to get into
The Club, and all their eyes seemed to turn at once
when Animal stepped onto the scene. He carried
himself with an air of confidence that Abel hadn't
seen since Ashanti had first convinced him to sign up
for a suicide mission for a dude he hardly knew. He
wasn't sure if it was due to the change of clothes, a
black, long-sleeved, graphic T-shirt with a picture of
Whitney Houston on it, black jeans, and construction
Tims loosely strung up, or the two rose, chrome
Glocks he knew Animal had shoved in the back of

his pants. It could've also been the signature Muppet pendant swinging from his neck. Abel couldn't put his finger on it, but something had changed. Animal was a legend, but the shell he had turned into after the murder of his wife and kidnapping of his children had given Abel pause. However, *this* version of Animal was one that Abel felt confident going to war for.

As they neared the spot where the line started, a couple was coming in their direction. A young dude in skinny jeans and colorful sneakers, and the girl on his arm was light-skinned, wearing a long black wig. From their unsure steps, you could tell that they were both tipsy. Finally, the girl's glassy eyes landed on Animal, and a light of recognition went off in them. "Say, ain't you that rapping nigga?"

"No," Animal said without breaking his stride.

"He looks just like him," he could hear the girl say to her companion as he continued steering her down the block.

"I forgot you were a celebrity," Diabolique said to Animal. "I can remember how proud I was of you the first time I saw one of your videos on BET. I was on Rikers at the time, fighting a robbery charge. I told all the girls in my dorm that you were my big brother, but, of course, them bitches thought I was lying. You were living the American dream."

Animal gave her a weak smile as he reflected on the life he used to have . . . the studio sessions, the tours . . . sharing it all with Gucci. "I was for a time.

I'm still trying to figure out how it all became a nightmare and when I'll finally be able to wake up."

Diabolique looked into Animal's eyes as they began to mist over. He tried his best not to show it, but she knew him well enough to know when he was hurting. She opened her mouth to offer him some words of comfort but couldn't find them. What could she say to him to ease the pain of losing his wife and children in one shot? She touched his cheek softly, hoping it would bring him some measure of comfort. He placed his hand over hers and nodded, letting her know he understood what she was trying to convey. The moment was a tender yet brief one.

Animal gently removed her hand, and his face went cold again. "Let's go do this work."

He didn't bother to wait in line. Even when he was still a street punk, Animal didn't do waiting in line. Standing in one spot for more than five minutes was four minutes less than what someone needed to plan where and when to get at you. He strode right up to the entrance. The Villain was at the door in the process of collecting money from someone when he spotted Animal. The Villain's internal warning system must've gone off at the sight of the grilled-up young man because he tensed before addressing him.

"The line starts back there." The Villain pointed half a block down where the line ended.

"I got eyes," Animal told him.

The Villain waited for Animal to either add to his statement or comply and move down the end of the line, but he just stood there glaring. Finally, after about a minute of awkward silence, the Villain found his voice. "Well, you either need to get in line or buy a table. Other than that, you ain't getting in."

"Homie, do you know who the fuck this is?" Diabolique stepped up aggressively. She was on *go* at all times and sized the Villain up as light work. Her eyes turned to Animal, waiting for him to give the signal that would spell the end of the cornball at the door, but instead, he motioned for her to be still.

"I don't think Don B. would take too kindly to you having one of his biggest artists standing out here in line like one of the common folk," Animal told him.

The Villain laughed. "You and ten other niggas with SoundCloud accounts have tried to run that *I'm with Big Dawg* line on me tonight. Let me guess. You want me to call Don B. to the door to validate you too?"

"No, because making Don B. aware of this grand ol' mistake you're about to make is likely gonna get you fired or fucked up. The safer bet is that you go in there, fetch Tone, and tell him that The Animal is here. He'll speak to who I am and likely be a side more forgiving than the Don. Pick your poison. I can use the entertainment either way."

The Villain ran the name through his mental Rolodex, and it stopped on a story he'd heard about a Big Dawg artist of the same, or a similar name, who had made the news for murder. Whether to let him press the issue or let him in was proving to be a decision that he no longer felt qualified to make or shoulder the consequences that came with it. So he decided to defer.

"Wait right here," he told Animal before calling for someone to cover for him while he went inside.

Five minutes had passed, and Diabolique had begun to get impatient. "Man, how come we didn't press the issue and just roll up in there? Dude was soft. We could've gotten it off."

Animal turned to the girl. "When you've been around the block as often as I have, you'll discover that sometimes your name can move more mountains than your muscle."

To punctuate his statement, the Villain came back to the door. Tone was behind him. When Tone spotted Animal, you could see the color drain from his face. He barked something at the Villain before shoving him forward.

"Y'all good. That was my fault," the Villain unclamped the rope and stepped aside for Animal and his group to enter.

Animal let Diabolique and Abel precede him before stepping through. He stopped, laid a reassuring hand on the Villain's shoulder, and whispered, "A bruised ego beats a cracked skull any day."

"Man, I thought somebody was playing a trick on me when they told me you were outside trying to get in." Tone pulled Animal into a hug. "How you be, Blood?"

"I'm well, all things considered." Animal clapped his back. Tone was one of the few members of Big Dawg that Animal respected. Granted, Tone could be as much of a shitbird as Don B., depending on the circumstances, but for the most part, he was a straight shooter.

Tone held Animal at arm's length and gave him a quizzical look. "Homie, you talking like you ain't living a good life. I've seen the numbers on what our bookkeeper wires into your account every quarter, so I know you ain't hurting. All you gotta do for the rest of your days is make bank transfers and spoil that fine-ass wife of yours. How is Gucci, by the way?"

"Dead," Animal said flatly.

Tone was dumbfounded by this revelation. "I . . . ah . . . I'm sorry. My condolences to you and your family," he said sincerely. "Was she sick?"

"No. Murdered," Animal told him, trying to keep his voice steady. He still hadn't quite wrapped his mind around it to the point where he could say it and not get choked up.

Tone kept his ear close enough to the streets to where he had already heard Animal was in New York and back on his bullshit, though he hadn't been sure of the motivation for his latest rampage. Hearing that his wife had been murdered filled in that blank, and for such an affront, whatever led Animal to him that night couldn't have been good. He looked over his shoulder at the Villain, who was now lingering near some of the other bouncers and chatting in hushed tones. Every so often, their eyes would turn to Tone and Animal, but none of them moved in their direction. When Tone turned back to Animal and saw the predatory look he was giving him, a frightening thought sprang to mind.

"Wait a second. I hope you didn't pop up here because you think—"

"Nah, man. If I was off that, you should know better than anybody that I wouldn't announce my presence. You and everyone you love would've simply ceased to exist," Animal said seriously. "I'm not here for blood; just a little information."

Chapter 18

Don B. was whispering deep into the ear of a girl who didn't look like she was old enough to be in the club, let alone in the middle of the nest of vipers which were Big Dawg when he heard Devil blurt out, "You have *got* to be shitting me." Don B. stopped his whispering long enough to look to where Devil's eyes were fixed. His mouth immediately went dry. Of all the ways an already lukewarm night could've been totally ruined, the worst-case scenario had just walked in the door.

Tone returned, and he wasn't alone. Animal, and a young couple Don B. didn't know, trailed closely behind him. He watched suspiciously as Animal said something to the couple, after which they broke off and disappeared into the crowd. That was a bad sign. As Animal neared the table, Don B. shoved the girl away and stood, mustering his most convincing smile. "It must be Halloween because I'm seeing ghosts."

"'Sup wit' you, Blood?" Animal gave Don B. dap. His greeting was neither cold nor warm.

"Out here trying to live right and enjoy the best of things," Don B. boasted.

"One out of two ain't bad, I gather." Animal's dark gaze shifted to the young girl who had been hugged up with Don. Some things never changed. All eyes in the section seemed to be on Animal, but he felt the most heat coming from Don B's bodyguard, Devil. He was staring daggers at Animal. "For as still as you're over there standing, one of these pigeons might mistake you for a statue and try to take a shit on you," he addressed Devil.

"You know me. I'm forever vigilant," Devil told him.

Animal nodded, satisfied with his response. "A soldier at all times. That's one of the things I've always respected about you, Devil. I often bump into you in my travels, and your energy is always the same."

All Devil could do was shrug awkwardly. Animal's remark was a low-key threat, and they both knew it. Unbeknownst to everyone there except Animal and him was that this was the second time he had seen the young killer over the last few days. Devil had been guarding the door at Original Sin the night Animal showed up and went John Wick on everybody inside. Don B. required that all his wolves serve his pack exclusively, and hearing that Devil had been moonlighting would carry unknown consequences. He tensed, waiting for Animal to expose his secret, but thankfully, he didn't.

"Where'd your two friends get off to?" Tone asked, directing the attention away from Devil.

"They're around. Not too close, but not too far either," Animal said with a sly grin. He'd purposely waited until they were in front of Tone to send Abel and Diabolique on their little recon mission. He knew the uncertainty of not knowing where his accomplices were but that they could pop up at any second would keep everyone honest.

"So, what brings you out to this fine establishment tonight? I thought your parole forbid you to hang out with undesirables?" Don B. joked.

"If a cage couldn't hold me, a piece of paper sure as shit can't," Animal said coldly. He waited until everyone fell uncomfortably silent before cracking a gold-plated smile. "I'm only fucking with you, Don. Let me find out money and age have stolen your sense of humor?"

"Sometimes it's hard to tell when cats like you are joking," Don B. said.

"Probably because we don't." Animal plucked one of their bottles off the table and examined it. It was a brand of tequila that cost at least two hundred if you bought it in the store, so he could only imagine how much the venue had inflated the price. There were four of them on the Big Dawg table. "I see you haven't lost your taste for overpriced liquor." He set the bottle back down.

"C'mon, son. You ain't been gone from the team that long to where you forgot that we don't indulge in anything but the best. Liquor, drugs, bitches . . . This is what we do," Don B. capped.

"Oh, I remember. That's actually what's brought me to you tonight . . . your affinity for the finer things and the smart hustlers' overwhelming urge to make sure they're the ones to provide you with them. I've come to break bread, but this meal ain't for public consumption." His eyes drifted over the unfamiliar faces in the crowded section.

Don B. knew that whatever his former artist wanted to talk about was serious. "If I don't sign your checks, disappear. Take a ten-minute break from my presence," he addressed the group.

"But we just got here," one of the trio of girls Tone had called over to replace Tess and her friends complained.

"Don't worry, baby. You'll still get your tonsils played with tonight. For now, take a walk." Devil helped the girl to her feet and motioned for her friends to follow her out of the section. He was anxious to hear what Animal had to say and be rid of him.

"Animal, I know you didn't come looking for me to put you on a train you've been riding for years," Don B. said suspiciously.

"Nah, I ain't trying to catch this train to ride it. I'm trying to derail it," Animal told him. "I'd look kindly on anyone who could help me get a line on the conductor of this particular locomotive. They'll likely be a new player in the game looking to cut into the New York market. Their angle would be to get the word out on their product hard and fast. Who better to do that, though, than the voice of the city? Sound like someone you may have come across?"

Don B. shrugged. "You know I've been getting my narcotics from the same people for years. The Don doesn't believe in fixing what isn't broke, and we don't trust new faces."

"This one you might. Pretty Puerto Rican thing, with a head full of red hair." Animal went on to describe Red Sonja. He watched Don B. closely for a reaction, but the man was unreadable as usual. The same couldn't be said about the small, light-skinned dude sitting with their crew. Animal couldn't remember his name but knew his face from working with Big Dawg at their studios. He was a producer or something, if Animal remembered correctly. He looked as if he were about to say something but then thought better of it.

"Doesn't sound familiar," Don B. said with a shrug.

"You sure?" Animal pressed. The question was directed to Don B., but Animal was looking at Hollywood. He was damn near melting under the killer's predatory gaze. Animal suspected that he knew something, and Hollywood confirmed it when he hopped up and excused himself.

"I meet a lot of bitches in my travels, but none of them came looking to sell me anything," Don B. said, which was half true. He'd seen the redhead, but she hadn't tried to sell him anything. "I'll be sure to keep my eyes peeled for her, though."

"You do that." Animal wrapped his knuckles on the top of the table before standing to leave.

"Yo, I haven't seen you in a minute. At least stay and have a drink before you dip off." Don B. offered one of the bottles.

"Thank you, but no. I don't drink when I'm hunting. Need my aim to be true when me and this pistol get to showing out." He patted his waist.

"I feel you. Seeing how this chick you're looking for has you back in your bag, I don't expect her movie will have a happy ending," Don B. pried.

Animal didn't answer. As he was turning to leave, Devil called after him. "What did chick do to bring the wrath of the Boogeyman down on her head?"

Though it was Devil who had asked the question, it was to Don B. where he directed his answer. "She lied to me."

No one was more relieved to be rid of Animal than Devil. The whole time Animal had lingered amongst them, Devil's hand had been close to his gun. He knew from personal experience how quickly Animal could turn a seemingly friendly conversation into a situation. That quiet voice, with almost a childlike quality about it, had rocked many a man to sleep and made them blind to the end that was coming until the curtain was lowered on their show. Devil almost being one of them. Only by the grace of God had he lived to learn from the experience. He wouldn't leave his life in the hands of fate again.

Even after Animal had gone, his presence could still be felt in the Big Dawg circle. Tone had rounded up some fresh girls and tried to get the party back in swing to ease the tension, but you could still see the impact of the visit weighing on Don B. He hadn't touched the fresh bottle of champagne he'd sent the waitress for and barely gave the girls a second look. One of them was practically trying to force herself on him, but Don B. barely noticed. He just sat there, chain-smoking weed and wearing a worried expression.

"You good?" Devil shoved the girl away and took a seat beside Don B.

"Yeah, I'm straight. Just thinking," Don B. told him.

"A visit from The Animal is always food for thought," Devil said. "Something tells me that the broad he's in here hunting is the same one we saw Sammy slide off with."

"We on the same page with that," Don B. confirmed.

"Then why didn't you give her up? Having a man like Animal in debt to you is worth its weight in gold."

"And trouble," Don B. added. "I've seen that look in Animal's eyes before. He's on a suicide mission, and we don't wanna get soiled by the mess I'm absolutely sure he's about to make."

"So, you not telling him that the bitch is here was a kindness?" Devil was surprised at the gesture.

Don B. laughed. "Nigga, the Don doesn't do kindness. This is about being smart. Animal is about to make it rain blood over the city, and I don't want me nor any of mine to get wet. I don't want anything to do with this."

"That's the smartest shit I ever heard you say, Don." Devil laughed. He was secretly happy that Don B. had kept his mouth shut. Sometimes, with men like Animal, the messenger could become a casualty. He was about to ask Don B. if he was about ready to head out when he heard what sounded like a gunshot, followed by the venue erupting into chaos.

Chapter 19

Hollywood sucked in a chest full of smog-tainted Midtown air when he came pushing out of the side door into The Club's parking lot. It was hot as hell inside the venue, but the temperature went up another hundred degrees when the spawn of Satan walked in. He hadn't seen Animal since back in the days when he was the wild-haired kid who used to make all the Big Dawg studio sessions uncomfortable when he showed up. It was crazy how he still had the same effect even years later when he entered a room. Animal was the one dude Hollywood knew that Don B. feared, and seeing Don B. squirm brought him untold amounts of joy.

He had almost allowed himself to be tempted to punch holes in the bullshit story Don B. had fed Animal about not having seen the redheaded girl just to see how Animal would react to Don B. lying to him. It would've probably been a reaction of biblical proportions, and the only thing that stopped Hollywood from exposing it was the fact that he couldn't guarantee that Animal's rage would've been focused exclusively on Don B. There was a very strong possibility that everyone in the entourage could've found themselves casualties of his wrath by association. That wasn't a risk Hollywood was willing to take, so he felt it best to remove himself from the equation.

Hollywood dug into his pocket and pulled out the last bent half of the blunt he had stubbed out earlier that evening. It was of an exotic strain that he had pilfered from Don B.'s personal stash the night before. The buds had been a gift from a private firm that was so exclusive that they hadn't even touched the East Coast yet. Getting everything first was one of the perks of being the Big Dawg's personal gofer and occasional whipping boy. Hollywood was just putting fire to the weed when he caught the flash of an SUV's brake lights in the parking lot. Upon closer inspection, he recognized the truck as one of the caravans of vehicles that had carried the members of Big Dawg to the venue. Curiously, he crept alongside the ride and peered in. What he saw gave him a chuckle.

One of the groupie girls who had been in their section, he believed her name was Shay, was straddling the driver's seat, facing the rear of the car. She was biting her lip almost hard enough to draw blood, and her eyes were rolling in the back of her head. Beneath her was Low. A thin film of sweat had broken out over his bald head. He was pushing slowly and methodically into her guts. From the way she had his chain in her mouth and was biting the medallion, Hollywood reasoned that Low was hitting her spot. From the things Hollywood was sure were being secreted on the front seat, he was glad he was riding in the back.

Lucky bastard, Hollywood thought to himself while watching the freak show. He was low-key jealous that though he did most of the grunt work for Big Dawg, he reaped very little of the rewards. Outside of free weed and liquor, Hollywood was always the last man picked for everything else. So when it came time to divide the groupie spoils, Hollywood always found himself left with whatever no one else wanted. If he had a hundred dollars for every cast-off chick he fucked for the sole purpose of not wanting to be the only one going to bed with a dry dick, he'd be rich.

Hollywood made himself comfortable, leaning against the vehicle while watching the freak show inside. Shay let Low throw his cock in every hole on her body and took it like a champion whore. Hollywood slipped his hand into his pants and tugged at his dick while still hitting the blunt. From the ugly faces Low was making, Hollywood knew that the pussy was probably super tight. He imagined himself sliding up in Shay and wondering if that box was as hot as he imagined. He was so preoccupied with his fantasy that he never felt the presence behind him. In fact, he'd thought that he was the lone spectator to the show . . . until a hand clamped over his mouth, and something cold and hard was pressed into his kidney. "*Scream, and you bleed,*" a voice whispered into his ear. He didn't have to turn around to know who it was.

"Animal, be cool," Hollywood raised his hands without turning around.

"*Cool* was yesterday. Today, I got ice running through my veins," Animal told him. "Now, put your fucking hands down, dickhead. You look like you're trying to wave a plane onto a runway." He waited until Hollywood complied before continuing. "Let's take a walk." He shoved Hollywood away from the SUV.

Hollywood reluctantly allowed Animal to steer him to a dark corner of the lot, just out of view of the security cameras that watched The Club. He was terrified but held onto the fact that Animal could've killed him at any point without Hollywood ever knowing that he was in the parking lot, but instead, he had made his presence known. He was hopeful but not very. Animal glared at him for what felt like a long while, the panther trying to figure out which chunk to bite off first from the boar he's just cornered. Hollywood felt his bowels shift, and for an instant, he felt he would shit himself. It was then that The Animal spoke.

"I thought after all these years of getting shitted on, you would have learned to find comfort somewhere else than at the feet of your masters," Animal observed.

"Not like I had much of choice," Hollywood replied.

"Die on your feet or live on your knees. We always have choices, but it seems you picked the wrong one. Let's hope you're smarter in dealing with me than you were with Big Dawg. Tell me a story, Hollywood." It was more of a command than a suggestion.

"I ain't no storyteller; I'm a producer," Hollywood said with an awkward smirk. It was a small joke

meant to ease some of the tension, but it didn't work
that way. Instead, pain exploded in Hollywood's
cheek when Animal slapped him. He never saw
Animal move, only felt the impact of his palm on his
face. The slap jarred Hollywood's brain to the point
that he briefly forgot where he was until the second
slap landed and brought him back to exactly what
was happening. This was The Animal that Hollywood
knew and the one that Don B. feared.

"How dare you try to play me like a sucker," Animal
said in a low growl, a fist full of Hollywood's shirt,
shaking him like a child. "Fu-ass-nigga, I'll waste you
and your mama before I let you play me like a nigga
who ain't never been outside. You think I don't know
your boss looked me in the face and lied? I need you
to fill in the blanks before I get on some bullshit. I
don't wanna do you like that, Hollywood, but you
know I will."

"Animal, I don't want no parts of whatever it is
you got going on. I'm a civilian," Hollywood told him,
rubbing his cheek. His response earned him another
slap.

"You lost the right to claim civilian when you threw
in your lot with Big Dawg. How many rapes or shady
deals you turned a blind eye to in your service to the
Don?" He shoved Hollywood, causing him to stumble.

"Bro, you out here bugging." Hollywood threw
up his hands as if he planned on defending himself.
However, it was more of a reflex reaction than actually wanting to get into a fight with Animal.

Animal chuckled at the gesture. "Nah, me slapping you around ain't bugging. *This* is me bugging." He drew his second gun and aimed the barrels of both pistols at Hollywood's face. He knew Hollywood was a sucker and hadn't planned on having to go this far in his information extraction, but he was growing tired of the lackey's games. "Spill your guts or your brains. Don't make me no never mind at this point."

The threat inspired Hollywood, and he sang like he was trying to win the final round of *American Idol*. Hollywood confirmed what Diabolique had suggested; Sonja had indeed passed through The Club that night. Why Don B. had chosen to lie about it was anyone's guess, likely trying not to jeopardize whatever he was trying to piece together. Animal would settle with him at a later date. All he was concerned about that night was finally having a solid lead.

Hollywood continued talking while Animal plotted his next move. In his cowardly rambling, he had not only given Animal what he asked for but had unwittingly provided a sweetener. What no one outside of Don B's inner circle knew was that the Big Dawg's bite wasn't what it used to be. Between the lawsuits, the growing popularity of streaming, and dwindling demand for the brand of gangster rap that Big Dawg Entertainment had built its legacy upon, the Don had started to feel the economic pinch. He had to resort back to dabbling in the streets to maintain the lifestyle he had become accustomed to.

"I guess it's true what they say. Every dog has its day," Animal thought aloud.

"Shit and a dark day it's gonna be from the looks of things." Hollywood assumed Animal was addressing him. "Dig, I would appreciate you keeping our little conversation to yourself. People can get the wrong idea, and I've got a reputation for being a stand-up dude."

Animal laughed at the request. "Save that bullshit for someone who doesn't know you. You couldn't stand up if you had four legs and a spotter. You've lived your entire life like a bitch. I suspect you'll die like one too. But seeing how your ho ass has helped me out tonight, your blood won't be on my hands."

"Thanks, man. I'm gonna take my free pass and slide," Hollywood said. He knew that somebody would likely die for what he had shared with Animal, and he wanted to be long gone before anyone figured out that he had been the rat.

"One question before you go, Hollywood. Did the redhead give you any idea where she was going before she slid off?" Animal reasoned that if he moved fast enough, he might still be able to catch up with Red Sonja before she fled the area.

"Yeah, to the other side of the venue," Hollywood told him.

"Say what?" Animal wasn't sure he had heard him right.

"Yeah. She was meeting with some old nigga that Don B. knew. They slid off to one of the tables on the other side," Hollywood told him.

"I been out here pressing you about this bitch's whereabouts for the last twenty minutes, and she's been inside the whole fucking time?" Animal was livid.

"Hey, man, all you asked was had I seen her. I wasn't trying to do no unnecessary talking while you were waving those pistols in my face. Speak when spoken to, feel me?" Hollywood offered in the way of an excuse.

"No, I don't." Animal slapped Hollywood to sleep. He stepped over the unconscious man and moved double time back toward The Club's rear entrance. The same one he had followed Hollywood through. He prayed to every higher power he could think of that he not be too late to catch Sonja. The contents of the bag she had stolen from him was the only leverage he had to use against Tiger Lily and his best shot at ever getting his children back.

He'd just reached the door when it swung open. He found himself nearly knocked over by a group of people that came spilling out. They looked terrified. Inside, he could hear screams and what he thought were gunshots. Something had gone down while he had been interrogating Hollywood. Animal was about to rush back in when one last person came running out, slamming into him. Their eyes met and caused a psychological explosion in his head. "You!" he snarled and went for his gun.

Chapter 20

When Ashanti rounded the corner of 151st Street and headed back to his car, two things stood out to him. A blue and white car was sitting at the curb in front of him. It wasn't uncommon to see a police cruiser on any New York corner, but the number on the car caught his attention: 1558. It was the same marked car that he'd seen when he was going to talk to Dice. Ashanti had been in the streets long enough to know this was no coincidence. The blue and white raised a red flag, but the brown Buick on the northbound side of the street confirmed his suspicions. He'd know that car anywhere. He should've because the whole Dog Pound had been evading it for nearly a decade. Ashanti sensed that he was about to be lined up for some bullshit, but he peeped it far enough in advance to give himself a fighting chance.

While he was trying to figure out the best escape from the trap, a group of people came walking out of the store. They would be just what he needed. He got down on one knee at the same moment the group passed him, and the view from the cop car was obstructed. He took the gun from his waist and tossed it behind the ice machine outside the store. When they moved on him, at least he'd be clean.

Ashanti was just finishing up his phony shoe-tie when, from his peripheral, he saw both doors of the squad car open and the uniforms spill out. That was when the Buick threw on its dash siren and almost hit another vehicle while making a hasty U-turn. It was going down.

Ashanti heard one of the cops call out from behind him, "Hey, Ashanti!" The fact that they knew his name told him that this wasn't some routine stop. They planned on taking him down. Had he known that, he wouldn't have bothered tossing his gun. They could've got what they were looking for and then some on the spot.

"Don't make me chase you," one of the uniformed cops called behind him.

Chase who? Ashanti was in the wind if he could make it to the corner of 152nd. This would be no chase but a manhunt. The driver of the Buick must've read his mind because it was positioning itself to cut off his escape. A few more yards and Ashanti would round that corner like an Olympic sprinter. He waited until he heard the slap of the cop's boots close the distance. He was directly behind him now. The driver's-side door of the Buick opened. It was now or never. The moment Ashanti felt the fingers of one of the uniformed cops graze his T-shirt, he took flight.

Ashanti had always been the fastest of the crew, and the uniformed cop found that out when he

tried to grab him and found himself clutching air.
His partner was quicker and managed to get out in
front of Ashanti. The younger man planted his foot
and cut hard left, hitting the cop with a spin that
sent him stumbling harmlessly past. The driver
of the Buick closed on him, a Black dude with a
box-shaped Afro and a suit straight out of the Sears
sale section. He closed in on Ashanti, arms spread
like Lawrence Taylor anticipating a sack. He was the
only thing standing in between Ashanti and freedom.
Ashanti timed it perfectly, and when the man with
the box Afro tried to take out his legs, Ashanti leaped,
pushing off the cop's back and hurdling over him.
It was a move that would've made Barry Sanders
proud. Ashanti backpedaled, pumping his fist in
victory in a show of defiance to the flustered cops.
He felt like he'd just won a gold medal in the street
nigga Olympics . . . but the moment was a short-lived
one. Ashanti found himself tripped, arms flailing
helplessly, as he fell to the ground and scraped his
hands and elbows. He was trying to get up when a fist
connected to his forehead and put him back down.
The world swam, and Ashanti heard birds chirping
in his ears. When he was finally back to himself, he
found himself at the mercy of one of the Dog Pound's
archenemies.

"See, now, why I gotta go through all that to get
your attention?" the tall Hispanic man standing
over Ashanti asked. He wore jeans, a T-shirt under
his blazer, and a pair of crisp white Air Force 1's.

A shiny gold badge swung from around his thin neck. This was Detective Alvarez. He was one-half of the crooked duo known throughout the hood as the "Minority Report." He flipped Ashanti over and slapped a pair of handcuffs on him before patting him down for weapons. Once he was satisfied that he was unarmed, he pulled him roughly to his feet. "He's clean," he announced.

The cop with the box Afro came hobbling over. One of the knees of his trousers was torn and stained with blood. He was the other half of the Minority Report, Detective Brown. Ashanti smirked at the fact that he was in pain, which turned out to be a mistake on his part. He slapped Ashanti in the mouth so hard that he saw stars.

"You little shit. These were a pair of brand-new pants you ruined," he barked at the dazed young man.

Ashanti wiggled his jaw to make sure it wasn't broken. His lip was busted, but he was otherwise okay. Then with defiance in his eyes, Ashanti spat blood onto the detective's white shirt. "Now, your whole outfit is ruined instead of just your pants, pussy."

"Muthafucka, I'm gonna waste you." Detective Brown reached for his pistol, but Detective Alvarez stopped him.

"Too many witnesses," Detective Alvarez whispered.

Detective Brown didn't like it but knew his partner was right. There would be no way he could justify the shooting of a handcuffed man, even if he were one of the most dangerous young dudes in the city.

Unfortunately, he couldn't take his anger out on Ashanti, so he turned it on the uniformed officers on the scene. "And are the two of you illiterate? Or did you skip the note in the bullet we sent out that states *don't try to apprehend*?"

"Uh . . . We were only trying to help. We figured since we had the drop—" one officer said but was cut off by the detective.

"You're lucky he didn't drop you," Detective Brown barked.

"Your partner just said he doesn't have a weapon." The second officer spoke in his partner's defense.

"Maybe not on him, but Ashanti is never without a weapon. I'll bet he ditched it somewhere when he realized you two were onto him. Ain't that right, *Blood*? C'mon, what do you think we'd find if we turned over the right rocks on this block?" He taunted Ashanti. The youth remained silent. "Why don't you two take a walk? We got it from here," he dismissed the uniforms.

"But don't we need to write this up?" the first officer asked. He didn't want to miss out on the credit that would come with being a part of the collar of the wanted man.

"So, you boys are hard of hearing *and* illiterate? Take a fucking hike," Detective Brown ordered them.

One of the uniforms looked like he wanted to raise a stink about being cut out of the bust, but his partner motioned for him to let it go. And so they did.

"You know it's bad when even your own people don't fuck with you," Ashanti mocked the tension between the detectives and the uniforms.

"That ain't our people. That's an example of the academy letting anybody graduate to keep the force's numbers in the black. They don't train them worth shit, and only about 10 percent will make it to see a gold shield. I'll give those retards five years, max, before one of them gets spooked out here and accidentally shoots some unarmed little Black bastard. Not that I'd lose any sleep over another one of you roaches getting stomped on," Detective Brown smirked.

Ashanti shook his head. He didn't care for cops, but he had always had a particular dislike for Detective Brown. Not because he was a cop. Everybody had a job to do. But for as long as he had been ducking the detective, he'd always been one of the most self-hating Black men he'd ever met. He was hard on criminals but took special care when mishandling little Black and brown boys. Every black mark on his service record resulted from doing some foul shit to people who looked just like him. It was like the detective was ignorant that all their ancestors had come to that country under the same set of circumstances.

"So, what's up? You see I ain't got shit, and I ain't did shit. What y'all pressing me over this time?" Ashanti got right to it.

"Same thing we're always pressing one of you Dog Pound niggas over—murder," Detective Alvarez said as if it should've been obvious.

Ashanti breathed a sigh of relief. He had been quite the busy little demon since Animal came back, but he hadn't done anything that could be traced to him. Even with the sinking of the *Red Widow*, nothing could've placed him at the scene. "Man, y'all beating a dead horse trying to put some other nigga's misfortune on me. All these years, and y'all still ain't that?"

"I got a couple of stiffs in Brooklyn, laid out near the Barclay's, that might say different. You getting sloppy, Blood," Detective Brown taunted.

Ashanti's mind immediately returned to the confrontation he'd had with the gangbangers who had tried their hands. He had gone to see Fatima at her job and had just gotten the news about her pregnancy. He was so distracted by her revelation that it had allowed the kids to catch Ashanti in a rare moment of slipping. Had it not been for an angel of mercy interceding on his behalf, Ashanti would likely be dead and them off somewhere, counting their bounty. Death had been dealt that night, but it wasn't Ashanti who shuffled the cards. Instead, the killer was someone who raised yet another question in an already complex equation. Still, it didn't change the fact that the detectives had obviously picked up on their scent.

"Y'all been chasing me a long time. I ever strike you as a man who would leave a witness to anything he's done?" Ashanti asked. It wasn't an admission of guilt, but when you'd been playing cat and mouse as long as Ashanti and the detectives had, sometimes, it was easier to cut through the bullshit and deal with facts.

Detective Alvarez snorted. "Apparently, you ain't hip to the fact that technology has made our jobs a whole lot easier. You don't need a living witness when you've got DNA."

Though he tried to hide it, the revelation rocked Ashanti's world. Though he hadn't been the killer the detectives were looking for, they could indeed place him at the scene. When he was 16, he caught a charge that landed him on Felony Probation. One of the stipulations was that he submit his DNA. Had Ashanti had the benefit of a lawyer or even been more knowledgeable of the law around that time, he'd have told them to "fuck off," but he was naïve and agreed. The uninformed decision had come back to bite him years later.

"That stupid-ass look on your face tells me that there's some truth in this story," Detective Alvarez told Ashanti. He didn't respond. "You ain't gotta say nothing, champ. Your body language is telling me everything I need to know."

"So, if you know so fucking much, why are y'all still standing around shooting the breeze instead of hauling me off to the gas chamber?" Ashanti asked.

"That's simple, grasshopper," Detective Brown spoke up. "You're a shark, but you ain't the biggest fish in the pond. We hear your boy, Animal, is back in town."

"Who?" Ashanti faked ignorance.

"The same dude who is in some way responsible for every murder that we're about to hang on you," Detective Alvarez cut in. "It's no coincidence that since Animal has returned, the body count in this city has spiked. We also know that until that butcher you call *big homie* is brought under control, things will likely get worse before they get better. You're a wicked little demon, but Animal is the spawn of Satan. So if giving you a pass will get him off the streets, we're okay with dealing with the lesser of the two evils."

"Man, y'all bugging." Ashanti rolled his eyes.

"No, you're the one bugging if you're willing to risk not being here for the kid you got coming for a guy who has nothing to lose." Detective Brown played their trump card, drawing his partner a sour look. Their finding out through the grapevine that Fatima was pregnant was supposed to be information they held as a last resort if the murders couldn't convince Ashanti to flip. In an unexpected twist, Brown had taken it upon himself to push all their chips into the center of the table. Ashanti and his crew had made the detectives seem like conspiracy theorists for years, which provoked Brown to go all-in with this. Alvarez didn't like it, but there wasn't much he could do about it but see how the hand was played, being that it had already been dealt.

Ashanti was silent for a time. It seemed that the detectives were smarter than he gave them credit for. The fact that they were not only aware of Fatima but also that she was pregnant gave him pause. How much else did they know about what was happening in his life, and how much could they tie to her? He thought of his conversation with Fatima earlier and her certainty of how great of a man he'd become. Great men became such by making unpopular decisions, regardless of the consequences.

"Y'all got better odds at choking to death on a dick than you do with me speaking against my loved ones. So do what you gotta do."

Detective Alvarez smiled. Contrary to whatever outcome Detective Brown hoped for, Alvarez expected nothing less from Ashanti than to stand tall. He represented the last of a rare breed, and though they might've operated on different sides of right and wrong, Alvarez couldn't help but respect his gangsta. "So be it then." He ushered Ashanti toward the Buick.

As they shoved Ashanti toward the car, he kept his head high, and his chest poked out, but inside, he felt defeated. They had him dead to rights, and even if they couldn't prove that he had been the killer, with his record, just being at the scene of the murder could put him away for a very long time. He would never get to see the child he loved so much come into the world. The game was over for him.

By then, a crowd had started to gather. People looked on as Ashanti was shoved roughly by the Black cop toward the waiting unmarked car. Some weren't too happy about the detective's aggressive handling of the youth and were vocal about it. Things took a turn for the tense when Brown made sure to bounce Ashanti's head off the car's door frame while shoving him inside. Chants of "Fuck the police" could be heard reverberating through the crowd. Someone even tossed a bottle that barely missed Alvarez's head. A situation was brewing.

"You might want to be careful, Officer. In this age of camera phones and social media, it's getting harder to murder Black men and get away with it," Ashanti taunted Detective Brown.

"Then maybe we'll get sidetracked on our way to the station. Find a nice dark block where I can—"

"What? Suck my dick?" Ashanti cut him off. "What you think, Brown? You give better head than that ugly-ass wife of yours?" He laughed mockingly at the detective, which sent him into a rage.

"You little bastard," Brown jumped in the backseat and began pummeling Ashanti.

"Are you fucking crazy?" Detective Alvarez pulled his partner off the young man. "Look at all these cameras." He motioned around at all the cell phones pointed at them with people recording the incident.

"I don't give a fuck, Jay. I will off this murderous muthafucka in broad daylight on the steps of the capital," Detective Brown barked.

Ashanti, bloodied in the backseat, grinned and blew a kiss in the detective's direction.

"You see what I mean? He wants to die," Detective Brown pointed out. Ashanti had been a thorn in their sides for years, and it would bring Detective Brown no greater joy than to wipe him off the map once and for all.

"I want him dead too, but not here and not like this," Detective Alvarez tried to soothe his partner.

"I saw what you did." A voice startled them. An older woman was standing a few feet away. She was stooped, wearing a tattered overcoat and leaning heavily on a cane. Her curled salt-and-pepper hair was covered by a floral scarf, and black glasses sat on the tip of her broad nose. They were so thick that her vision must've been terrible. "Seen it all . . . What you did to that young man and what y'all fixing to try to do."

"This is a police matter, ma'am. I'm going to need you to back up and let us do our jobs," Detective Alvarez said politely. This was the last thing they needed right then.

"Your jobs are to serve and protect the community, not beat our young kings like dogs. Y'all ain't right, and this has got to stop," the woman scolded them.

"I ain't got time for this shit." Brown stepped forward. "Listen, lady, if you wanna file a complaint, we'll gladly give you our badge numbers when we're done here. Until then, I need you to back up," he said harshly.

The old woman's eyes narrowed to slits behind her glasses. "That ain't no way to speak to your elders. Ain't you been raised with no home training? If you were one of mine, I'd have put you over my knee and given your hide a good tanning."

"I guess it's a good thing I ain't one of yours. Now, I'd appreciate it if you just step back off the curb." Detective Brown took her by the arm to escort her out of the way. When his fingers closed around her bicep, he found it firm and muscular—not like that of a withered old woman.

The elder's hand shot out and punched Detective Brown with enough force to knock the wind out of him. She then twirled the cane like a baton and pointed it at him. A stiletto jutted from the tip of it, which she drove into his stomach. She twisted the spear in the detective's gut, driving him back and against the car. Gasping for air, Detective Brown clawed at the older woman's hair and came away holding a salt-and-pepper wig when it slid from her head. Beneath it was a spill of long dreadlocks. This was no old woman at all but a young girl who wore a face very similar to that of the young man currently bleeding in the backseat.

"Brown!" Detective Alvarez finally shook off the shock of seeing his partner speared and found his voice. He snatched his gun from his holster and pointed it at Ophelia. He had a clear shot at her head and pulled the trigger. His bullet might've struck true had Ashanti not shot his feet out of the backseat and kicked him in the ass, which threw his aim.

The bullet missed Ophelia and struck the window of the bodega. She brought the cane up like an MLB batter and scored a double play when it connected with Detective Alvarez's chin. Ashanti wasn't sure, but he could've sworn he saw a tooth fly from the Hispanic man's mouth. Ophelia brought the cane around a second time, connecting with the back of Alvarez's head, and laid him out. She raised the cane/spear and was about to deliver the killing blow when Ashanti stopped her.

"No!" Ashanti shouted.

Ophelia looked at him. "You that much of a trained dog that you'd beg for the life of the masters who were about to put you in a cage for the rest of your days?"

"I'm a dog, but I ain't got no training or no master. I'll bite whoever the fuck I get a mind to. Don't you forget that. This ain't about my bite. This is about your face." He nodded at a man who was filming her with his smartphone. He was one of about a dozen still filming them. "You've gone viral. The whole internet is watching your little temper tantrum. How do you think the elders will react to a member executing two police officers on a live stream? That's gonna be a lot of heat on an organization that prides itself on secrecy."

Ophelia stayed her killing blow. She wanted to kill the detective . . . wanted to watch the life drain from his eyes, but she knew that Ashanti was right. She'd lost her temper and allowed herself to be exposed. Ophelia didn't care what the elders under the Mountain would think about her outburst. Soon enough, their voices would all be silenced. She was more concerned about disappointing her mother.

So, instead of executing the Hispanic detective, she stomped on his head until he was unconscious.

"Smart girl," Ashanti said. It was a long shot, but he had managed to appeal to her sense of reason, which meant there was still enough of his sister there to have a civil conversation with. It was a small thing but a start, nonetheless. "Now, why don't you grab them keys and let me out of these cuffs so we can—" Ashanti's words were cut off when Ophelia unexpectedly struck him across the face with the cane, and everything went black.

PART VI

LOVE HER MADLY

Chapter 21

"It's too fucking loud in here," Abel said in irritation as they picked their way through the crowd inside The Club. The music was playing at almost deafening levels.

"This is a nightclub, not a library. So what the fuck did you expect?" Diabolique inquired.

"Fuck you, cunt," Abel spat.

"Maybe when this is all done," she replied with a wink. She liked giving Abel a hard time. He was so easily riled. He lacked the deviousness of his brother, Cain, and the brooding demeanor of Animal. He was a killer, same as the rest of them, but the fact that he wore his emotions on his sleeve added humanity to him that the others lacked. "So, do you think you'll be able to pick this broad out of a crowd if she does happen to be here tonight?"

"Sho-nuff. I'd know that redheaded devil anywhere. I hope we come across her because me and ol' girl got a score to settle." Abel patted his waistband where his 9 mm was tucked.

"You heard what the big homie said about not doing anything stupid. Our job is just to spot her and make sure she doesn't leave. No extra shit," Diabolique reminded him.

"Yeah? Well, I'm an extra nigga. Bitch damn near gave me a concussion. At the very least, I'm going to pistol-whip her," Abel said.

"With that little-ass gun? I hope she feels it when you do clock her," Diabolique laughed.

"Well, if she doesn't feel this one, I guarantee *this* one will get her attention." He rolled up his pant leg to show her the small .38 he had strapped to his ankle. "It ain't the biggest, but you'll know it when it hits you."

"You know, they say you can tell a lot about a man's dick size based on his choice of firearms. So, which one are you? The 9 mm or the cap gun?" Diabolique asked.

"Neither. I'm a rocket launcher," Abel told her, walking ahead.

The deadly duo took their time moving across the dance floor, trying their best not to get trampled or pulled into a dance battle. It seemed like everyone in the place was super high. It was customary for there to be a constant flow of drinks and drugs in any New York nightclub, but this was different. A man stood off in the corner, staring at the ceiling as if waiting for it to open and reveal the sky. A girl sobbed uncontrollably while mumbling to herself and pacing in a tight circle on the dance floor. In a quiet corner, a girl was eating another girl's pussy, while the one receiving the favor swapped spit with the guy they were with. It's like the clubgoers were all high off something more than weed, alcohol, or any designer drug that either of them had ever seen at work.

"Blue Dream," Abel whispered, thinking back to the blue substance that had stained Animal's clothes after he escaped the *Red Widow*. It was the dream that had started it all in the first place. Things were good . . . until that red witch and her blue bag of tricks had pulled them all down a rabbit hole that none of them were likely to be able to climb out of.

"You good?" Diabolique asked, noticing the dark expression on Abel's face.

"Yeah, I'm just tripping off this freak show." Abel watched in disgust as a dude rushed past them toward the bathroom. He looked like he was about to be sick. He never made it. Instead, he spewed whatever he had eaten for dinner onto the floor.

"Just say no," Diabolique said, looking shamefully at the young man who had gotten sick being carted off by security.

"Kinda hard when everybody and their mamas are doing it. In today's society, using drugs to chase the pain away is the new norm," Abel told her.

"That's because you new-age niggas are weak-minded. You feel like you gotta do shit because everybody else is doing it," Diabolique countered.

"Shorty, we gotta be about the same age, so why you coming at me like you're an old head?"

"I'm actually younger than you," Diabolique corrected him. "I'm cut from a bit of a different cloth, though. The dudes I came up around didn't spend their days chasing a high; they were chasing money.

They did what they did but in moderation and never tried to push that shit to the shorties, which were us. So, I didn't have the same temptations dangled before me like a carrot."

"Shit, I heard you came up under Animal, and I know that dude dabbled in all kinds of drugs." Abel recalled some of the war stories he had heard about Animal and his tolerance for drugs and alcohol. He was said to be a dude who partied to the brink of death but always made it back.

"Yeah, the big homie had his vices. That's for sure, but for the most part, he kept it away from us. Animal played a huge part in my development. He was the one who placed the steel in the fire, but it was another who forged the sword . . . shaped me, made me what I would come to be. Once the blinders were snatched off, I couldn't un-see what was revealed to me." She absentmindedly rubbed the tattoo at her temple. She could feel her emotions welling but kept them in check as best as she could.

"And what's that supposed to mean?" Abel asked curiously.

"Nothing . . . I'm just thinking out loud," Diabolique downplayed it. "I gotta use the bathroom. You think you can behave yourself until I come back?"

"I can't make you any promises, but whatever." Abel shrugged. He remained standing there for a few ticks, watching her push through the crowd, swatting off thirsty advances from guys until she reached the safety of the bathroom. Abel was still on the fence about Animal's protégé. Part of him still didn't trust her, and part of him wanted to follow her into the bathroom, bend her over the sink, and fuck her brains out. But that wasn't like him. Abel had always been a lady's man: handsome, charismatic, and confident. So, why was it that since Diabolique showed up, he had been feeling anything *but* that? She had been able to occupy space in his head without being invited and could get under his skin so easily. He wasn't sure what her interest in him was or why he was having such a hard time ignoring her, but what he *did* know was that at some point, he would either have to sleep with her or blow out her brains. There was no way they could continue to coexist so long as whatever tensions between them lingered.

Abel continued to float around, eyes scanning the people for signs of their mark. The deeper he moved into the crowd, the more irritated he became. Abel had never been a big fan of nightclubs. He became even less of a fan after his last visit resulted in him killing a cop. Although in front of Animal and the others, Abel pretended that his popping that pig was a small thing, they all knew that it changed the dynamics of their crew *and* him. Cop or not, it was either his life or Animal's. Abel was protecting his pack, just as Ashanti had schooled him to do since putting him down with the Dog Pound. It wasn't the first man Abel had killed, and it surely wouldn't be the last. However, taking the life of a police officer and still being able to walk around to pounder it put him in a different weight class. He was in the big leagues now, so it pissed him off that Animal still treated him like a pup.

In Abel's mind, his killing that cop should've upped his status amongst the crew. He wasn't in the same weight class as Animal, as he had taken down some very notorious and dangerous targets, but it should've put him in the same category as Ashanti or, at the very least, Zo-Pound. Yet, he still wasn't getting the props that he felt he deserved. The fact that Animal had him in that hot-ass club on a scouting mission instead of in the streets with the rest of them spoke to that.

Abel wasn't stupid. He knew that Animal was keeping him close because he felt like he needed to babysit him, and so did everyone else, which made it worse. That was probably the reason Diabolique felt like she didn't have to respect him because no one else did. Before it was all said and done, Abel would show the entire Dog Pound, including Animal, that he was a full-grown dog, not a pup.

He continued picking his way through the venue, trying his best not to get trampled by the partygoers. Finally, the next act took the stage, a light-skinned dude whose body was covered in tattoos, and a heavy chain hung from his neck. He had so many dudes with him that it was a wonder that they could all fit on the small stage. Abel had seen him somewhere before but couldn't remember his name. He didn't keep up with the new rappers too much, preferring the old-school rappers like Biggie and Pac. The crowd loved him, though. The moment he opened his mouth and his voice came through the speakers, the place went crazy. Women sang along with the lyrics, and dudes shoved each other aggressively. It was like his music was bringing out the worst in them. Before Abel knew it, he was in a violent mosh pit and needed desperately to get out before he ended up smoking something.

Abel was already hot and frustrated, and the swarm of people knocking him back and forth only added to his irritation. He had decided to swing on the next muthafucka who stepped on his feet and didn't beg his pardon. The universe must've heard him and decided to give him what he asked because a well-built Italian man bumped past him and stepped on Abel's boot while walking by him. Trailing him was a Black dude who looked too old to be in a party full of twenty-somethings. He ignored the older man and zeroed in on the Italian, anger building. Not only did he not apologize for bumping Abel, but he never even looked back to acknowledge the youth. He was about to become an example.

Abel was easing up behind him, ready to pop off, when he caught a flash of crimson at a table across the room. It was her. Red Sonja. Animal had given orders for them not to engage, but fuck that. She had damn near split his head open when she had betrayed them at the port and made off with the bag. It was a slight that he was about to make her answer for. With her locked in his sights, Abel moved in.

Chapter 22

Thirty minutes. That's how long Tess had been in the restroom attending to her friend, but it felt far longer. After pulling Tasha away from the table, she half-carried, half-dragged, the girl to the unisex restroom. She urgently pushed through the smoked-glass door, almost hitting a guy behind it. The bathroom was teeming with people. Some were relieving themselves, but for the most part, it was a mess of people getting high or committing lewd acts. She managed to get her intoxicated friend to one of the empty stalls near the end. Someone was about to enter it, but Tess was quicker on the draw. She had barely gotten Tasha into the stall before she threw up the liquor on the floor and splashed the new shoes that Tess had planned to return to the store in the morning. That plan was a wrap.

"I'm sorry, Tess," Tasha slurred as she clutched the edge of the bowl and began to vomit again.

"It's fine," Tess lied, holding Tasha's braids out of her face so she didn't ruin them like she had done Tess's shoes. As she watched her friend heave up her guts, she couldn't help but think about all the things she would've rather been doing with her night. "I should've stayed the fuck home."

"Oh, damn," Tasha blurted out, clutching her stomach.

"What's the matter?" Tess asked, thinking that she was about to throw up some more. But instead, she hiked up her dress and pressed her ass against the toilet a split second before her ass exploded like a geyser, erupting a river of shit. "Oh, hell no!" Tess backpedaled out of the stall, fanning the fumes. Tasha was her girl, but this was taking friendship too damn far.

"I'm sorry . . . I'm so sorry," Tasha whimpered as her ass continued to leak.

Tess allowed her friend some privacy and went over to the long mirror that took up one side of the bathroom wall. She examined herself and wasn't pleased with who she saw staring back from behind the looking glass. Her hair was frizzy from sweating, and a small tear in the shoulder of her dress stood out. It likely happened while trying to lug her drunk friend into the bathroom. Her night seemed to be going from bad to worse, and she was ready to get the hell out of there and get home to her bed.

As she thought back on it, the night hadn't been completely horrible. The dudes they had met earlier seemed pretty cool, at least the dark-skinned one. She didn't care for the light-skinned cat, Valentino. He gave her serious creep vibes. His friend, Zion, seemed to be okay, though. She had been apprehensive at first because that's just how Tess was, but she hadn't missed how hard he had tried to ensure they were at ease. She had toyed with the idea of getting to know him a little before the rug was pulled out from under their little flex when the real occupant of the private table had shown up. One thing she couldn't stand was a poser, which is what the two of them appeared to be. Still, she couldn't help but feel bad for the boy they called Zion. He seemed genuine enough, but Tess would never know. Despite his sincere vibe, if he hung with a kid like Valentino, she reasoned that he probably had some creep in him too. *Birds of a feather*, as they said.

Tess was over that whole night and was ready to get up out of there. She pulled out her phone and called Shay but got no answer. She was probably somewhere still being a slut with the dude she had slid off with. Her friend was shameless, and sometimes, Tess wondered why she even still rocked with her other than the fact that they had history. Sometimes, familiarity bred complacency. Fuck it. Once Tasha could stand on her own again, they were leaving, regardless of whether Shay was ready. If she could let dude get the pussy, at the very least, he could provide her with a ride home.

A girl walked into the bathroom. Tess probably wouldn't even have given her a second look had it not been for two things: her fire-engine red hair and the air of menace that she carried with her. She was a pretty girl, aside from the tattoo on her face, but something about her felt off. Tess wasn't the only one who felt it because everyone in the bathroom parted like the Red Sea to let her pass. She gave Tess a passing glance that chilled her blood. She held her breath until the girl entered one of the stalls and slammed the door shut behind her. It was definitely time to go.

"All these damn ants," Tess heard Tasha mutter from the stall.

"Girl, what are you in there babbling about?" Tess asked with an attitude. She had had about enough of Tasha's shit as well.

"These red ants. Don't you see them?" Tasha's voice was more urgent now.

Tess pushed the stall door open to find Tasha swatting at her arms and legs as if something were crawling on her, but Tess saw nothing. "Girl, your ass is high. Ain't nothing crawling on you."

"Get them off me . . . Get them off me." Tasha was in a panic now. In her mind, troops of fire ants were crawling up and down her body. She began clawing at her face, raking red welts down her cheeks.

"Tasha, calm down. There's nothing on you." Tess grabbed Tasha's arm, but the girl pushed her away. The unexpected force behind the push sent Tess staggering backward out of the stall and hitting her back against the sink. Tasha was a petite girl whom Tess outweighed by at least twenty pounds, so how the hell was she able to manage that?

Tasha jumped off the toilet, panties still around her ankles, and dress now hiked up over her hips.

She dug her nails into her ass and thighs so deep that they left blood trails in their wake. "They're biting me . . . They're trying to eat me alive," she rambled, duck-walking to the sink. She turned the hot water on full and dropped her hands directly in the line of the scalding spray. If she couldn't scratch the ants off, she would boil them off.

By now, people had started drifting to that end of the bathroom to see what was happening. Tasha looked quite special, trying to boil herself like a lobster in the small sink. Then suddenly, phones came out, and people started recording the girl having a meltdown as if it were the funniest thing they had ever seen.

"What's wrong with you people? Why isn't anybody trying to help instead of doing it for the Gram?" Tess barked angrily at the spectators while trying to block her friend's naked ass from their cameras. Tasha was having a full-scale meltdown from whatever drug Valentino had given her earlier. Tess had no clue what the hell it was, so she wasn't sure what to do for her friend. This was above her pay grade, and she needed to get some medical help. "C'mon. I'm going to get you out of here." She tried pulling her from the sink, which only seemed to agitate Tasha.

"Nowhere is safe. They're all over the place!" Tess shouted. She jumped out of the sink and clumsily tried to reach the door. But unfortunately, this was about when Diabolique came out of the other stall. Tasha took one look at her, and instead of seeing a redheaded girl, her mind convinced her that she was a demon with hair of flames. "Devil!" she screamed and charged with her claws bared.

Diabolique was caught totally off guard by the feral girl coming in her direction. But it only took her warrior's brain a split second to identify a threat and start walking through scenarios to neutralize it. She planted her foot behind her, pushing off and throwing a punch from her shoulder. Tasha ran straight into it with her momentum taking her legs out from under her and planting her on her back. "Nut-ass bitch." She looked down at the girl, still trying to figure out what made her attack her. As she pondered this, Tasha sprang back to her feet like a creature from *Night of the Living Dead*. Diabolique knew that she had hit her with enough force to lay most men out, but the skinny girl ate it and was coming back for a second helping. "Shit." She drew her gun and was about to plug the crazed girl, but her friend jumped between them.

"Don't . . . please. She's not in her right mind. These dudes gave her something . . . I don't know," Tess rattled off, pleading with Diabolique not to kill her friend.

Usually, Diabolique would've shoved Tess out of the way and still made Tasha eat fire anyhow, but the mention of the girl having been drugged gave her pause. Not just because she was there tonight hunting a drug dealer, but because she knew firsthand what it was like to be drugged by someone and stripped of her free will. Before she could figure out an alternative course of action, the girl attacked again.

This time, Tasha's fury wasn't on Diabolique but on Tess. She caught her from behind and raked her nails over the girl's face, leaving nasty scratches. Tess fell to the floor, screaming with her hands over her bleeding face. Tasha was out of control, and somebody had to stop her.

Mind your business . . . this isn't your fight . . . stick to the mission . . . All logic screamed for Diabolique to leave it alone, but she couldn't. Her conscience wouldn't allow her to leave Tasha in that condition to possibly end up someone's victim later in the night as Diabolique had some years earlier. Diabolique couldn't exorcise whatever demons were raging in Tasha's head, but she could help quiet them.

Wild-eyed, Tasha was in the process of choosing another random person in the crowd of onlookers to attack when Diabolique stepped into her line of vision. The tactic had the desired results because Tasha was now locked in on Diabolique. She came at her like an animal—all teeth and claws. Diabolique calmly socked her in the gut, and when she doubled over, she brought the butt of her gun down across the back of her head. Tasha did a face plant onto the linoleum . . . and the fight was over.

"You good?" Diabolique asked Tess, who was using a fistful of tissue to wipe the blood from her face. Her friend had done a number on her but hadn't scratched her deep enough for the wounds to leave scars.

"Did you really have to do all that?" Tess asked, looking at Tasha, who was on the floor moaning. A bloody gash had opened up on the back of her head.

"Ungrateful bitch. I'd say it beat the alternative, wouldn't you?" Diabolique held up her gun.

"I'm sorry. I didn't mean to come off like that. Thank you for helping me. I just hope she's gonna be okay." Tess was a bit calmer now. She might not have agreed with Diabolique's method of stopping Tasha, but it had been more effective than anything she'd tried.

"A few stitches and a seventy-two-hour hold at Bellevue, if you're lucky. If I were you, I'd get this girl to a hospital sooner than later." Diabolique turned to leave. A crowd had formed, and damn near everyone had their phones out, recording the confrontation. This meant that her face was going viral, which wasn't good. Staying anonymous and off anyone's radar had been the key to her being able to come to Animal's aid without ruffling any feathers. But because she couldn't mind her own business, all bets would be off as soon as those videos were uploaded. Diabolique's image would probably send up red flags in several databases.

At that point, what was done was done, and she could do nothing about it. There was no way she could confiscate all the bathroom phones. And even if she could, she was sure the videos had already gone up. So all she could do at that point was get out of the public view as quickly as possible and hoped she could get out ahead of a shit storm that she was sure was coming.

She plowed through the crowd and ran out of the bathroom. As she was coming out, security was rushing in. No doubt someone had alerted them about the fight in the bathroom. Within a few minutes, they'd probably be swarming through the crowd looking for her. She planned to be long gone by then. This mission was a wash. She needed to gather her people and get the hell out of there. Animal wouldn't be happy about it, but putting their hunt for Sonja on hold for a time beat the alternative, which was more people that she loved dying over a promise that she had made . . . and broken.

Diabolique pushed through the crowd on the dance floor. She looked around frantically, trying to find her comrades. There was no sign of Animal, but she could spot Abel. At first, she thought he was having a friendly conversation with someone he might've known in the spot, but then she saw the redhead. Not only had Abel disobeyed a direct order by engaging Red Sonja, but he was unknowingly about to make an already bad situation worse.

Chapter 23

For the second time that night, Zion found himself at the same private table. The difference was that this time, he had been invited by the person who paid for it rather than just trying to post up like a broke nigga just trying to stunt. Red Sonja had been the name of their benefactor. From Valentino's reaction and learning what he had attempted to do to her, the last thing Zion had expected was for her to offer them a seat at their table. Yet, she did. Zion didn't trust it and had tried to decline her offer respectfully, but the redhead wasn't someone who was easy to take "No" for an answer. From how her Italian companion grilled them with his hand in his pocket, Zion reasoned that they didn't have a choice.

The first thing Sonja did was order bottles, and then from a place Zion couldn't identify, pulled out a half-ounce of weed, which she placed on the table. The bud was so loud that you could smell it through the Ziploc. Next, she encouraged the two young boys to get as high and drunk as they wanted; it was on her. Valentino was quick to fill his cup with champagne, but Zion declined. He didn't trust the situation. After learning of what Valentino had attempted to do, how could he?

Zion had suspected that something was fishy with Valentino's story from when he had run it down to him, but that was the homie, so he rode out with him anyway. The story got more suspect when Valentino showed him the synthetic drug and told him how he had come to get his hands on it. What sent up the red flag was that though Valentino was Zion's best friend, he was also a notorious greaseball. Nobody in their right mind would trust Valentino with their drugs and expect him to return with the count being straight. It wasn't a knock on him; it just spoke to who Valentino was. For most of the night, Zion had been trying to figure out the real story of how Valentino could come up, but it wasn't until they had sat with Sonja that the blanks were filled in.

What Valentino had said about Sonja being the plug and his uncle her new chemist was true, but he hadn't been entrusted with the drug samples. He had stolen them. Sonja had given Valentino a package of beta samples to take to his uncle, who was supposed to deliver them to some potential buyers. The samples weren't quite street-ready yet and would need another round or two of testing before they could flood the city, but all Valentino saw was an opportunity for him to get the jump on something that was about to change the drug game. With this in mind, he kept the drugs for himself instead of delivering them to his uncle as instructed.

He hadn't planned on keeping whatever profits he could turn from the drugs, only to show Sonja that he could be an asset to her organization, but he ended up looking like a petty thief who couldn't be trusted. What was worse was that he had now roped Zion into his bullshit. Zion had expected Sonja to be upset with the theft and prepared himself for whatever she and her Italian companion had in store for them, but instead of going off, she simply laughed. She wasn't angry at all because she had orchestrated the whole thing.

Within the first ten minutes of meeting Louie's nephew, she understood his character probably better than he did. She had dealt with men like him in her father's organization since she was a girl. He was overly ambitious and wasn't above trying to snake himself into position when profit was involved. She saw Valentino trying to flip the drugs on his own long before she handed them to him. She had even planted the seeds for him to try to hustle them at The Club that night by leaving the promotional flyers on Louie's coffee table for Valentino to find. He'd tried to sell the drugs to impress Sonja enough to let him eat from her plate but ended up showing how easily he could be manipulated. He wasn't very sharp, but he showed moxie, so she hadn't yet deemed him totally useless.

"What? My hand no longer good enough to eat from?" Sonja directed the question to Zion.

"How you mean?" Zion didn't understand the remark.

"I invite you boys to my table, pop a few bottles, and you don't partake?" Sonja gestured to Zion's empty glass.

"I'm not a big drinker," Zion said with a shrug of his broad shoulders.

Sonja nodded. "Right. Can't get caught off point. I guess you need to be constantly on guard when you go around ripping off strange women."

"I ain't no thief," Zion told her.

"So, that wasn't you I saw drinking it up with those hoodrats? No doubt with money that rightfully belongs to me. Regardless of whether you took my shit, there was a glass to your lips right along with his." She thumbed at Valentino. "So, consider this a case of guilt by association."

"Sonja, this was all on me. Zion didn't know anything about it," Valentino said honestly. He felt terrible about getting Zion caught up, but a part of him was happy that he didn't have to face his fate alone.

"I know whose hand was in my cookie jar. That's what makes this even worse. Your friend doesn't know me from a hole in the wall, but you . . ." Sonja jabbed her finger into Valentino's chest. ". . . know exactly who I am and how I play."

Valentino's mouth got incredibly dry. Something about those steel-gray eyes latched on him made him feel unwell. He was glad that he was already sitting because if he hadn't been, there was a good chance that his knees would've buckled. He instinctively looked at Zion, who was watching the exchange. His face never changed, but Valentino saw his fists curling on the table. One thing about him was no matter the odds, he would bang with Valentino to the end, even when he was wrong.

"Richie . . ." Sonja kept her eyes on Valentino but addressed the Italian man. ". . . What do they do to thieves in your family?"

Richie draped his arm over the back of the chair, letting his track jacket open just enough so the youths could see the gun hanging from his shoulder holster. "Make it so they can't do it again."

"Yeah, I could think of a few things I can do to Valentino to make me feel a little better, but something tells me that whatever I do to him, I'll probably have to get through his sober friend. Ain't that right, big man?" Sonja looked back at Zion. "Would you eat a bullet for this little nigga?"

Zion knew it was a loaded question, and how he answered could potentially drop or stay the guillotine Valentino had hanging over their necks. "Respectfully, anybody that tells you that they're willing to eat a bullet for the next man is either lying or has never been shot. Now, if you're asking me whether I'm gonna ride with my boy if it goes down tonight, absolutely."

"Even though he's as wrong as two left shoes?" Sonja asked, genuinely curious.

"We came to this spot together, and we're gonna leave together, either on our feet or our backs." Zion wasn't boasting, only being honest.

"Blind loyalty like yours gets men killed," Sonja told him.

"My loyalty isn't blind, just unwavering. If I'm with you, I'm *with* you," Zion told her.

Sonja leaned forward and studied him, locking him in with her steel-gray eyes as she had done Valentino. His face wore the story of his upbringing, while his eyes told his future. They were still the eyes of a child but beginning to get that hardened look about them. The dark-skinned young man reminded her of someone she'd once seen great promise in. Only Zion hadn't completely hardened by the streets just yet. Despite his brutish appearance, he was slightly more than a child, still trying to find his way. Sonja smiled, showing off two rows of perfect white teeth behind painted red lips. "In my business, a loyal man is a well-fed man, Zion."

For the first time that night, he mustered what passed for a smile. A simple twisting of his thick lips . . . a gleam in his eyes. "That's a good thing because I ain't ate a decent meal in weeks, and I'm starving."

After the conversation between Sonja and Zion, the tension lingering over the table drained away, at least in part. Though the threat of them being executed—at least that night—was gone, Zion was still uneasy. Sonja paid particular attention to Zion for the rest of the evening, even making Valentino switch seats with her so she could be closer to Zion while they spoke. Sonja was beautiful, probably the most beautiful woman that he had ever laid eyes on. Having her in such close proximity, invading his space, forcing the sweet scent of her into his nostrils . . . it was almost like sensory overload. It took some measure of concentration on his part not to allow himself to get so lost in her physical appearance that he forgot how dangerous she was.

Sonja's words were all business, but something about her delivery was intimate. She purred into his ear about the potential she saw in him and how pledging his loyalty to her and her organization could change his life. She was very persuasive. During the conversation, she made it a point to let her hand graze his arm or leg. The gesture was hardly sexual, but his brain kept sending signals to the rest of his body that it was. She was making him uncomfortable, and the playful glint in her eyes said she was aware of this. He couldn't have been happier when some other business she had at The Club that night drew her to the other side of the room. Being out of her proximity felt like a weight had been lifted from his chest. Finally, he was free of the spell she was attempting to cast over him . . . at least until she returned.

"A red widow." Zion could hear the low voice of his demon mumble.

"What?"

"The girl. She's like a black widow spider, only red. Still, the outcome will be the same. She will mate, and she will kill. So grab your simpleminded

friend and get out of here while she's got her back turned. You haven't fallen that deep down the rabbit hole yet," the demon urged. He seemed genuinely concerned.

"Since the day you hitched a ride in my skull, you've been pushing me to do wrong, and now, you want me to do right?" Zion chuckled. The demon had always been his biggest cheerleader when it came to doing things that would bring him harm. He advocated for Zion fucking up his life, so to hear him argue so animatedly about Zion not doing business with Sonja made him want to link with her even more. This had the potential to be something good for Zion, and the demon hated it.

"You think your wet-behind-the-ears ass is ready for what the girl is about to lay on your lap, but you aren't. Your flesh is too tender for the likes of her. Jump on the subway back to your ghetto and deal with the players in the game there. This one is out of your league," the demon told him.

"Shut up." Zion slammed his palms against the sides of his head as if trying to dislodge water from his ears.

"Shut up is what you should've told your idiot friend when he brought this dumb-ass scheme to you in the first place," the demon replied. *"You're a fool if you think that red bitch couldn't smell what we were when we walked in. Behind that pretty face, she's just like us, pal."*

"We aren't anything alike," Zion insisted.

The demon chuckled. *"You can keep telling your-self that if you want. You love painting the narrative of me being some malevolent spirit who is looking to drag you to hell, but we both know that the truth of the matter is, I am you . . . The things you fantasize about that are so dark and so twisted that you're ashamed to carry that kind of shit inside you are what created me. I'm your scapegoat, and that's the story you run with every time you do something bad, but we both know how much you love sipping from this poisoned well. I'm only the gas, baby boy. You're the engine that makes this monster move."*

"You done?" Zion asked with an attitude. Some of the demon's words had hit close to home. His demon always seemed to know him better than most.

"Nope, but apparently you are," the demon replied. *"I'll give you some food for thought. You treat me like the worst part of yourself because I encourage you to occasionally play in a little blood. Let's see how your precious moral code holds up when the red one has you swimming in it."*

"You good?" Valentino retook the seat that Sonja had evicted him from. He was sipping from one of the champagne bottles like he'd purchased it.

"What?" Zion asked as if Valentino were speaking a foreign language.

"I asked if you were good. I see you down here mumbling to yourself and wanted to make sure you weren't having another one of your episodes." Valentino had seen Zion step out of his skin before and become something he didn't recognize. His friend had an on/off switch in the back of his mind that seemed to flick one way or another of its own accord.

"My demon is under control. It's yours out here overplaying its stroke and getting us twisted in this bullshit. That stunt you pulled with trying to pass shorty's drugs off as your own could've gotten us hurt," Zion scolded him.

"But it didn't. Sonja was a little salty, but at the end of the day, she saw that I'm a man who takes the initiative, and that was the point I was trying to make all along. Sure, we took a risk, but look at what the rewards can be," Valentino said excitedly. It was as if he had already forgotten how, moments before, Sonja had almost made him shit himself out of fear of what she might do to the little thief.

"Yo, that was some gangster shit you ran down to shorty. You almost convinced me that you were all in on this thing."

"A man who knows he's about to die will say anything to save his life," Zion told him. "And it wasn't game. It was real shit. You said yourself that this Red Sonja broad is about to be a major player in the game. I don't know about you, but I'm tired of eating table scraps. I want an actual meal."

"Right, right, and we're gonna eat plenty good under her. It's just like I told you. I got us." From how Valentino was talking, you'd have thought he had just made a deal with the devil instead of Zion.

Sonja returned shortly after, and she wasn't alone. Trailing her was an older man who Zion had seen before in passing. His name was Sammy. From what Zion knew of Sammy, his thing was gambling and pumping a little weed, so what he did with Sonja was somewhat of a mystery, but Zion wouldn't have to wait long for it to be solved.

He sat back and quietly observed while Sonja, Sammy, and Richie spoke. Sonja did most of the talking, with Richie interjecting here and there as needed. From what Zion had picked up, Sonja was pitching Sammy on the idea of being one of her suppliers of the Blue Dream in New York. Sammy had his finger on the pulse of the streets and knew all the major players because most of them frequented his gambling spots. So they would use his games as a launchpad for the Blue Dream and gradually let it trickle into the streets.

"Sounds good, Sonja, but you know there will be some people who ain't going to take kindly to you stepping on their toes, and me by extension, if I throw down on your play. I ain't no pushover, but I don't have the kind of muscle behind me to deal with the blowback which will surely come from this play," Sammy pointed out.

"And this is where I come in," Richie spoke up. "Me and some of my outfit associates will provide you with the extra muscle you need."

Sammy studied Richie's face for a time as if he were trying to place him. "You're one of Gee-Gee's crew, ain't you?" He was referring to the current boss of the Cicero crime family.

"I was once until our business interests were no longer aligned. I've got my own thing going now. Me and my guys operate mainly out of the Bronx and Westchester."

"But you're still a Mafioso. I thought you boys had a thing against drug dealing . . . *deal and die,* isn't that how the saying goes?" Sammy asked.

Richie shrugged. "These days, a man earns any way he can. I can give you my word that you need not worry about it. A few coins every month placed into the right hands will ensure that the old-timers turn a blind eye to our business, so long as we keep it under control and away from them." He had already lined it up with some of the street capos he used to run with so that they could wet their beaks once things were up and running. Unlike some old-timers who held dear to the rules, the younger ones played a little faster and looser. All they were concerned about was making a profit.

"Sounds like y'all have laid the groundwork. The question remains: How do I know this fancy shit you're trying to push is everything that you say it is? For all I know, this could be nothing more than the next MDMA. People can get shit like that anywhere. So what makes this Blue Dream shit so special?" Sammy questioned.

"Look around you, OG," Valentino interjected, much to everyone's surprise. "Blue Dream got this whole party shaking." He motioned at a cluster of young people standing in the corner with spaced-out expressions on their faces. They were stuck on stupid. Valentino didn't mean any disrespect when he jumped into their conversation uninvited. He was just proud of the work that he had put in with spreading the drug throughout the club. All he wanted was to be acknowledged, and he was.

"Who is this little nigga, and why is he speaking to me?" Sammy asked, looking at Valentino as if he had just been caught with his dick in his hand under the table and jerking off.

"Excuse him, Sammy. Valentino is one of our new hires, and he's just a little anxious. Harmless, just anxious," Sonja said coolly.

"Well, you need to teach the rookie to keep his mouth closed while grown folks are talking," Sammy said. He hated dealing with young people because they lacked etiquette, as shown by Valentino speaking out of turn.

"I didn't mean no disrespect, OG. I'm just trying to assure you that the product is everything Sonja says it is," Valentino said in a rare moment of humility. He was trying to right his wrong, but the old man was stuck on what he was stuck on.

"I dig it, shorty, but the muthafuckas flipping burgers out front never got to speak to the McDonald's brothers, so we're gonna follow the same model of success with this here." To punctuate his statement, Sammy gave Valentino his back while he continued speaking to Sonja and Richie.

Zion could tell from his friend's face how deeply Sammy's slight had cut him. He looked down at his bottle of champagne, too embarrassed to make eye contact with anyone at the table. All Valentino ever wanted was to be at the table. He didn't need a seat; he just wanted his voice heard. Behind Valentino's misty eyes, Zion could see a poor decision taking shape. Zion placed a calming hand on Valentino's shoulder. His and his friend's eyes met, and Valentino knew that Zion knew what he was thinking, but Zion's eyes said, "*Not now . . . Not here.*"

Valentino nodded in understanding, but the sorrow in his eyes remained. It was a dead issue for the night, but Zion knew that at some point, Valentino would make the old man regret the flagrant way he'd handled him. He had no idea how, but he was sure it would come. Valentino wasn't the hardest nigga Zion had ever encountered, but he was undoubtedly the most spiteful. That was the Sagittarius in him.

Sonja and her collective continued to talk, Valentino continued to drink excessively, and Zion continued to watch. He was picking up on bits and pieces of Sonja and Sammy's conversation, and just when he thought he was getting an idea of what they were cooking up, the next performer at the showcase took the stage, and the room filled with deafening applause. It filled the place with so much noise that it drowned out their conversation completely, and Zion had to rely on poor lip-reading skills to fill in the blanks.

Zion turned to the stage to see who had riled the crowd up in such a way. A part of him knew who it would be. Even before his Tims touched the cheap plywood box slapped together to serve as a stage, Zion knew who the energy belonged to. Inferno was officially in the building. He remembered Valentino speaking about the young rapper and his strong following, which gave Zion an idea of what to expect. However, he still wasn't totally prepared for what he experienced. From what he understood, Inferno was known for inciting violence whenever they performed at a live show. He did not disappoint. Within a minute of his opening bars, the whole place had turned into a chaotic ball of flailing arms, feet, and youths screaming his lyrics at the tops of their lungs.

Two dudes who had obviously had too much to drink and were too vested in Inferno's lyrics had gotten into it. They engaged in a shoving and shouting match that spilled a little too close to Sonja's table. Zion moved to stand between the scrapping youths and their table. It was more of his protective instincts kicking in than actually wanting to involve himself in the fight, but the two youths must've felt otherwise. Before he knew it, they had abandoned their beef and designated Zion the common enemy.

He tried the diplomatic approach and let the dudes know he didn't want any problems. For this, he was met with a slug to the jaw, and it was all downhill from there. They were both drunk and/or high, which made them easy work for the bruiser. By the time security came to break up the fight, Zion had knocked one of the kids out and was strangling the other boy. The bouncers were about to jump on him, but Sonja stepped in on his behalf.

"I got it," Sonja assured the bouncers.

"We can't have this shit in here. I don't care how much money you're spending, get me?" one of them told Sonja.

"Whatever, nigga." She tossed some bills at them for the damages and led Zion away from the table. "Foolish boy, have you lost your mind?" She scolded him once they were away from the ruckus and Zion had calmed down some.

"You showed me love, and I was only trying to show it back by making sure you were good," Zion explained. He was a bit embarrassed and, for a minute, feared that Sonja would rescind the offer she had made earlier. But once again, she surprised him by showing amusement instead of anger.

Sonja laughed. It was a thoughtful and cute gesture but hardly necessary. "Zion, one thing you'll learn from being around me is that I'm always good, even when it looks like I'm not. That's my gift . . . deception."

"Meaning you're a good liar?" he questioned.

"I'm an amazing liar, among other things, but that's not what I mean in this case," Sonja clarified. "If you're going to stand next to me, I must know that you know how to control yourself. I can't have you popping off and ruining deals. We got people to handle petty skirmishes."

"I thought it was only you and Richie here," Zion said.

"Again, deception. If I wanted to, I could've made it run hellfire in this bum-ass spot, but I'm here trying to catch a bag, not a body. Blood isn't always the first course of action when doing business. It can make things uncomfortable for the squeamish," Sonja told him.

Zion's eyes went to the table. Valentino was now alone, looking around nervously, and there was no sign of Richie or Sammy. Zion figured he had scared them off with his little outburst.

"Sammy had other business to attend to, and Richie is taking care of some last-minute details for delivery of our product to him," Sonja said as if she could read his mind.

"I thought I had messed things up," Zion said with a hint of embarrassment.

"Nothing short of God or the devil can fuck this up for me. Me and God have an understanding, and I'm trying damn hard to stay one step ahead of the devil," Sonja said cryptically.

"I'll fall back and play my position from now on," Zion assured her.

"And if you play your cards right, your position will be with me. Zion, I know exactly what you are, even if you don't yet. I can promise you that you'll see as much action as a part of my crew as you will cash, but we need to be clear about something before moving forward. You are auditioning for the part of my new champion bulldog. This means that you only bite who I tell you to, when I tell you to. And when you bite, you make sure you devour the whole meal and clean your plate like a good boy. Do you understand?"

Zion didn't like her dog reference, but he wasn't about to raise a stink over it and risk getting cut out before he even got in. "Don't worry. I won't disappoint you."

"That's too bad because she's for sure going to disappoint you right before she double-crosses you." Abel appeared just behind the two of them. Sonja tried to hide her surprise at him being able to track her down, but her eyes couldn't hide it. "I'll bet I'm the last person you expected to see again."

"I guess that little love tap I gave you last night must've knocked all the common sense from your head. Otherwise, you wouldn't have been dumb enough to roll up on me alone," Sonja said to Abel.

"And who says that I'm alone?" Abel taunted. He saw Sonja's eyes dart around. She was no doubt looking for Animal, knowing he had to be somewhere lurking in the shadows. "No need to worry about the big homie. He's around, but I need my fifteen minutes of fame with you before y'all settle whatever differences you got going on. The last bitch to put her hands on me was the last bitch to put her hands on me," he said menacingly.

"Li'l fella, this isn't a problem you want," Sonja said coolly.

"Oh, I can guarantee I want *all* the smoke." Abel lifted his shirt, exposing the handle of his gun. "Let's take a walk, Sonja. I got somebody who is really anxious to speak with you."

Sonja needed to think fast. She was pretty confident that she could kick the shit out of Abel without breaking a sweat, but by engaging one of the pups, she would risk being slowed long enough for the alpha wolf to appear. Animal was a problem she didn't need. Not when she was so close to claiming the prize. She needed an exit strategy. "Zion."

"'Sup?" Zion stepped forward, eyes locked on Abel.

"Do you remember that conversation we had about finishing your food?" Sonja asked him, keeping her eyes on Abel.

"Indeed, I do."

"Good, because it's chow time."

Chapter 24

Floating. That was the best way to describe the feeling that had come over Abel. It was as if he were floating on a groovy wave that he never wanted to end, but unfortunately, it did when he landed on his back and banged his head on the hard dance floor. His skull cracking the hardwood snapped him out of the euphoric dream and brought him back to the reality of his situation, which was a fight for his life.

Before he could adequately gather himself, the brute was back on him. Zion grabbed Abel by the front of his shirt and yanked him to his feet with the ease of a parent scooping their child. Abel tried to bring his gun into play, but Zion smashed one of his massive fists into Abel's wrist and caused him to drop the gun, which got lost in the stampede of people trying to get out of the way of the two combatants. Abel hit Zion with a right cross, which stunned him enough to loosen his grip. Then he wiggled free of his shirt and put some distance between himself and the bigger man. When Zion tried to rush him, Abel danced out of the way and hit him with a combination. Zion had the height and weight advantages, but Abel was the more skilled boxer.

Zion tried to grab Abel, but every time he did, he was rewarded with a shot to the face. His lip was bleeding, and he could feel a knot forming over his right eye.

"*He's kicking your ass. You might want to do something before you get embarrassed in front of your little girlfriend,*" the demon taunted.

"Shut up," Zion grunted and pressed his attack. He attempted to grab Abel in a bear hug, which was a mistake. The smaller man's fist moved in a blur, raining blows into Zion's midsection. Zion could feel his wind fleeing his lungs. For the briefest of moments, he dropped his guard, and Abel went in for the kill. He hit Zion with a right that sent him stumbling and crashing through the table where they had been sitting.

"Bet that'll hold your big ass," Abel huffed. He was exhausted, and his jaw was killing him. He looked up and saw Red Sonja making a beeline for the back door. He was about to pursue her when someone jumped on his back.

"Raise up off my homeboy!" Valentino had put Abel in a reverse chokehold. He was no fighter, but Zion had stood up for him more times than he could count. He had to try to help. Abel grabbed Valentino and flipped him onto the ground with so much force he saw spots. When he looked up and saw Abel standing over him, he knew things were about to go very badly for him.

"Bitch-ass nigga," Abel spat and began stomping out Valentino.

Zion was in pain and wet from all the liquor that spilled on him, but more than anything, he was embarrassed. He'd gotten his ass kicked in front of Red Sonja. He looked around and noticed that there was no sign of the girl. She must've slipped away during the fight. *"I'm always good."* Her words from earlier echoed in his head. He didn't see Sonja, but he did see Valentino. He was on the floor being stomped to a bloody mess by Abel.

"That one there is a real spark plug, isn't he?" The demon was speaking again. *"I'd say there's a good chance that he will stomp your little friend to death unless someone intervenes."* He sensed Zion's hesitance. He wasn't afraid, just not sure it was a battle he could win. *"You and I both know that there's only one way for you to save him. Let me out to play. C'mon, you know you want to. It's either that or let that guy kill your best friend. Make your choice. Say the words."*

Letting the demon out was the last thing he wanted to do, but what choice did he have? Abel was a monster, and it would take a monster to defeat a monster. *"I release you."*

Abel was opening up a can of whip ass on Valentino. He fully intended to kill him for raising his hand to him, but his murder would have to wait because he felt a presence looming behind him. He turned around and found the bruiser he had put on his ass moments before. Something was different about him, though. There was a darkness in his eyes that Abel hadn't noticed before. Also, he couldn't be sure, but Zion seemed bigger than Abel remembered.

"Back for more, huh?" He cracked his knuckles. "Sit tight," he told Valentino. "This won't take long." Abel had beaten Zion once and thought their second round would end the same, but he realized that he was in trouble when he threw the first punch.

Zion moved with speed that a man of his size should not have possessed, avoiding Abel's punch and following up with one of his own. He hooked his fist into Abel's gut with so much force that it lifted him off his feet slightly and knocked the wind out of him. He followed with a massive overhand to the back of Abel's head, dropping him on his hands and knees. Abel tried to crawl away, but Zion wrapped his hands around his neck and lifted him.

"You touched my friend," Zion snarled, choking Abel and shaking him like a rag doll. The man's thin neck felt good in Zion's hands, and he squeezed harder and harder. In fact, he was squeezing so tight that the tips of his fingers were nearly touching at the base of Abel's throat.

"*That's right . . . Snap his neck. Kill him for what he did to us. Kill him!*" the demon squealed excitedly. This had been the furthest he had been able to provoke the youth since he had almost beaten his father to death. The demon was getting drunk off Zion's rage, and the pending death of his opponent would be oh . . . so sweet.

Abel kicked and scratched at Zion's hands, but he could do nothing to break the man's grip. He tried to get to the gun he had strapped to his ankle but found that he didn't have the strength to lift his leg high enough. Pain and then numbness shot through Abel's limbs as he felt his neck crack. The lights in The Club began to blink in and out as he started to lose consciousness. Finally, the darkness came, blanketing him little by little in a beautiful death. He had always envisioned that when God called his number, he would die the soldier's death that Ashanti and the others always spoke of. Never in a million years did he imagine that he would meet his end at a hole-in-the-wall club at the hands of a man barely out of his teens. He steeled himself against the end, which he could almost taste by that point, but fortunately, the universe had deemed that it wasn't his time just yet.

There was a thunderous crash, and suddenly, Abel found himself free of the brute's grip. He hit the floor in a heap, gasping for air. Abel had never been a praying man, but at that moment, he thanked God with all his heart for the miracle he had sent him. Then ignoring the pain in his neck, he managed to look behind him and saw that it hadn't been a miracle that had snatched him from the jaws of death but a woman. Diabolique stood over Zion's prone body, holding what was left of the chair she had smashed over his head. She was barking something at Abel, but he couldn't hear her over the thumping of his heart in his ears. Abel had been involved in some dangerous capers during his young life, and there were times when he had been 50/50 on whether he would make it out, but that was the closest he had ever come to death, and the feeling left him unsettled.

"Nigga, do you hear me talking to you?" Diabolique's words had finally managed to penetrate. "Are you okay?"

"I'm good," Abel said in a hoarse voice. Even free of Zion's grip, he was still having trouble breathing. Moreover, he was certain the youngster had damaged his windpipes.

"Then get your simpleminded ass up, and let's get back on this mission." Diabolique pulled Abel to his feet. His legs were still clearly shaking, but he managed to stand on his own. "What part of 'do not engage' weren't you clear on?" She was heated.

"I thought I had the drop on her, but then—"

"Blood, I don't even wanna hear it," Diabolique cut him off. "I told Animal not to bring you novice niggas in on this, but he wouldn't listen, and now look where the fuck we are." She went off. She was more upset at herself for what had happened in the bathroom than at Abel jumping the gun, but he was the most convenient target for her rage. "Where's Animal?"

"I ain't seen him, but the bitch darted out the back door," Abel told her.

"Then you better hope we can catch her before she gets too far to salvage this clusterfuck of a mission, or you're going to be the one to tell Animal that you blew his best shot at getting his kids back."

***

When Red Sonja set out that night, she had expected it to be one of high risks, and if God showed her favor, it would be a high reward. She was on fire in the streets. Tiger Lily's agents were leaving no stones unturned in search of her, making it difficult for her to bust the necessary moves she had set out to make, and she was getting desperate. It was desperation that made her double-cross her best chance at coming out on top. The Animal.

When Sonja first showed up on his doorstep, she had been genuine about needing Animal's help. If anybody could protect her daughter from the bullshit her *stepmother,* Tiger Lily, was trying to pull, it was him. She had planned to keep Animal on watchdog duties while she quietly made her play to usurp Lilith as the distributor of the Blue Dream pipeline, but then the unthinkable happened. Gucci was murdered, and both their children were taken hostage. Animal now had skin in the game.

Shitting on Animal and snatching the formula from Abel had been a decision she hadn't made easily. Outside of her father, Animal was the only man she could recall that had put her first. In all the time she had known him, whether she was right or wrong, he would always rise to the occasion when it came to defending her honor or heart. He had so quickly fallen head over heels for Celeste and the story Sonja had packed with her that she'd almost felt shameful for using his one weakness against him—his heart.

And then she recalled how he had rejected her for, in her opinion, a woman who would never understand him like she did. With Sonja, he could've been great. With Gucci, he was simply pitiful. The man she had met in that California beach house that night was a far cry from the man she had watched singlehandedly turn the tide of a drug war in Old San Juan. Still, he was all she had at the time. Gucci had fed his heart but snuffed out his fire, which forced Sonja to take matters into her own hands and fast-track her plans.

Red Sonja's plan was a simple one. She had tapped into her father's network and managed to piece together a small crew of some of his lesser-used contacts. Small-timers who were under the radar. They would be crucial in helping her get the ball rolling regarding manufacturing and distributing the drugs. She could've made a bigger play if she could've reached out to some of the heavier guys who did business with Poppito, but they were all tucked into Lilith's pocket now. She didn't mind starting out small because she knew that the floodgates would eventually open once she got the drugs processed and on the streets. Sonja had been raised around drugs and drug dealers all her life, so one thing she knew was how to bubble. Her pot would boil quietly and then bubble over.

She reasoned that she had a decent enough head start on Animal, and by the time he managed to track her down, she would have pieced together a crew at least big enough to keep him off her back, but she should have known better. Behind those tender brown eyes and infectious smile beat the heart of an apex predator. Animal was the ultimate hunter, and once he was set on you, nothing short of God could stop him, and considering how many times he had cheated death, that was still up for debate. She had been stupid in her handling of the situation. If she would double-cross him, she should've killed him and saved herself a major headache.

Abel showing up unexpectedly had thrown a hitch into her plans. It wasn't that she feared the twin. He was a formidable adversary but nowhere near the monster his brother, Cain, was. On the other hand, his presence meant that her baby daddy and his merry band of serial killers likely weren't far behind. His catching up with her so quickly was a problem she wasn't prepared to deal with, so she hauled ass out of the spot.

She felt bad about abandoning Zion the way she had. The youngster had impressed her with the way he handled the situation. He tore into Abel with a fierceness that she hadn't expected. Zion was holding his own for a while, and then things started going left. When Sonja dipped out, Zion was on his back, and Abel was stomping Valentino like a roach that refused to die. She couldn't bring herself to watch the fight until the end, but she didn't hold it against Zion. There was no doubt in her mind that Zion was a tough kid. He just wasn't as seasoned as Abel. If Zion managed to survive the confrontation, their paths might cross again, and she'd see if she could extract the killer she suspected was hiding in Zion. If not, it just wasn't to be. For as much promise as Zion had shown, at the end of the day, she was lining him up to be a pawn, just like the rest. On the upside, she kept her word when she promised Zion that she would make good use of him. Had it not been for his sacrifice, she may not have had the opportunity to escape.

Sonja pushed and bumped her way through the frenzied crowd. Then she heard a loud crash somewhere in the distance like furniture being smashed. However, she never broke her stride. She spied a group of people stampeding through a fire door in the back and headed straight for it. She breathed a sigh of relief only when she had made it out of the spot and felt the night air on her face. She was thankful that she had dodged a bullet and was now home free . . . But her moment of hope was dashed to hell when she heard a familiar voice snarl, "You!"

Red Sonja coming out of that door had both shocked and enraged Animal. It was as if seeing her again brought on a flood of emotions and hurtful memories. Here was someone who had once claimed to love him, then who had recklessly burned down his entire life. Anything akin to the passion he had once felt toward her was gone and replaced by pure fury.

The first thing Animal did was go for his gun. Knowing him like the back of her hand, Sonja had expected as much. She grabbed his wrist, pausing his draw, and hit him on the side of his head with her elbow, hard enough to daze him. "Now, is that any way to greet your baby mama? Give me a kiss and show me how much you miss me," she taunted.

"Rotten whore. Only thing I'm going to give you is what you gave me . . . pain!" Then to both Animal and Red Sonja's shock, he hauled off and slapped her. The slap was so vicious that it busted her lip and shifted a tooth. Animal had never raised his hand to a woman, let alone one who had gifted him a child, but the slap was more of a reaction than something he'd thought about. For the briefest of seconds, he allowed himself to feel pity for Red Sonja, and that was all the time she needed to react.

Sonja kicked Animal in the nuts, doubling him over in pain. She tried to run, but he grabbed her by the back of her jacket and yanked her back. She threw two more wild punches, which Animal blocked. A few years before, she could've caught him with that move. "So, the student thinks he's better than the teacher now?" She smiled devilishly. "It was Gladiator who taught you how to kill, but me who showed you how to fight. Let's see what you've learned."

Red Sonja broke Animal's grip on her jacket, and they both took a backward step. Animal tried to grab her, but Sonja danced out of his reach and hit him with two quick punches to the jaw. She tried the move again, but this time, Animal was ready and countered with another slap. However, he held back on it that time. Animal didn't want to hurt her, and she could see it in his eyes, which would give her the advantage. One of the most important lessons her father had taught her while growing up was: *When in battle, leave nothing on the table. You go all in.* And so, she did.

Sonja was coming back at Animal. He was expecting her to throw a punch, so it caught him off guard when she caught him with a whirling kick to the ribs. He gasped, trying to keep the air from escaping his lungs. Another elbow was launched at the side of his head, this one connecting with his ear. She struck him so hard that, for a minute, Animal thought she had deafened him because he was now hearing everything as if he were underwater. He wanted to keep the fight respectable, but it was clear that Sonja was out for blood. She threw another kick. This one he caught and held her leg suspended. She tried some movie stunt and left her feet to bring the other leg around, intent on taking off Animal's head. This blow, he didn't bother to block. He simply let her leg go. Sonja fell hard on her ass. She now found herself looking up at a very armed and very angry Animal. She had seen many men on the business end of Animal's pistol and knew what came with it.

"I didn't teach you that one," Sonja half-joked, trying to ignore the pain shooting from her tailbone to the base of her skull.

"You'd be surprised what you learn when handling snakes," he replied.

"So, I'm a snake now?" Sonja faked hurt.

"I could think of some more fitting names that I'd like to call you, but I'm trying to keep in mind that you're still my daughter's mother. What the hell is wrong with you, Sonja? I'm out here risking it all to save our babies, and you sabotage my plan. I'd think the fact that Lilith took our daughter along with my son would make you at least try to be honorable for once in your life, or don't you even give a fuck?"

"How dare you question my love for my daughter? I've been the one busting my ass to raise her for the last three years on my own," she spat.

"A daughter that I knew nothing about until you dumped all this shit on my front door," Animal fired back. "If I'd known anything about Celeste, I would've been in her life from day one, same as I was with T.J. I would've thought you knew my heart enough to see that I ain't no fuck nigga who shrugs off his responsibilities."

"And that's exactly why I never reached out," Sonja revealed. "Tayshawn, I don't even know what to call what we had in Puerto Rico, but I know it wasn't what you had with Gucci back here. She occupied a space in your heart that I had never even glimpsed. For once in your life, you were at peace, and I knew that telling you about Celeste would've destroyed that peace. Gucci didn't strike me as a woman who would've readily accepted a side chick's baby." Tears welled in her eyes at the admission.

"You weren't a side chick, Sonja. And whether Gucci would've accepted Celeste or not, I still would've stepped up. Instead, you robbed me of the choice," Animal said passionately.

"And that's my one regret."

"I hear all that, but that still doesn't explain why you would run off with the only bargaining chip we had to save these kids." Animal returned to business.

"You still don't get it, do you?" Sonja shook her head sadly. "Lilith was only toying with us, making us think that we had a snowball's chance in hell of forcing her hand on this. The Blue Dream is only important to her because cocaine and heroin are dying off, and designer drugs are the new wave. That Blue Dream can open doors for her that cocaine never could. It's important but not a deal-breaker. In addition to her Brotherhood contacts, Lilith has an army behind her. Most of the men loyal to my father are gone, and those left are mercenaries who will stand with the highest bidder. The only way to beat Lilith is at her own game, and that's by becoming the plug. Women like Lilith only respect people who can do something for them, and by us cornering the market on this, it creates a dependency. That's where our *real* negotiating power will come from."

Animal ran his hand through his curly mop in frustration. Had this been a younger version of him, when he was still heavy in the streets, his brain might've tricked him into finding the logic in Sonja's plan. Of course, that was a lifetime ago to him, but obviously, all Sonja could see was the broken young man who had helped her family overthrow a rival cartel. "There was a better way to go about this, baby girl. If only you had trusted me."

"You mean like I trusted you never to break my heart, and you ran off to another woman?" Sonja questioned.

"That isn't fair."

"Tell me about it," she chuckled. "So, what, now? You gonna shoot me if I don't give you the formula back?"

Animal looked at the gun in his hand. His pistols had become such an extension of him that he hadn't even realized he was holding them. He shoved the gun back into his pants. "Sonja, I'd never hurt you. At least not intentionally." He extended his hand to help her up.

"Forever the gentleman . . ." she smiled ". . . and that's where you always fuck up." Then she produced a gun and shot him in the chest twice.

"Bitch," Animal collapsed. He rolled around on the concrete, clutching his chest and gasping for air.

Sonja knelt over him and yanked down the front of his shirt. Just as she had hoped, he was wearing a vest. Fortunately, the Kevlar had taken the worst of the impact. He would be sore for the next few days but would live. "Good job, papi," she whispered before disappearing into the night.

***

The last thing Diabolique expected to see when she came out the back door, which led to the parking lot, was Animal on the ground. She immediately rushed to her mentor and fell on her knees beside him. He was clearly in pain, and for a minute, she thought that he had been shot or stabbed. "You hurt?" she asked in a concerned tone, hands exploring him, checking for wounds.

"Only my pride." He allowed her to help him to his feet. His chest was throbbing like someone had hit him with a hammer.

"What happened to you?" Abel asked.

"Probably the same thing that happened to your face. Red Sonja." Animal noticed the bruises and scrapes covering Abel's face. Someone had done a number on him.

"Got into it with two of her soldiers inside the joint," Abel explained.

"From the looks of your grill, I hope whoever did this to you is no longer amongst the living," Animal stated. Abel was silent.

"Pretty boy was about to blow dude's brains out, then security came, and we had to slide or risk getting caught," Diabolique interjected. "I was wrong about him, and he's Dog Pound material after all."

Abel gave her a look that said thank you.

"She was in there rolling heavy. I didn't expect her to have put a crew together so quickly," Diabolique changed the subject.

"That ain't on you. I should've seen this one coming. Sonja is the ultimate puppet master, good at getting people to do shit for her right before she bleeds them and leaves them for dead. I'd forgotten how ruthless my baby mama was, but she graciously reminded me." Animal fingered the holes in his shirt.

"You think the cats we clashed with are the ones who are gonna help her get this shit on the streets?" Diabolique asked.

Animal thought about what Sonja had said earlier about her plans to become the plug. "No, those were foot soldiers. Sonja wouldn't risk anyone instrumental to her plans by having them in a dive like this. There's another piece on the chessboard that we haven't seen yet."

Chapter 25

Raffa Khan drew more than a few curious stares from the people going in and out of the establishment he was lingering in front of, a seedy-looking building that stood in the shadow of the West Side Highway in Manhattan. He was dressed in a dark-colored business suit and leather shoes that cost more than some of the residents in the building made in a month of working or hustling. Seeing him standing at the suspect location, dressed in his expensive finery, most probably assumed that he was either law enforcement or a john looking for a cheap thrill. Still, neither of those assumptions would've hit anywhere near the truth of who or what Raffa Khan was.

By day, Khan held an executive position at an accounting firm based in Washington, D.C., but under cover of darkness, he was an agent of the Brotherhood of Blood. These days, Khan didn't do much fieldwork anymore. In fact, he rarely left the comforts of the cushy life he'd built for himself in D.C. He only dropped the façade of accountant and stepped into his true self when it came to matters sensitive enough that required his personal attention.

That's why he spent most of the day driving up from D.C. to New York.

He looked down at his silver Rolex to check the time. The hand had only moved five minutes since he'd last looked, but it felt like five hours. He hated waiting. It wasn't that he was an impatient man. In fact, Khan had made his bones by being patient. He always took his time when it came to getting something he wanted, whether it was something as complicated as planning a hostile takeover of a rival company or as simple as selecting a steak from the supermarket. He always took his time going over every possible route of success or consequence of failure for his action. Only then would he make his move. So, it wasn't that Khan was impatient; he just hated to be kept waiting.

After trying to be solicited by a prostitute for the third time, Khan was ready to call it and leave. He was retrieving his cell phone from the pocket of his suit jacket when a silver Denali pulled to the curb a few feet away from him. The heavy bass from a rap song that Khan couldn't identify rattled through the truck every time it dropped. Thick clouds of weed smoke billowed out from the partially cracked tinted windows like a small fog threatening to sweep over the neighborhood.

The first one from the car was the driver. He was well-built, with long, black hair he wore in two Pocahontas braids that spilled from beneath his fitted Yankee cap. He gave Khan a curt nod before taking up a position leaning against the truck's hood, thumbs hooked into the belt loops of his jeans and his size thirteen Tims crossed over each other.

The passenger came next. Like Khan, he was also dressed in a suit, but he wore no tie, and the first three buttons of his black shirt were left undone. However, where the driver wore a mean scowl, a smile was plastered across the passenger's face. It wasn't a toothy grin. More like that of someone who had a secret he couldn't wait to tell. Khan couldn't help but think how much of a demon he looked like with his coal-black skin, perfect white teeth, and green eyes. They weren't like regular green eyes. It was more like someone had pressed two jades into his sockets. As harmless as he might've appeared, the green-eyed man was one of the most dangerous that Khan had ever met who the Brotherhood hadn't trained. The young Black dude's name rang bells all over North America and even in a few third world countries.

"Raffa Khan." The green-eyed man extended his hand.

Khan hesitated for a second or three before shaking it. "You're late, K-Dawg. That shit may be okay in the hood, but punctuality counts for a lot in the circles you're trying to move in."

"Wise words spoken by a wise man," K-Dawg acknowledged. "I won't insult you further by wasting your time telling you why I was late, but I can assure you that it won't happen again." What K-Dawg was reluctant to say was that he had been trying to track Justice down for most of the day. He'd finally found him about noon that day at an after-hours spot, shit-faced drunk and entertaining two skanks. He was in such bad shape that K-Dawg had considered making him sit out the meeting and go alone. The only things that stopped him were that there was nobody in his crew that he trusted more than Justice and that you didn't meet with a man like Raffa Khan without having eyes in the back of your head.

"I appreciate that," Khan said honestly. Generally, when dealing with the young street guys, respect and etiquette were like a foreign language to them, but K-Dawg had proven to be different. Though in the short time Khan had known him, K-Dawg showed a knack for doing the unexpected, which was part of why Khan was suspicious about why K-Dawg was there to meet with him instead of the man he was expecting. "Where's Shai?" He got right to it.

K-Dawg shrugged. "He had some other shit to do. I'm here, though."

"The information that'll be traded here is too sensitive to be carried by a third party," Khan explained.

"Which is why I've come personally, so that you can pass the information directly to the source," K-Dawg countered.

The cagey look in K-Dawg's eyes let Khan know he wouldn't let it go until he told him something, so he decided to be blunt. "This was supposed to be a meeting of bosses. Respectfully, you ain't a boss."

K-Dawg's green eyes flickered when the statement sparked the fuse of that side of him that nobody wanted to see. However, thanks to years of practice, he could swallow the urge to test Khan's chin. Instead, he decided words would better serve him instead of fists. "I'm gonna ignore that slight and hit you with a fact. Only one of us is standing here with somebody to answer to. I ain't that dude by a long shot. That boss talk is cute when you ain't in the presence of people still bleeding out onto the asphalt. King Shai Clark agreed to turn a blind eye and let us take this little leap of faith, but rest assured, it'll be me doing all the jumping. You got something to say, then I'm the one who needs to hear it."

Khan waited a few ticks before responding. He had already fleshed out what he planned to say to Shai, but K-Dawg showing up forced him to revise his pitch. "There has been an adjustment to the scheduled delivery date."

"An adjustment as in . . . We'll have to wait another few days to pick up the product? Or an adjustment like y'all managed to get the supply sunk by a kid with a gun and a broken heart?" K-Dawg smirked knowingly. He could see Khan trying to come up with the proper response to spin him, so K-Dawg saved him the trouble. "The sinking of the *Red Widow* has been on the news all day. I hear it's being played up as an oil leak that started the fire, but I think we both know different, don't we?"

"Animal was supposed to be a La Peste Negra problem," Khan said.

"Li'l bro was our responsibility, but the bullshit you and your homegirl pulled with his wife and kids have now made him everybody's problem," Justice cut in from his position at the curb.

K-Dawg flashed Justice a disapproving look before turning back to Khan. "Justice has a bit of a personal stake in this, so sometimes he can't help speaking from his heart even if it's out of turn."

"Never apologize for having someone in your company who doesn't sugarcoat his feelings. A man with a strong opinion could be the difference between life and death in this game we've chosen to play."

"This we can agree on. As I recall, you generally keep the company with the same type of man. Where's your shadow?" K-Dawg asked. He was referring to Bastille.

"Tying up a loose end," Khan replied.

"I hope that loose end is getting this delivery straightened out. I've been on the campaign trail pushing this dream you and Tiger Lily sold me on like a presidential election. Many players are lined up waiting to spend their coins with me because I made them guarantees on this package. Once K-Dawg gives his word, the only thing that can make him break it is death."

"No need for the theatrics. You'll get what was promised. We managed to salvage enough of it from the wreck of the *Red Widow*. We'll make up the rest once we're done manufacturing the new batch."

"And how long is that going to take?"

"Shouldn't be more than a few days at most," Khan assured him, trying to sound more confident than he was. He still hadn't heard back from Lilith about whether they had recovered the chemical formula that had been stolen from the courier.

"That may be too long," K-Dawg told him, wheels already spinning as to how he would solve this new problem of being short on the supply he'd promised the streets.

"You can't rush greatness, K-Dawg," Khan said cockily.

"Nor can you keep hungry wolves at bay for too long before the pack turns on you," K-Dawg countered. "I'll take whatever drugs you have for now so we can get the ball rolling, but I need the rest of what's owed to us ASAP."

"Fair enough," Khan agreed. "I'll text you an address where your people can pick up the stuff."

"No need. I already know about the garage on Bedford Ave.," K-Dawg told him, much to Khan's surprise. "Surely you didn't think the Brotherhood were the only ones with eyes and ears all over this city." He strolled back to the car. "Make this right, Khan," he said over his shoulder before hopping in.

Justice gave Khan a final, hard stare before climbing behind the wheel and pulling the SUV out into traffic.

***

"Bitch-ass nigga," Justice grumbled more to himself than anyone else. He pushed the SUV through Manhattan while K-Dawg was resting in the passenger seat, putting the finishing touches on the blunt he was rolling.

"Who? Khan?" K-Dawg asked, licking the ends of the cigar to seal it. "He a'ight, at least as long as he's still putting money in our pockets, which he is."

"All money ain't good, Keyshawn," Justice told him, weaving in and out of traffic, slapping his horn occasionally to alert the slower-moving drivers that he was coming through. He hated driving in Manhattan, especially Midtown.

"So, what you saying? You ain't trying to get this paper no more?" K-Dawg gave him a quizzical look.

"Nigga, you know I'm always about a dollar. Since we were kids, I was on my shit, even before you were, grasshopper," Justice reminded him.

"Yeah, you put me in the game, but I taught you how to play to win," K-Dawg shot back. "What's with you and this shitty-ass attitude the last couple of days?"

"What you talking about?" Justice faked ignorance.

"I'm talking about this chip you've been walking around with on your shoulder," K-Dawg clarified.

"You know I don't trust Khan or none of these Brotherhood muthafuckas, for that matter."

"And you'd be a fool if you did. Don't think for a minute that just because I'm smiling and being all diplomatic that I don't understand the nature of these people we're dealing with. My head is on swivel at all times," K-Dawg said.

"Then why crawl so deep into bed with someone you don't trust?" Justice asked.

"Because they're a means to an end. Doing business with the Brotherhood will change our lives, bro," K-Dawg promised.

"And that's what I'm afraid of. K-Dawg, we've both seen what these jokers are capable of, and I think we can both agree that they're playing on an entirely different level, even bigger than Poppito, when you put all the pieces together. This cult, organization . . . whatever the fuck you wanna call it, is tied into some heavy shit, and I don't know. This is the deep end, brother."

"Then I guess it's a good thing I can swim." K-Dawg exhaled a large puff of smoke. Justice's face was still sour, which was starting to irritate K-Dawg. "Justice, me and you are closer than brothers. I never had a reason to question you, but right now, I'm having a hard time understanding your attitude. We're on the verge of closing a deal that isn't just going to make us rich . . . We'll have generational wealth. We'll be able to ball until we die and still leave our kids and grandkids with more money than they'll ever know what to do with. Right now, I'm happy enough to bust a nut in my jeans, but your ass is sitting over there like the girl fresh off a breakup and scared of getting hurt again. This ain't the nigga I came up out of the mud with."

"I just wanna make sure that we're not left hanging if this shit all blows up," Justice downplayed his apprehension. It went far deeper than that, but pouring his heart out to K-Dawg wouldn't do him any good, at least not at that moment.

"Justice, I got no illusions about who and what Tiger Lily is, but I also know who and what we are. The Brotherhood isn't the only one capable of changing small countries' fates, and we did it with less to work with. I know this, which is why you'd be a fool to think I'd get into bed with her without having a surefire way to declaw the tiger if it comes to it."

"This shit is just so deep, man," Justice said with a sigh.

"Then put on your hip boots and watch where you step." K-Dawg fired up his blunt. "Justice, you act like we ain't never been the flies on the wall before. These secret spy games Lilith and Khan are playing ain't got nothing to do with us. Our job is to flood these streets with product and stack. Anything beyond that is above your pay grade."

"Don't you mean *our* pay grades?" Justice corrected. "I know you like to think that you're the sharpest pencil in the box, but I've always been the one with the long-range vision. Our strengths have always gone hand in hand, which is why we've succeeded."

"Has that changed, and somebody forgot to tell me?" K-Dawg asked accusingly. "Bro, don't think I haven't noticed that you been acting real funny style over the last couple of days. What? You still in your bag because of that shit with your niece and nephew getting snatched?"

"I don't know them kids well enough to care about them like that," Justice lied.

"Bullshit. You forget that we've known each other all our lives. You value family more than anything, Justice. Even when your mom let that dope-fiend-ass Eddy treat y'all like shit, you still worshipped her trifling ass. I get it. Love is important, but love ain't gonna take your ass out of poverty. Besides, them kids will probably be better off with the Brotherhood. Probably end up at some fancy school and grow up to speak all proper and shit."

"Or trained killers," Justice countered.

"Like growing up with Animal would be any different. No disrespect, but what would happen if Animal had lived and was left to raise them kids on his own?"

Justice was silent. K-Dawg was still under the assumption that Animal had died on the *Red Widow*, and Justice hadn't seen fit to correct him. Admittedly, he wasn't too sure about his baby brother's survival either. He had been in bad shape when Justice pulled him out of the drink, and a lesser man would have likely succumbed to his injuries, but Animal had never been a lesser anything. Justice had been pleasantly surprised when he spotted Animal back on his feet and on the hunt so soon after his near-death experience. It spoke volumes to a resiliency that Justice had only heard whispered about over the years. To see it firsthand made him proud. He was every bit the demon that the streets said he was, and every bit the headache Justice had raised him to be.

"I'll tell you," K-Dawg continued. ". . . They'll grow up to be just like us, if not worse. Homie, if I thought that they were actually in harm's way, then I'd be the first one to grab a strap and lead the charge straight down that old bitch's throat to get them back, but I haven't, and it's probably for the same reason you ain't made a move. Now, the way Tiger Lily handled this was foul, but is she totally wrong? You're salty because of the collateral damage, but deep down, a part of you knows that those kids have a better chance of becoming something with her than they do out here with us mixed up in how we live. Letting Lilith keep those kids and raise them up beats the alternative, which would be going into the foster care system and coming out as the next generation of Road Dawgz. So for the good of everyone involved, let it go."

"This bitch snatches my family and kills my little brother and his wife, and you think I'm just supposed to let that ride?" Justice asked.

"I never said all that. Animal was a soldier, so he understood the risks. But the minute he decided to bring a knife to a gunfight, he was doomed. Baby bro should've never been on that boat. His death was tragic, but it's all a part of the game. As far as what they did to Gucci, that's another story. On my sister's soul, somebody is gonna wear that, Justice. But right now, I just need you to fall back and trust me."

*****

Khan took his time walking back to his car, processing information in his head as he did. His brain was like that of a supercomputer, constantly whirling and problem-solving. His current problem was K-Dawg. He had some nerve speaking to him the way he had. Khan had sat in the presence of kings and commanded their respect, so who was this street punk who dared to address him as if they were equals? It took all his resolve not to kill K-Dawg where he stood when he had ordered Khan "*make it right.*" Men like Khan didn't take orders; they gave them. This was something the leader of Los Negro Muerte would learn soon enough.

Khan was upset with K-Dawg, but Lilith was the real source of his anger. It had been her mishandling of the situation that forced Khan to have to suffer K-Dawg's presence. When she approached him with her plan of flooding the streets with drugs to finance the war she planned to wage against the Brotherhood, it had been a sound one, which is why Khan had agreed to help. By right of succession, he would've inherited a seat on the Order's council when one of the elders passed next, but he was impatient. He didn't want to wait to hold the reins of power, and Lilith had promised to be able to fast-track his ascension. Siding with her had been risky, but the potential rewards were too great for him not to take the gamble.

Upon their initial execution of the scheme, things had been going smoothly. Khan had arranged for Nicodemus to die, which would open up his seat on the council, and Lilith had brokered a deal with Shai Clark to receive his blessings for them to distribute the Blue Dream on the streets of New York. They had a clear path to victory, but Lilith deviated when she went after Red Sonja and her daughter. Khan tried to make her understand that they didn't need the girl. Lilith had already nearly taken total control of Poppito's cartel, and once he sat on the council, her path back to the Brotherhood would be cleared, but Lilith was determined to bring the child into the fold. She believed that the girl would fulfill some type of prophecy that would give her domain over the Order and the streets. It took some doing, but she was eventually able to kidnap Sonja's daughter, but in taking possession of the child, she also inherited all the problems that came with her, the biggest being her estranged father.

Lilith had downplayed the threat Animal repre- sented, assuring Khan that it would be dealt with as if it were that simple, but Khan knew better. What Lilith didn't know, and he had no plans on telling her, was that he was already familiar with Tayshawn Torres. Anybody who dealt in the business of mur- der had likely heard the seemingly tall tales about the baby-faced killer known as The Animal, but he hadn't officially made it onto Khan's radar until Priest. Priest was a member of the Brotherhood that

Khan had a great deal of respect for. He was a member of the council, although not of the same standing as Tiger Lily or Nicodemus, but a respected member, nonetheless. What adhered Khan to Priest was that he was no puppet of the Order like so many. Instead, he was a man of his own ideals. It was evident from the first time Khan met Priest that he was different, but he wouldn't find out why until he got to know him.

When Khan was first initiated into the Brotherhood, Priest had only recently returned to the fold after being absent for several years. There were whispers throughout the halls about his return and the circumstances surrounding it. After serving in the last American war at the behest of the Brotherhood, Priest hadn't returned directly to the Mountain. Instead, he had spent the years immediately following in Miami to service a drug lord they called Poppa. No one could say why Priest was so fiercely loyal to the gangster, nor why the Order chose to turn a blind eye to Priest's extracurricular activities with Poppa.

Since his return, Priest had started drinking heavily, and sometimes when he'd had too much, he would sit with the initiates and wow them with tales of the battles he fought and the wicked men he had killed in Miami as well as New York. His stories were frowned upon by the elders, but the initiates loved them. None more than Khan.

One of those nights when Priest had been drinking heavily, he told Khan how he had lost his eye and the woman and child he had been forced to abandon by the Brotherhood. Priest was a hard man and made no excuses for what he had done in life, but when he spoke of his family, there was genuine regret in his voice. This made Khan think of his friends back in Cuba and how he had watched them slaughtered when Tiger Lily and Nicodemus claimed the then teenaged Khan for the Brotherhood. He too was forced to give up those he cared about because of the Order.

Not long after that, Priest would take a leave of absence from the Brotherhood once more. It would be years before Khan would see him again. By this time, Khan had come up through the ranks of the Brotherhood, and Priest only made the occasional visit to the Mountain when bound by his duty as a council member, which is why it surprised Khan when Priest showed up at his accounting office in D.C.

He had come to Khan for help with his son, who had managed to earn himself some very powerful enemies. Khan was familiar with Animal, or at least his résumé. In Khan's line of work, it was important that killers knew other killers, especially ones as skilled as Animal. He was familiar with his exploits but had never made the connection that he was the son Priest had abandoned all those years earlier. Priest wanted Khan to use his influence to support his claim that Animal be allowed into the Brotherhood by birthright. It was a last-ditch attempt to save the life of a kid he had never done anything for. Unfortunately, Khan had to deny his request. It wasn't just because Animal was already far too old and far too street poisoned to be allowed membership. In truth, Animal would've made a welcome addition to their ranks. No, Khan had to deny Priest because, by that point, he was already knee-deep in planning his own little coup of the Order, and to get involved with Priest's cause could have potentially exposed what he was up to. For him, saying no to someone he had once considered a brother and inspiration wasn't personal. It was a business decision. Thinking back on it, if he had agreed to support Priest in the matter, he could've probably avoided the headache he was currently dealing with.

His thoughts turned back to his coconspirator, Bastille. He'd sent his executioner in pursuit of the Black Lotus, and from what he heard, the mission hadn't been going well. The Lotus had managed to murder a half dozen of Khan's agents and badly injured Bastille. Khan tried to rescind Bastille and have someone else take up the cause. Bastille was too important to Khan's plans to lose, but the executioner wouldn't hear of it. Instead, he insisted that the blood of the Lotus stain his hands. Khan had known Bastille long enough to know there was no swaying him when his mind was set on something. The last time Bastille checked in, he had tracked Black Lotus to Virginia, which surprised Khan. There was only one reason he could think of for her to be in the state—the Mountain. Khan had launched a successful campaign that marked her a traitor, so she would be hard-pressed to find refuge within the Brotherhood. Still, the Black Lotus was a legend within the halls of the Mountain, so there was the off chance that she could dredge up some who still respected her enough to lend assistance—much like the crew who had rescued her from Bastille in New York.

Too many variables came into play when dealing with the Black Lotus. She was the thread that could unravel the whole quilt. She needed to die before she could cause more trouble than she already had. This was part of why Khan didn't raise too much of an argument when Bastille insisted that he be allowed to continue his hunt. His executioner had never failed him when dispatched, but the fact that Bastille had missed his last two scheduled check-ins made Khan insecure. Had he succeeded in killing the Black Lotus before she reached the Mountain, Khan would've known about it. Even if he had failed, and the Lotus had reached the Mountain and found refuge, there would've been talk of it. The fact that a wall of silence had been erected between Khan and all his agents told him that something was wrong. He needed to get back down I-95 to find out what.

He had just arrived back at his car, a modest Lexus 350, parked on a side block lined with residential buildings. He stopped short of the SUV and was fishing around in his pocket for the key when he caught movement in his peripheral. A Hispanic woman stepped from the doorway of one of the buildings.

She was pale with bleached blond hair with dark roots. A cigarette dangled lazily from her painted lips that she seemed to be having trouble lighting with the cheap plastic lighter. She was fairly attractive, but hard living had started to catch up with her. From the too short skirt and the imitation leather jacket with nothing but a bra underneath, it didn't take a rocket scientist to know what her game was.

"What's good, papi? Can I trouble you for a ride?" She swigged from the pint of cheap whiskey clutched in one of her bony hands.

"I doubt we're going anywhere near the same direction," Khan said over his shoulder, hitting the remote to disarm his car alarm. He had pressing issues to deal with and no time to dismiss yet another prostitute. He couldn't wait to get out of the cesspool of a city and back to D.C.

"Don't be like that." She invaded his space. "I'll give you a good deal on account of you being so handsome. I'll let you get the ATM special for a hundred bucks." She flipped her skirt up to flash her shaggy love nest. Khan's eyes instinctively went to her exposed sex. It was only for a second, but that was more than enough time.

The lighter in her hand suddenly found its spark at the same time she spat a mouthful of the cheap liquor at him. The fireball singed Khan's face and stung his eyes. Then reflexively, his arms went up to cover his face, and he felt the searing pain of the blade as it bit into his forearm. He reached for the pistol holstered under his suit jacket, but something snaked around his neck from behind before he could clear it. A second attacker had joined the fray, choking him with a cord.

"Raffa Khan, your presence is requested back at the Mountain," the man holding the cord hissed in his ear as he pulled it tighter. His voice was slightly muffled by the wool ski mask he wore.

Initially, Khan had thought K-Dawg had sent the couple to double-cross him, but he had been wrong. Instead, they were agents of the Brotherhood.

"Stop struggling and come along quietly. I'd hate to have to mess up that pretty face." The woman inched closer, holding the bottle and lighter up threateningly.

Khan threw himself backward, slamming the man against his SUV, which caused him to loosen his grip on the cord. Then moving swiftly, he went for his pistol again. Without removing it from the holster, he fired the gun twice through his jacket and hit the man in the stomach, causing him to lose his grip on the cord. Now that he was free, he was ready to play.

The blonde took another swig from the bottle and geared up for another fireball. Khan waited until the moment she flicked the lighter to fire a high, straight kick to her hand. The woman howled in pain as the fireball turned on her and ignited her hair and the imitation leather jacket. Khan wouldn't go quietly . . . nor would she.

He then turned his attention back to the man trying to crawl into the street. He was likely trying to get

himself run over by a car, but he would have no such
luck. Khan had questions that he needed answers to.

"Not so fast." Khan pulled him back onto the curb.
He grabbed the man's shirt and laid him on the hood
of the car. Khan ripped off the black ski mask to get
a look at him. He was a young Black man, about 20
or 21, with a close-cut fade. Khan didn't recognize
him, so he doubted he was a Brother of any standing. He was probably only slightly higher on the food
chain . . . cannon fodder. This is what made the attack
such a slap in the face. Still, he had been sent by the
Order, and he needed to know why. "Who sent you?"

The man remained silent.

"We'll do it your way then," Khan told him before
slinging the man over his shoulder and stuffing him
in the trunk.

Khan drove down near the South Street Seaport.
At that hour, the streets were empty, which would
serve his purpose nicely. He found an isolated area
in the shadow of where FDR Drive met the Brooklyn
Bridge, killed the engine, then opened the trunk. The
assassin looked in bad shape but hadn't yet passed
due to all the blood he'd lost. That was good because
Khan needed him to be lucid enough to answer his
questions.

He yanked the man from the trunk and let him
collapse at his feet. "I need a name. Who sent you to
bring me in?" The list of Brotherhood members with

balls enough to move against Raffa Khan was short. The list of those with authority to give the order was even shorter. Khan waited a few seconds. It looked like his hostage was ready to talk, but instead, he spat blood onto one of Khan's expensive shoes. He was a tough nut, Khan gave him that. Little did he know, though, Khan had ways of breaking even the hardest of men.

"You know my name, little one, but you are about to learn my title." Khan opened the passenger-side door of his Lexus and retrieved something from the glove box. He returned carrying what looked like a small men's grooming kit—the kind that usually held a small nail file and a comb. "It was a title bestowed upon me by far better men than you or I." He spread the case open on the car roof, just out of sight of the man lying on the curb. He rummaged through the case until he found the instrument he sought, a thin set of pliers. "To most, I am simply Raffa Khan, an accountant and a businessman. That is the skin that I wear in this world. But in the shadow of the Mountain, I am known as the Grand Inquisitor."

Khan spent the next fifteen using the pliers to break off teeth in the man's mouth. He could've yanked them out, which would've been painful, but breaking them ensured the pain would last. To the man's credit, Khan had to work through nearly the entire upper row of his mouth before the man finally croaked a name weakly. "Nicodemus."

"Impossible!" Khan said, unable to hide his surprise. He had personally procured the poison that one of his attendants had slipped into the elder's food. It was a particularly nasty toxin created from the venom of a box jellyfish, administered in small doses over several weeks. Even someone with as high a resistance as the Master of Poisons couldn't have recovered from that. "How?"

By the time he finished with the man, he had extracted not only all his teeth but his secrets as well. There was hardly anything left of the would-be assassin, yet he still lived. "If you're going to kill me, then be done with it. I am a sworn Brother, and to die in service to the Order is an honor," he said defiantly.

Khan pitifully gazed at what was left of his face. "The young ones are always in such a rush to die. You've spent so much time under the Mountain with your head up the elders' asses that you've actually convinced yourself that it is an honor to die for them," he chuckled. "I was once like you—until I could get out and sample the world's pleasures. What my experiences have taught me is there is no honor in dying broke and subservient to a group of old farts who could give less than a fuck about you. Still, I'm happy to accommodate you."

Khan pulled the man's pants down to his knees. He prodded the soft flesh of his inner thigh with his fingers until he found what he was looking for, a gentle pulse just beneath the skin. "You took on a hunt without being totally familiar with your prey.

This tells me that you're a gambling man. So, I offer you a game of chance." He jabbed the thin pliers into his thigh, nicking the femoral artery. Blood squirted out and began to pool beneath the man. "If you're lucky, someone will come along and find you before you bleed to death. Then you can wait on one of the members of the Brotherhood to come and snuff you out for failing at your mission. If not . . ." He shrugged before wiping the excess blood off the pliers on the man's pants before returning them to their case. "Either way, you'll know death, but I'm afraid there'll be no honor in it. Die well or don't. I don't give a shit."

Leaving the man to whatever his fate would be, Khan got back in his car and pulled off. He pushed through the streets of New York, engine and mind racing. His interrogation had yielded a story that seemed almost impossible to believe, but it made too much sense to be a lie. It filled in too many blanks. According to the assassin, a dark-haired woman had been responsible for Nicodemus's miraculous recovery. He claimed it had been the work of black magic. Khan knew the woman he spoke of had to have been the Black Lotus. Khan knew the Lotus well, and though she may have been many things, a trafficker in the dark arts wasn't one of them. Maybe there was more to the Maiden Sword than he knew.

If the Black Lotus had indeed reached Nicodemus and managed to stir him, no less, it confirmed two things that Khan had already feared: Bastille was certainly dead, and his problems had gone from bad to worse. Lilith's plan be damned. It was time to bring this little game to an end. With that in mind, he pulled out his cell and played his trump card.

PART VII

PEOPLE ARE STRANGE

Chapter 26

Kahllah and Artemis went to his quarters to grab a few essentials that they would need. His small apartment was right off Nicodemus's chambers, so he was always close to his master. She had expected to walk in and find some musty library as she had with Nicodemus's room or possibly some other drab space more fitting of a monk than a man in the prime of his life. She was wrong.

The place Artemis called home wasn't a chamber but a quaint studio apartment. It sported hand-carved black wooden bookshelves loaded from floor to ceiling with books, a plush velvet couch, a glass coffee table cluttered with old issues of *Popular Science* magazine, and a couple of other periodicals. When he touched a switch on the wall, the track lights lining the ceiling illuminated the room in a soft glow. The place was more fitting for a young bachelor than a member of a secret order who had vowed to forsake all life's pleasures.

"What? Were you expecting me to be living in a hovel with dirt floors?" Artemis asked, noticing how she was studying the place.

"Yes, kind of," she admitted.

"I love my Order, but I love being comfortable more." Artemis gave her a wink. He grabbed a duffle bag from a small closet and tossed it to Kahllah.

"Thanks, but I'd rather have a blade." Kahllah looked at the empty bag. She saw a marine stamp on the side of it and wondered if Artemis had spent time in the military before entering the Brotherhood.

"Nicodemus said that you were impatient, and the more time I spend with you, the more I'm inclined to agree." Artemis walked past her to his bookshelf. He scanned the titles until he found the one he was looking for: *War and Peace* by Leo Tolstoy. He removed the book, and there was a clicking sound, followed by the shelf folding inward to reveal the hidden room behind it. The room was barely the size of a closet, but what it held made Kahllah's eyes widen. At least two-dozen weapons . . . pistols, rifles, swords, and axes were stored there. Artemis had a small armory hiding in his apartment.

"This strikes me as the cache of a man who was preparing for a war that he claims he didn't believe was coming," Kahllah said, inspecting the weapons.

"I've been preparing for war since the day I was born. And I never said I didn't believe it was coming. I just didn't expect it to come here," he replied. He started pulling weapons from their racks and putting them into the duffle bag, mostly bladed, and a few handguns. He also added what looked like a pipe bomb that was heavily bubble-wrapped.

Kahllah selected two pistols, a Glock and a P89. Part of her was tempted to snatch the AR-15 that he had on the wall too. It would serve them well if they found themselves outnumbered while trying to escape the Mountain, but it would also slow them down. In light of the situation, she felt they would have to make their exits as speedily as possible. With the guns tucked into the holsters at her hips, Kahllah was ready.

She was about to leave the weapon closet when something caught her eye. It was a sword with a blade that thickened as it went and curved to a thin needlepoint. She took it from the hook on the wall and held it in her hands, letting her eyes roam over the finely crafted weapon. The guns would be helpful, but this was more her speed. Its design reminded her of a stingray, and that's what she decided to name it. Now armed, the two headed out.

"So, what's the plan?" Kahllah asked once they had left Artemis's apartment.

"Once we're away from the Mountain? Get to the safe house as fast as possible and hope we can catch Nicodemus before he walks into whatever trap has been laid for him. He was headed for New York. If we hurry, we can get there before nightfall," Artemis told her.

"Sounds good, but there's only one problem. Most under the Mountain probably think that I'm a traitor, and Nicodemus has, no doubt, left word that I'm not to leave this place until he returns. So the guards at the gate aren't going to let me walk out of here, even in the company of the Lord of the Lash," she pointed out.

"That's why we aren't going through the gates. Instead, we'll use the same tunnels that got you in to get you out. The next town is only a few miles over. Once we reach it, we can procure transportation to New York."

"And if the tunnels are guarded as well?" Kahllah asked.

"Then we fight." He patted the duffle bag.

They continued their path to freedom, which took them past Nicodemus's quarters. The two guards who usually stood vigil outside his door were gone, which struck Kahllah as odd. As she thought on it, she hadn't seen much of anyone since their skirmish in the Hanging Garden with the Apes. The Mountain had been buzzing with activity earlier, but now, it felt deserted.

"You'd think that with all that's going on, including the recent attempt on Nicodemus's life, that security would be tighter. Where is everybody?" she asked.

Artemis had been thinking the same thing. Of course, the members under the Mountain had been spread thin as of late, but even still, certain areas were to be constantly guarded . . . such as Nicodemus's quarters. "I don't like this." He removed one of his whip handles. "We need to get out."

The two hurried down the corridor that would take them to the tunnels. Suddenly, a man appeared in their path a few feet ahead. He was tall and gangly, wearing a stained white linen shirt. A bloodied sword hung from his hand.

"Behind me, Lotus." Artemis put himself between her and the man, who shambled down the hall like a wounded animal, and it was then that Artemis could make out the blood on the young man's shirt. "Elan?" He recognized the young man.

"Lord Artemis, thank the elders!" Elan collapsed into Artemis's arms. He was a youth of about 20 or so with a handsome face and soft blond hair. One of his blue eyes was swollen shut, and the other was filled with blood. His shirt was covered with so much blood that there was no way to tell where the wound was.

"What happened to you?" Artemis asked in a concerned tone. He knew Elan very well and was fond of the boy. He was currently finishing his third circle of training, and in the next few months, was supposed to be starting his long walk. But from the looks of him, he wouldn't be going anywhere.

"Killed them . . . cut them down like they were dogs . . ." Elan began rambling.

"Slow down, brother. Who has been killed?" Artemis pressed.

"All of them! They came in force and caught us by surprise. We never had a chance . . . all dead now. The whole class."

"Who has done this to you, brother?" Kahllah asked, but she felt she already knew the answer.

"The Apes! Curse them all for what they've done! Curse them all!" Elan shouted emotionally.

Just then, Kahllah picked up on the faint sounds of a battle coming from somewhere down the corridor. Ignoring Artemis's warning for her to wait, she ran to investigate. She found herself standing outside one of the half dozen or so libraries scattered throughout the Mountain. It was one of the smaller libraries the initiates sometimes used to hold study sessions. She had fond memories of the place, but what she saw when she looked inside would taint those memories forever.

Blood was everywhere. The floors, the walls, and even the books on the shelves were soaked in it. The library looked like a scene of a massacre. Bodies of initiates littered the floor. Most of them were children, barely in their teens. They had all been cut down in cold blood. In the center of the carnage were three Apes. They laughed as they made the rounds about the room, using ax handles or whatever else they could get their hands on to bash in the skulls of those who hadn't been fortunate enough to die during the initial attack. Kahllah had seen some truly gruesome things in her life and never lost much sleep over it, but the sight of those dead young men would haunt her for a long time.

One of the first things they taught you when you started your education in the Brotherhood was control of your emotions. Emotions were a distraction and could be the difference between life and death in battle. Kahllah had mastered this over the years, the art of being cold and calculating, but there was something about the sight of those dead children in the library that caused something in her to snap . . . and she lost it.

"Murderers!" she screamed as she charged into the library. The handle of her Stingray curved almost perfectly to her hand. It was as if the blade had been waiting for her to find it. The sword sang a sweet song as it slashed through the air and the right forearm of the ape closest to her. The cut was so clean that the ape never felt his arm when it came off, nor did he feel it when the next strike removed his head. She turned to the two remaining Apes, sword raised and slick with their comrade's blood.

"To kill children is the act of a coward. Neither of you deserves the honor of calling yourselves members of this Order or wearing those masks. I'll be sure to remove them from your corpses after I kill you."

Kahllah tore into the Apes like a woman possessed. Steel met steel, and fists met flesh as the trio danced around the library, locked in what to her was a battle for the souls of those murdered children. To their credit, the Apes fought fiercely and with great skill, but she was the Black Lotus. One of the Apes tried to take her head with the fire ax he wielded. The same ax that he had used to cave in the skulls of the initiates. Kahllah grunted, swinging Stingray with everything she had. The sword cut through the ax handle, sending the head flying across the room and burying itself in the side of an ape's skull. A crack opened his mask before the whole thing split and fell away, revealing the unremarkable face beneath. His eyes blinked at her dumbly as if what remained of his brain was still trying to process what was going on.

"When you sit before God, tell him the Black Lotus sent you." She pulled the blade from his head and allowed him to bleed out.

"For the tribe!" A roar came from behind Kahllah. The remaining ape was moving against the Black Lotus. He held a heavy wooden chair above his head, intending to bring it down and crush her skull. However, he and his plan died when Stingray sang his sweet song again, and the ape found himself sliced in half. His legs fell in one direction, and his body another.

A hand touched Kahllah's shoulder, and she instinctively spun, ready to attack once more, but her strike was stayed when she realized who it was.

"It's me!" Artemis raised his hands in surrender.

"The children . . . They killed all these children," Kahllah said as if he weren't standing in the middle of the same horrid scene as she.

"And those who have created this chaos will be made to answer for it, but that will have to wait. Right now, we must go. The Mountain has been overrun." He grabbed Kahllah by the arm and began pulling her toward the door.

She didn't fully grasp what Artemis meant until they stumbled back into the outer corridor, and she had a chance to lay eyes on it for herself. Two dozen or more members of the Brotherhood of various ranks and sects had stormed the Mountain, accompanied by outsiders armed to the teeth with heavy artillery. Mercenaries, no doubt. If she had to guess, they were on Lilith's payroll. The mixed group swept through the Mountain with bullets and blades, laying down anyone who wasn't loyal to the traitor, Tiger Lily. All this time, Kahllah had been living in fear that a civil war would break out within the Brotherhood, but this was no civil war. It was genocide.

"My God!" Kahllah clasped her hand over her mouth in disbelief. It only took a second for her to come back to herself before her vow to protect the Order returned to her, and she tried to join the fight.

"Are you out of your fucking mind?" Artemis held Kahllah by her shoulders. She tried to break free, but he held fast.

"But they are our Brothers. We must—"

"Survive," Artemis cut her off. "I love the Brotherhood more than anyone except those who founded it. I would gladly lay down my life to serve my Order, but this isn't service. It's suicide. We will do the ones who fall here no favors by dying with them just to say we did. You and I must live so we can one day make right this wrong."

Kahllah ignored the screams of her falling brothers and allowed Artemis to lead her through the bowels of the Mountain. Dead bodies were scattered everywhere while the rogues swarmed the Mountain like insects, helping themselves to what they wanted and burning what they didn't. The whole place seemed thrown into chaos.

They'd finally arrived at the entrance of the tunnels. It was a hatch that was only slightly bigger than a manhole. Once inside, they could follow it to the secret entrance that would let them out on the blindside of the Mountain. That was how Kahllah could slip inside unseen; hopefully, the same would hold true for them getting out. She guarded their flank while Artemis worked to open the hatch. "Fuck," she heard him curse.

"What's wrong?" Kahllah moved to look over his shoulder.

"It's locked!" Artemis jerked at a thick lock that had been placed on the entrance. "They probably put it on right after your breach." He sounded defeated.

"It's the traitor, Black Lotus!" they heard someone shout. Several mercenaries, led by a rogue member of the Brotherhood, were headed in their direction. They were now trapped.

"If you've got another idea, I'm listening." Kahllah drew Stingray and took a defensive stance.

"We make our stand," Artemis brought his whips to life. As their enemies drew closer, their numbers began to swell. The handful was now a dozen strong.

Behind them, there was a loud sound. It blended into a jumble of battle cries at first, but it was more distinct the second time. Something heavy was slammed against the hatch leading to the tunnels from the other side. By the time it hit for the third time, the lock had broken, and the hatch flipped open. Sticking up from the hole were two bronzed gauntlets. It was the Iron Monkey.

Kahllah, thinking he was a part of the attack, was about to bring Stingray around to take his head when the Iron Monkey raised his hands to show that he was not a threat. "I didn't come here to fight. I'm trying to pull your asses out of the fire. If you want to live, come with me."

"Why would you want to help a traitor? For all I know, the Apes could be waiting for us down there," Kahllah said suspiciously.

"Better than what's waiting for you up here. Follow me or don't. The choice is yours," Iron Monkey told her before disappearing back down the hole.

Kahllah looked at Artemis. "I don't trust him."

"Nor do I, but I trust *them* even less." Artemis swung his whip and took off the face of one of the mercenaries that had wandered too close. "Down the rabbit hole, Lotus. I'll cover you."

Kahllah put Stingray back into its sheath but kept the gun in her hand as she backed down the ladder into the hole. She couldn't see past her waist and had no idea what was waiting for her below. She was so busy looking for an ambush that her foot missed one of the ladder's rungs, and she slipped. She fell the rest of the way down and would've likely broken her neck had Iron Monkey not caught her. He cradled her like a groom about to carry his bride across a threshold, creating a moment of awkwardness.

"I'm good." Kahllah slid from his arms.

"You're welcome." Iron Monkey picked up the assault rifle at his feet and slung it across his back.

"What are you doing here? Are you responsible for the destruction your Apes are causing up there?" Kahllah pressed him.

"If I were responsible, would I risk my neck to save yours?" Iron Monkey questioned. "When you and Artemis left the jungle, I found Prime gathering our forces to stage this little uprising. When I tried to stop them, they voted me out as tribe elder." He lifted his vest so that she could see the bruises over his ribs and abdomen.

"And now you're looking to throw in your lot with us?" she asked suspiciously.

"The only thing I'm looking to do is save the Order from being destroyed," Iron Monkey said honestly. "Were you serious earlier when you vowed to stand on the side of the righteous in all this?"

"As serious as the day when I took my oath to put the needs of the Brotherhood before all else, including my own." Kahllah recalled her vow.

"Then let me help you repair some of the damage my people are up there doing. I have a way to get us out of the Mountain," the Iron Monkey announced.

The conversation was interrupted by the sound of gunfire coming from above. Kahllah looked up, wondering what was keeping Artemis. Above her, she could hear the sounds of battle and saw the flash produced by Artemis's whip over and over. What the hell was he doing? Kahllah was about to start back up the ladder when she finally saw him swing his long legs over the rim of the hole.

"Hurry!" she shouted up to him. Artemis gave her the thumbs-up and began his descent. He had made it about halfway down before gunfire exploded from somewhere above. A bullet sparked off the ladder, causing Artemis to lose his grip. He bounced from one side of the tight space to the other before finally landing on the ground below with a heavy thud.

"Son of a bitch!" Artemis yelled, clutching his leg. The place where his shin met his knee was bent at a painful-looking angle.

"I've got you." Kahllah tried to help Artemis to his feet, but it only seemed to cause him more pain. Above them, the mercenaries had begun to climb down the hole after them. Kahllah let off two shots with the P89, dropping one of them and giving the rest food for thought.

"I'm not going anywhere on this." Artemis grimaced, holding his broken leg.

"No, we can do it. Iron Monkey, help me move him," Kahllah demanded.

"Even with both of us carrying him, there's no way we'll outrun the mob," Iron Monkey told her.

"That's bullshit. Come fucking help me!" Kahllah's voice was almost pleading as she tugged at the heavier man.

"He's right, Lotus. I'm never going to leave this Mountain," Artemis said in a matter-of-fact tone.

He was living his last moments and knew it. "The responsibility of finding Nicodemus and saving the Order is now yours."

"So, I'm just supposed to leave you for the traitors to capture—or worse?" she asked emotionally.

"I've been a prisoner of war before, and it's something that I have no plans ever to experience again." He reached into the duffel bag and removed one of the pistols and the pipe bomb. "My task to find Nicodemus and salvage what we can of this once great Order now falls to you." He extended one of his whips to her.

Kahllah didn't trust that she could keep her voice steady if she spoke, so she simply nodded and accepted the whip.

"Move swiftly, and I will buy you as much time as possible." Artemis armed the bomb and then removed a compact machine gun from the duffel, which he placed on his lap. More men had started down the hole and would be on them soon.

"You don't have to tell me twice." The Iron Monkey started down the tunnel.

Kahllah was about to follow but stopped short. Then unexpectedly, she swooped in and hugged Artemis. "It was an honor to have fought by the side of the Lord of the Lash."

"And an even greater one to say that I died for the Black Lotus," Artemis replied. He flipped the machine gun's safety to the off position.

"I'll make sure all who come after us know that whatever is left of the Order only remains because of the sacrifices made today by the Lord of the Lash." She released him and took off after the Iron Monkey.

Kahllah ran down the long corridor. She could hear the sounds of gunfire behind her but didn't dare turn around because she didn't trust herself not to go back and do something stupid. The relationship between Artemis and she started off rough, but she eventually came to respect Nicodemus's protégé. He was an honorable man and loyal to what he believed in.

She had just reached the end of the corridor where the Iron Monkey awaited when she heard the explosion. The Lord of the Lash was gone and was now free of his vow. Kahllah hoped that his death had been a beautiful one, but considering how he chose to go out . . . she doubted it.

"I'm pretty sure we passed the path that would've taken us out of the side exit a few yards back," Kahllah said. She was following the Iron Monkey through the tunnels. The explosion Artemis caused had knocked out what few lights were in the tunnel except the blinking red emergency lights that appeared every few feet. The constant flashing made it hard for her to focus and even harder to see where they were going.

"We're not taking the secret entrance," Iron Monkey revealed.

"What? Why not? I assumed that was how you planned to get us out. What would you have us do? Walk through the front gates?" Kahllah was upset. She feared that she had made a mistake by following him.

"I would have you stop bitching at me and let me concentrate," Iron Monkey snapped. He was running his hands over the wall as if searching for something. "Between the brothers who have sided with Tiger Lily and those damn mercenaries, all our main points of entry and exit are either guarded or barricaded, including the one you used to get in. It was one of the first to get shut down. The traitors can't risk anyone getting out and spreading the word about what they've done here. This means we'll have to get creative about this." He depressed one of the stones in the wall, and a small panel opened.

Kahllah followed him through the small entrance and found herself in a dimly lit garage. Several vehicles were lined up, most in different stages of disrepair. They were in the Brotherhood motor pool. "How did we get here?"

"During my exile to the catacombs, I made it a point to familiarize myself with every inch of this Mountain and its tunnels. These . . ." he ran his hand over the wall ". . . have been here since long before the Blood tribes gifted this place to our ancestors. They needed to move freely without having to venture into the light of day. So I learned to do the same, using these very same secret passages."

"For someone who came into the fold so late, you sure seem to know a lot about our history. What's *your* story?" Kahllah said.

"A long one, which will keep for another time," Iron Monkey replied. "The past is irrelevant. It's the future that I'm trying to ensure. The future of both brothers and Apes, and I think you're our best shot."

"Why the sudden vote of confidence?" she wanted to know.

"This isn't about confidence; it's about faith. I've got some people in place that I think can help us turn this around. They're just waiting for my signal. Tiger Lily thinks she's a chess master, but she'll soon discover I'm a pretty fair gamesman myself." Iron Monkey moved from car to car, checking their conditions. He came across a minivan that looked to be in a little better condition than most of the others. He jumped into the driver's seat and began searching the car, hoping the keys might still be in it. No such luck, but that wouldn't stop him. He yanked out the paneling beneath the steering wheel and searched for the correct wires. He struck them together until he achieved a spark, and the van sputtered to life. "Bingo."

"I take it this isn't your first time stealing a car?" Kahllah asked.

"You'd be surprised at what you can learn when you grow up dirt-poor and hungry," Iron Monkey told her before getting out of the van. "Take the wheel. I'll open the door. No matter what happens from here, you drive this bitch like you've got the devil on your heels. Don't stop for anything," he warned before heading toward the garage gate.

Kahllah sat behind the wheel and waited. It would've been a lie to say that she was waiting patiently because patience was something that had abandoned her hours ago. She needed to get out of Virginia and back to her people. She would honor her promise to Artemis and find Nicodemus, but first, she needed to check on Animal. The information she had gathered during her time at the Mountain would prove invaluable to him and might help turn the tide against Lilith. The gate rattled to life and began to rise slowly. Kahllah revved the engine, eager to be away from the Mountain. In a few hours, she would be back in New York. She just needed Animal to hold on until she got there.

When the garage door rolled back completely, she realized this was not to be. Standing between her and freedom was a wave of Apes. Leading them was Prime. She had placed her faith in the Iron Monkey, and he had crossed her.

"Leaving us so soon, Lotus?" Prime stepped into the garage. He signaled the men, and they proceeded to surround the minivan. There would be no escape. "Well done, brother. I knew you would eventually come around and see things my way." He placed a hand on the Iron Monkey's shoulder.

The Iron Monkey knocked his hand away in disgust. "This has nothing to do with what you want but the good of our tribe."

"And both these things require the death of the Black Lotus. Now, bring me the bitch." Prime ordered the Iron Monkey as if he were one of his subordinates instead of the other way around.

Kahllah looked at the Iron Monkey in disgust as he approached the driver's side of the van. When he opened the door, he couldn't even meet her gaze. "You must believe me, Lotus. I didn't plan for it to go this way."

In response, she spat in his face. Her saliva dripped down the side of his mask and splashed on his vest.

"Don't worry, brother. When we get her back to the jungle, we'll put out that fire," Prime joked, drawing laughter from the Apes surrounding the van.

"Let's get this over with," Kahllah said and made to exit the van, but the Iron Monkey stopped her.

The Iron Monkey took her hand and pulled her from the car. He leaned in and whispered to her. "Sometimes, when we run out of everything else, all we are left to hold onto is our faith." He turned his machine gun on Prime and gunned him down. "Floor this bitch!"

Kahllah didn't think twice before she pressed her foot on the gas pedal and forced it to the floor. She gunned the van, but it didn't have the pickup she had expected, and it only sputtered forward. The Iron Monkey stood on the floorboard, holding onto the rack on the van's roof with his free hand and blasting the machine gun with the other. Those who hadn't been hit by the vehicle were mowed down.

Apes swarmed them, grabbing at Iron Monkey and busting the van's windows. When Prime's machine gun clicked empty, he began punching them off with one of his bronzed gloves.

"There's too many of them!" Kahllah swerved the van from side to side, trying to dislodge an ape that had jumped onto the windshield.

"Just keep driving. No matter what. Don't stop!" Iron Monkey commanded, kicking away an ape who grabbed at his vest.

One of the Apes hit him in the head with a spiked mace, knocking his mask away. For the first time, Kahllah got to see his face, and it surprised her that he appeared to be little more than a child. He was coal black and had a stern face that looked like it had been chiseled from stone. He resembled an ape more without the mask than he did with it. As she studied him, she couldn't help but notice that he bore a striking resemblance to the man she had first heard whistling the Executioner's Song. Now, it made sense.

They'd cleared the garage and were now on a narrow road leading them to the main highway. Ahead was their final obstacle, an iron gate. It was closed, so she would have to bust through it with the van and hoped it would hold up. Some Apes had fallen behind, but others were still clinging to the truck. They were knocking out windows and trying to hack away at the tires. Then suddenly, she heard a loud pop, and the van began to wobble and slow down.

"We're not going to make it," Kahllah said.

"We don't have a choice," Iron Monkey replied. The Apes who had fallen behind were catching up with them. "When you reach your destination, look for my mark, Lotus."

"What does that even mean?" Kahllah asked, wondering if it was some kind of code.

Iron Monkey reached into his vest and removed something, which he tossed onto her lap. It was an old cell phone. "Look for it," he repeated before releasing his grip and throwing himself from the van.

Kahllah watched through the rearview mirror as he hit the ground in a roll. The Apes pursuing the van abandoned their chase and went after Iron Monkey. He put up a good fight, but there were too many of them. As she burst through the iron gate in the hobbled van, the last thing she saw was the Apes swarming their former elder. In less than an hour, two men she barely knew had sacrificed their lives for her. She would make sure that their deaths weren't in vain.

Chapter 27

"Man, he should let me get some of that," Nef said, leaning against the wall. They were in one of the back bedrooms of the small apartment in which they had been held up since leaving Animal and the others. It was a secret crib that Nef kept where he could take his jump-offs. There was a look of excitement in his eyes, which were locked in on the scene unfolding in the middle of the room.

"Stop acting like you're really trying to be a part of this shit show," Bizzle said over his shoulder. He was sitting on a milk crate near where Nef was standing. He too was watching the scene. It was like a horrible train wreck, but he just couldn't bring himself to pull his eyes away. For the last hour or so, he had been a spectator at Lilith's baby boy, George's, interrogation at the hands of Cain. Bizzle encountered plenty of violent men in his life, but few were on Cain's level.

Cain stood in the center of the room, breathing heavily like he had just run a marathon. He was naked from the waist up, wearing only jeans, boots, and yellow dish gloves. He was covered in a sheen of sweat, and drying blood covered his face, arms, and

chest, but he didn't seem to notice or care. Before
him was George . . . or what was left of him.

Cain had started out beating George, landing vicious punches to his head, face, and stomach. He was
mindful not to hit him in the jaw because he needed
him to be able to talk. The beating hadn't done much
to loosen his tongue, so Cain broke his fingers one
at a time. To George's credit, he was a tough bastard.
Cain had broken three fingers on his right hand, and
still, George wouldn't talk. This was when Cain decided to try something a bit more extreme. He went
to the kitchen and got a knife which he heated with
a cigarette lighter. A look of horror painted George's
face as Cain began pulling his pants down. He begged
Cain not to do what he expected was coming, but his
pleas fell on deaf ears. Cain licked his fingertip and
tapped it against the blade, watching his spit sizzle.
Then satisfied that it was hot enough, he pressed the
knife against the shaft of George's dick. His scream
was bloodcurdling, and it was fortunate for them that
they were in a project apartment in a rough section of
town, so the neighbors weren't likely to call the police.
Then Cain reheated the knife and was about to poke
George's balls, but Lilith's youngest boy decided that
he'd had enough and finally cracked.

According to George, his mother was held up in a
mansion out in Westchester County. She needed to
be close to New York because it would serve as her
launchpad when she was ready to put her product on
the streets. That's why the *Red Widow* had been at

Port Newark. The *Widow* was carrying the first batch of street-ready drugs scheduled to go out. George had been locked in a storage unit the whole time, so he had no way of knowing they had sunk the boat. Cain and the others knew most of these things, but then he revealed something they hadn't known. While Lilith was becoming the next Godmother in New York, a separate plot was unfolding in Virginia.

For months, Lilith had her loyalists slowly inserting themselves into the Brotherhood power structure and strategically taking out anyone who didn't go along with her plans. As they spoke, dozens of her cartel mercenaries were already in the area, waiting for a signal from one of Lilith's agents inside to launch an all-out assault. The few brothers left who were still loyal to the Order would find themselves fighting a war on two fronts they never saw coming. They wouldn't stand a chance. More alarming was that if the Mountain had indeed fallen under Lilith's control, the Black Lotus would be walking into a trap.

"Fuck!" Cain cursed and began pacing the room.

"Why don't we just call her and give her the heads-up?" Bizzle suggested.

"The Lotus ain't big on cell phones, and she never carries one while working. Besides, she's had more than enough time to reach the Mountain. Whatever was going to happen has probably happened already. Nothing we can do about it at this point," Cain said sadly. Knowing of Black Lotus's already fragile relationship with the Brotherhood, he wasn't hopeful about her ever leaving the Mountain alive. He just hoped they gave her the respect of a soldier's death. Cain was fond of the Lotus, and someone would bleed in her name.

Nef's phone rang. He looked at the screen and exited the room to take the call.

"You think he's lying?" Bizzle asked, speaking of George, who was hanging limply in the chair, whimpering.

"It's possible, but I doubt it. Nothing a man holds dearer than his dick," Cain chuckled.

"I say we strap up and ride out to that mansion in Westchester and make it rain on that old bitch," Bizzle said hastily. He was tired of playing the sidelines and was ready for some action.

"Now, that's a plan that I can go along with. Only problem with that is we don't know how many soldiers Lilith has in the crib or exactly where Animal's kids are in the place. We go in blasting, and we put them at risk. I won't do that to him," Cain said.

"Then get him on the line and see how he wants to play it," Bizzle suggested.

Just then, Nef came rushing back into the room. There was an excited look on his face, and they hoped that the phone call had been good news.

"That was the homie, Animal. He's got a lead on Red Sonja and needs the whole team on deck to take this bitch out," Nef broke the news.

"*That's* what I'm talking about." Bizzle grabbed his gun and chambered a round.

"Let me clean off some of this blood and get Ashanti on the line." Cain began wiping himself down with one of Nef's bed sheets.

"I already tried reaching Ashanti, but he didn't pick up. Animal says this is our one window to take her, so we can't waste time trying to track him down. It's now or never," Nef said.

"Between your brother, that crazy broad Diabolique, Animal, and us, we should be able to get the job done. Shorty is tough, but not five against one tough," Bizzle said.

Cain didn't want to ride without Ashanti, but he had no choice. He slipped on his hoodie and grabbed his pistol. He was about to head out when he remembered George. "What about him?"

"I'll keep him under wraps and keep trying to reach Ashanti," Nef offered. Everybody in the room knew he wasn't built for what was about to go down, so no one argued about him sitting out the fight.

"A'ight, you can play babysitter, but keep trying Ashanti, and don't stop until you get him on the phone. I'm not trying to lose any more of our family." Cain glanced at Bizzle, who nodded in understanding. Then the two gunmen raced from the apartment, leaving Nef and their hostage.

Nef waited until he was sure the two men were gone before picking up the knife that Cain had left behind. He tested its sharpness with the tip of his finger. A small dot of blood appeared. He looked at George and smiled sinisterly. "I know you already spilled your guts to my boys, but I have a few questions of my own that I need answered." He loomed over George, whose eyes were wide with fear. "Where do we start?"

Chapter 28

The ride back uptown was a quiet one. Diabolique sat behind the wheel, eyes focused on the road ahead. She hadn't said much since they had left The Club. Something was obviously weighing on her, but she didn't seem inclined to talk about it.

Abel was in the backseat, licking his wounds. It had been a long time since he had lost a fight, so the feeling was no longer familiar. He felt like he had let down the team. He had been going out of his way to gain Animal's approval since the shooting of the cop at the other spot, and once again, he had shit the bed. Subconsciously, he was starting to question whether Diabolique had been right in her assessment about him not being cut out for the Dog Pound. With sad eyes, he looked at Animal.

Animal too was silent, save for giving directions to their next destination. When they'd left The Club, he'd received a text message that made him hopeful, but it still didn't do much to pull him out of his funk. The crew likely thought he was upset with them over how things had jumped off at The Club, but he wasn't. Instead, animal was more disappointed in himself, allowing someone to drag him back into a world of madness.

Over the last couple of days, he had crawled deeper down the rabbit hole than he had in many years, and he was uncertain if he could pull himself back out. Violence came naturally to him. It was as if it was what he had been put on earth to do. In his opinion, he had been a far better killer than he was a father. He'd always had Gucci to shoulder most of the load with raising T.J., but she was gone. With the way Sonja was moving, she likely wouldn't be long for the world either, and it would be left to Animal to raise both T.J. and Celeste on his own. What kind of father would he be to those kids? What kind of Karma would he attract to them? One thing that the years had taught Animal was that no matter how far he ran, death would always be just a few paces behind. It was a generational curse passed down to him from his father, and he could only pray that he didn't pass it on to his children.

"Pull over on the next corner," Animal directed Diabolique as he saw his destination looming.

Diabolique looked up at the tall, brown project buildings. "What are we doing here?"

"Got one last lead I wanna follow up on before calling it a night." Animal slipped from the car, followed by Abel.

"Let me park the car, and I'll come with you," Diabolique offered.

"Nah, it may be nothing, but I don't wanna leave any stones unturned," Animal told her.

"Big homie, I told you I was going to be with you on this until the end," Diabolique reminded him.

"And you have been, little one." Animal gave her an approving smile. "It's been a long night for all of us. You ain't gonna be no use to me if you're burned out. Go home and get some rest. I'll call you if something pops off."

"If you say so." Diabolique was clearly disappointed. "I got something I need to follow up on myself." She thought of the videos taken of her in the bathroom. She had been getting calls from a private number, back-to-back, for the last hour, so she was sure it had been viewed already. "I'll be out in the streets for a while, so make sure you hit me if you need me." With that, she pulled off.

Diabolique tried not to show it, but she was extremely worried. The deeper she got into the situation, the more apparent it became that they had no real chance of success. Her heart wept for her former mentor. Animal had already gone through so much in life, and every time it looked like he would find a measure of peace, the universe took another dump on him.

She had been sincere when she had told Animal that she planned to ride with him to the end of this, but she hadn't been honest with him about the costs.

What no one but Diabolique probably realized was that she and Animal had led parallel lives in the time since they had been apart. She too had seen her fair share of tragedies. From the loss of her mother to her being drugged and made an unwilling participant in a gang rape orchestrated by the man she thought she loved.

Diabolique had been young and naïve then, but you couldn't tell her she didn't have the world figured out. In her street running, she met a slightly older man who went by the name of Buck. Buck was a player in the game. Not on a grand scale, but his name rang in certain circles. He wasted no time in snatching up Diabolique's young ass and making her his personal arm candy. Let him tell it, he had plans to change her life, and he hadn't been lying . . . but it would be nothing like she expected.

Being chosen by a sporting street cat, especially one who was as generous as Buck had been, was a big deal for a young and naïve girl. In the beginning, Buck spoiled her. He would buy her new clothes and shoes and occasionally let her drive his BMW. But she wasn't a total dolt. She knew that Buck dealt with other women. He never made a secret of that. He could often be seen whispering in the ear of what he playfully liked to refer to as his "business associates." She would find out later that the girls worked for him at his escort service. Diabolique didn't like the idea that Buck was into the Flesh Game, but so long as that world never overlapped with hers, she turned a blind eye to his dealings. So she allowed him his occasional fling. In her mind, the girls could have his dick so long as she had his heart and bankroll.

The other shoe had dropped about four months into their relationship. Buck often made jokes about how much money she could make if she were "in the life." He would always follow up by telling her he could never see his little princess in the game to mask the truth behind the joke. One night, they had been partying with some older dudes who Diabolique had never been around before. She remembered the beginning of the night clearly. They had both been drinking heavily, and Buck was coked up out of his mind. All night, the guys Buck had her partying with kept looking at the young girl as if they wanted to eat her alive. The looks made Diabolique's skin crawl, but she said nothing to not cause friction between him and his friends. He had made it a point to tell her beforehand how important they were, so she remained silent.

As the night wore on, Diabolique continued to drink and found herself fairly twisted. This was when the wolf gave her the first glimpse of his fangs. Buck had come to Diabolique and informed her that one of his friends was smitten by the lovely young lady on his arm and was willing to pay top dollar for a few minutes of her time. He insisted that she didn't have to do anything sexual, but he'd be willing to pay extra if she did. Of course, Diabolique cursed him out and told him where his friend could shove

his money. She demanded that Buck take her home
immediately. He agreed and asked that she just let
him finish up his business. Half an hour later, Buck
apologized for making the request and brought her
a glass of champagne as a peace offering. She smiled
inwardly, thinking about how she had her older sugar
daddy sprung on her in such a way. Had she been a
little older or wiser, she would've never let her lips
touch that glass.

The rest of the night after the champagne came
to her in pieces. She could remember feeling sick
and needing to get to the bathroom. Her legs were
shaky, and her vision kept going in and out. A masculine hand, which she had assumed was Buck's, took
her by the arm and steered her through the apartment toward what she thought was a bathroom. To
her surprise, it was a bedroom, and the man who had
steered her there wasn't Buck but the one who
had been ogling her. Buck was also there, standing in
the doorway.

She was so loopy that she couldn't do much when
he tossed her onto the bed. She managed to find
the strength to push him off her and ran to Buck.
Of course, he would protect her. She was his little
princess. That notion died in her head when Buck
punched her in the face. She staggered back, holding
her busted lip. With fury in her eyes, she attacked
him. Diabolique was scrappy, but Buck was a grown
man and far stronger than her. When she refused to
stop fighting, he twisted her arm behind her back and

applied pressure until she heard something pop, and pain shot through her entire body.

Between the pain and whatever Buck had given her, Diabolique found it hard to maintain consciousness. She drifted in and out, and she found another man on top of her every time she did. She wasn't sure how long this lasted, but it felt like an eternity. By the time they were done physically and sexually abusing her, she was in terrible shape. Fearing that they had accidentally killed her, Buck and his friends dumped Diabolique's body under the Brooklyn Bridge. To her, death would've been mercy. She had been violated in ways that she never knew were imaginable and had no desire to live with the memories of what had happened to her. Death didn't come for her that night, but the man came who would give her a second chance at life.

Her "*Champion*," as she liked to call him, had found Diabolique and nursed her back to health. When her body was strong enough, he instilled the skills to ensure she would never be a victim again. In the months she had been with him, she often wondered what had ever become of Buck. It wouldn't be until years later that she would learn that Buck and the men involved in the rape had all met unfortunate and mysterious ends. Her Champion would never confirm nor deny whether he had been involved, but she felt he had been behind it. This made her love him even more.

She would spend the next few years with her Champion, conditioning her mind and body until she became a fine-tuned weapon. The things she saw and learned while in the company of her Champion would change her life for the better. With him, she finally found a place she belonged and would be protected. It was something that she hadn't felt since her time with Animal in The Below. For all that her Champion had done, all he ever asked of her in return was for her loyalty. Diabolique had promised to remain by his side for as long as he would have her, but that changed when she received the news of the death of Animal's wife, Gucci. This forced her to break her vow and leave her Champion to be with Animal during his time of need. It was a decision that she hadn't made easily and one that she knew would have consequences. She had been running ever since.

Her cell phone vibrated. She looked at the screen and saw that the call was from a private number. She knew who would be on the other end of the line and how the conversation would go. "No more running," she told herself and answered the phone.

PART VIII

THE LAST SONG

Chapter 29

After Diabolique had gone, Animal and Abel ventured into the heart of the projects. It was late, but there were still people out hustling or hanging. Animal could feel their eyes on them as they entered the building, likely wondering who the new faces were. They managed to make it to the elevator not accosted. They had to stand on their tiptoes in separate corners to avoid stepping in the puddle of urine someone had left in the elevator.

"I never understood why people did shit like this." Abel looked down at the piss in disgust.

"Learned behavior," Animal replied. "If the kids see that their parents don't respect where they live, they likely won't respect it either. Niggas been pissing in project elevators since the beginning of time, and I doubt that it'll change in either of our lifetimes."

"It's fucked up, but you're probably right," Abel said, shaking his head sadly. He was silent for a few ticks. He had something on his heart that he needed to get off but wasn't sure how to word it. "Animal . . . about earlier. I know I fucked up jumping the gun back there with Red Sonja, and I'm sorry."

Animal stared at Abel for a bit before responding. "I'd be lying if I said it wasn't foolish on your part, but I understand. You made a stupid decision in the heat of battle. Shit happens."

"I know, but why does shit keep happening to me? By now, you probably think I'm a world-class fuckup and not fit to fly the Dog Pound flag," Abel said in a defeated tone.

"No, I think you're a young nigga suffering through some growing pains," Animal said sincerely. "Look, ain't no instruction manual for this shit. We learn as we go through trial and error. That comes with time. It took Ashanti awhile to get his shit together too."

"You shitting me?" This surprised Abel. "Man, I'd have thought that a dude like Ashanti would've come out of the womb banging."

"He did, but that doesn't mean he was any good at it right off. Ashanti had suffered through his fair share of lumps and bumps over the years, but he eventually got it right and became a solid soldier. Judging by how thorough you and your brother are, I'd say he's also made himself a pretty decent leader. My point being, don't force it. Let the game come to you, and I'm sure you'll be fine. Then when it's your time to rise to the occasion, I'm sure you will."

"Damn right, I will. Before it's all said and done, I will make you proud of me, Animal. That's on the hood," Abel declared.

The two men stepped off the elevator on their desired floor. They walked down the hall to an apartment at the end. Animal double-checked his text message to make sure that it was the right one before knocking. A few seconds later, the locks came undone, and the door opened.

"Took you long enough," Nef greeted them. He was wiping his hands on a kitchen towel stained red.

"Is that blood?" Animal asked.

"Long story, man. Y'all come in out of the cold." Nef opened the door wider so that the two could enter. "How'd everything go at The Club?"

"Listen, I've had a fucked-up night, and I ain't got time to play twenty questions with your ass. You said old boy gave y'all some new information, so spill it, nigga," Animal said angrily. He was in a bad mood and didn't feel like dealing with Nef's shit. He wanted to go home, crash, and get a fresh start on his hunt.

"Yeah, man. You ain't gonna believe this shit. Come on in, and I'll run it down to you." Nef started toward the living room.

"Where's my brother?" Abel thought it strange that Cain hadn't come out to greet him yet.

"Him and Bizzle went to the store to get some cigarettes, so we just been in here chatting while waiting on y'all to get here so I can tell you what I learned," Nef said.

We? The question exploded in Animal's head. If Bizzle and Cain went to the store and Ashanti was still MIA, who the hell could Nef be talking to? He wouldn't have to wait long for an answer to his question. When they rounded the corner into the living room, they saw a beaten and bruised George sitting on the couch, sipping a glass of water.

"What the fuck?" Animal reached for his gun, but his hand was stayed when he felt the press of something cold at the back of his head.

Standing behind him was a Hispanic man armed with an assault rifle. Two more men came from the kitchen with weapons trained on Animal and Abel. "Easy, papi," one of the gunmen warned. He wore a thick mustache and had oily, black hair. He reached beneath Animal's shirt and relieved him of his pretty bitches, while one of his associates disarmed Abel. They were then ushered into the living room and forced to their knees.

"Nef, you set me up?" Animal asked in disbelief. He and Nef went back to the sandbox. He had been one of the founding members of the Dog Pound and Animal's closest friend. "Why?"

"I didn't set you up. I set myself up," Nef explained. "See, while you were off living your best life, and Ashanti was off traveling the world with Kahllah, I was out here starving. When the lawsuit money ran out, I was flat on my ass with no money and no idea how to feed my family. Meanwhile, my homies were out balling."

"Nef, why didn't you call me if you needed something?" Animal wanted to know. He'd have given Nef, or any other member of the Pound, the shirt off his back.

"When you got out of prison, you went underground with your family. You cut all ties with your day-one homies except that selfish-ass Ashanti. When he got his turn at the top of the food chain, he never once reached back. My number has been the same for years, and neither one of y'all even so much as reached out to see if I was still alive. Instead, y'all left me for dead."

"Man, that's bullshit. The Dog Pound would never abandon their family," Abel declared. It had been nothing but love since he had been inducted into their gang. Ashanti had taken care of him and his brother, making sure that they wanted for nothing.

Nef laughed. "I see they've got you good and brainwashed too. I used to be like that, a stupid little nigga begging for his big homie's attention. What did it get me? Not a damn thing. I put in work for this crew, but when it was all said and done, the two people I looked up to most acted as if I never even existed. You think I'm lying? Ask Animal how many times he's reached out to me over the years."

Abel looked at Animal, who wouldn't meet his gaze.

"See, it's just like I told you. That Dog Pound for Life shit died once Animal and his family was out of harm's way. After that, all bets are off. I can guarantee you that he would've left you for dry too once he got his kids back, and you'd outlived your usefulness."

"What did Lilith promise you to get you to cross us?" Animal asked angrily.

"It didn't take much, really. See, I've hated your guts for years, Animal. Even when we were running the streets, and you treated me like a whipping boy, I couldn't stand you. So I secretly prayed for the day to come when somebody finally laid your ass down. Not Mr. Nine Lives, though. You just wouldn't die, so I had to suffer in silence," Nef confessed. "What Lilith gave me was only more of what she's already been giving me for the last couple of years—cold cash.

"See, when I was at my lowest point, this guy named Khan approached me and offered to change my life. I thought he was bullshitting until he dropped that first bag on me. Khan and some of his people had a plan to take over the city. A damn good plan at that. This was before the Blue Dream when they were still mainly moving Poppito's coke. He gave me a little block to call my own, promising more to come once I'd proven myself. Then when the Blue Dream came into the picture, he made me an offer I couldn't refuse. Once the Blue Dream move is up and running, I will be Lilith's right hand in the city. Can you imagine? Ol' sorry-ass Nef as the king of the city? Khan and Lilith saw value in me when y'all didn't. So, the same way you said fuck everybody and did what you needed to do for your family, I'm doing what I gotta do for mine."

"My brother is going to waste you for this!" Abel spat. He knew it was over for him, and his only regret was that he wouldn't be there when Cain peeled Nef's skin off—layer by layer.

"I doubt that. Before you boys showed up, I sent Cain and Bizzle on a little dummy mission they'll likely never come back from. Setting those two up was too easy. All I had to do was tell them that their big homie needed them, and they took off running, no questions asked. You won't get any help from them. If you're banking on Ashanti, I heard he got snatched by some bitch in a mask. He's probably dead already."

"This shit is so foul," Animal said, still not believing what was happening.

"It ain't foul; it's Karma. Y'all always said that I wasn't street smart, but right now, I'm looking like a genius," Nef laughed.

"I'm gonna kill you!" Abel lunged at Nef, which proved to be a foolish move on his part. One of the armed Hispanics clocked him with the butt of his rifle and knocked him to the floor. A nasty gash opened up on his forehead. He sat on the floor, glaring murderously at Nef.

"Show some respect for your new king," Nef taunted him.

"You ain't gonna be king of shit but corpses. Lilith will never let a nigga like you sit at her table. One thing I've learned about that old bird is that she only respects the strong—and that ain't you. You were a weak-ass nigga when we were shorties, and you're still weak. Lilith will gut you like a fucking fish and pay you what she owes in blood," Animal told him.

"That's where you're wrong. I was able to do something that she couldn't and cage The Animal," Nef said proudly.

"Don't be so quick to stroke your dick, Nef. No matter how this plays out, *you* are going to die. I may not be the one to kill you, but you have my word it'll be a member of the crew you betrayed that will send you to your final reward," Animal warned.

"There you go overestimating yourself again. Your run has been over for a while. Sitting up in that big house, changing Pampers, and eating pancakes have made you soft. Everybody knows it. Had this been a few years ago, I'd have never been able to take you down this easily," Nef boasted.

Nef continued to belittle Animal while the armed men looked on in amusement. They were so entertained by the show Nef was putting on that they weren't paying much attention to Abel, but Animal was. He saw his hand inching toward his ankle. Animal knew what he was about to do and how it would play out. He tried to warn Abel with his eyes and tell him not to do it, but it was useless. Abel snatched the small pistol from its hiding place at his ankle and turned it on Nef. He fired a shot that struck Nef in the throat. He clutched at his throat, trying to stop the blood from squirting all over the living room, but it was pointless. The self-appointed king of New York met his end unceremoniously in a dirty project apartment.

Abel brought the gun around to get off a second shot, but the gunmen were prepared. The one with the mustache swung his rifle on Abel, and Animal knew what would come next. He didn't want to see it but couldn't bring himself to turn his eyes away.

"No!" Animal screamed, but the sound of machine gunfire drowned out his voice.

Mustache did Abel filthy, hitting him at least ten to a dozen times. His body flopped around like a fish out of water for a time before finally going still. He looked like a bag of chopped meat, but his chest still rose and fell faintly. Animal wasn't sure how, but Abel was still alive. Ignoring the gunmen and their warnings, he crawled over to Abel. Animal cradled Abel's head in his hands and tried to give him a measure of comfort in his final moments. "Abel," he said softly.

"Is that you, big homie?" Abel asked. His eyes were darting around as if he were trying to focus but having trouble.

"I'm here, little one," Animal told him.

"Tell Cain that I'm sorry for not being a better brother. I always wanted to be better," Abel rasped.

"You're a great brother. Better than my own brother, in fact. And whatever message you have for Cain, you can give it to him yourself."

"Man, you ain't a very good liar," Abel tried to laugh, but his body was racked with pain. "You said I would rise to the occasion when my time came, and

I did, didn't I?" Those were Abel's last words before his body shook . . . and he was gone.

"Mourn your buddy on your own time. Right now, somebody wants a few words with you, and we've got a long ride ahead of us," Mustache said. Animal glared at him as one of the gunmen pulled him to his feet while the other helped George.

"You're going to suffer for what you've done," Animal said in an icy tone.

"By the time Tiger Lily is done with you, I doubt there'll be enough left for you to be considered a threat anymore," Mustache told him.

"I'm the least of your concerns, but when that boy's brother finds out what happened here, you're going to wish I was the one who did you in. Cain's wrath will be biblical, and I only hope I live long enough to witness it."

Chapter 30

Cain and Bizzle entered Central Park at the East Seventy-Second Street entrance and started heading south toward their destination located on Sixty-Fifth. It was not long before dawn, and the park was beginning to come alive. Birds chirped in the trees, and the things that walked the park at night were returning to where they hid from the daylight. Cain had lived in New York his entire life and could count on one hand how many times he had ever been to the park. It was like that with most New Yorkers. Tourists came from all over to behold the city's wonders while the natives hardly gave them a second look.

One of the reasons that Cain didn't bother with the park was because of the painful memories that it stirred. Many years ago, he suffered a terrible accident. It was the day his mother's crack pipe exploded in his face and left him with the scars he would have until the end of his days. While in the emergency room receiving treatment for his burns, he had the pleasure of meeting a young man named Jonas. He and Jonas were about the same age and from the same walk of life, so they ended up striking up a conversation while they were in the hospital.

While Cain was in the hospital due to neglect, Jonas was there because of an accident. From what he told Cain, he had been trying to get his football from the frozen lake when the ice cracked, and he fell into the icy water. Cain could recall overhearing one of the nurses telling Jonas's sister that he had been dead for nearly three minutes and how it had been a miracle that he hadn't suffered any brain damage. When they were alone later that evening, Cain had asked Jonas how he'd gotten out of the lake. His response made Cain wonder if the nurses had been wrong about him not having suffered any brain damage. According to Jonas, God had sent an angel to pull him from the frozen lake. A beautiful white angel with blue eyes. This made Cain laugh. It wasn't to mock Jonas, but because Cain didn't believe in God, he had a hard time believing that any God would have allowed innocent children to suffer as he and his brother had. Although Cain didn't believe in God, he knew the devil was real. The fact that he was living in hell was a testament to that.

Social Services had come for Cain the following day, and Jonas was allowed to go home with his family. They promised to keep in contact, but it would be years before seeing each other again. By then, they were both in the streets, Jonas heavier than Cain. They ran in similar circles, so from time to time, they would bump into each other on the street or at some random gangster function. They were always cordial to each other but would never be closer than they had been that night spent in the hospital. Cain was sad when he heard that Jonas had killed himself. He never saw him as that type. Jonas was getting money, and every time Cain saw Jonas, he always seemed to be in good spirits. It just went to show that you never knew what kind of demons people were carrying around with them.

Sometime after Jonas's death, his best friend, Ace, found his name on a piece of paper and his head at the wrong end of Cain's pistol. Ace had been one of Cain's first, the hit where he had made his bones. Ace had made the mistake of crossing the wrong person, and for that, his life was forfeited. He had knocked up the sister of a man of influence. Ace tried to get the girl to abort the baby, and when she refused, he pushed her down a flight of stairs. The baby lived . . . but Ace didn't. It wasn't personal for Cain, just a business arrangement. After the fact, he would learn that the girl had been lying about the baby belonging to Ace and was only trying to extort money from him. Cain would reflect on the hit over the years and wonder if maybe he should've turned that one down on the strength of his relationship with Jonas. However, what was done was done, and Cain couldn't change it, but it was the one murder that he felt anything close to regret over.

"Why in the hell would he be here?" Bizzle asked, looking quizzically at the Central Park carousel when they arrived.

"Fuck if I know," Cain told him while examining the perimeter. It was early, so the carousel wasn't open to the public yet.

"I don't like this, man. It doesn't feel right," Bizzle said, looking suspiciously at the still, plastic horses. Something about the way the slowly rising sun was kissing the ride gave off an eerie appearance.

"Nothing about this does, but we've got jobs to do," Cain said, walking in a slow circle around the carousel, searching for clues. Finally, he spotted what looked like a torn piece of fabric sticking out of the mouth of one of the horses. Upon closer inspection, he realized it was what was left of a tattered red bandanna. "One of ours has definitely come this way." He examined the cloth.

"Then why are we the only ones here? You been able to reach Animal yet?" Bizzle asked.

"No, I called but didn't get an answer. I'm about to try to reach Abel."

Cain whipped out his cell, and the moment he went to punch in his brother's number, his chest was racked with pain. The world began to spin, and he dropped his phone on the ground while trying to steady himself against one of the horses. It felt like he had a minor heart attack.

"What happened? You good?" Bizzle checked Cain for injuries. From his reaction, you'd have thought some unseen enemy had just shot him.

"Something is wrong." Cain tried to catch his breath. He suddenly found himself overcome with a feeling of dread. Something had happened to his brother. He couldn't explain how he knew except to attribute it to their twin bond. Even when they were kids, one brother always knew if something wasn't right with the other. "We shouldn't be here."

"Which is what I've been trying to tell you since we set out on this dummy mission. You sure that was Animal that Nef was speaking to on the phone?" Bizzle asked suspiciously. Nef had never been one of his favorite people. He never cared for the kid, even when they were all younger and the Dog Pound was just forming. He always struck him as sneaky because of the way he skulked around watching everyone and always managed to avoid getting his hands dirty when the shit went down.

"Nope, but I sure plan to ask him. We gone, Blood." Cain reached down to pick up his phone. No sooner than he did, he heard something whistle past his head. At first, he thought it might have been an insect or a bird, but then he looked at Bizzle and knew something was wrong. There was a puzzled expression on his face. His hand was over his heart like he was about to recite the Pledge of Allegiance. "You good?"

Bizzle removed his hand, and a small red dot on his shirt gradually spread. "No, I don't think I am," he replied before falling.

Cain barely had time to react before a spray of bullets ripped through the spot he had previously been standing. They were under attack. More shots followed, ripping through the plastic horses of the carousel as he made for cover behind one of the carriages. The carriages were made of metal, so they were a bit sturdier than the horses, giving him a second to assess his situation. Bizzle was down but still alive. There was no telling how long that would hold true as long as he was lying out in the open. Cain had no way of knowing where the shots were coming from or how many shooters there were, but he had to do something. He couldn't just leave his comrade like that. Throwing caution to the wind, he made a move.

"You want me? Here I go, pussies." Cain ducked out from behind the carriage, firing his gun blindly while making a mad dash in Bizzle's direction. More shots came, but this time he could see the muzzle flash. The shooter was behind a tree to his left. Cain paused and looked around as if he were still trying to identify the enemy, and when the shooter poked his head out, Cain put a bullet in it. By the time he reached Bizzle, the OG was trying to push himself to his feet but didn't seem to have the strength. "I got you." Cain assisted him. He took Bizzle under the arms and tried to drag him as best he could back into the carousel.

"That faggot set us up . . . I knew that nigga was foul!" Bizzle said through clenched teeth.

"I know, and he will get everything coming to him. I promise you that." Cain vowed. If he was lucky enough to survive the night, Nef was a dead man, and he didn't give a fuck how far back he went with Animal and Ashanti. The reality of it was that if something happened to his brother, he would kill Nef slowly.

"Look out!" Bizzle shouted unexpectedly.

Cain's head whipped up in time to see a man darting from the tree line, armed with a rifle. Cain's hands were full with Bizzle, and he couldn't clear his gun to get a shot off. So the shooter had him dead to rights. Cain's hands might've been occupied, but thankfully, Bizzle's weren't. He leveled his pistol and shot the charging man in the chest, flipping him backward. That was two down, but they weren't out of the woods yet.

Three more men came rushing at them. Two were Hispanic, dressed in street clothes, and armed with machine guns. The third was wearing all black with a mask covering his face. Across the mask was a red tiger print. If they hadn't been sure before, that mark confirmed that these were agents of Tiger Lily. One of the men fired a shot, and the slug hit Bizzle in the gut. The force of the impact caused him and Cain to fall clumsily. It took a lot of effort for Cain to wiggle out from beneath the heavier man. Cain tried again to pull Bizzle to safety, but another barrage of bullets forced him back. When he tried for the third time, Bizzle waved him off.

"You gotta go, Blood," Bizzle said. His breathing was labored, and blood started to spill over his lips.

"No man left behind," Cain said.

"You and I know it's a wrap for me." Bizzle pressed his free hand against the wound in his gut. The rifle had ripped a hole in his stomach.

"I can't leave you," Cain said emotionally.

"You can, and you will!" Bizzle insisted. "All I ask is that you honor the last request of a dying man."

"Anything, OG. Name it."

Bizzle threw Cain his gun. "Take these mutha-fuckas to war!" Those were Bizzle's last words before their enemies fired again and ended him.

Cain looked from the bloodstained gun in his hand back to his comrade. "This, I can do."

What happened next unfolded like an out-of-body experience. Cain saw the men, heard the gunshot, and felt the proximity of the bullets as they passed him, but he no longer cared. The reality of the situation was that Nef had betrayed them, and Cain was pretty sure he wouldn't have moved to take him and Bizzle out unless he had gotten Animal out of the way first. So, this meant that his brother was likely dead at that point too. There was nothing left for him but revenge.

The first shooter, a squat, dark-skinned Hispanic man, closed the distance between them. His machine gun made him cocky, but Cain's gun made him dead. He shot him twice in the chest, dropping him, then put another bullet in his head for good measure as he stepped over his corpse. A bullet creased Cain's thigh, sending him to one knee. It was only a flesh wound, but it hurt like he had been set on fire for the second time. Before he could get up, the butt of one of their rifles came down across the back of his head. Spots danced before his eyes, and his mouth was filled with the taste of dirt when his face hit the ground. His guns were kicked away, and then the ass-whipping commenced. One of the shooters clubbed him in his head repeatedly, and Cain felt like he would lose consciousness until the gunman's partner stepped in.

"Chill out, fool. Lilith says that she wants the one with the long hair alive," Cain could hear one of the men say to the one trying to bash his skull in. From the slight muffle of his voice, he reasoned it was the one wearing the mask.

"There's a few of them with long hair, and you know all these Black bastards look alike," Skull Basher replied.

"Just help me get him up and out of this park before the police come. I know one of these Fifth Avenue crackers has already called the cops by now," Tiger Mask said. So he and the remaining shooter scooped Cain up and dragged him out of the park, each man holding him under one arm like a drunk.

"Christ, I hope I didn't kill him," Skull Basher said, noticing that Cain was limp and not moving.

"For your sake," Tiger Mask added. "I can only imagine what Tiger Lily will do to you for breaking one of her toys."

"Fuck him. How many of our guys did he knock off? If it were up to me, I'd put a bullet in his head and leave him here," Skull Basher said.

"Well, it isn't up to you. Tiger Lily says the one with the hair isn't to be touched. Let's just take him in and let her sort out the shit," Tiger Mask said. He hated working with Tiger Lily's mercenaries but hated being in the company of the scarred man even more. He'd seen what he was capable of and didn't want to remain in the company of Cain for any longer than he had to. It had been dumb luck that he and the mercenaries had even survived the attack, and he didn't want to tempt fate any more than they already had. So the sooner he delivered him to Tiger Lily, the better.

"I don't know why she's even bothering with this one. He's got to be the ugliest son of a bitch I've ever seen," Skull Basher remarked.

"I'm with you on that," Tiger Mask agreed. "You ever hear the expression, 'a face only a mother could love'? No way that applies to him."

"Ironically, my face is the only gift the bitch has ever given me," Cain said to both of their surprise. They'd assumed he was unconscious, considering the vicious blows he'd taken to his head.

"Fuck," Skull Basher cursed. He released one of Cain's arms and fumbled with his rifle. Unfortunately for him, this would prove to be a fatal mistake.

Cain produced his trusty hunting knife, which he always kept tucked in a sheath clipped to the back of his pants. Ashanti and Abel had always teased him for carrying it, but it was the thing that would now turn the tide for Cain. "Behold, the beast has risen!"

He drove the knife into Skull Basher's side and brought it around to the other side of his stomach, opening up the man. Skull Basher clutched at his stomach as his intestines spilled out onto the grass. Then he snatched the gutted man's rifle without missing a beat and turned it on his accomplice. There was a silent exchange between Cain and the man in the mask. They both understood how this had to go. Tiger Mask made the first move, lunging at the twin. Cain waited until Tiger Mask was almost on top of him before pulling the trigger. The impact knocked Tiger Mask several feet back and deposited him into a patch of grass.

Cain retrieved his knife from Skull Basher's body and limped over to where the other man was lying. He was in bad shape but, thankfully, still alive. Ignoring the pain in his leg, Cain knelt beside the wounded man. "You were right about my mother, you know? Having no love for this face . . ." He pushed his hood back so that his victim could get a good look at his deformity. "Most my days were lived shunned, but it wasn't because my mother didn't care about me, but because she feared me. Do you know why she feared me?"

"Your face," the downed shooter said just above a whisper. He wasn't even sure why he answered the question outside of the fact that it may have prolonged his life by a few more moments.

Cain pulled his scarred lips into a twisted smile. "A common misconception, but I'm going to let you in on a secret. My mom didn't fear me because I'm ugly, but because she was one of the first to realize that I'm just as ugly on the inside as I am on the out." And with that, Cain went to work with his knife.

He was pressed for time so that he couldn't give the Brotherhood member the complete interrogation treatment, but he could glean some additional information from him while peeling strips of flesh from the wounded man's forearms and one of his thighs. When Cain was sure the shooter had told him everything he knew, he cut his throat. Then he sat on the grass, watching the man bleed out while processing the new information. Just when they thought they had it all figured out, another twist was thrown in. The question now was how to use this new information to his advantage.

Killing a sworn member of the Brotherhood brought him some measure of comfort, but it was nothing compared to the joy that was sure to fill his heart when he claimed Tiger Lily's life. This all started because she had wronged Animal and his family, so in the beginning, Cain was content to let Animal have the honor of killing her, but Abel's death changed all that. Lilith was now food for the beast, and Cain planned to eat his fill before he even considered letting anyone else have her, including Animal.

Chapter 31

The sound of a ringing phone awakened Ashanti. It was a familiar tone . . . the ringing was coming from his phone. He reached for it to see who was calling and found he couldn't move his arms. At first, he feared being paralyzed but could still feel his legs. They were cold and damp, like maybe he had pissed himself. Finally, he opened his eyes and found himself in a dark room, with the only light from the rising sun shining through the window. When he tried to shift his body and heard the familiar jingle of handcuffs, everything that had happened earlier came rushing back to him. Ashanti sat up, probably too fast, because his head began to spin.

"Careful," someone spoke just outside his line of vision. "You may have a concussion, so sitting up too fast might cause you to black out again or throw up. I suspect neither will be pleasant for you."

Ashanti turned himself so that he could see who was speaking. She was cloaked in shadow, but the light of the rising sun highlighted her profile. She had abandoned her mask, and he found himself staring at a face resembling his. "Angela?"

"Why do you insist on calling me that?"

"Because it's your name," Ashanti insisted. "Does Tiger Lily have you so brainwashed that you don't remember who you are?"

"Who I was is irrelevant. All that matters is who I am now. I am Nightshade, right hand to the true elder of the Brotherhood of Blood," Ophelia said proudly.

"That's bullshit." Ashanti managed to sit up and turn so that he was facing her. The motion was awkward, considering that his hands were still cuffed behind his back. "You're Angela, my big sister. The same girl I used to follow back in the projects and beg to take me to the store for candy. Don't you remember?"

"I remember a great many things." Her eyes took on a faraway look. "I remember the little girl sold by her mother to pay off her drug debt, the putrid smell of sweat and tobacco coming from the men who had their way with her, the pain she felt when her pelvis was fractured as she was passed around a dozen times for entertainment. Also, the despair of waiting to be rescued, only to realize that no one would ever come for her. These are the things I remember," Ophelia said emotionally.

Her words cut Ashanti deep. "I'm sorry that happened to you. I wish that I could've done something . . . anything, but I was only a kid," he said sincerely.

"And when you became a man? What then?" Ophelia questioned. "For years, I toiled in bondage while the man who calls himself my brother rose to power in the streets. Sometimes, I would dream that you would come breaking down the doors of my captors and rescue me from that hell, but you never did."

"I didn't know where you were. If I'd had a way to find you, then I would've come. You're my family, and there's no mountain I wouldn't move for my blood," Ashanti said.

"By *blood,* I can only assume you mean your gang, not those you share DNA with. You couldn't find me, yet you were able to track the enemies of The Animal to the ends of the earth," she shot back.

"Whatever Tiger Lily has been pumping into your head has got you blinded to what's real and what ain't," Ashanti said.

"Quite the contrary, little brother. For the first time, I can see things with perfect clarity." There was a hint of madness in her voice when she spoke. "When Tiger Lily found me, I was a broken child, and she pieced me back together. My new mother has shown me the world through fresh eyes, a world where little girls are not victims but goddesses. I will help her usher in this new world by cleansing the old one of the things that plague it."

"She's using you, Angela," Ashanti told her.

"No, as Angela, I was a thing to be used, but I am Nightshade. Tiger Lily has given me a gift that no one in my life, including my brother, has ever seen fit to—purpose," Ophelia said with confidence. "Once, your opinion of me may have counted for something, but not now. You have chosen your new family as I have chosen mine." She dropped two guns on the floor between them.

It took Ashanti a few seconds to realize what he was looking at. One gun was a .45, and the other a .357. Ashanti knew those guns almost as well as he knew his own. There was only one way that Zo-Pound could've been separated from his precious pistols. Over the years, Zo had become so much more than a friend; he was his brother. They had gone on countless missions together and forged a bond that came only second to the one Ashanti shared with Animal. Ashanti had never been big on showing emotions but couldn't keep his eyes from misting up.

"If it helps to bring you any comfort, I gave him the honor of a soldier's death," Ophelia offered.

"I wish you hadn't done that," Ashanti said in a low tone. "Zo was a good dude and deserved better."

"You'll find no sympathy from me on that account. Zo was a soldier, same as you and I. We live our lives knowing that each day is borrowed. We have no real right to life, but death is ours for all time," Ophelia told him.

"This we can agree on." Ashanti glared up at her.

"I know that look." Ophelia moved closer. "You're probably thinking of what you would do to me if your hands weren't shackled. I'll admit, a part of me is curious as well. I've heard some amazing stories about you, and I can't help but wonder how much is truth and how much is lore."

"Take these bracelets off, and I'll be happy to show you," Ashanti said. A slow-burning fire lit up in his heart.

"You wouldn't hurt your big sister, would you? Not again?" There was a hint of scorn in her voice.

Ashanti didn't resist when she used her finger to lift his chin so that he could look into her eyes. Staring back at him were two pools of hatred. Whatever bond that existed between them before had officially been broken beyond repair. He knew what needed to be done but wasn't sure if he had it in him to do it.

"Ironic, isn't it?" She removed her finger. "I've brought you to the same place to meet your end, the same place Angela met hers." She motioned around the space.

For the first time that morning, Ashanti took stock of his surroundings. He was in an empty factory that had once been used as a mirror manufacturer. From the dilapidated look of the place, it had been down for quite some time, but remnants of what it had once been remained. Broken pieces of mirrors littered the floor, and some that were still intact rested against emptied shelves. Yet, for some reason, the factory stuck a chord of familiarity. Ashanti felt like he had been there before. It took his brain a few seconds to register why the place looked so familiar, and when it hit him, his heart grew heavy. It was where the men who had kidnapped him and Angela herded all the children they collected before they were sold off for profit. That factory had been the last place he'd seen his older sister.

"I feel your pain" was the only response that came to mind.

"Like hell you do. Tell me, little brother, do you remember the touch of a man? How it was to be defiled in a way that no child should?" she questioned. "Of course you do," she answered for him. "I can still hear your screams from those nights when they visited you too and repeatedly took your innocence. I'll bet those few weeks were a living hell for you. Now, imagine how it would've felt if it had dragged on for years. *That* is my pain, so don't you dare pretend that you feel it."

"Ophelia, we can still fix this if you would only listen," Ashanti urged.

"We have no more words to exchange, little brother." She went to the window, and leaning against it was the cane/spear she had used to impale the detective. Clutching it firmly, she moved to stand over the still-kneeling Ashanti. "What remaining blood ties that exist between us will be severed today."

All Ashanti could do was watch helplessly as his sister moved in for the killing blow. The girl he had known was gone, and she was under the control of the Brotherhood. There would be no mercy. She suddenly stopped and cocked her head to one side as if she had heard something. Then without warning, she snatched one of the daggers from her belt and threw it across the room. The blade sailed into a dark corner, and Ashanti heard a scream. A split second later, a man staggered from the darkness, the blade embedded in his chest. He was wearing all black, and his face was covered by a mask marked with a red tiger print. It was the mark of the outlaw, Tiger Lily.

"Stay your weapons, Nightshade." Another man appeared. He too wore a mask, but this one bore not a tiger print but a totem of the Brotherhood. "You're amongst friends."

"Sno, we've never been friends and never will be. The only thing we have in common is that we've both pledged ourselves to the Order," Ophelia spat. "You're no friend of mine, Sno, but a lapdog of my mother." Sno was one of Lilith's new enforcers who had gone against the elders to side with her. He was a low-ranking member of the Brotherhood and, in Ophelia's opinion, didn't deserve to wear the totem on his mask. "What are you doing here?"

"When you left the mansion, your mother sent us to keep an eye on you. She had a feeling that you might do something stupid, and her suspicions were right from the looks of things." Sno looked at Ashanti. "Why have you brought him here instead of returning to the mansion as your mother commanded we do with all this street trash?"

"That is none of your concern. You can crawl back to Westchester and tell my mother that I'll return when she's done entertaining her guests or has word on Animal," Ophelia said dismissively.

"You mean you haven't heard? We've already captured the Bastard Son and wiped out most of those who would be loyal to him, save for this one." Sno was speaking of Ashanti. "The war is over."

"Taking down the Bastard Son was an honor that was supposed to go to me," she said angrily. When she'd left the mansion, she had intended to track down the members of the Dog Pound one by one and snuff out their lights. Animal, she had planned to save for last. She couldn't wait for the praise her mother would heap on her when she brought the son of Priest back in chains to kneel before her, but someone had robbed her of the opportunity. "How could you cage that which could not be held?"

"I'm afraid I can't take credit for this one. It was his own blind loyalty that proved to be his undoing." Sno went on to tell Ophelia of the trap laid by Nef, which claimed the lives of several members of the Dog Pound and eventually led to Animal being trapped.

Ashanti listened in disbelief as the man called Sno went on to tell the tale of the demise of the only family he had left: Bizzle, Abel, and even Cain had fallen to Lilith's killers. Ashanti felt sick, and if it hadn't been for the fact that he was already on the ground, he would've probably fallen out from the grief of it all. The only two things that kept him upright were knowing where Lilith was held up and that Animal was still alive. So long as the big homie still breathed, Ashanti held onto the hope that they could turn the situation around, but before he could turn his attention to rescuing Animal, he had to figure out a way to save himself. He had one last card to play but just needed the opportunity to lay it on the table. Sno would be the one to give it to him.

"This little game of yours is over, Nightshade. We'll be taking you and the prisoner back to the mansion." Sno waved his hand, and two more Brothers dressed in black appeared. They also wore tiger print masks and carried assault pistols. They stank of mercenaries and were not members of the Brotherhood.

Ophelia stepped between Ashanti and Lilith's men. "His life is already spoken for. Touch what belongs to me, and both of you will die before he does." Ophelia leaned on her cane/spear.

The two looked at Sno, uncertain of what they should do. Sno was their commander, but Ophelia was the elder's daughter. None of them wanted to risk offending Tiger Lily and ending up at the wrong end of her claws.

"What are you waiting for? I've given you an order!" Sno commanded them.

Hesitantly, the two masked men moved toward Ashanti. Ophelia never moved. She simply watched them. The minute the one closest to her laid hands on Ashanti, she made good on her threat. She drove her spear up through the bottom of his chin, causing it to explode through the top of his head. His death was a clean one, but his comrade wasn't as fortunate. Mimicking a move she had learned from her mother, Ophelia pinched his Adam's apple between her index finger and thumb, giving it a little twist. This prevented him from breathing, causing him to die a very nasty death. Ophelia retrieved her spear from the other mercenary's skull and turned to Sno.

"On second thought, you were right. I'll tell your mother that we lost you, and this never happened." Sno backed up fearfully.

"You should've left when I asked you to." Ophelia stalked toward him, flicking the blood from the tip of her spear. Sno took off running, as she had expected. She liked it when they ran. It made the hunt that much sweeter. Sno had a decent head start on her, but it didn't matter. Ophelia hoisted her spear, making sure the balance was right, compensating for the distance, and threw it. He'd just reached the exit when the spear plunged into his back and sent him spilling onto his face.

Sno resembled a harpooned whale, trying to drag himself out of the factory with the spear protruding from his back. Every so often, he'd spare a glance over his shoulder, only to see Ophelia closing the distance between them. She was stalking him like the predator that she was, taking her time and savoring the moment before the kill. Finally, Sno rolled over onto his side, breathing heavily as his life's blood spilled onto the dusty floor. "To kill a member of the Order is a crime punishable by death. It's one of our oldest laws."

Ophelia wrenched her spear from his back, making a wet, puckering sound. "The old ways are dead, and so are you." Now, she drove the spear through his heart. After dispatching Sno, she returned to the factory to deal with Ashanti. When she arrived at the spot where she'd left him, she found only the discarded handcuffs. Ashanti was gone, and so were Zo's revolvers.

There was the sound of something being kicked over coming from her left. Ophelia turned in time to see Ashanti dart between one of the aisles of shelves. He was trying to run . . . good. Ophelia moved with caution through the aisle where he had disappeared. There were mirrors everywhere, in different states of disrepair. They cast reflections from different angles, like walking through a funhouse.

"Angela, you don't have to do this," she heard Ashanti's voice bouncing off the factory's walls.

"Oh, but I do. You are a grim reminder of everything I was . . . weak and victimized. I must destroy my past to embrace my future," she called back.

"Regardless of what Lilith has been filling your head with, know I love you. I've always loved you. So please, just let me try to make this right between us."

"This will be right when your blood stains the tip of my spear," Ophelia shouted. There was a flicker of motion, and she caught a glimpse of Ashanti. She struck with her spear . . . only for it to contact glass instead of flesh. It had been a reflection. "Parlor tricks won't save you. Step out into the open and die with honor."

"Fine." Ashanti appeared a few feet ahead of her. His form was shadowed, standing amongst some discarded mirrors stacked against one of the shelves. Zo's revolvers hung loosely at his side. "I don't want to do this, and I think in your heart you don't want to either. So stop this before we reach the point of no return. We're family," he pleaded.

Ophelia wouldn't be tricked the same way twice. "Blood doesn't make us family; deeds do. I've made my choice." She raised the spear, but instead of throwing it forward, she spun and struck behind her, breaking yet another mirror. She assumed that Ashanti was trying to use his reflection to misdirect her again, but that time, the target in front of her had been the real thing.

When Ophelia turned back, she found Ashanti standing before her, both barrels of the revolvers pointed at her. Tears danced in the corners of his eyes. "And I've chosen mine." He pulled the triggers.

Ashanti spent the next twenty minutes weeping over the corpse of his sister. He'd wanted so badly to reconcile with his last living relative. They were all that they had left. As it turned out, Lilith's brainwashing outweighed genetics. When he left, he would call 911 and hope that emergency services would get to her before the rats did. She might've just tried to kill him, but she was still his sister.

He reflected on what she had said about killing her past to embrace her future. In a sense, that's just what he had done. Angela . . . or Ophelia, had left him as the last surviving member of a very dysfunctional family. When she died, she took his past with him. He would now turn his attention toward the future, which involved helping Animal rescue his children and killing Lilith. She had taken out almost everyone he loved in one shot, and he planned to make her bleed. Until that day, finding her had been like trying to find a needle in a haystack, but thanks to the conversation between Ophelia and Sno, he now at least had an idea of where to look.

He could remember when they first came across the messenger bag that exposed Lilith's role in Nyack. There had been a list of residential properties in the company's name, one of which happened to be in Westchester. Ashanti had an idea that was where he would find his enemy and put an end to this madness. He wasn't fool enough to think he'd be able to take Tiger Lily out on his own, especially not on her home turf. He would need a carefully laid plan and a whole lot of luck to pull it off. It was time for him to sift through the ashes of what remained of the Dog Pound and see if there was enough left to put together a good old-fashioned war party.

Chapter 32

Animal sat alone in the dark cell. At least it was dark at the moment. In a few minutes, a blinding light would come on and go back off just as suddenly. They were doing it to screw with his senses, and it was working. His eyes hurt, and he had a splitting headache. It had been going on like that for hours: on, off, on, off. The light flashed on every eight minutes. Animal knew because he counted the seconds between flashes. That was also how he had been able to determine that he had been in the cell for roughly twelve hours.

His hands were shackled by two chains anchored to the floor. He'd been trying to free himself for hours, but he only succeeded in cutting one of his wrists on the shackles. Being chained in that cell reminded him of darker times as a child. Those cold nights at the mercies of his mother's boyfriend, Eddie. He was a wicked man, but it wasn't a man who was the cause of his current set of circumstances. Instead, this was the work of a woman.

This whole time he had always seemed to be one step behind Tiger Lily, or she one step ahead of him, depending on how you looked at it. Nef's betrayal placed him in that cage, but the situation as a whole had been his fault. *"That bleeding heart of yours will be your downfall,"* he could hear his father's warning. He had been right. If only he had told Sonja to go fuck herself instead of taking pity and agreeing to help her in her time of need, Gucci would still be alive, and T.J. would've been sleeping in his own bed instead of in the company of strangers. These things were true, but what about Celeste? She was an innocent child dragged into all this by her troublesome mother. She hadn't asked for this and didn't deserve what was happening to her. The girl had already been through so much and deserved a chance at a normal life, and it fell to Animal to ensure she got it.

The light unexpectedly flashed on again. Eight minutes hadn't yet passed, so it caught him off guard, and he found himself temporarily blinded. When his vision cleared, he was no longer alone in the cell. Leaning against the wall near the cell door was Lilith's eldest son, Peter. As usual, he was dressed in army fatigues and combat boots. His head was freshly shaven, and you could make out the devil horns he had tattooed on each side. He and George wore nearly identical faces, resembling their mother, but Peter was the more well-built of the brothers. That was because he constantly trained, preparing his mind and body for war.

The room was silent, with Animal and Peter staring at each other from opposite sides. The last time

Animal had seen Peter had been when he and his men killed his friend, Brasco, back at the twins' apartment. Like a coward, they'd shot Brasco in the back, denying him the soldier's death he deserved. Nevertheless, animal had vowed to avenge his dying friend, and he planned to keep his word.

"Pardon me for staring, but I want to savor this moment," Peter finally spoke. He moved closer to Animal and studied him. "They talk about you like you're some kind of boogeyman, but I know better. I don't know what you might've been in your prime, but you ain't nothing but a bitch now. I smelled it on you the first time we met, right before I smoked your punk-ass homeboy."

"Take these chains off me, and we'll see who the bitch is." Animal faked like he would lunge at Peter, making him flinch. "Pussy," he laughed.

"You think you're so fucking tough, don't you?" Peter asked angrily. Animal had struck a nerve. "Tell me this, tough guy. Did you cry when you found out that your bitch was dead?"

"Watch yourself," Animal warned.

"Oh, did I touch a sore spot?" Peter taunted him. "Yeah, I'll bet you cried like a fucking baby. I sure would've if someone had done my lady that way. She died bad, you know? *Real* bad."

Animal shifted, causing his chains to rattle. Peter was poking a bear.

"Broken jaw, fractured orbital socket, a cracked skull, a few broken ribs. She really had a number done on her," Peter continued.

"What? Did Mommy have you steal the medical examiner's report?" Animal asked sarcastically.

"She didn't have to. I was there," Peter revealed, much to Animal's surprise. "Oh, you mean you didn't know? It was me and my guys that broke into your house. Nice place, by the way. I guess those royalty checks from that trash-ass album you put out have you living the good life. I think it'll be a little too much space for you now that you're a widower with no kids. If it makes you feel any better, your wife didn't go down easily. She even killed one of my men, which is why the guys worked her over that way. They would've probably beaten her to death if I hadn't stopped them. Nobody deserves to die that way, so *I* choked the bitch. Call it mercy, but you don't have to thank me. I was happy to do it."

The whole time Peter talked, a fire was slowly building in Animal's gut. Lilith's boy was pushing all the right buttons. He could ignore the taunts for the most part, but when he heard Peter admit to being the one who killed Gucci, he exploded. A roar erupted from deep in Animal's soul. He lunged at Peter, only to find that the chains prevented him from reaching him. He continued yanking at the chains until he was exhausted and finally dropped to his knees with his head down. "You are going to die," he said just above a whisper.

"Not any time soon and not by your hand." Peter kicked Animal in the face. Animal's nose bled, and blood dripped onto the floor. "I can't wait until my mother is done with you so I can do you like I did your bitch."

"What the hell are you doing?" Lilith's voice startled Peter. She was standing in the doorway with Mustache, one of the mercenaries who had brought in Animal. She looked at Animal's bloodied face and knew precisely what Peter had been up to.

"Mother, I—" Peter's words were cut off when Lilith slapped him across the face.

"Beating a man when he can't defend himself? I hadn't realized that I had raised a coward. Get out. It's making me sick to look at you right now," Lilith commanded.

"Yes, Mother." Peter lowered his head and left the cell.

"I'm sorry about that," Lilith told Animal.

"He's an asshole, but I guess he got it honest, huh?" Animal spat blood on the floor at Lilith's feet. "You come here to gloat?"

"Not at all. Just because I defeated you doesn't mean I don't respect you. On the contrary, you have proven to be a very worthy adversary, Animal," Lilith said honestly. "A part of me wishes that things didn't have to go down like this."

"You snatched my kids. There's only one way this could go down," he told her.

"Still, I can't help but wonder how great we could've been as allies instead of enemies," she told him.

"Lady, no way in the hell we would've ever found ourselves on the same side of anything but the law since it's something we've both spent our lives break-ing," Animal said.

"I wouldn't be so sure about that if I were you. There are a great many things that I see you are still blind to."

"Such as?" Animal questioned.

"In time, my violent friend . . . in time," Lilith said with a sly grin. "I can give you a history lesson later, but we have more pressing business right now." She motioned Mustache forward.

Animal watched Mustache timidly approach him. He wouldn't dare get close enough to Animal for him to grab him, so he tossed the plastic bag he was carrying over to him. Inside, there were fresh towels and a change of clothes.

"What's this?" Animal asked suspiciously.

"I can't have you show up to dinner dressed in those bloody rags. So I'll send someone for you shortly, who will take you to clean yourself up before bringing you to the dining room," Lilith explained.

Animal looked at Lilith as if she had lost her mind. "And what makes you think we'll be breaking bread?"

"Because if you don't, I'll be forced to take back the gifts I brought you. *Traerlos adentro!*" she shouted in Spanish to someone in the hallway. A few seconds later, one of the women who worked for Lilith came into the cell. With her were T.J. and Celeste.

"Daddy!" T.J. squealed and rushed to his father.

"Son," Animal's voice trembled. When T.J. wrapped his arms around his neck, Animal felt like his heart would burst with joy. Even little Celeste came over and embraced Animal. There was no way to describe what he was feeling at that moment. He tried to hug them back, but the shackles made it awkward.

"Daddy, why are you all tied up like that?" T.J. asked, touching the chain curiously.

"Your dad and I were playing a game," Lilith told the boy. She turned to Mustache. "Remove the chains."

"Have you seen what this kid is capable of?" Mustache asked. He didn't want to be anywhere near Animal if his hands were free.

"I don't think we'll have any problems out of The Animal, not with his children in the room. Isn't that right?" She directed the question to Animal.

At that point, Animal would've agreed to anything just to be able to touch his children, so he nodded. Mustache cautiously undid the chains that bound Animal, and, after, got away from him as quickly as possible. Animal never gave Abel's murderer a second look. Instead, his focus was on his children, who he pulled into a tight hug. Tears rolled down his eyes and splashed onto their little heads.

"Why are you crying, Daddy? Did someone make you sad?" T.J. asked, wiping the tears from Animal's face.

"No, I'm just really, really happy right now." Animal rubbed T.J.'s head. He looked at Celeste, who was glaring at Lilith. "Are you okay?" He stroked her hair. Celeste nodded but never took her eyes off Lilith.

She probably hated her grandmother more than her mother did.

"She got in trouble yesterday for choking the lady who brings us our food. She was trying to stick Celeste with a needle. I told her that hurting people is bad. That's what you always tell us at home, right?" T.J. remembered the long talks that he would have with his father about it being wrong to hurt people.

"Yes, but sometimes there's an exception to the rule," Animal chuckled. She was definitely his kid.

"Where's Mama? I haven't seen her since the men came to bring us here." T.J. was curious.

Animal wasn't sure how to respond. How did one tell a sweet, innocent child that their mother had been viciously murdered and it was their fault? "I . . . um . . ."

"Mommy went on a vacation," Lilith answered for the tongue-tied dad. "You'll see her again soon enough. Of course, how soon will depend on your father." She was speaking to T.J. but looking at Animal. He hadn't missed the threat in her words. "Okay, children. Your dad and I have some grown-up things to discuss, so back to your rooms for now."

"Too soon! Too soon!" T.J. huffed.

The caregiver who had been watching over the children moved to collect them. T.J. was cooperative, as usual, but Celeste was a different case. The little girl clung to Animal, baring her teeth and hissing like a feral cat at the young girl.

"It's okay, baby. You go with her and be a good girl. I'll be coming to get you guys real soon, and we'll walk out of here together. I promise." Animal stroked Celeste's red hair. Reluctantly, she released her grip on him and allowed the girl to lead them out of the room. The moment they were gone, Animal's smile faded, and his angry scowl returned. "Okay, now you've got my attention."

"I figured as much. Dinner will be in half an hour. I've got some people I want you to meet, so don't be late," Lilith told him and exited the cell.

Chapter 33

Twenty minutes later, Animal was showered, dressed, and escorted by two of Lilith's men to the upper level of the house, where he was supposed to meet Lilith in the dining room. Calling it a dining room was an understatement. The place was more like a banquet hall. Men and women dressed in maids' and butlers' uniforms moved about, ensuring the needs of Lilith's guests were met.

A massive fireplace dominated a large portion of one of the walls, and in it, a fire raged, making the room warm and cozy. Above it was a large painting depicting Lilith, dressed in all her finery, with her hand on the shoulder of a pretty young woman. Animal recognized Ophelia. Seeing her made him think of Ashanti, and he wondered how he was fairing. The last Animal had heard, he was still MIA, and Animal was beginning to fear that he might be dead. If that were the case, he hoped that his friend was given the honor of a soldier's death.

There were about a dozen people in the hall already, primarily muscle. On one side of the room stood Lilith's forces, a combination of her mercenaries and men dressed in black and wearing masks bearing tiger prints across their faces. One of them, a thinly built man with a wide buck knife strapped to one hip and a pistol on the other, stared at Animal as he passed. Animal couldn't see his eyes behind the mask, but he imagined hate filled them, like every other eye in the room. Animal could only guess what kind of warped picture of him Lilith had painted for her brainwashed followers. Fuck 'em. They'd all be dead soon—or he would.

Seated on one side of the table were three serious-looking men wearing suits. The looks they gave Animal ranged from curiosity to disgust. Peter and George were also at the table. Peter was drinking tequila straight out of the bottle, brooding over something or another. George still bore signs of the work Animal's people had put in on him. He glared hatefully at Animal. When Animal got a good look at Peter, he had to do a double-take. Not because he had finally taken off those fatigues and put on a suit, but because resting in two holsters under his arms were Animal's beloved Pretty Bitches.

"Beautiful, aren't they?" Peter taunted Animal, caressing the grips of the guns.

"Don't get too comfortable. They're coming home where they belong," Animal told him.

"Keep moving." One of the mercenaries who had been escorting Animal shoved him forward.

Also seated at the table was Raffa Khan. He wore a gray suit and white shirt with no tie. One of his slender fingers traced a line around his water glass. He looked like he would've rather been anywhere *but* there. Animal had never met him, but he knew him from the intelligence that Kahllah had provided them when they were preparing to go against Lilith and her people. Animal knew that Khan held rank within the Brotherhood, so something major must've been happening if he were there.

Seated at the head of the table was an older man with silver hair and deeply tanned, leathery skin. His cold blue eyes remained on Animal as he was directed by one of Lilith's men to take the chair to the right of the silver-haired man, who continued to stare.

"Do we know each other, friend?" Animal asked, finally tiring of the man's gawking.

"By extension . . ." The silver-haired man nodded, ". . . but it'd be a stretch to call us friends," he said in a nasty tone.

"From the way you're looking at me, I figure you're either looking for a kiss or a slap," Animal matched his tone.

The silver-haired man shook his head. "Just like your father—no respect for your betters. I don't know why the Lotus has even bothered to risk all that she has worked for to help the likes of you. When I return to the Mountain, she and I will have to speak about her poor choice in the causes she's been championing lately."

His statement told Animal that Kahllah was still alive, which was a relief. With the way Lilith and her agents had been plucking off members of their crew, he feared that Kahllah may have also fallen victim. He knew she didn't have many friends left in the Mountain fortress, and going there had been a considerable risk.

"Nicodemus, is that any way to talk to someone who is also a guest at my dinner party?" Lilith entered the dining room, escorted by Mustache. She was wearing a long, flowing black gown and high heels. Her signature claws dangled from a beaded belt around her waist like a fashion accessory.

"Is that what we're calling this, a dinner party?" Nicodemus snorted. "It must be an Easter dinner since you seem to have been resurrected."

"Yes, I'm afraid the rumors of my death have been greatly exaggerated." Lilith walked to the end of the table, where Nicodemus and Animal were seated, and kissed Nicodemus on both cheeks. "As have the rumors of your death. The last I'd heard, you were knocking on death's door."

"And now, I am not," he replied.

"Yes, and how did you manage to accomplish this miracle?" Lilith studied him.

"I'm not the one being interrogated here. This is about you and the things I've been hearing. You have a lot to answer for, Tiger Lily."

"Answers that I will be more than happy to give. Shall we discuss it over dinner? The main course should be coming out shortly." She picked up one of the bottles of wine sitting on the table and filled the crystal glass in front of her. She offered some to Nicodemus, but he declined.

"I have not come all this way for food or drink. I have come for answers. You have been accused of conspiring to overthrow the Brotherhood of Blood. Do you deny this?"

"Why would I? It's the absolute truth," she confessed. "I have indeed been conspiring against the current leadership of the Brotherhood, but not to overthrow . . . to remake it."

"I've never made it a secret about my displeasure with how the elders have been running things for the last few years. We were once a proud Order of assassins, feared and respected throughout the world, but the things that worked for us twenty years ago have no place in the new world. Instead of adapting, the older men who lead us toil away in their chambers and whisper to each other while we've become a shell of what we once were. The Brotherhood is dying, my love, and I intend to save us." She took a sip from the glass.

"And how do you plan to do that? By throwing in with mercenaries, traitors, and street punks?" Nicodemus looked from Khan to Animal, respectively.

"I'm not a traitor; I'm a capitalist. You, of all people, should know this, Master," Khan said scornfully. "Much like many of us, I'm tired of sitting at the feet of my elders' table waiting for scraps to fall. It's like you always taught me; if you want something, take it. That is the will of the strong."

"I should've left you in the trash where we found you," Nicodemus spat.

"Your bad, not mine," Khan shot back.

"Khan has played an intricate part in all this. In fact, much of this was made possible by him. And regarding Mr. Torres, I can see how someone like you would overlook the value of a man with his particular skill set. That's because you're not looking at the bigger picture. Men like him and Khan are the future and the key to restoring the Brotherhood to its former glory," Lilith said.

"Okay, now you've even lost me," Animal interjected. "I'm not a member of the Brotherhood."

"Aren't you?" Lilith questioned. "Let me ask you something. Did your father ever speak to you about the Grand Design when he was alive?"

Animal thought about it. "I heard him mention it several times but never knew what it meant. I always assumed it had something to do with making me a better killer."

"In part, yes. That's not the whole of it, though. Your father and I were never friends to speak of, but we did share some of the same philosophies, especially regarding the elders and their reluctance to embrace the new world. The Brotherhood has been rotting from the inside out long before even Priest or I became members of the Order. We aren't the only ones who saw it, but we were amongst the few who weren't afraid to speak out about it. Priest and I were part of a small group who understood that to save the Brotherhood, we couldn't just oust the current body of leadership. That would've done more harm than good. Death was not the answer, but life. This is where you and several others like you came in."

"So, you planned to use us to replace the current governing body of the Brotherhood?" Animal looked at her as if she had taken leave of her senses.

"Well, if you put it in layman's terms, yes. Still, it's a bit more complicated than that. The Brotherhood usually recruits its members at an early age. For the most part, they all become solid and loyal Brothers, but the most efficient of our lot tend to be the legacies, those who are born to existing members of the Order. Members like you, Khan, and even my beloved, Ophelia, would form the new council of elders while I sat at the head of the table until the time came when you were ready to take what is yours by right of your bloodline. As a child of Priest, you carry the blood of old in your veins, and a seat at the table is your birthright. No one, not even the elders, could deny you this if you had chosen to accept it. The Grand Design was never about killing, but leading."

"And when I wouldn't play along, you snatched my kids," Animal said with the pieces finally falling into place.

Lilith nodded. "I'll admit, the kidnapping of those children wasn't one of my proudest moments. I only wanted Celeste, as she is a legacy too, but finding out you had two children was a bonus. But of course, I never intended to hurt either of them. My plans for

Celeste were solely to validate my claim to be on the Brotherhood high council. With me, your daughter would've had the very best that life had to offer, and then Sonja went and got you involved and brought us to this point."

"Kidnapping, mutiny, deception . . . Does your treachery know no ends?" Nicodemus asked disappointedly.

"Honestly, I don't know yet. You'll have to see what I pull next to answer that," Lilith laughed.

"If you think that the rest of the elders and I are just going to sit by while you install your puppets into our leadership and take the Mountain, then you are truly as insane as they say," Nicodemus told her.

"But it's already happening," Lilith informed him. "As of this morning, my people launched a twofold attack on the fortress. As we speak, all who remain who would oppose me on the Mountain have fallen, and the Brotherhood is now mine."

Nicodemus's eyes widened at the revelation. "This is going too far, even for you, Lilith."

"I haven't gone far enough," she shot back. "But have no worries, my love. You have always been dear to my heart, so I hope you see my vision and help me bring it to life."

"I will bring you death for what you've done!" Nicodemus slammed his fists against the table and rose to his feet. "Tiger Lily, I am officially charging you with treason and demand that you return with us to the Mountain." Then from somewhere within his jacket, he produced a tightly coiled bullwhip. "Take her!" he commanded his men.

Khan was the first to react. He rolled up his sleeves, exposing the two armlets on his wrists. With a flick of his hands, two spring-loaded darts attached to retractable chains shot out and buried themselves into the chest of one of the men. Khan leaped onto the table, pulling his victim closer to him like a fish on a line. When he was within arm's reach, Khan wrapped one of the chains around his neck and strangled him.

The other suited men died far less ceremoniously, cut down in a hail of bullets delivered by Lilith's mercenaries. This left Nicodemus alone and outnumbered.

"Traitors, the lot of you!" Nicodemus snapped his whip thunderously in the air. "You have betrayed that which gave you life, and now I will show you the penalty of your actions."

"Stand down, my beloved. This doesn't have to end this way. Let it be like it was, with you as my king and I, your queen," Tiger Lily pleaded. She genuinely loved Nicodemus and had hoped not to have to kill him.

"Queen?" Nicodemus laughed mockingly. "You were never anything more to me than an experiment, something I created in my lab as I do with my poisons. I am a sworn Brother of the greatest Order the world has ever known. I am royalty in the court of death. You . . ." he gave her a pitiful look, ". . . are a whore who I took pity on."

Nicodemus's admission shocked Lilith into a deadly stillness. His words cut her deeper than any blade her skin had ever tasted, and there had been a few. She held no illusions about what their relationship had been when he'd first found her, when she was still working as a whore and a thief, but through the years, she thought they had grown to more than that. The intimate moments they'd shared, the dreams conspired. After her reconditioning, when he had remolded her in his own image, Lilith became utterly subservient to him. She was like a loyal dog who wanted nothing more than to please its master. It had all meant nothing to him. Lilith was about to open her mouth to say something. What? She wasn't sure just yet. The moment was stolen from her by the sounds of two thunderous gunshots. Blood squirted onto her face and dress from the two lemon-sized holes that had appeared in Nicodemus's chest. He pitched forward, knocking over several platters from the table before falling to the floor.

Her heart broke in her chest. She didn't know if it was due to her reconditioning, but even after how he had belittled her, she couldn't bring herself not to love him. Tears welled in her eyes when she whipped around to see which one of her men had the audacity to do that. She spotted Peter standing just behind her. In his hands were the two smoking Pretty Bitches. Her eyes asked what her mouth could not: *Why?*

Peter's voice was emotional when he answered, "After watching my father do it all those years, I promised that I would never allow another man to disrespect my mother."

Lilith approached her son. The sadness was still in her eyes, but she managed to muster a weak smile. She laid her hand lovingly on his cheek. "You are a good son, Peter. Dramatic, but a good son nonetheless."

"And I thought *I* came from a fucked-up family," Animal remarked, scanning over the dead bodies.

"What the fuck?" George blurted out.

Animal instinctively turned to him. All the color had drained from George's face as his eyes locked on something just behind Animal. When Animal turned around to see what had spooked George, he leaped from his seat. It was impossible! Animal had taken many souls with the Pretty Bitches, so he knew that what he was seeing was impossible—yet, there he was.

Nicodemus's slender fingers gripped the edge of the dining room table as he pulled himself to his feet. The motion looked awkward and painful. He managed to push himself into a chair and let out a deep whine. He looked at his chest and recoiled when he saw the holes. When he looked up, there was a look of genuine confusion on his face. "What in God's name did she do to me?"

Lilith approached her former lover, sliding into her signature tiger gauntlets. "The witch has cursed you, my love, but I will be your exorcist." Her hands flashed, and six crossing wounds appeared at Nicodemus's throat . . . right before his head fell from his shoulders and bounced to the floor. She stood over him for a while, looking down at the body that had been separated from its head. Her lips moved quietly as if she was praying over him before turning to the rest of her guests. "My apologies, but it seems I've made a mess in the dining room. I suggest we have dinner in the parlor instead."

"How the hell can you still be thinking about food after all this?" Animal asked.

"Murder helps to build my appetite," Lilith said coldly. "No worries, Animal. I suspect you'll appreciate what my people have prepared."

It was a short walk from the dining room to the parlor. Lilith led the group, with one of her sons on each arm. Animal's eyes took in everything they passed, noting all the entrances and exits. He needed to get his kids and get out of that place. He had always known that Lilith was more ruthless than most, but one thing that night had taught him was that she was not only cruel but as mad as a hatter, and there was no way he was going to trust anything that came out of her mouth. All he needed was to get his hands on a gun, and he was out of there.

They saw more of Lilith's mercenaries assembled when they entered the parlor, who, upon seeing their mistress, all stood at attention near the fireplace that took up a large portion of the wall. An intense fire burned inside, casting flickering orange lights on the thing the men seemed to be guarding. It was a hospital gurney; on it lay a body covered in a sheet. Whoever was beneath it squirmed. He hoped Lilith wasn't about to ask him to participate in some Brotherhood ritual that involved a human sacrifice because he wasn't with it. He watched as Lilith approached the gurney. She made sure that she had his attention before snatching the sheet away, revealing what she had been concealing: Red Sonja bound and gagged.

"How?"

"I'll let the one responsible fill you in." Lilith motioned to someone who had just entered the room.

When Animal's eyes landed on the newest arrivals, all he could see was red.

Chapter 34

Earlier . . .

Woods had been parked across the street from the high-rise apartment building since nine a.m. This was his fourth day laying on the place since he'd first gotten the tip. He liked to stalk his prey before he moved in for the kill. The original plan had been to rush the apartment and strong-arm what he was after, but thanks to his patience, he had discovered an easier way to go about it. About a day earlier, he noticed a pretty redhead coming in and out. Sometimes, she would come with a bag and leave without one or vice versa. There was no doubt in his mind who she was coming to see because he had seen her with Louie before. So she was either the plug or a courier. Either way, she was getting jacked.

Woods was still pissed about Dice backing out at the last minute. He had never known Dice to let anyone or anything scare him away from a lick, so he couldn't understand why he acted like a bitch over this Ashanti nigga. For all he knew, Ashanti could've been asking about the score for the same reason; planning to rip the drugs too. If his ass snooped around, the score must've been bigger than Woods had been led to believe because he knew that Ashanti had been out of the robbery game for years. The only good thing about Dice not being with him was that he would've had to split the money down the middle with him. He could give the hired muscle he had brought with him whatever he wanted and keep the lion's share. Besides the small piece he had to kick back to his man who had given him the tip, the rest was for Woods.

Although he didn't have Dice with him, he wasn't going in alone. He had two kids he knew, Mac and Brad, with him. He knew Brad from the neighborhood. He was one of those dudes with one foot in and one foot out of the game. Woods had just happened to catch Brad when he needed money, and that's how he convinced him to come along. Mac was another case. Woods had met him during a brief stint in prison, and they became friends. Mac was down to do anything and everything for a dollar. This was the team he had assembled for the score.

"There she goes," Woods said when he saw Red Sonja exit the building. He pulled down his ski mask in anticipation of the heist.

Mac sat up, his beady eyes scanning for their intended victim. He spotted Sonja hurrying down the street. Over her shoulder was a large shoulder bag that looked like it had some weight. "Damn, you didn't tell me the bitch was that fine. We should be trying to fuck her, not rob her," he said thirstily.

"Nigga, keep your mind on this money," Woods barked.

"You think she got money, drugs, or both in the bag?" Brad asked.

"I don't know; let's go find out." Woods put the car in gear and proceeded to make a U-turn.

Sonja couldn't get out of Louie's apartment fast enough. She had called him that morning and told him to stop manufacturing Blue Dream in his apartment. The heat was on, and by "heat," she meant Animal. The run-in with her daughter's father had been too close of a call for her. She had been lucky to escape him once and knew he wouldn't allow it to happen again, especially considering that she had shot him. He was getting too close, so Sonja decided to play it safe and move her operation. Louie was responsible for getting rid of the lab, and Sonja came and collected the supply of the Blue Dream he had already manufactured. There wasn't as much as she had expected, but there was enough for her to deliver the shipment she had promised Sammy and maybe have some left to reach out to a few more people. She wasn't worried about the temporary shutdown because that first wave of Blue Dream would shake the town. By the time they were back up and running, she expected the demand for it would be through the roof. Sonja was playing the long game with this.

She came out of the building at a brisk walk, clutching her shoulder bag that held the Blue Dream. Her eyes constantly scanned the streets for danger. She had almost reached her car when she saw a green Honda make a U-turn and start down the same side of the street where she was walking. Her heart fluttered, initially fearing that it might be Animal, but if it had been, she'd have never seen him coming. Whoever was in that car definitely didn't have good intentions for her, but they were amateurs.

Mac jumped out of the car and stepped into her path. He was loud talking and waving his gun around menacingly. It reminded her of a rap video she had seen.

Sonja never said a word; she just pulled the trigger on the pistol she'd been holding and shot him through the bag. Seeing their accomplice go down gave the robbers food for thought, but it was too late for that.

She no longer hid the gun in the bag now. It was raised and blasting at the would-be robbers. She dropped Brad next, hitting him once in the head and twice in his stomach. Woods was now trying to run, but there would be no escape from her. She placed her bag on the ground and steadied her shooting hand. Woods was almost a half-block away when the bullet struck him in the ankle and sent him crashing to the ground. She had been aiming for his knee, but she'd take her victories where she could get them.

Sonja approached the wounded man and snatched off his mask. She didn't know him from a hole in the wall, so why did he target her? It was no coincidence that the heist just "happened" to go down outside Louie's. Something smelled rotten.

"Who sent you?" She jammed her gun in his mouth. Woods tried to play the strong, silent role, so she hit him in the mouth with her gun and knocked out two teeth. "Who sent you?"

"I sent him," a voice called from behind Sonja. She turned to find herself face-to-face with a grinning K-Dawg. He held a very nasty-looking handgun in his hand, which was pointed directly between her eyes. "Drop your gun, please."

"You set me up to get robbed, K-Dawg? That's low, even for you." Sonja tossed the gun onto the ground. She and K-Dawg had history, so she was disappointed that he was behind her misfortune.

K-Dawg looked over at Woods, who was on the ground in a world of pain. K-Dawg decided to put him out of his misery and shot him. "Not robbed, baby girl. I just needed you distracted long enough for me to get the drop. I fought alongside you for years, so I'm not dumb enough to go at you head up. The element of surprise makes this less messy."

"What do you want?" she asked harshly.

"The same thing everyone else does." K-Dawg scooped her bag. A car screeched to a halt in front of them, and the back door slid open. Justice was behind the wheel, looking up and down the street nervously. "Somebody would like a word with you. Let's go." He nudged her with the gun toward the car.

Sonja climbed in the backseat, with K-Dawg cramming himself next to her. "I can't believe after all we've gone through, you let that bitch buy you off."

"Then you must've forgotten that I'm a mercenary," K-Dawg replied. "Jus, you take care of that other thing for me?"

"Yeah, right after she left." Justice raised a blood-stained folder for K-Dawg to see.

"My nigga."

"Dawg, how did you know that the little dudes were gonna move on her and where it was going down?" Justice asked. The question had been eating at him since they set out.

K-Dawg grinned slyly. "Who do you think gave Woods the tip? Now, let's head up. I don't want to miss any of the festivities."

Chapter 35

"Little brother," Justice greeted Animal with a nod.

"Dick sucker," Animal replied. He had wondered if he would see his brother sometime during all this. A part of him didn't want to because he knew that it would mean that he was able to stand by while all this was happening to Animal . . . the kidnapping, the murder of his wife. His brother knew all of it and still remained loyal to the enemy. Animal had nothing left for the man who had also come from his mother's womb.

"Now, now, boys. Regardless of what's going on, you're still brothers. Ain't that right, Tay?"

"Fuck you too, you black-hearted bastard!" Animal spat on the floor. "If I get out of this, I'm putting both you niggas' lights out."

"Enough," Lilith commanded. "Your assistance in this has been greatly appreciated, K-Dawg, by Khan and myself, isn't that right?" She turned to Khan, who just shrugged. "Were you able to find it?"

"No, only the drugs. The chemist was long gone, and he left in a hurry from the looks of things. They were expecting company." K-Dawg glanced at Animal.

"There's only so far he'll be able to run. My people will catch up with him sooner or later," Lilith said. She'd have loved to have been able to capture either the formula or the chemist, but once again, they had eluded her. "This is all your fault, you know? What do you have to say for yourself?" She snatched the gag roughly from Sonja's mouth.

"Fuck you. You threw the first shot when you tried to take what belonged to me and my brother. I should've cut your fucking throat in your sleep when I had the chance," Sonja spat.

"Then let that serve as a lesson to you." Lilith gave her a light scratch with one of her claws and opened up a cut on her leg. "I believe you know everyone here." She motioned to her guests.

Sonja craned her neck and looked at the assembled faces as best as she could. When her eyes landed on Animal, she felt a tinge of guilt. She gave an apologetic look, to which he responded with one of disgust before turning his eyes away. She had hurt him, and as warped as it may have sounded, she was glad. At least she knew that he still felt something for her.

"It's time for us to end this little game. Animal . . ." Lilith turned to him. ". . . You've heard my vision, and now, let's have your decision." She took a knife from one of the soldiers. "Will you stand with me . . . with your children and step into your new life? All I require of you is to kill what remains of your old one." She held the knife out.

Animal stared at the knife as if it were something alien. He was no fool. He knew that no matter what Lilith said or promised, he would never be allowed to be a father to his kids under her watch. "Respectfully, if you put that knife in my hands, I'm more likely to cut your throat than hers."

"A fool for love to the end." Lilith retracted the knife. She turned to her men. "Take him and his bitch in the back and prepare them for execution."

Lilith's men pulled Sonja from the gurney, binding her hands in front of her. The same was done to Animal. They were about to be ushered out into the backyard to face whatever fate Lilith had planned for him, but just as they were being led out, Mustache came rushing into the parlor. From the smile on his face, Animal knew he was in for another dose of bad news.

"I know you said you didn't want to be disturbed, but I figured you'd want to see this right away," Mustache said apologetically. He waited until she gave him the nod before ushering in someone who had been in the foyer.

Animal's heart broke into a thousand pieces when he saw Kahllah, Ashanti, and Diabolique ushered into the room. Their hands were on their heads, and two of Lilith's black-masked soldiers were covering them. A third held their weapons, including Kahllah's Stingray. Animal had prayed that they had made it out, that they wouldn't be pulled down the rabbit hole with him, but once again, his curse had spread. "I'm so sorry," he said to his friends emotionally.

"Who wants to live forever anyway, right?" Ashanti half-joked. Men covering them forced the trio to their knees.

Lilith approached and examined each new face. Her eyes lingered on Ashanti. "If Ophelia is not here and you are, I assume she's dead?"

Ashanti nodded.

The news rocked Lilith, but she tried not to show it. Despite her methods when raising Ophelia, she had genuinely come to love her as one of her own. "This one dies last. I want him to hear his friends scream before he goes." Then she moved on to Diabolique. "I don't know you, little one. I have no gripe with you, but unfortunately, you've thrown in with the wrong lot, and you'll be going along for the ride."

"So long as it's a fast ride," Diabolique said defiantly.

Last but not least, she came to the Black Lotus. "And you, one of the Brotherhood's greatest disappointments. I had so much hope for you when you were coming up. You were like me, one of the few women in the Brotherhood. Do you realize how rare of a thing that is? We could've ruled as queens, but you chose to die like a pawn instead. Since you announced your presence, I assume you've come to beg for your life, Lotus?"

Kahllah gave her a cold look. "I have not come to beg for my life. I've come to take *yours*."

Lilith laughed. "Have you looked around? You are surrounded by my soldiers and two sworn members of the Brotherhood of Blood. What chance does one lone member of the Order stand against these odds?"

"Not one, but two," Diabolique spoke up. "I was born Rose, but in the shadow of the Mountain, I was given the name Wildflower."

Lilith shook her head disappointedly. "Women like you are the problem with the Brotherhood now. They'll allow anyone to join."

"I never said that I was a member of the Brotherhood. I said, the *Order*." Diabolique rose to her feet, followed by Ashanti and Kahllah. "Apes!" Her voice bellowed through the room.

One by one, several of Lilith's hired mercenaries took their guns off their prisoners and turned them on Lilith's men. The one now pointing his gun at Lilith's head sported a tattoo on his hand. It was a mark that Lilith knew well. "The Apes," she hissed, "but how?"

"I found his mark," Kahllah replied triumphantly. Diabolique pushed her hair back so that all in the room could see the gorilla tattoo at her temple. Kahllah hadn't understood what Iron Monkey meant when he told her to look for his mark. It wasn't until she called the number in the cell phone he had given her, which led her to Diabolique, did it all make sense. By his "mark," he meant his protégé. In his death, Iron Monkey had sent her to find the one person, besides Prime, whose word the Apes would trust and who they would fight for.

One of the mercenaries loyal to the Apes returned the trio's weapons to them. Ashanti chambered a round into his weapon. "Big homie, I think you're standing on the wrong side of the gun line."

Animal approached Peter, who was being covered by one of the ape mercenaries. "I believe these belong to me." Then with bound hands, he removed his Pretty Bitches. He held them both together and smashed Peter in the face with them.

"You broke my fucking nose." Peter crashed to the floor, blood spilling over his hands as he tried to slow the bleeding.

"That ain't all I'm gonna break. Me and you gonna dance, boy," Animal promised before crossing the room to stand with Ashanti and the others. When Kahllah cut his hands free, he flexed his fingers around his beloved guns. "How did you find me?" he asked Kahllah.

"Tommy Clark," Ashanti answered, much to Animal's surprise. "One of his people reached out to me with an address. Don't know why, and I don't care. He did have a message for you, though."

"And what's that?" Animal wanted to know.

"He says to tell you that this makes the two of you even."

Animal couldn't help but chuckle. "Yeah, until next time. Now, let's get back to the business." He turned to Tiger Lily. "Where are my children?"

"You still don't get it, do you?" Lilith shook her head. "Why would you deny your children the opportunity to be something far greater in life than you could ever push them to be? *I* will give them the world."

"And *I* will give them love," Animal countered. He turned the gun on George, sitting on one of the chairs. "You make me ask you again, and you'll be one kid short."

Lilith looked at Peter, who was still nursing his broken nose. "Bring them," she commanded. Peter left the parlor and returned a few minutes later with T.J. and Celeste in tow. T.J. tried to run to Animal, but Peter held fast to his hand.

"Not so fast, Animal. You want something from me, then I'm going to need something from you. Take T.J. and leave me with Sonja and the girl. I can still do what needs to be done with one legacy. Sonja is a bitch, but she's still the girl's mother. I'll find some other way to punish her rather than killing her. You agree to this, and I'll let you and T.J. walk out of here and return to your lives," Lilith offered.

"Animal, you know the minute you walk out of here, I'm as good as dead, and she's going to take Celeste," Sonja said frantically. She was still tied up and in the hands of their enemies.

"Think about it, Animal. You did not know the girl until a few days ago, so there's no real attachment to her. Go home with your son, mourn your wife, and live your life," Lilith urged him.

For the briefest of moments, Animal actually weighed the offer. He was tired of the fighting. All he wanted to do was get his children back and try to pick up the pieces of his shattered life. Then he saw Celeste, who was watching him with pleading eyes. She was the flesh of his flesh, and there was no way he would leave her behind. "No, dice. I leave this house with both my children, or you'll leave this world."

"Very well," Lilith sighed. "I've tried diplomacy, and now I will speak to you in a language which you may better understand . . . death. Kill them all, starting with his children."

"Noooo!" Animal screamed as the first shot was fired.

The room was thrown into chaos. One of Lilith's mercenaries had opened fire, which caused a chain reaction, and bullets now flew all over the room. Lilith stood in the center of the carnage, oblivious to the bullets whipping past her, cutting into anyone who got close enough for her to strike with her claws. The Apes fought valiantly, but they were outnumbered and began to fall.

There was no sign of Kahllah, but Animal doubted if she had gone far, not while Lilith lived. He knew this was as personal to her as it was to him, though for different reasons. Ashanti and Diabolique had taken cover behind the gurney, which Sonja had previously been strapped to. The two youths exchanged fire with Lilith's mercenaries.

Animal looked at his children. They were cowering in the corner when all hell broke loose around them. Then with no thoughts for his own safety, he ran through the fire zone toward them. He needed to get his kids out of harm's way.

Animal made it across the room in time to see Peter flee up the stairs, dragging both children behind him. Animal made to go after him when Mustache blocked his path. He was armed with a machine gun, and his eyes held a murderous look.

"I tried telling her she should've killed you, but she wouldn't listen. Now, I have to clean up the mess." He opened fire.

Animal barely escaped before bullets ate through the parlor floor. He dove behind a couch, which was peppered next. He tried to return fire, but Mustache had him pinned. He looked at the doorway where Peter had disappeared with his children. He needed to get to them at all costs. He was about to risk it all when he saw a blur of motion.

The air whistled as Kahllah brought her Stingray around and sliced off Mustache's gun hand. He shrieked, holding his bloody stump, but his screams were soon silenced when Kahllah took his head. Mustache's head fell one way and his body another.

"That was for Abel." Animal spat on the corpse.

"Are you hurt?" Kahllah asked him.

"No, but the kids . . . I need to go after them," Animal told her.

"Do what you gotta do." Kahllah's eyes were locked on Lilith, who fled down the hall. "I'm about to bring this little game to an end."

"Well, that escalated quickly," K-Dawg joked. He and Justice were crouched behind a table they had turned over when the shooting started.

"I told you that fucking with this broad was going to go bad," Justice told him before letting off his gun. He was shooting Apes and mercenaries alike.

K-Dawg happened to notice that there was no one guarding the front door. So they would have a clear path. "Let's get while the getting is good." He tugged at his friend.

"What about *him?*" Justice saw Animal running up the stairs.

"Above my pay grade. I captured Sonja and delivered his bargaining chip to him wrapped in a bow. He could've walked out of here but chose to try to save the world," K-Dawg told him.

"He didn't because it would've meant he had to leave one of his kids behind. Ain't you never loved something enough that you couldn't bear to walk away from it?"

"Honestly? No," K-Dawg said, hunkering down lower as wave of bullets hit the table. It was taking heavy damage and wouldn't hold much longer. "Listen, man, what we got in that folder we snatched can set us straight for the rest of our days. Louie is the only one, besides us now, who had access to that information, and you took care of him. We're the only game in town, Justice. Animal made his choice, and now it's time for you to make yours."

"You're right." Justice came out from behind the couch and went after his brother.

"Just like old times, huh?" Diabolique told Ashanti before letting off several shots from her pistol.

"Yeah, except it's usually *us* getting *you* out of some shit instead of the other way around."

"I told you when I showed up that I had the Apes on deck," she joked.

"I didn't know you meant *literally*. What's up with you and that ape shit?" Ashanti wanted to know. When she got down, he went up and fired. They alternated that way throughout the battle, like a finely tuned unit.

"Long and painful story. If we live, I'll tell you all about it," Diabolique promised. She was about to come up and take her turn in their shooting routine when pain exploded in her shoulder. A dart attached to a chain sticking out of it was stuck there. Holding the end of that chain was Raffa Khan. Before either of them could react, Khan yanked the chain and dragged Diabolique into the kitchen.

Ashanti was about to follow when he saw Justice going up the same stairs Animal had. He knew where Justice stood and that he was on the wrong side of this war. He had a difficult decision to make: rescue Diabolique or go after Animal.

"You know, I tried to tell the elders to wipe out the lot of you stinking Apes the day the Iron Monkey led that bootleg-ass tribe up from the catacombs. I said it was a mistake to give a group of lunatics any authority, but no one listened—and now look." Khan was ranting while dragging Diabolique through the kitchen. He pulled the dart free when he got her to his desired location.

Diabolique howled, not sure if the dart hurt worse going in or coming out. She was now on her back at the foot of a large rack holding dishes from the dishwasher. The bottom was where the pots and pans rested, and utensils were at the top.

Khan grabbed a butcher's knife from the rack and tested its weight. "I toiled under that crazy bitch, Tiger Lily, for years while trying to wait for this deal to come together, and you and your monkeys blow it all to hell within seconds." He straddled Diabolique, holding the knife above her. "You claim to be a part of the Order, but not the Brotherhood, when it's all one blood. Here, let me show you." He brought the knife down.

Diabolique waited until Khan had committed to the strike before raising the frying pan she had pulled loose from the shelf while Khan was ranting. The knife kissed off the bottom of the pan, and the stab missed its mark, but it did open up a cut on her arm. Ignoring the pain, she brought the pan around and smashed it into the side of Khan's head.

"You little bitch." Khan rolled off her and to his feet, clutching his head. Diabolique tried to get up, but Khan kicked her in the stomach, sending her back down. "I was going to kill you quickly, but now, all bets are off."

Pain shot through Diabolique's skull as Khan pulled her by her hair to her feet. She felt like he was trying to rip out each follicle. He cocked her head back and slammed it into the top of the stove. Diabolique always laughed at the part of the cartoon when the character would get hit in the head and see little birdies. She didn't find it as funny now that it was happening to her. Her hands desperately searched the stove for something she could use for a weapon. Her fingers found the gas switch, and she turned on the burner . . . hoping that it was the right one.

"Bitch!" she heard Khan scream before releasing her.

Diabolique would've hit the floor had she not grabbed onto the refrigerator door handle for support. Khan was flailing his arms, trying to extinguish the fire quickly consuming his suit. Diabolique looked at her reflection in the steel refrigerator. Her face was bloodied and bruised. The reflection staring back at her was the same one as the little girl who had been raped and tossed in the trash all those years ago.

Khan was so busy trying to get out of the jacket before the fire engulfed him that he didn't see Diabolique approaching him from behind, holding the knife he had dropped when she hit him with the pan.

"I'm *not* a victim," Diabolique chanted, plunging the knife into Khan's back. He staggered forward, instinctively throwing his arms out, and accidentally ignited the kitchen curtain. "I am *not* a victim." She stabbed him again. "Not a victim." Diabolique didn't stop stabbing Khan until her arms had grown tired, and the kitchen was up in flames.

Chapter 36

Animal cautiously made his way up the stairs to the upper level of the house. He found himself in a long hallway lined with several rooms. At the end of the hall, he heard T.J. scream. This added speed to his steps.

He found them in the last room on the left. Peter was backed into a corner near the window. His forearm was encircled around T.J. and Celeste's little necks in a reverse chokehold. With his free hand, he held a gun to the side of Celeste's head. His eyes were wild, like those of a trapped animal.

"Take one more step, and I'll air these little muthafuckas out," Peter warned.

"Daddy," T.J. yelled. The little boy was terrified.

"I'm here, son. I got you . . . both of you." Animal tried to calm the situation. "Peter, this is between you and me. Let the kids walk out, and we can deal with this like men."

"You ain't no man; you're a demon. My family has had nothing but bad befall them since getting mixed up with you and these fucking kids," Peter shouted.

"All the more reason you should let them go."
Animal risked taking a step. Peter fired his gun into
the air before returning it to Celeste's head. She
winced as the hot barrel burned her skin, but she
would not cry.

"You think this is a game? Am I a fucking joke?"
Peter was agitated. "Put the guns down and kick
them over here."

"You got it." Animal placed the Pretty Bitches on
the floor and kicked them in Peter's direction. One
of them ended up sliding under the bed. "No more
guns, see?" He raised his hands. "Now, let's have a
nice, calm conversation. One that doesn't involve you
hurting innocent children."

Peter shoved the children, still keeping the gun
trained on Animal. He picked up one of the Pretty
Bitches closest to him and pointed it at Animal. "Bet
you never thought you'd see yourself at the wrong
end of one of these. They say that these guns are
cursed. Does that mean your soul will go to hell when
I shoot you?"

Animal looked at his children. They were huddled
at the foot of the bed. T.J. was sobbing uncontrollably, trying to get to Animal, but Celeste held him
back. She stood in front of her baby brother protectively. T.J. might not have been sure what was about
to happen, but there was no mistaking Celeste's
understanding. There was a silent exchange between
them. At that moment, any doubts Animal may have
had about the girl being his were washed away. She
was without question the blood of his blood.

"Don't look," he told them. Animal closed his eyes and heard the shot . . . but felt no pain. When he heard Peter cry out, he opened his eyes. There was a lemon-sized hole in his stomach. A second shot rang out, this one striking Peter in the head. He staggered once before falling through the nearby window. That was the end of Peter's story.

Animal looked around to see where the shot had come from, and his heart leaped into his throat. Celeste stood there, the gun clutched in her tiny hands. She was crying and looking at the window Peter had fallen out of as if she feared he would return. "Give Daddy the gun, baby," he urged her softly. Celeste turned those steel-gray eyes in his direction as if she were trying to decide whether she could trust him. Eventually, she relinquished the weapon and fell into his arms, sobbing. T.J. joined her. "It's okay. I got you now . . . I got you."

Animal stayed there for a time, consoling his children. What they had experienced was sure to traumatize them and leave some very deep psychological scars that he wasn't sure would ever fully heal. He kissed the top of his baby girl's head. Passing his generational curse onto his children, as his father had done to him, was something that Animal had always been afraid of. He tried his best to ensure that it never happened . . . but had failed. He had indeed passed his curse on to his offspring; now, he knew which one. Allowing his daughter to be put into a position to be robbed of her innocence was something he would never be able to forgive himself for.

Kahllah descended the steps she had seen Lilith go down and found herself in the basement, though it looked more like a dungeon. Lilith had cells and torture devices set up throughout the spacious room. She expected to have to search for Tiger Lily, but she didn't. Instead, she found her standing in the center of the room, waiting for her.

"Guess it comes down to you and me," Lilith said.

"I would've expected this to end no other way. You are an enemy of the Brotherhood, Tiger Lily, and I have come to administer justice," Kahllah announced, tightening her grip on her blade.

"You're the second person to tell me that tonight. Unfortunately, the first one is dead, and I suspect you'll end up the same way." Tiger Lily raised one of her clawed hands.

From the shadows appeared two of Lilith's disciples, both wearing the black masks and markings of her cause. They came at Kahllah swinging blades. She took a defensive stance, fending off their strikes with Stingray. They were good, but they were no Black Lotus. She dispatched one easily enough, and when she turned her attention to the second one, she felt the pain in her back, causing her to cry out. She staggered forward and turned to see Lilith behind her. Her claws were slick with the blood of the Black Lotus.

"That's the Black Lotus I know. I'd almost forgotten how sweet the sounds of your screams were." Lilith launched another attack.

Kahllah danced around the basement, trying to keep Tiger Lily and her disciple off her. If she let them sandwich her in, she would be dead. She decided Lilith was the greater threat and tried to keep her attention focused on her. For an old woman, Tiger Lily was still quite fast. She lashed out with her claws, trying to gut her former pupil. Steel sparked off steel as Stingray tested Lilith's claws. The man in black managed to distract Kahllah enough for Lilith to get off another strike. This time, she opened up her thigh. Kahllah hobbled. She knew that she couldn't keep this up much longer.

Lilith's disciple moved in on Kahllah, swinging his blade back and forth wildly. Kahllah let him get close, and when he struck, so did she. Stingray bit into the disciple's neck at the same time his blade pierced her side. Warm blood leaked down her side and pooled on the floor where she was standing. Kahllah was wounded and at a disadvantage.

Lilith pressed her attack, knowing Kahllah was wounded and on the ropes. She attacked her ferociously with her claws, finally knocking Kahllah's sword from her hand. Kahllah fell onto her back, and Lilith jumped on her with murder in her eyes.

"Scream for me, little bruja. Scream for me like you used to."

It had been many years since Kahllah had been in that type of pain. Wherever Lilith's claws stuck left a wound. It was like she was dying the death of one thousand cuts. She tried to claw at Lilith's face, only to have one of her fingers sliced off.

"Bleed for me, little bruja . . . Bleed for me." Lilith laughed maniacally as she continued to cut into her.

Kahllah felt like she was about to pass out from blood loss. A million things ran through her mind in those final moments. She had failed Animal, Iron Monkey, Artemis, and anyone else who had put it on the line for her. What was worse? She had failed her Order. There would be no beauty in her death—only pain. Then something strange happened. Lilith's cutting stopped, and her weight was lifted off Kahllah. She dragged herself into a sitting position and looked at Lilith. She didn't quite understand what she was witnessing.

Another of Lilith's disciples had appeared, face covered by a black mask. He had a fistful of Lilith's hair, with her head drawn back and a large buck knife pressed to her neck. "This is for my brother," he whispered into her ear before opening her throat.

The man in the mask released Lilith and allowed her to fall to the floor. She instinctively clutched at her throat where she had been cut, but only did more damage because she was wearing the claws. It only took Lilith a few minutes to bleed out, but it felt like forever. Kahllah sat there for a while, staring at the corpse and wondering what could've been. Tiger Lily was a legend amongst the Brotherhood. She was a trailblazer in the Order and one of the women who had made it possible for Kahllah to rise in her rank. Tiger Lily could've been great, but she couldn't see beyond her own ambitions.

The masked man moved toward Kahllah, knife still slick with blood. When he reached for her, she recoiled. "Relax," she heard a familiar voice behind the mask. When he removed it, she was surprised to see Cain's face staring down at her. "I borrowed this from a nigga I left stinking in Central Park." He helped Kahllah to her feet, and she looped her arm around his neck. "Let's get our people and go home."

Kahllah wasn't used to asking for or receiving help, but she didn't refuse Cain's offer. She was beaten to hell and had lost so much blood that she probably couldn't have walked on her own anyhow. She stopped short as they neared the stairs that led back to the main level. "Is it me, or do you smell smoke?"

Animal rushed down the hall carrying his children. The house was filling with smoke, and he needed to get them outside. He had almost made it to the stairs when there was the sound of a shot, and plaster flew from the wall near his head. He lost his balance, trying to protect his children as he fell. He also lost his last Pretty Bitch. He looked down the hall and saw

George coming in their direction, holding a gun. He must've hidden in one of the upstairs rooms when the fighting had started.

"You killed my brother," George raved, firing again.

Animal was thankful that George was a poor shot, or he would've died. Still, there was only so long even George could miss with Animal being out in the open like that. So he pushed his children toward the staircase. "Take your brother and run," he told Celeste. The girl wasted no time in obeying.

Animal rolled as another shot hit the floor. He scrambled for his gun and almost reached it when something heavy hit his shoulder. He knew long before his arm went numb that he had been shot. He waited until he saw his kids descend the stairs before turning over onto his back to face George. There was a crazed look in the man's eyes as he stalked toward Animal.

"You guys kidnapped me, beat me, and were probably going to kill me. All for what? I'm not a soldier; I'm just the moneyman. You could've just let me go," George said. He sounded like a man on the verge of a nervous breakdown.

"You became a soldier when you started dabbling in your mama's business," Animal told him. "You gonna kill me, do it and be done with it."

"Fine." George aimed, but a high-powered slug took him off his feet before he could pull the trigger. He was dead before he hit the ground.

Animal looked toward the stairs and saw his brother, Justice, holding a smoldering pistol. "You good?" Justice moved closer to Animal.

"Oh, so now you wanna play the concerned brother? This don't make us square because you and your people are partially to blame for this shit," Animal said. He hadn't forgotten or forgiven Justice for his role in his troubles.

"And now, I'm trying to help fix it." Justice extended his hand.

Animal tried to get up on his own but realized he couldn't. His shoulder was in a bad way from the bullet. Reluctantly, he allowed his brother to help him up. "When this is over, and my shoulder is healed, you still owe me a fade. I ain't saying it'll make us right, but it's a start."

"Fair enough," Justice agreed.

The two brothers had just reached the stairs when they met up with Ashanti. He took one look at Justice and Animal's bleeding shoulder and got the wrong idea. "Strike two. Your ass is out." He trained his gun on Justice. To his surprise, Animal stepped between them.

"This isn't his work. In fact, he's why I'm only shot and not dead," Animal explained.

"Say the word, big homie, and this nigga is dead." Ashanti took aim.

Animal placed his hand on Ashanti's gun and forced him to lower it. "They'll be no more death here tonight, Ashanti. It's over."

***

By the time they reached the bottom of the stairs, the house was full of smoke. The fire in the kitchen had spread to the living room and was eating its way through the rest of the mansion. Parts of the ceiling had even begun to collapse. It seemed that all Lilith's men had either fled or lay dead, their bodies were littering the floor.

Cain was coming from the opposite hallway with a badly beaten and bloodied Kahllah hanging from his neck. Animal, Ashanti, and Justice met Kahllah and the others at the bottom of the stairs. She was covered in blood and leaning on Cain for support.

"Didn't expect I'd ever see you again," Animal told Cain.

"Nor did I expect to find you in the company of a bitch-ass nigga." Cain glared at Justice.

"I'm gonna let that slide, but it's the first and last one I'm gonna let you get off," Justice warned.

"Lilith?" Animal asked.

"Gone," Cain told him. "My brother's account has been settled."

"Where are my kids?" Animal looked around.

"I got them." Diabolique came into view. She had both children in her arms. Her face was badly bruised, and she felt like her jaw was broken. She saw the pitiful look Animal gave her. "You should see the other guy."

Justice heard a crash in the other room. The fire was getting bigger. "Let's get the fuck out of here." He threw one of his arms under Kahllah's and helped

Cain carry her outside. Diabolique followed with the children, with Animal behind and Ashanti bringing up the rear.

Animal was about to cross the threshold when he stopped short. He thought he heard a woman screaming. When he looked outside and scanned the faces of the people gathered on the estate's front lawn, he realized that Sonja wasn't one of them. It occurred to him that with all that was going on, no one ever bothered to untie her, which meant she was likely still somewhere in the house. "Keep going. I'll be right behind you." He started back inside the house.

Ashanti grabbed his arm. He knew what Animal meant to do. "You can't be fucking serious. She *caused* all this. Let that bitch burn."

Animal jerked from Ashanti's grip. "I won't let my kids lose another mother." He disappeared back inside the house before Ashanti could protest. Ashanti tried to follow but was cut off when a chunk of the burning ceiling collapsed in front of the doorway and blocked his path.

"Animal . . . Animal . . ." Ashanti shouted, but his friend couldn't hear him over the roar of the flames.

"Sonja!" Animal called her name as he ventured deeper into the burning house. It was like an oven in there, and there was so much smoke he could barely see his hand in front of his face.

Risking his life—again—for someone who had done nothing but repeatedly cross him at every

chance she got wasn't one of Animal's most brilliant
moments. Still, he wouldn't be able to look his baby
girl in the face knowing that he had let her mother
die in such a horrible way without even trying to save
her. He had done more for people that he was less
connected to.

The smoke-filled air made breathing almost impossible, but he pressed on. He managed to make
his way to the last spot he remembered seeing Sonja,
and near a burning chair, he spotted the silhouette
of someone lying on the ground. From the outline,
he could tell it was a woman. A lump formed in his
throat as he raced to her. Animal flipped the body
over, and it was indeed a woman, but not Sonja.
Instead, it was the girl from earlier who had brought
the children to his cell. That's who he had heard
screaming. Her eyes stared lifelessly at the ceiling,
and black soot covered her face. The smoke had
taken her long before Animal ever reached her.

Not far from where she had fallen, Animal saw the
ropes used to bind Sonja, but she was long gone. His
daring rescue mission had been in vain. One thing
Sonja had proven time and again was that she was
the ultimate survivor. He had to give her that.

The heat was now so intense that Animal felt like
his blood was boiling under his skin. He needed
to get out. He tried to make it back the way he had
come but found himself disoriented in the smoke.
His lungs burned in his chest, and his eyes stung as
he tried to feel his way out of the room. The front
door was blocked, but he remembered seeing a side

door off the kitchen. Then as he made his way back through the house, he heard what sounded like groaning wood. He looked up in time to see part of the wall collapsing, trapping him under the rubble. Animal tried to free himself, but he was tired . . . so very tired. All he wanted to do was rest. As he lay there, choking and waiting for the end, his last thoughts were he hoped that the smoke took him before the fire did. Being burned alive was a bad way to go, or so Cain had told him.

What remained of the Dog Pound stood on the front lawn of Lilith's estate, watching helplessly as it went up in flames. Lilith's men were gone. Once again, the members of the Dog Pound had been the last men standing . . . but at what cost?

Diabolique cried openly while Justice cursed and raged. It took the combined efforts of Cain and Diabolique to keep him from rushing back into the house after his little brother. There was nothing he could've done at that point. There was nothing any of them could've done.

Ashanti stood there, watching the flames consume the house, and thought fondly of his friend. He hoped he would rise from the fire unscathed, as he always did, but this time, it wasn't to be. As he had been doing all his life, Animal gambled everything for someone he cared about . . . only this time . . . he'd lost.

Epilogue

Pain . . . that was the signal Animal's body kept sending to his brain. The thing that forced him to wake. When he opened his eyes, he immediately knew that something was wrong. The first thing was that there was something wrong with his vision. He could only see out of one eye.

He was in a dimly lit room with stone walls, lit only by candles. From the stale air, he reasoned that he was somewhere underground. Beneath him was an uncomfortable cot that smelled of musk and something else he couldn't identify. A tattered blanket covered his body from the waist down. When he went to move it, fire shot up through his arm. That's when he realized that his arms were wrapped in heavy bandages.

"Try not to move. Your burns are still fresh, and the bandages could rub more of it off," a familiar voice said from somewhere in the darkness.

Animal was dreaming . . . He had to be. Or worse. He peered into the darkness, trying to see as best he could through his one good eye. "Who is that?" he called out in a shaky voice. When the figure stepped from the darkness into the light of the candle closest to him, his mouth went dry, and his eyes welled with tears. This had to be a trick . . . It couldn't be real.

"I told you that I would always love you in this life and the next," Gucci said with a smile.

"I don't understand," Animal choked on his tears. "If you're here, then that means I'm dead, but why am I in so much pain if that's so?"

"You're not dead, just in bad shape." Gucci sat on the cot beside him. She touched his face lovingly, but there was a chill to her fingertips.

Animal just stared dumbly. Gucci was as beautiful to him as the day he had met her, but something was different about her that he couldn't quite put his finger on. The glow of her skin? The glimmer in her eyes? What was it? "This can't be. They told me that you died . . . We mourned you. What kind of shit is this?"

"I imagine you have a lot of questions. I've got a few of my own, and I'm still trying to figure all this out. So maybe it's best if *he* explains it to you." Gucci looked to a dark corner of the room.

"Who is he?" Animal asked.

"He would be me." A figure stepped into view. He was tall and dark with a shaven head and wore a long, black leather duster. At a glance, Animal almost mistook him for Priest, but this man had two eyes, two piercing green eyes. "You look like shit, Gang Lord."

"Do I know you?" Animal eyed the man suspiciously.

"No, but I suspect we will soon become great friends. I am called The Cross, and I need a man with your skill sets."

Animal didn't trust him. "Fuck you want with me?"

"To help me right a wrong done to our family." Cross opened his hand, and in the center of it was a small glass vial filled with a red liquid. "To do this, I would like to offer you a bargain."

Sonja sat in a beach chair on a nondescript patch of sand somewhere in Old San Juan, Puerto Rico, looking out at the rolling blue waters. It felt strange being back home, considering the circumstances under which she'd left before. After what she'd done in New York, Sonja found herself a hunted woman. She was on the watch lists of law enforcement, the Dog Pound, and the Brotherhood. So she figured the best place to hide would be where they were least likely to look for her—right under their noses where it had all started.

Home.

The doctors who treated the burns she had suffered while escaping Tiger Lily's burning estate had suggested that she avoid the sun for a while. Still, she had never been one to follow doctors' orders . . . or anyone else's, for that matter. Sonja was the conductor of her own orchestra, and her last symphony had been a masterful one.

Animal going all Liam Neeson on her at the last minute had complicated her plans but hardly thwarted them. Sonja always had a scheme within a scheme within a scheme. Working with Louie and Sammy to get the Blue Dream onto the streets was a plan she set into motion when it became apparent that Animal was about to go off script. Louie and Sammy were weak, but they were a necessary evil. She just needed to get her operation up and running, and then she would make her pitch to the one man in the city who she knew had the power and influence that she would need not only to make her a global brand but protect her from the likes of Lilith.

But before she had a chance to make that play, K-Dawg had fucked her. She'd promised him a piece of her action once she became the sole distributor of the Blue Dream if he had acted as a decoy with Lilith and Khan, but she should've known better than to think he'd have done what he had promised. Men like K-Dawg were never content with a piece. They always wanted the whole thing. He had double-crossed her and stolen the only copy of the chemical equation, and left her to die, but she had lived, and that's where he had fucked up. Sonja was as patient as she was vindictive. Before it was all said and done, the Dawg would know the sting of the Widow.

Being captured by Tiger Lily and nearly being burned to death had been an unforeseen hitch, and she had narrowly escaped being executed and burned alive. Neither was an appealing prospect. Sonja had never been very religious, but as she was lying in that living room, hog-tied and about to meet her end, she prayed harder than ever. Her prayers were answered when the girl Lilith kept on staff appeared. She had cut Sonja free of her restraints, and to thank her, Sonja had clobbered the girl and left her to die. It wasn't personal, but Sonja knew that the only way to keep her enemies from hunting her until the end of her days would be if they thought she was dead. She reasoned that once they found whatever the fire left of the girl's remains, they would assume it was her, and she would be in the clear. Then she heard his voice.

It amazed Sonja that even after all she had done to Animal, he would still risk his life to save her. She watched him from the back window she was about to climb out of as he pitifully cried out for her, feeling around blindly in the burning house. She was relieved when he seemed to have finally given up his search and tried to make his way out, and then the wall collapsed. It took everything in Sonja to keep herself from going to him and meeting the same horrible fate. She and Animal were at odds, but she still loved him. She couldn't bring herself to watch him burn alive, so she stole away through the window with tears stinging her eyes. Differences aside, there was no doubt that Animal was her one true love, and not handling him differently would be one of her greatest regrets. At least she was still alive to have regrets. He was now the past, and she turned her attention to her future.

Sonja unwrapped the parcel on her lap and looked at it. The sun kissed the rose-colored barrel and cast a red-tinted light on her thigh. She discovered it while escaping from Lilith's mansion and decided to take it with her. It would be all she had left to remember Animal by . . . a keepsake of sorts. It was strange that it was at least ninety degrees on the beach, yet the gun was ice cold to the touch. Was it missing its twin? Or was it missing its master as much as she was?

"That is one beautiful piece of hardware." A masculine voice reminded Sonja that she wasn't alone on the beach. Tommy Guns sat in his wheelchair, a large brim hat and dark sunglasses pulled low over his head protected him from the sun. He was wearing a long-sleeved linen shirt and pants, overdressed for the heat, but he seemed comfortable enough.

"Yes, it is." Sonja covered the gun again. It was like Tommy had intruded on an intimate moment.

"You miss him, don't you?" Tommy asked, noticing the solemn look on her face.

"More than you know," Sonja said honestly.

"Your cousin came through on his end," Tommy changed the subject. "Our pipeline of pistols between San Juan and New York is up and running. Thanks for helping to push this deal through."

"I didn't do it out of the goodness of my heart. You needed something from me, and I need something from you." Sonja was speaking about her father's cartel. Lilith's death had created a vacuum in the power structure. With Lilith gone, and her father in a

vegetative state, it was a free-for-all with the top lieu-
tenants fighting for control. Sonja was the rightful
heir, but considering her wanted status, she couldn't
just stroll in and stake her claim. She needed help . . .
powerful help. This is where Tommy came in. He had
agreed to use the Clark resources to sort out the mess.

"Right, Daddy's kingdom," Tommy said with a
smile. "I'm going to do what I promised and sort that
out, but first, I must ask you a question. If you loved
Animal as much as you claimed, how could you cross
him like that?"

Sonja thought before answering. "It was for the
greater good. Animal was a man of tunnel vision, and
it kept him from seeing the bigger picture."

"You're right about that. Once that man had his
mind set on something, there was no deterring him."
Tommy thought about the years of war between
Animal and the Clarks. It was still hard to believe he
was gone, and the Clarks' days of looking over their
shoulders were done. "And your daughter? You plan
on going after her?"

"No, she's probably better off without me. The road
I'm walking ain't no place for a kid," Sonja said. The
statement sounded cold, but she hadn't meant it that
way. Her primary reason for even having Celeste was
to keep a piece of Animal with her. She had always
hoped that, in time, the girl would be the thing that
brought them back together. But now that he was
dead, there was no chance of that happening.

Tommy shook his head. "Takes a cold piece of work for a mother to abandon her kid so she can chase a dollar."

"I'm not chasing a dollar; I'm building a legacy," Sonja countered. "Now, if you're done getting into my personal business, I need you to keep your word. Honor your debt to me."

"If it's one thing you can be certain of, it's Tommy Guns always honors his debts."

"Even those owed to a dead man?" a third voice joined their conversation.

Sonja turned and found a man standing over her. The sun was at his back, so she had to shield her eyes against it to see his face. He wore a dark hood, but she could see the burn scar and milky white eyes glaring at her. "No," she gasped.

"Yes." Cain smiled wickedly. "The beast has risen."

Sonja reached for the Pretty Bitch on her lap, but Tommy snatched it away. "That ain't gonna happen." He held the wrapped gun out of her reach.

Sonja sank into her beach chair, defeated. "I guess that bullshit about Tommy Guns being the honorable one of the Clark brothers was bullshit, huh?"

"Not at all. I am a man of honor, but that only applies to honorable people. Ain't no honor in you, bitch. Animal and I have more often than not found ourselves on opposite sides of the gun, but he didn't deserve to go out like that. He tried to do right by you, and you did him filthily. So consider this me settling up the tab between him and me. We are truly even now."

"So, because of what happened with me and Animal, you set me up to die at the hands of this monster?" Sonja was speaking to Tommy but glaring at Cain.

"Death?" Cain cocked his head as if trying to figure out what she meant. "No, sweetie. Death is too tender a mercy for someone like you. I haven't come to give you the gift of death . . ." He drew his buck knife from his sheath. "I've come to give you my mark."

Several years later . . .

"It's not fair. Why can't I go?" T.J. sat on the bed of the hotel room, arms folded and the heels of his feet tapping against the bottom of the bed. He had started to grow his hair out and looked more and more like his father every day.

"Because you're too young," Kahllah yelled from the bathroom, where she was fixing Celeste's hair. Her red locks now reached her back. Kahllah stood behind her, hands on her shoulders, looking at their reflection in the mirror. Celeste had her mother's build, but that face was all Animal's. Sometimes, it was painful to look at her because it made her think of him. She missed her brother dearly. After the fire, Kahllah reached out to some of her contacts to see if Animal's remains had ever been found. Unfortunately, there were so many corpses, and most of them burned beyond recognition, that there was no way to be sure. Since they couldn't give him a proper burial, they held a small, private memorial service for the family. Kahllah was sad that her brother was no longer with them, but at least now he had been reunited with his beloved, Gucci. She knew that they were somewhere up there watching over them.

"Are you okay, Auntie K?" Celeste asked, noticing the sadness that had come over her. She was very intuitive for a child her age.

"Yes, doll. I'm just thinking how beautiful you look." Kahllah stroked her cheek.

"Do you think they'll like my dress?" Celeste tugged at the black velour dress Kahllah had picked out.

"I'm sure they'll love it."

"I hope so because I don't like it. It makes me feel sweaty, and I wish I could wear my jeans instead," Celeste said, sounding like her father. Animal hated to dress up too. She still wasn't the most overly chatty child, but she was doing better than when she first came under Kahllah's care. She couldn't remember Celeste saying more than the occasional few words here and there for the first year. The therapist said it was likely due to her childhood traumas. Kahllah had shared with the therapist that the girl had lost both her parents violently, but, of course, she couldn't tell the whole truth.

"Your dress looks fine, but something is missing." Kahllah studied her with her finger on her chin. "I know what it is." She fished around in her pocket and came out holding a gold rosary. It had been a gift handed down from father to son and now to daughter.

She slipped it around the girl's neck and adjusted it to ensure the cross was straight.

"It's beautiful." Celeste ran her fingers over the beads.

"And so are you." Kahllah stroked her cheek.

"You two are going to be late," Ashanti said as he entered the hotel suite. He was carrying a pizza box. His daughter, Tayshawn, followed closely behind. She was growing like a weed and already nearly T.J.'s height. That must've come from Fatima's side because Ashanti had always been short.

"We're leaving now." Kahllah picked up a briefcase that had been resting by the door. "You guys gonna be good while we're gone?"

"We're good." T.J. grabbed the pizza box from Ashanti's hand and rushed to the table to open it. He squealed with delight when he saw it was topped with pepperoni and extra cheese.

Kahllah led Celeste from the hotel suite and took the elevator to the lobby. They walked down a long hallway, following the signs that pointed to the conference room. Standing outside the door, they found Diabolique. She no longer dyed her hair red, returning to her natural black. She wore fitted slacks and a plain white blouse with black heels. Kahllah didn't think she would ever get used to seeing Diabolique dressed like a girl, but jeans and boots were no longer appropriate for a woman of her standing. Her face was flawlessly made up, but the gorilla tattoo at her temple was still visible. It was the one mark on her body that she was proud of.

"Hey, pretty girl," Diabolique greeted Celeste with a hug. "You ready for your big day?"

Celeste paused to consider how she would answer. "I guess, but I'm a little nervous."

"No need to be. You are a legacy." Diabolique planted a kiss on the girl's forehead. "You'd better get inside. They're waiting."

Celeste followed Kahllah into the conference room. It was dimly lit, save for a single high-powered light that created a circle. Sitting around the conference table were men cloaked in shadows. The girl could feel their eyes on her, and she squeezed Kahllah's hand for comfort.

Confidently, Kahllah stepped into the light and stood at attention, facing the men in the shadows. Celeste lingered behind the protection of her leg.

"Greetings, noble Black Lotus, Maiden Sword of God, and commander of the Black Hand," one of the men in the shadows greeted her. "You have requested an audience with the elders, and it has been granted."

"I have come to you today hoping you will honor my request to increase our ranks." She nudged Celeste forward. Celeste looked back at her with uncertainty. "Do it just like we practiced," she whispered.

Celeste stood with her back straight and addressed the elders. "I am Celeste Cruz, daughter of the Bastard Son, son of the Priest. Mine is the blood of old, and my place is within the Order."

There was a moment of murmuring amongst the elders. "And you would sponsor this initiate and be held responsible for her actions under the penalty of death if our traditions are not upheld?" This voice was different than the first one.

"I would," Kahllah agreed.

More murmuring. Kahllah waited patiently for them to reach a decision, though she was never worried about Celeste being accepted. It was her birthright. She, and others like her, would be the ones who rebuilt the fallen Order.

"Your request is approved, Black Lotus. We would welcome Celeste as one of our own, as we did her grandfather. And now, she will be named in the shadow of the Mountain."

"With respect, the child has chosen her own name," Kahllah informed them.

This was unusual. Typically, the elders or whoever sponsored the initiate would give them their name.

"And what name would you choose, little one?" a third elder asked.

Celeste took the briefcase from Kahllah and approached the conference table. "I would take the name of my mother." From the case, she produced a gray mask with a spider totem on the forehead. The girl slipped the mask over her face and addressed the elders. "*La Viuda Roja* . . . the Red Widow."